KEEPER & KINDRED

KEEPER & KINDRED

MEOW: MAGICAL EMPORIUM OF WARES
BOOK TWO

TONI BINNS

To those who find joy in the magic surrounding us every day. May you find those who share your joy, may your coffee cup always be full of warmth and goodness, and may your days be good, even when they are full of trolls and dragons.

ONE

I stared up into the skylight, wondering what to do with this new information. The Cat wasn't a cat. He was some Fey Lord that had screwed up so badly the Fates cursed him to run a magical shop. Now, he was stuck until he'd fixed the wrongs he'd created.

What did that say about the bookstore?

My fingers rubbed against the green velvet chair. I needed to get up and deal with the rest of my breakfast. I hadn't finished eating yet when Lady Twilight had interrupted.

Why had she brought the Elven woman for me to hear the story? Even more importantly, why did she consider it a gift? There was something I was missing, some connection I needed to figure out.

The Cat's sad statement that there wasn't anything to do echoed in my mind. While he had screwed up, he shouldn't be punished forever.

I climbed out of my chair and grabbed my mug, which still had half a latte in it, and marched to the kitchen. It was time to finish the bacon and figure out how this all connected to me.

Dragons weren't dumb, far from it. Lady Twilight had brought Liluth to me for a reason. Now, I needed to live up to the Elder's expectations and connect the dots.

An hour passed and I had no better idea than before, but I'd had a second latte and I'd finished half the bacon. Now I sat on my stool behind the front counter, even though we weren't open. The Cat hadn't reappeared, and I wondered what was on the docket for today.

"Hey, Betty, is it safe to go find the Cat?" I asked softly.

Light drew my attention upward, and I quickly dashed up the stairs. As soon as I reached the balcony, I saw the Cat. He lay in the cat tree I'd gotten him, staring down at the tiny oak tree. The one red leaf glowed against the others. I slowly approached before sitting down in the chair next to it.

"Is that leaf Liluth?"

The Cat huffed. "Yes. I don't know what the dragon did, but it hasn't died yet."

"So the rest of those leaves are your kids?"

The Cat said nothing, but he closed his eyes slowly before nodding.

My heart clenched in my chest. While I was separated from my family, this was worse. How long had he been separated from his family? From what Liluth said, it had literally been centuries, or longer. Who knew how long a dragon meant when they said ages.

"So what was in the book for today? I'm guessing Lady Twilight threw us a curveball..."

The Cat's tail twitched. "A simple drop off we can do this afternoon if you'd like."

I nodded. "That sounds like a plan." I stood up from the chair with a soft smile. "How about I make you a coffee before we get ready for our day? Something warm and sweet."

The Cat turned to look at me, his green eyes glowing. Slowly, he stood up. "I'd like that." He jumped to the floor and padded around the balcony. I followed, keeping pace with him.

I quickly pulled out his teacup and set it on the counter. Then I made some fresh espresso and steamed milk. This time I added honey to it, and the smell of summer took over the shop. A floral hint with that warmth of sunshine.

It only took a little of the steamed milk to fill the little teacup, and I used the rest to fill my mug. I didn't need any more caffeine, but I couldn't let it go to waste.

"Let me know when you're ready to open the shop," I said to the Cat. I didn't want to rush him to drink his coffee, but I wanted to reassure him that everything was okay.

The way his eyes lingered on me occasionally said he expected me to act differently. The Cat was the Cat, and hearing about his past didn't change what I thought about who he was now. I knew him. That was what mattered.

I sat on my stool and slowly sipped the honey latte. It made me think of the flower garden on the farm.

My mother tried to grow flowers, but she wasn't that good at it. Umber really shined at growing things, and he'd helped create the flower garden of my mother's dreams.

The bees would fly from flower to flower. They loved the zinnias in the late afternoon sunlight. Sometimes, you would catch a small green frog sitting on a flower head or nestled in among the petals.

The sunflower seeds that I'd passed along to Cerulean, to give to Umber, would grow, I was sure. I wondered what color they would be. Maybe a burnt yellow or orange, something striking if they were magical.

"Are you ready?" asked the Cat.

I smiled at the question. He sounded more like himself, and at least a little less sad. More determined. More centered.

"Yep."

The door unlocked with a snap, and I smiled, ready for whoever would come inside.

Yet, somehow the old woman who entered, wrapped in a shawl, threw me. The door slowly closed behind her as she hobbled toward the counter with a basket in one hand. She was not what I'd expected, even though I hadn't known I'd had expectations.

"Good Morning, welcome to the shop." I kept my voice warm and a smile on my face.

"Oh, aren't you a cutie," she said as she slowly approached, setting the basket on the counter. "Much better than that grumpy man who used to work here."

She flipped the basket lid open with ease and started pulling out goods. Knitted goods. Beautiful knitted goods.

I glanced at the Cat as scarves and gloves were stacked on the counter.

The Cat nodded as she pulled out the various items. "Perfect, she has everything for our inventory."

"These are amazing, did you make them yourself?" I asked, picking up a purple scarf that'd match Indigo if she was down here.

"Of course, of course. Got to keep busy, otherwise I get bored and sad." She pointed to a knitted hat in the same color, with green trim. "That one would be a better fit for you."

I couldn't help but pick it up. The yarn was super soft. I let the sigh of amazement slip out. "You are going to make it easy for me to do my shopping for the winter holiday..."

The old woman chuckled.

"Let her know we will add the money to her account. Same as always," mumbled the Cat, counting the pile.

I quickly repeated his message, and the woman chuckled.

"Good, good." She nodded expectantly. "I love knowing that things I created are out in the world, being loved by others I'll never meet."

"That's a wonderful way to look at it." Being loved by others, I'll never meet, I repeated inside my head.

"It is all about creating connections." A bright smile covered her face as she hobbled toward the door, carrying her basket.

Then she headed out, the door closing softly behind her.

"Cat, can I really do some shopping from this pile, or will that screw things up?" I asked, completely serious.

"I'll pull things to the side that are marked for others," mumbled the Cat. Yet, his tail flickered in joy as he moved the things that were reserved closer to the register.

While the day had started rough, this was nice. It felt normal, and a little normal was just what we both needed right now.

CHAPTER

TWO

Breakfast this morning was simple. English muffin sandwiches, with an egg and cheese on top. Quiet without Indigo since she slept in a growth spurt.

Somehow, the Cat ate it, though since he wasn't a real Cat his odd habit of disappearing food made more sense. Did I only see a Cat, and his true form was actually in the room? How did that work?

Thinking about it made my head hurt, and instead I finished my sandwich with a little hot sauce and then headed toward the front of the shop. While the shop was warm and bright, and sunlight drifted down from above, I was inclined to make a warm fall drink. It felt like fall, somehow.

Hot chocolate with some cinnamon was just perfect. I even topped it with some whipped cream. The Cat received a smaller version, which he promptly demolished.

"That hit the spot," said the Cat.

His praise made me smile as I sipped on my drink.

"Anything special about today?"

The Cat shook his head. "Another easy day, though they will be shopping, I think, and buying a few things."

I studied the store in front of me, trying to spot anything different.

The children's area wasn't there, just more bookshelves, and another table with various goods on it. Candles, books, and crystals covered the big center table, and the newer small one contained some of the knitted goods from yesterday. Plus a few pillows, which I hadn't seen before.

The bookshelves along the back wall were arranged differently, and the hanging signs that dictated the genre were in a different order. Still, everything looked ready to go.

"I'm ready when you are..." I quickly removed the Cat's teacup as the door unlocked.

The door shot open as two women entered the shop.

"Welcome to the shop," I called out, then quickly took a sip of my drink to study the newcomers. Yet, they weren't the only ones who entered. Another set followed them in as well.

All the women had fuzzy ears poking out of some kind.

It took a second before I realized that they weren't just headbands. These were some sort of animal people, not beings I'd met before. They weren't like the cat worshipers, instead they were like humans, with various animal characteristics.

Fur, sometimes whiskers, and pointed ears.

One of them waved in my direction while the others

grabbed baskets by the door that I hadn't noticed. Then, off they went in various directions.

"Cat, are those...?" I couldn't finish my question since they did not look like the cat person who I'd gotten the painting of the Cat from. The painting hung up in my room and was one of my cherished objects.

"Forest Creatures, usually very good customers. They are preparing for a holiday festival focused on giving a gift to the one they want to...be with over the winter."

My jaw dropped, but I quickly closed it, as the ladies moved fast around the shop.

Faster than a human could. One carefully sorted through the knitted goods on the smaller table. She focused on the green-colored goods, stacking them in a pile. Her bright red fur made her stand out, along with her whiskers.

Nearby, one lady studied the books with an intense focus. She had little horns in front of her brown ears.

The other two spoke softly next to the bigger table, looking at the crystals and candles.

"So, they are picking out gifts for a significant other..." I whispered to the Cat, for clarification.

"Kind-of. Partners only commit for one winter, then everyone goes their own way in spring."

That was new, and not something I'd heard about before. I'd need to check my book to see if anything else popped up, since I'd now met a few different species, and it'd been a while.

The one studying the bookshelf pulled a book down and then marched my way. The two near the table went silent, and the one still sorting through the yarn goods snapped her head up.

"I'd like to get these two books," the horned girl said, setting her basket on the table.

I smiled at her, then quickly rang her up.

She paid using weird metal coins, but they matched what the register said.

"Good luck."

She blinked a few times, then smiled at me.

"Ah, I know she will love them. They're from one of her favorite authors." A light blush covered her cheeks, but she headed out the door with a swagger in her step.

The others moved faster as soon as she left. The one looking through the knitted goods was next, purchasing a bright green scarf with darker leaves. The red-eared one looked less certain, and fretted as she paid for what she'd found.

"Thank you," she whispered quietly, before fleeing the shop.

That left the two next to the table, still whispering back and forth. Finally, they both approached with a few different candles and crystals.

"We would like your thoughts," one of them stated. Her brown ears twitched back and forth, while her tail flickered behind her. "The person we desire loves warmth and stones, and we can't decide."

They placed two candles on the table, both dark gray, along with a crystal that flickered with an orange light.

"Better you than me," grumbled the Cat.

"Do they have any color preferences? Things they like to eat?"

The two girls turned to one another, shrugging. "They are a bear creature, nice and fuzzy..."

I resisted the urge to ask more questions and instead motioned back to the table. "I think there is a beeswax candle there. It would smell like honey. That, plus the orange crystal, would be a delightful gift."

The two of them quickly turned to the table, almost running into one another. I waited until they brought over the candle I had pointed out. Both smiled.

"You are brilliant," whispered one of them, though I couldn't tell who as I rang up the purchases.

"I appreciate that. Good luck."

Both nodded at me, but one of them gave me a lingering look. She went to say something, but the other girl yanked her out of the store.

"I think you were going to be propositioned there," added the Cat.

"What?"

"Yep."

My head tilted to one side as I thought through that whole shopping experience.

The forest creatures gave gifts to see who would stay with who through the winter. If the system worked for them, more power for it.

That would make dating a ton easier. First dates were the worst. They were why I hadn't dated anyone in a while. Maybe after my contract was up, I'd find someone. Then again, with the Cat and Indigo, I wasn't exactly bored, or lonely. Dating wasn't something to consider too deeply at the moment.

Plus, how would I date while at the shop?

THREE

I knew as soon as I opened my door that today would be a longer day.

Cafe mode was back. The gorgeous, long table was back near the window, along with the benches. The smaller wooden tables were scattered about, and it all made me smile.

While the Cat didn't appreciate the business of these days, I liked them.

Mostly.

Figuring out what we were meant to do was frustrating, but it was a delightful change of pace. The hanging plants in the window looked happy, and I moved with a small jump in my step.

Indigo didn't stir as I closed the door behind me. Whatever growth spurt she was experiencing, it was a long one. Hopefully, not too much longer. I missed her.

First coffee, then breakfast.

The Cat jumped up on the counter as I approached. "We have trouble again today."

"It'll be fine," I said with a smile. "What sounds good today?"

"Something highly caffeinated."

I chuckled and made him a simple latte with an extra shot of espresso. I went with something cold.

Last time it'd warmed up in the shop, and something cooler felt right. Espresso, some cold cream and a little brown sugar. Sweet, caffeinated, and milky. I popped a straw in it, but as I turned toward the kitchen one of the cake stands caught my eye.

"Is that coffee cake?" I moved closer.

The Cat nodded after finishing his drink.

"What do you say to some coffee cake for breakfast?" I asked with a grin, though I pulled the lid off without waiting for a reply. I pulled out two slices of the giant treat and set them on little plates. "I'll warm them up in the kitchen. Wait here..."

It only took a few minutes before I returned, sat down on my stool, and placed the Cat's treat in front of him. I used a fork and took little slivers of the cake to enjoy every moment.

Coffee cake was a favorite, especially if I didn't need to bake it.

"We have to be running low on baked goods at this point," I mumbled between bites.

"Maybe, though a long time ago one of the shop-keepers baked."

I turned and looked at the Cat. "Really? So you're telling me there is a stockpile of outstanding baked goods hidden by magic?"

The Cat didn't answer, just took another bite of the

coffee cake.

This coffee cake was perfect, cinnamony and sweet, but fluffy. The crumble on top wasn't too crunchy, which I knew from experience was difficult to get right.

I took my sweet time with the treat, taking small bites, but eventually I reached the end. I cleaned up my plate, along with the Cat's, and sat back down on my stool.

"Are you ready?" asked the Cat, staring at the door, his whiskers drooping.

"Of course, are you?" Between the coffee cake and the amazing sunlight coming in, today would be an amazing coffee shop day.

The Cat huffed. "You do all the work on these days."

"That isn't a problem for me. Any hints for today's task?" Today would be a great day for me.

"None, just that we are helping people connect." His voice slipped lower. "Whatever that means."

"Let's do this, then." I scratched behind his ears before he could respond. "You can take a nap in the warm sunlight."

The lock on the door snapped open as I took a sip of my cold coffee. My eyes drifted back over to the cake stand of coffee cake.

I didn't need another piece, but I really, really wanted one.

The bells on the back of the door rang as it opened.

"Good morning, welcome to Meow."

A familiar face walked inside with a nervous smile. It was the same troll as before. He was dressed the same, in a linen button-up and jeans, though It looked like his horns were polished this time.

I didn't really have a lot of experience with trolls, though, so I couldn't be sure.

He headed directly to the counter and held out the rewards card. "Can I please get an Americano?"

"Of course," I said, getting started with a big, dark slate mug for him. "Any treats?"

"Not yet, maybe later." He glanced toward the door, then turned back toward me.

This time I had a chance to ring him up before the door opened again. He hastened to claim the big table after I stamped his card. He had a free drink coming soon.

A group of five elves came in, though they weren't the same as Liluth.

The Cat sat down next to the register with a huff.

The ears were the biggest difference; they weren't as long. Not to mention they didn't have the same feel, though I couldn't really describe it. They ordered a bunch of drinks to go, and I quickly got to work as the door jangled again.

The rush didn't let up, though most folks got drinks to go.

I recognized one shifter from last time, but he didn't stick around. The two Elven girls came back with a friend, and they stayed put with books all around them.

Economics.

Somehow, no matter the world you were in, the concepts were the same.

The whispers from their table revolved around

passing the class and figuring out what they wanted to study.

Once things calmed down, the troll approached for a refill.

"No study group today?" I asked as I pulled the espresso, trying to figure out how much time had passed since the last time we were here.

"I got an early start. I wanted to finish up my reading for a different class." He glanced toward the door again. His shoulders slowly crept closer to his ears. "Though, they should be here soon..."

The door jingled as another troll walked in. This time it was clearly a woman. Her long dark brown hair was brushed back, and her horns were a little smaller. Dark brown eyes searched the space until they landed on the troll at the counter.

"There she is..." Everything about him suddenly melted.

I nodded to myself with a small smile. Young love was clear as day. This was better than a romance novel. I glanced at the Cat, but he just napped on the counter like I'd suggested.

The lady troll headed to the counter, her eyes staying on him.

"Samantha, can I get you anything?" he asked her.

"Something warm, and maybe sweet..." Her forehead winkled a little as she tilted her head to one side..

He turned to me, eyes wide as his shoulders inched up a little.

"Do you like vanilla?" I asked with a smile, turning my attention to her.

She nodded slowly, biting her lip.

"I have just the thing." It didn't take long for me to make a simple vanilla latte in a bright blue mug which I placed next to the Americano. "Here you guys go."

He held out the rewards card and started to fumble with his wallet.

"You're all set." I grabbed the rewards card from him.

He opened his mouth, but then snapped it shut before picking up both drinks and leading her over to a table.

For a split second, a gold outline shimmered around them both.

FOUR

I reached out to the Cat to ask about it, but it was gone so fast, I doubted what I'd seen.

A gold outline shimmering around them both, almost touching, I thought. Like they both reached out to one another but didn't make it quite yet.

I snagged a mug from behind the counter and started wiping it down with a rag, so I wouldn't be caught staring. But, still, I wondered what I'd seen. I'd have to ask about it later.

One of the elven students approached with a soft smile. Her gaze didn't linger anywhere, sweeping around the counter. "Can I get some coffee cake?"

"Of course, let me grab a slice." A simple white plate with small blue floors waited under the counter, so I grabbed that one. Using the tongs I added one of the biggest pieces. Maybe then I wouldn't end up eating it all.

"Did I really see a dragon last time?" she whispered, leaning closer across the counter.

"Yes, she's napping at the moment." I leaned in like we were telling secrets.

"Do you think she'll be up soon?" Her face fell at my response, pulling back. "Everyone doubts I've seen one. No one believes me and, well, Tash... doesn't care. All she focuses on is finals."

"No, you really saw her. Her name's Indigo, but she's going through a growth spurt." I shrugged. "I don't know how long she'll be out, but I'll let her know you asked about her."

She nodded with a brighter smile and paid for the coffee cake.

My stomach grumbled, and I forced myself to look away from the goodies. Actual food would be better.

"Hey, Cat...?" I asked.

His eyes flickered open slowly before he stretched.

"Can you watch the counter? I'm going to make us some food really quick. Proper food this time." We still had an hour till lunch, but sugar and carbs didn't last long.

"Then can I have another coffee?"

"Sure." I hurried into the kitchen and pulled out some leftover cooked bacon, along with eggs and wraps. Breakfast wraps were super fast, all I needed to do was cook the eggs, which took no time at all.

I peeked my head back out, but no one had entered and I quickly scarfed down my wrap. I left the Cat's on the island and walked back to the front.

"Any requests?" I asked, feeling settled with food in my stomach. "You have a wrap on the island, I'll make a coffee for you."

"Your choice." He jumped off the counter, padding to the back.

My empty glass sat next to Betty, and I wondered if I wanted to stay with something cold. Opening the fridge, I pulled out some heavy cream, and some toffee. A toffee cold coffee with a drizzle of chocolate sounded good. Sure, it had lots of sugar and caffeine, but today was going to be long and I did just eat some real food, after all.

I didn't notice the troll approach, and her voice almost spooked me.

"That looks tasty," she commented.

I glanced up quickly with a grin. "Thanks, I'm in a cold drink mood today."

"Can I get one of those?" she asked, looking down at her hands.

"Of course. How's studying going?" I quickly pulled another two shots of espresso.

She shrugged before running her fingers through her hair. "Good, I just wish he would get the hint and ask me out already."

Oh this was gonna be fun. "You can ask him out, you know... take the initiative?"

Her eyes grew wide and she leaned back. "I mean, I could... Maybe."

"Do it." I didn't want to encourage her too much, but those gold outlines had to mean something.

She turned to look at him sitting at the table and caught him checking her out. His cheeks turned a dark green.

"I mean, he has a thing for you, that's clear…" I added, seeing the glances between the two of them.

"You might be right…" She quickly paid for her drink, then wandered back to the table.

Within seconds, he was an even brighter red, and that same golden outline appeared again before vanishing.

This time I *knew* I'd seen it.

The Cat jumped up on the counter.

"Did you see that?" I asked quietly with a grin. Young love.

"See what?" asked the Cat, as he padded in a circle on the counter.

"Between the two of them, that flash of golden light?" I kept my voice down.

The Cat looked at me like I was crazy before laying down.

"Nevermind." I placed a much smaller version of my toffee-chocolate iced coffee in front of him. "Here's a drink for you."

"What do you say we split a piece of coffee cake?" asked the Cat without even glancing at me.

I chuckled, my willpower failing as I grabbed two plates.

"Well, since you asked…"

Thankfully, no one else entered until the crumbles were gone and the plates cleared away.

The moment the cleanup was done, though, three people entered, all human. They ordered fall drinks and took a table near the door.

They chatted louder than the five people already in the coffee shop were. Both the elves and the trolls sent looks their way, but the trio of humans didn't notice.

Next a mixed group entered. Some shifters and elves, plus someone with magic.

I could feel it around them. They took the table next to the humans. Something was up there.

My eyes kept wandering to the human table. It felt like trouble was brewing.

"Cat..." I whispered.

He blinked at me.

"Can you go knock over one of that group's to-go cups?" I asked.

The human group didn't get mugs, I'd used to-go cups for all of them. It'd made sense at the time, and it felt like the right move.

One thing that being the Shopkeeper had taught me was to go with my gut.

"They're being rude..." I caught one of them glancing around at the other tables with a smirk.

The Cat jumped off the table and headed in that direction.

The mixed group shot darker looks at the table of humans, but did nothing.

Then the Cat arrived.

"Oh, look at the kitty," said one of the humans, way too freaking loud given the overall mood in the coffee shop.

The Cat jumped on the table and let one of them pet him. Then he twisted around, accidentally knocking into a cup. It crashed onto the table and he jumped out of the way to not get his paws wet.

The coffee splashed onto the lap of the one I thought was the leader. He jumped up with a frown.

One of the others, a girl, tried to use some napkins to wipe up, but he stormed in my direction.

"Your cat spilled my drink!"

The temperature in the coffee shop lowered by a few degrees, and I studied him. Then I pointed at the sign on the wall behind the counter.

> Do not upset the Cat
> The Cat is always right
> Do not go behind the counter
> Do not upset the Cat

"The rules are pretty clear, so maybe it's time you headed out." I kept my voice firm, and the skylights darkened for a moment.

"Let's get out of here..." He took a step back, eyeing the sign, then me. "We have better things to do."

It didn't take long for the entire group to storm out. Seconds later the temperature returned to normal, along with the lights.

"Sorry about that everyone, had to take out the trash." I grabbed a rag and moved out from behind the counter to clean up the table.

The troll laughed, as did the mixed group. They beat me to the table and tossed the remaining to-go cups, pitching in to help clean up.

"How about cookies for everyone?" I asked with a smile at the thoughtful gesture from them.

Everyone in the shop quickly lined up, and I passed out either a chocolate chip cookie or a peanut butter.

It felt like things were getting back on track, though that feeling of a storm coming remained.

CHAPTER

FIVE

"Maybe that was our goal today..." the Cat muttered as he jumped onto the counter once the line for cookies was gone.

The mood in the coffee shop quickly returned to normal, and he lapped at his coffee.

"Not at all," I said. My gaze flickered out to the trolls.

The two trolls packed up the books from the table and headed out. The guy gave me a quick wave before the door closed behind them.

"They were the assignment," I added quietly with a smirk.

The Cat's head snapped in that direction. "How can you tell?"

"Just a feeling I got..." Not to mention that weird trick of golden light. "Though, kicking out those asshats felt good. I appreciate your help there."

"Of course, although if we are done, do you think we could get everyone else to leave and close up the shop?"

I chuckled at the Cat's question. "I'm not going to

close early. You can go nap in your chair. We need to stay open at least until mid-afternoon. Keep consistent hours and such."

Plus that strange feeling remained.

The Cat grumbled in reply, but didn't leave the counter. He curled up into a ball and appeared to nap yet again.

The rest of the afternoon passed quickly, and sadly we sold out of the coffee cake. By three o'clock the place was empty.

"Betty, can you lock the door?"

It snapped shut at my request and I turned to the Cat. "You really don't like coffee shop days?"

"No. They make little sense to me, but you do well with them." His voice came from the center of a tight ball of fur.

I nodded and picked the Cat up, pulling him close. "I'm thinking that we sit on the roof for a bit and rest our feet. Maybe get some take-out if that sounds good."

The Cat purred in my arms in agreement and that remaining tension vanished.

It'd come from the Cat, but why?

I didn't need to rest my feet since I'd worn my boots. My feet felt amazing, though my suggestion was an excuse to try to relax for a bit. "Have you ever seen a TV?"

"What's a TV?" asked the Cat.

"Oh, do I have a surprise for you." My mind raced as I wondered if I could get a TV delivered and connected to stream TV shows and movies. "I can show you on my laptop."

Already, I was trying to think of the best shows to

introduce the Cat to. I even had a TV show in mind that involved elves, magic, and an evil lord. Hopefully, the Cat would enjoy the show.

Once in my room, I set the Cat down on my bed, and checked on Indigo.

She hadn't moved from her spot, and I gave her a little pat before grabbing my laptop.

"I'll order our normal Chinese order, in case she wakes up." Yet, I doubted she would wake up soon. It didn't feel like she was done yet, and she slept deeply without snoring.

I set my laptop up to watch the first episode of the show, then ordered food. It wouldn't take long to get here. The entire time before the food arrived, the Cat hadn't moved an inch. His eyes were locked on my little screen, mesmerized at what was going on.

I paused the show, and he turned to look at me.

"Are elves like that on your world?" he asked seriously, without blinking.

"It's a story, like a bard would tell, only you can see it..." I tried to explain how TV worked, what actors were, how special effects were created, but the Cat didn't care about that. He just wanted to finish the show.

I plated up food for him and myself, but he didn't touch it at all. Instead, I ate spicy noodles as the Cat stayed glued to the screen.

A chirp, followed by a flash of purple that landed right next to my plate, almost caused me to dump my food over my bedspread.

"Indigo!"

The bookdragon didn't look different. Her size hadn't changed at all.

"Food!" She dove headfirst right into my plate, chasing after my noodles.

I chuckled and held the plate steady as she devoured every noodle that was left.

"Dumpling soup?" she asked, looking at me with gigantic eyes.

"Of course," I said with a smile. "It's downstairs. That is not an eating-on-the-bed type of food. Cat..."

He still watched the screen, and I picked up Indigo to head to the kitchen.

"How was your sleep?" I asked, carrying her down the stairs.

"Long, but I feel better. Hungry..." Her wings remained tight next to her body.

"Well, there's lots of food." Now, I was glad I'd ordered food for her anyway. Maybe the smell woke her up.

Indigo nuzzled into my chest, leaving bits of red spicy sauce on my T-shirt, but I didn't care. Clothing could be washed.

"I missed you, too," I mumbled as I entered the kitchen. One-handed, I pulled out her soup bowl and poured in her favorite.

Then she climbed into the bowl and chased after the dumplings like she always did.

At least she was awake, safe, and could now speak better. Though, that might be me, too.

I ate some spicy chicken, along with the rest of the

noodles, as she finished the entire bowl of soup. The physics didn't work, but I tried not to think about it.

Once she was done, she crawled back into my arms after rinsing off.

"Tired again..." she mumbled.

"It's okay if you need to rest more..." I lied. I didn't want her to go back to sleep for days at a time, but if that was what she needed, that was what she needed.

"Just nap..." Her eyes fluttered closed. This time she snored a little.

I carried her back upstairs. The Cat pawed at the screen near the next button. The credits rolled.

"How does this thing work?" he growled, then he spotted Indigo in my arms. "When did she wake up?"

"You were in the middle of the show." I didn't set her in the tower. Instead, I kept her in my arms. "She said she needs to nap a little more but she can speak much clearer."

"Well, she's growing up."

I frowned at that. I thought dragons grew up slowly, over centuries, not this quick.

"I see food has arrived as well," added the Cat, now eyeing the plate of chicken next to him.

"Yep. You really liked that show." He had gotten completely sucked in.

"Your world's magic is strong," said the Cat around bites of what was probably cold chicken. "Very strong."

SIX

I wrapped my fingers around the mug of basic coffee as I sat at the counter. Breakfast had been simple, just some oatmeal with chocolate chips in it.

Indigo now zoomed around the store, flying better than she had before.

"Chocolate is the best," she sang as she flew, clearly burning through the sugar.

The Cat's eyes tracked her, but he said nothing in response. Instead, he finished up his own teacup and turned to me.

I nodded without him even asking the question. Since he had said nothing about Indigo, I assumed she was free to fly about today.

The only thing missing from the shop's Earth mode was the children's section. Instead, there were some wingback chairs set around for people to sit and read in.

The big table in the center of the store still sat covered in books.

Sunlight streamed in from the skylights and the front window, yet a breeze blew across the outside as dead leaves floated past. Whatever world this was, it was late fall or early winter.

I shivered and took a sip of my coffee. It was way too early to be thinking of winter, though pretty soon here the harvest holiday would be upon us.

That was another thing I didn't want to think about.

I needed to call my mom and be blunt that I wasn't going to make it. No caramel apples or cider donuts for me. My stomach rumbled, and I wondered if I could get the bakery we ordered stuff from to make some cider donuts.

The bells rang on the door and snapped me back to attention.

Indigo pivoted in the air and headed toward the counter.

The man paused just inside the door, letting the icy breeze in. His eyes locked on the little dragon.

"Welcome to Meow," I said with a smile as I recognized him. "Carter, can you close the door?"

His cheeks turned a little red as he stepped the rest of the way inside and let it shut. "Sorry about that; the little dragon surprised me."

I couldn't believe I had remembered the man, but he wore the same uniform as last time. Though, the aura surrounding him had increased substantially. That same draw to stare that the angel had before now completely covered him.

Indigo chirped as she landed. *Magic, he has magic.*

The Cat couldn't resist chuckling. "Looks like they beat the Demon King after all."

It came back to me as Carter approached. The price for the boots had been a feather after they had beat the Demon King. At the time, I hadn't really thought it was a thing.

Now? The talk of Demon Kings worried me, for Indigo's sake.

"Let me make you a coffee. Americano?" I asked.

"Yes, please," he gazed around the shop, but his eyes kept going back to Indigo. "I don't mean to stare, but I've never seen a little dragon before."

Indigo stretched out her wings all the way, giving him a good look. If she had been human, I'd say she was flirting with him. She padded closer to him.

"May I?" he asked.

She nodded, and he scratched under her chin.

I chuckled as I made him an Americano in a to-go cup. "So, I take it you finished whatever the Cat said you would?"

"Thank the Fates we did," he said with a frown, shaking his head. "Betha did most of the work, along with something related to your friend here, something called a dragnus. The Demon King is dead, and the portals between the worlds are being guarded by gargoyles again."

That sounded like something I didn't want any part of.

His eyes landed on the Cat. "Though, I'm guessing you knew that would happen."

"You can tell him I didn't, but I hoped they would solve the problem."

I set the to-go cup in front of him. "He hoped, but you exceeded expectations."

Carter chuckled.

I paused then and really looked at him.

"Are you okay?" I motioned to him. Normally, I wouldn't ask something like that, but I just had a feeling that something was up with him. "You feel different. Not that it's a bad thing, but I know that sometimes injuries don't show on the outside."

"I'm good, and I have a good friend who's getting trained in that sort of thing. We're chatting..." He gave me a bright smile and pulled away from Indigo. "Though, I owe you a feather."

Now that he was here, I really wanted to tell him the deal was off. Though, I couldn't make that call, only the Cat could. It was his deal after all.

One moment Carter stood there looking like a buff army guy, the next a bright gold light shimmered into view and wings appeared behind him. The white feathers had a touch of gold along the edges.

I felt like I couldn't breathe.

Magic streamed off him, and Indigo took a step back, her little eyes wide.

"It happened, then," muttered the Cat, almost too quiet for me to hear.

Carter reached over and pulled carefully on one of the lower feathers. It came free in his hand. Then the wings faded out of view, along with the intense feeling of awe.

I knew I wouldn't forget the sight.

He held the feather out toward me. "Here you go, though I need to warn you. I don't know what good it will do. While feathers from archangels have power, I'm not an archangel…"

The Cat nudged me after a few seconds and I realized I hadn't moved, I was just standing there, staring.

"Sorry, I haven't seen an angel before." I chuckled weakly as I took the feather carefully from him. "See something new every day, right?"

Carter laughed. "That's how I feel about the little dragon…"

"Indigo. Her name's Indigo."

She chirped twice and stepped closer again. *"He has wings! Can he fly? Can you get wings?"*

The Cat moved toward Indigo, and her head snapped to pay attention. Whatever he said to her, I couldn't hear it.

"Well, it was nice to meet you Indigo, and those boots saved Betha's life more than once."

"I got a pair for my birthday." Mine hadn't saved my life, but my feet never hurt from standing. "They are pretty amazing."

"Well, I need to get back. Thank you both again." He nodded and took a sip of his coffee. He waved before he strode out the door.

"What do I do with this?" I asked, holding the feather. My fingers tingled.

"Hold on to it till the next dragon lesson, then ask if they can attach it to your necklace. It's very powerful magic," replied the Cat.

"A real freaking angel," I muttered, staring at the feather in my hands.

"Archangel, actually, or he will be soon," added the Cat. "He just doesn't know it yet."

CHAPTER

SEVEN

The rest of the afternoon passed quickly, with only a few easy deliveries. Adam the driver dropped off some boxes, but it was all normal boring things that went into the storage room. Then it was over, and the time I'd dreaded was here.

I stashed the feather on my bedside table, then crashed down on my bed.

No matter how old I was, it always felt the same when I needed to call home with bad news. Not that this was bad news, it was just that my mother would take it that way.

Finally, I hit the contact button and speaker phone. It rang three times before she picked it up.

"Hey, Mom," I tried to sound like my normal self.

"Hey, honey, just give me a second. I have brownies in the oven...and I don't want them to burn."

That surprised me. My mom could bake most things, but brownies were one of those specialties she only made when she was worried. I heard a ding and a few sounds over the speaker.

"All right, I'm here. Those need to cool anyway, so you had good timing."

"How come you're making brownies?" I asked, trying to keep my cool.

"I felt like chocolate would be a good thing. Have you figured out when you're coming to visit? The town's harvest festival is coming up in two weeks, and I haven't heard anything." She snorted before continuing her ramble. "It doesn't help that Cerulean has been in a mood since he visited you."

That was a ton of information in not a lot of time.

"The harvest festival is why I'm calling, though now you have me worried about Cerulean…"

"Let's focus on your trip home first."

"Well, I can't really make it." I paused and scratched my ear swallowing hard. "Like I said before, I don't have enough time off to make the trip worth it with the flight. I really wish I could be there, but it just doesn't work out."

My mom sighed on the other side of the phone. "That's okay, honey, I get it. Plus, it's only until you get some more vacation time."

"So, what's going on with Cerulean?" I asked quickly, changing the topic. I didn't really get vacation time with this job, only weekends off until the contract was up. The winter holiday would be a much harder conversation that I didn't want to touch right now. Not at all.

"No idea what's gotten into that boy. He and Umber

have been at the farm nonstop getting corn in for the festival, plus a load of giant pumpkins."

"They got pumpkins to grow?" That was new.

"For once." My mom chuckled. "Umber is so proud."

"And you're worried because they're spending time together? Isn't that one of those things you are always harping on Cerulean about? Spending more time with the family?"

She paused on the other end of the phone.

"I do, but this feels different. One sec." I heard her place something over the end of the phone.

"Hey, Sis," said Umber.

"Whoa, didn't realize you were home," I said with a smile, leaning back on my bed. "Shouldn't you be admiring your pumpkins?"

"I could smell the brownies all the way from the fields. I had to come get one." He paused for a second and took a breath. "So, those sunflower seeds you got? Can you get more? They're pretty rare, and I've been looking for something like that for ages…"

I blinked, not expecting the question. After handing them off to Cerulean, I hadn't really thought much about them. "I don't know, but I can check. Like I said, someone didn't pick up an order, and I thought of you."

I swallowed at the lie. Worry crept in, wondering if Umber had realized they were magical somehow. Magic he shouldn't know about.

"Well, if you can, I'd really appreciate it. Mom's staring at me, so I'm gonna give the phone back. Too bad you can't have one of these brownies."

"Jerk…" I'd love one of her brownies.

"None of that, now," said my mom as she took back the phone. "Well, he was here for all of five minutes and half my brownies are gone."

"You love all of us stealing your baked goods."

That got her laughing, which was my goal. It gave me a moment to reset my brain away from giving my family magical goods, and the problems likely to be associated with that.

"Well, I want to eat one of these before any more go missing. Keep in touch. I miss you."

"I miss you too, Mom. Send everyone my love. Oh, and the cupcake was perfect. Let Dad know the journal has me thinking."

"I will, honey. I will." Then she hung up on me.

I turned off my phone, wondering.

She'd ended the conversation pretty quickly there. That, plus the brownies, felt off. Yet, I didn't know who to bug.

Without thinking too much, I sent a text to my dad. "Hey Dad, thanks for the journal. Hope all is well."

He wasn't one to check his phone often, so it might take forever to get a response.

Yet, my phone beeped almost immediately.

"I hope you get good use out of it. Love, Dad."

Now I knew something was up. My worry grew, but there wasn't anything I could do. Hopefully, my brothers would keep me in the loop. Or get me back into the loop.

I got up from my bed and headed to the door. The Cat was outside.

"Hey, I was just looking for you," I said with a smile.

"Can I get some more of those flower seeds for my brother?"

The Cat blinked at me twice.

"We can try to order them, but magical seeds can be hard to find." The Cat paused. "Did your brother mention the magic?"

"No, but he said he's been looking for seeds like that. Weird, right?" I asked.

The Cat nodded in response, but then continued on his walk around the balcony.

I COULDN'T BELIEVE the shop let Sable catch me eavesdropping outside her bedroom door on the conversation she'd had with her mother. If I could be embarrassed, I would. Instead, though, she hadn't realized I'd been listening in, and wanted to order more of those magical sunflower seeds.

First, one of her brothers had a spark of magic, then her next brother had more than a spark. Now, the farmer has been searching for extremely rare magical sunflower seeds that concentrate and spread magic within a set area, like he knew what they were.

Who was Sable's family?

EIGHT

I missed the hustle and bustle of the cafe.

Compared to a normal day of one or two customers, the day passed slowly. Yet, I reminded myself it was okay for the day to be slow. This wasn't like a normal job where I'd be getting a six-month review and let go if I hadn't hit some unknown metric.

Here, each day mattered, even when it didn't feel like it.

The Cat napped on the counter while Indigo listened to a story on her MP3 player.

She hoped a dragon would show up for lessons, but the Cat had said it might take a few days. That made me wonder if he was in contact with them somehow, even though it shouldn't be possible from what I could gather.

For now, I sipped on my warm tea and worked on the crossword puzzle in front of me. The shop was open, but so far no one had arrived.

The Cat had reassured me once already that we

would have a customer, and that timing wasn't always perfect.

Books were piled everywhere today. The normal bookshelves were around the back wall, plus an additional row. Toward the left of the room were even more shelves than usual.

The table in the center also had random stacks of books. It was a bit disorganized, more random than usual, and it made me twitch a little, but I had to trust that Betty knew what she was doing.

At first, I'd wanted to see what I could find, but then I noticed the dust. It covered everything, and it bothered me. No matter where I looked beyond the counter, there it was. I didn't know how Betty could handle it. A thick layer was making my skin itch.

Indigo hadn't even gone to her hideaway. Instead, she lounged behind the counter in a tiny cat bed I'd found for her.

The Cat had said it was good enough, as long as she didn't come out when the customer was here.

Right now she was in her own world, listening to dragon stories, her tail flicking lazily.

My fingers tapped on the counter, and I wished whomever this was would hurry. Anticipation was getting to me, plus I was stuck on a word for the cross word puzzle.

"Eaglet's home..." I asked quietly to myself.

"Eyrie," came from the Cat, even though he appeared to be napping.

I filled in the word, but it screwed up the one I thought I'd gotten right crossing through it.

It took another hour before they showed up, right as I had decided to go prep lunch. Suddenly, the door opened and the bells rang.

The Cat snapped to attention faster than I'd ever seen before. It put me on edge.

I checked to make sure Indigo was in her own zone, and she was.

In walked a crocodile. Not really a crocodile, of course, but the being definitely reminded me of one. It stood upright and wore a loincloth around its midsection. It had a backpack made with some kind of leather on its back.

Water tried to push in behind it, but something held the liquid back at the door. The creature's tail swept along the floor behind it, leaving a trail of dampness.

"Welcome to Meow," I said, trying to figure this whole thing out.

"I've finally found it," he said. I assumed it was a he, given how masculine the voice was, but I didn't know for sure. "The temple of knowledge..."

Temple of Knowledge? That's a good name for a bookstore.

His small black eyes darted every which way, not landing on one spot for more than a few seconds. "The elder was correct."

"Cat, what's going on?" I asked in a whisper.

"Let him have his moment."

That caused me to stare at the Cat, wide eyed.

"This is the place where I can learn words, correct?" asked the crocodile, inching closer to the counter.

Everything in me snapped to attention.

"We have books, yes." This crocodile wanted to learn how to read? All of my concerns vanished. "What are you looking for?"

The crocodile lunged to the counter, and I wanted to step back, but I resisted. Just because they looked strange didn't mean I should be scared.

He pulled his backpack off and pulled out several books. They all looked like they were primers to learn how to read.

"I've made it through these, but I need more. I think I have the basics down, but I want to be a sage, and the elders agreed! No more hunting! Just learning and guiding the tribe. But I had to find this place; I have to learn first."

"Tell him to look at the stack on the main table, the big green book at the top," said the Cat.

"My friend says what you are looking for is on the table." I motioned behind him. "Start with the large green book."

The crocodile turned around and carefully picked up the first book. His claws clenched at the cover, but they didn't dig in.

Dust rose into the air and I carefully ignored it.

He then flipped through the pages, carefully keeping his claws from tearing the pages. His small eyes glowed with pleasure. "This is all about my kind, stories of us! Of our kin, ones who have left and changed!"

He picked up the next book and flipped through it as well, then the next one.

"I don't know if I can pay the price for this knowledge," he said sadly, as he turned back to the counter.

I glared at the Cat. If there wasn't a way to get this guy these books, I'd be pissed.

"The stones he has for payment will work," grumbled the Cat, his tail flickering around. "But make sure you ask about the gold as well."

"You have some stones, and some gold?" I asked.

The crocodile frantically nodded and hurried back to the counter, setting the books off to one side. Then he dumped his backpack. The blackest stones I'd ever seen tumbled out, followed by clumps of gold the size of my fist.

"Are you sure? We can't do much with these, but we trade them to outsiders and they seem to like them."

"Okay, we don't need all of that," said the Cat. "Maybe half, but make sure he takes at least five books."

I separated out the black rocks and the gold into two piles, then pushed half back. "Take those three books, plus three more. We will take these stones."

"You are generous with me!" His eyes grew wide as he twisted back to grab three more books. "I thank the forest spirits!"

Eventually, I got him to put the leftover stone back into his bag, and the books as well.

"I will not forget the temple of knowledge!"

I waved as he headed out the door, then stared at the gold. "How much gold is this?"

"You'd be rich on your planet. The black stones are Black Opal, used in jewelry, but more valuable when used in magic." The Cat nudged one. "You better put them in storage."

"Hey, Betty..." I asked, and the stones sank into the counter, along with the gold.

"You're getting good at that."

I shrugged.

"I appreciate Betty and her skills. She is an amazing partner." I nudged the Cat. "Just like you."

The Cat blinked a few times in surprise at my comment. His mouth opened, but no words came out.

CHAPTER

NINE

I decided to save him.

"So, what was the problem with Indigo being awake with the Crocodile?" I asked, curiously.

The Cat shuddered. "The Crocodiles, as you call them, hunt small flying creatures in the swamp they live in. Anything smaller than them is fair game. Nothing nearby is furry, so I wouldn't register, but Indigo? She looks similar to a flying lizard they eat regularly."

I opened my mouth, then closed it before nodding. That was a pretty significant reason to keep her where I could see her. Though, I nudged her cat bed lightly with my foot and her eyes opened.

A claw reached out and poked the stop button of her player.

"Done now?" she chirped.

"Yep, you are free of your comfortable bed."

Indigo crawled to her feet then shot into the air, carrying her player toward her hideaway.

"Smells weird," she chirped softly as she flew across the room.

I chuckled as I finished my tea. "Is that all today, or can we hit another task on the list this afternoon?"

The Cat blinked. "It isn't a race."

"I figured I'd ask."

He let out a sigh, turning away from me. "We can complete the next task this afternoon, after lunch."

It was about the time I normally made something for lunch, so I headed toward the kitchen.

"Are you interested in anything in particular?" Sandwiches were pretty normal, along with wraps, since I couldn't mess them up. We'd been eating a ton of take out for dinners, and I needed to get out of that habit.

My progress on learning how to cook had lagged after the newness of having whatever food I wanted wore off. Now, cooking felt like a chore, but maybe I just needed to reframe it.

Maybe pasta with a meat sauce. That wasn't hard, and the sauce came in a jar.

About an hour later, I placed bowls of shells in a meaty tomato sauce with cheese on top in front of the Cat. My bowl had a little more cheese.

"Indigo, how much cheese do you want?" I asked, holding up the shredded mozzarella. I sprinkled some on top.

"More," she chirped. *"Keep going..."*

Finally, I dumped the rest of the cheese I had onto her pasta, which had to be about half of what was on her plate. Hopefully, cheese was healthy for her.

I dug in with a fork and watched as the Cat's food disappeared like normal.

Indigo ate slowly, careful to cover each shell with at least three pieces of cheese and some of the sauce before eating it. It was the first time I'd seen her not just dive into her food, sometimes literally. Maybe her tastes were changing with the growth she was going through.

The pasta was decent, but I'd put a little too much red pepper flake into the sauce. My eyes watered, but I didn't comment, just made a mental note to watch it next time. Now I just needed to come up with something for dinner that was different. There was enough pasta left over to feed us for a week of lunches, so at least that was covered.

"So, what's the next customer?" I asked, changing my train of thought.

The Cat glared at me from over his food. "You know, you could wait until we're done eating before moving on to more work."

I smiled, and my focus went back to my food. Indigo's food was slowly getting eaten with her new method. I had to admit I was proud of her.

"Plus, this afternoon is weird, even by my standards," added the Cat, grabbing my attention again. Though, this time his plate was empty.

I quickly finished my food.

"Weird?" The Cat didn't usually use terms like weird.

"It involves a ghost, and a necklace."

"Ghosts are a thing?" I asked, though I wasn't sure why I was surprised. Magic itself was strange.

"Yes. We need to contain the artifact."

The last time we'd needed to contain an artifact, it had been that evil book. A shiver went up my spine, and Indigo's head snapped in my direction. I gave her a reassuring smile.

"It will be fine," I muttered, so she would go back to eating. Though, I didn't know how I felt about ghosts. Were ghosts just dead people? Or were they something else entirely?

It took Indigo forever to finish up her food, but we both waited patiently for her to eat until she was done. Then it was time to head back to the front of the shop.

The shop had changed from a dusty bookshop into more of what felt like a secondhand store. The center table was covered with crystals, bowls, and candles, while a case appeared on the right-hand wall filled with things that looked like expensive gems. It gave off the vibe of a witchy new-aged shop one would visit in some alley in London.

More importantly to me, that layer of dust had vanished.

"Let's get this done, so I can nap," stated the Cat.

I waited behind the counter as the door unlocked.

Indigo flew toward her hideaway and landed on the bookshelf with care before disappearing into her own private space.

It took about fifteen minutes for the door to open with the bells ringing. By that point, I had made myself an afternoon tea and sat on my stool, sipping it slowly.

In walked a young woman, someone near my age, with a stricken look on her face. Her brown eyes darted all over the shop before landing on me.

"Welcome to Meow, how can I help you today?" I asked with a soft smile. So far, there was no sign of a ghost.

"I heard from a friend that you might be able to tell if objects are cursed," she said, so softly I had to focus to hear her.

"We can help with that." At least, I hoped so.

The Cat added nothing, but he watched her carefully.

CHAPTER

TEN

The young woman approached the counter, then pulled a necklace out from under her T-shirt. It was a locket, of all things. Her fingers trembled as she tried to unclasp the latch.

A cool breeze drifted through the air, and my eyes narrowed. The store heated in response, and after a moment she was able to unclasp the necklace. She carefully set it on the wooden counter.

"I think it's cursed. I got it three weeks ago from an estate sale…" She shook her head frantically. "At first it was just weird dreams, but the picture I put inside keeps falling out. I think I'm hearing voices."

I reached out and touched the locket. The metal was ice cold, and it took everything inside me to open it.

For a second, the picture inside blurred, showing just a blob, before changing to two friends smiling at the camera.

"Interesting." I set it back down, wanting to jerk my hand back but resisting. "I think we can take care of it."

"We need to buy it from her," said the Cat. "It needs to be destroyed."

That's when the hair on the back of my neck rose. In the distance, someone whispered.

"I want to keep it if possible." The woman's fingers inched back to the locket. "Just get rid of the voices."

"Are you sure?" Everything inside me watched her fingers twitch. "It might be easier if we take care of it. I can't guarantee the process won't destroy the locket."

Her lips parted, and her eyes grew wide. "I..."

The Cat nudged her hand and purred. Warmth pulsed from the store, heating the wooden counter.

The whispering stopped.

"That might be best." She paused, fingers still stretched out. "How much?"

"It won't cost anything."

The Cat pushed under her hand, still purring.

She blinked. "You'd take it for free?"

The Cat stuck near her.

"Yes, things like this aren't safe."

A blast of cold rose from the locket and I grabbed a mug from under the counter. I used it to cover the locket, cutting off the chill.

"Better to clean them up. I'm sorry you're going to lose the locket, though."

"As long as the dreams get better," she said, shaking her head. "I thought I was going crazy."

"Sometimes things go sideways, and it's better to distance yourself from them. We can take good care of the locket, and you can be free of its burden." I really had no idea what to say here, and the Cat wasn't helping, though now she was more easily petting the Cat.

"It's for the best. Thanks for taking it off my hands."

"Of course, and good luck." Hopefully this took care of any ghostly problems for her.

The woman turned and gave one last pet to the Cat before fleeing the shop. She didn't even notice Indigo staring at her from on top of the bookshelf. The door closed with a snap.

"Evil necklace," chirped Indigo.

"What do I do with it?" I asked the Cat.

He moved closer, sniffing at the coffee mug. "You contained it for the moment, but we need to destroy it. The shop can do it. Much like you did with the book."

I didn't want to think about how I had destroyed the book with the demonic soul attached.

"What's going to happen to the ghost? Is it a person?"

"Not anymore. It was once, but now it's been twisted. Once destroyed, it will return to where we all come from." The Cat stepped back. "You don't even need to touch it again, just focus on the shop eating the energy."

I frowned and glanced at the espresso machine. Last time, I had imagined it turning into a warrior knight dressed in red metal that attacked the evil book.

"Betty, I'm going to need your help with this," I whispered, touching the bottom of the mug.

The mug under my hands grew warm, very warm.

"We need to destroy the locket." This time my voice came out strong.

The mug on the counter melted, almost like it was

metal instead of ceramic. Thankfully, it wasn't a mug I used. It soaked onto the counter, then a hand tried to reach up out of the melted mug.

"I don't think so." I focused even harder on the idea of Betty reducing the locket to nothingness. I pressed harder into the counter on either side as the hand tried to reach up again. It couldn't break through the liquid mug coating it.

"Now, Betty!"

The liquid contracted, then hardened.

All of the energy inside me vanished, and I stumbled back onto my stool.

The hardened ceramic puddle then crumbled into dust, leaving nothing on the counter.

My head spun, and I leaned to the counter, bracing myself on my arms.

"Thank you..." whispered a soft voice.

Something landed next to me and I heard the Cat speaking, but couldn't make out the words.

Warmth rushed into me from everywhere that I touched the shop. My stool, my boots on the floor, and my arms touching the counter. It felt like a jolt of caffeine and I sat up quickly.

"She's fine, it just took a bit out of her," said the Cat.

"*Okay...*" chirped Indigo.

"That was weird." I shivered, thinking of the voice.

"Spirits are strange," said the Cat. "Especially when they can't move on. They turn dark, and try to regain new bodies. They yearn for what they knew, even if the person they once were would never choose such a path."

I shivered again, and Indigo growled at the Cat before climbing into my arms.

"I'm okay, it was just creepy." I held her tight. "You knew the necklace was wrong, though."

"Bad feeling near it. You both are brave."

I hugged her again before letting her climb down. "I think a dip in the hot tub sounds like a great idea. Don't you?"

Indigo jumped up from the counter and quickly flew toward the balcony. She hadn't gone for a dip since she woke up. She made a cheerful sound as she flew up to the door leading to the roof.

"It is gone, right?" I whispered to the Cat.

"Yes, the shop ate the energy and the locket. The spirit has moved on."

"Just checking." I stood up from the stool and moved toward the stairs. "Cat, if I ever go in that direction, don't let that happen..."

"Of course not, Sable. That won't happen to you."

"Better not."

CHAPTER

ELEVEN

"I told you, I didn't mean to spill my coffee..." It had been a perfect cup as well, with lots of caramel and some toasted pecan on top, along with the whipped cream.

It actually hadn't been me, it had been Indigo, but there wasn't a chance I would ever say that out loud. She had been coming in for a landing, and hadn't noticed her tail hitting the edge of the tall glass.

That's what I got for having a cold drink instead of something in my trusty, heavy mug.

I wiped down the wooden counter, laughing at myself. The Cat stood on the floor glaring up at me, and his look was just so funny. Whipped cream covered him, and bits of caramel hung from one whisker.

My coffee had flown everywhere. Betty could clean it up for me, but I decided to do it myself since I couldn't stop laughing at the cream-spotted Cat. One moment he was covered in sticky stuff, and the next a green wave flashed over him and he looked like his normal self.

Indigo still pranced around like she'd had too much caffeine, but it was because she had a dragon lesson today.

I couldn't blame her at all.

Right now, she had caught up to all the stories they had sent to her, and she wanted more.

In addition, I'd added several other books from my world to her MP3 player about random things like dinosaurs, which she was very interested in, and then outer space. I resisted adding anything fantasy-related, since I didn't know what was true versus not.

The doorbells jingled and my head snapped up, ready to say something to Lady Borsal, yet in walked Lady Twilight. Her purple robes were freshly pressed, and her hair was coiled up in a bun. Her eyes landed on Indigo as she flew laps around the main shop.

"Good Morning, Indigo." She smiled at me. "Sable."

The Cat used the moment to jump on the counter. He nodded in her direction, and she nodded back.

"We have plenty to cover today, I hope you did your homework," she added, watching Indigo flying around.

Indigo started talking too rapidly for me to follow, but I caught some questions about why some Lord killed a cow, or something.

Lady Twilight chuckled. "You did your homework."

"I can't keep enough information flowing, and that's with additional audiobooks."

She broke out into a full laugh, making the room fill with sound. "She's in a major growth spurt; she'll take as much information as she can. I'll have to keep sending over stories as we get them in from the various Elders in the clans."

"Ask her about the feather," muttered the Cat, near my elbow.

Lady Twilight headed toward the open area to the right of the main shop. It had lots of pillows and great places to sit on the floor.

Based on what I'd seen, it also fit her full sized dragon, if needed. Though, I realized, there was no reason the dragon form I'd seen had to be her full size. I wondered how big she really was.

"Do you have a moment to help me with something before you begin?" I asked, tapping my fingers on the counter.

Her eyebrow lifted.

"I received a gift that the Cat suggested I add to the necklace Lord Bennit gifted me." I pulled the feather from Carter out from behind the counter. The white feather glowed in the sunlight, the edges glowing with golden warmth. My fingers tingled.

Her head snapped to the Cat and something unspoken passed between the two of them, until she stepped forward.

"That is a worthy gift, young Guardian. Powerful." She took a step closer and Indigo landed on her shoulder. Her hand reached up to stroke the back of the dragon. "This will be an excellent lesson for you as well. Receiving a powerful gift is a precious thing, and making sure to present them in such a way is important."

I didn't mean it to become a lesson.

Then she stood in front of the counter and held out her hand. "May I hold it, and the necklace?"

I handed over the feather, then unhooked the necklace holding the leaf. My bracelet from my brother jingled as I did so. Her eyes landed on it and widened again, but she said nothing. Still, it caught my attention.

"My brother got me a birthday gift as well," I said with a soft smile.

"Your family cares about you very much. Maybe someday I will get to meet them."

Indigo chirped in agreement.

"Maybe, though magic isn't common on my world, and I'm not sure how a little dragon would be received..." My voice trailed off as I thought about my mother meeting Indigo. "My family probably wouldn't have a problem. They've always gone with the flow. My mom would adopt her in an instant."

Now that I thought about it, I wondered if it would be possible for them to meet Indigo.

"Indigo, watch what I do here," said Lady Twilight.

The Cat moved closer on the counter, as did the young dragon.

"The goal is to not touch the source of the magic in the feather. We want to coat it with a layer of magic and make it smaller." Purple light pulsed through her fingers, which turned into talons. It slowly crawled up the feather, but it didn't dim the glowing edges. "See, it's coating, not mingling."

Indigo crawled down her arm and stared at it closely, before nodding her head.

"Now, I'm going to make the coating smaller, asking

the feather to get smaller. You must always ask items of power, never force them..." She waited until Indigo nodded before the purple magic flashed again. "Did you feel the consent? The feather doesn't mind getting smaller; it wants to help."

Slowly at first, the feather shrunk, then it moved faster until it was about the size of a charm on a bracelet.

"You're saying the feather wanted to help?" I asked.

"Yes, it was given in good faith. Whatever you did to help that archangel meant the world to him. He and the feather want to help you in the same way."

TWELVE

Magic was awesome, but wrapping my head around the fact that the feather wanted to help me just didn't click as easily as I wanted it to. It seemed wrong to think of inanimate objects as wanting things, though I knew better. Betty was a shop, and she clearly had a will of her own.

"I don't even know what it can be used for," I mumbled, staring as she connected it to the chain on the necklace.

Lady Twilight held it out to me. The charm sat right next to the leaf, and it looked like it belonged.

It hummed lightly as I snapped it back around my neck before tucking it under my shirt.

"Archangel feathers are powerful sources of magic. Usually, they're used for healing, or protection and defense. It can even be used to jump-start a witch's own powers, or permanently increase them. In most cases, other angels use them to move up the social ladder, so to speak."

That sounded way more important than giving someone a pair of boots.

"Oh, interesting..." Yet, it didn't help me figure out what I'd use this for.

"Alright, time for Indigo to work on her magic. We can even try making magical objects smaller, to see what you learned," said Lady Twilight. She turned toward the seating area on the right with Indigo still on her shoulder. They started chatting much faster than I could follow.

I leaned closer to the Cat. "I feel like you gave Carter the raw end of the deal there...but I appreciate the gesture."

The Cat snorted.

"Those boots saved the life of the woman he loves. It was more than a fair trade." He head-butted my elbow. "I'm glad you'll keep it close."

I patted the feather and the leaf under my shirt.

So many people were worried about my safety. I wasn't sure if it was that they knew something I didn't, or if everyone in the magical worlds was paranoid.

It helped me understand better why if you weren't magical, that world was hidden from you. Which meant my family wouldn't get to meet Indigo, it just wasn't safe for them.

Then again, look at what'd happened to Indigo. Her mother was kidnapped and the little dragon was born away from anyone else like her. It'd worked out, and in turn others had been helped, but still. They'd wanted to feed her that demonic book.

I pushed those thoughts away.

Though, it reminded me to ask Lady Twilight about something she had mentioned last time she was here. There had been others like Indigo, but for some reason Indigo's education was more important.

"So, Cat, what do you think about board games?" I asked slyly. In the most recent deliveries, I had ordered a game I'd played with my brothers when I was really young, called Snakes and Ladders. A used copy now sat in my room, and I knew Indigo would like it, but I wasn't sure about the Cat.

"Board games?" The Cat tilted his head, looking up at me.

"You play them for fun," I explained. "They are games, like cards, but with more pieces. Some are based on chance, others on skill."

"I've played cards, a long time ago, but no board games."

"Let me get the game and the instructions. This one is more based on chance, so it should be a good introduction."

It didn't take long for me to grab the game and hand over the booklet.

"So, no one dies during this?" asked the Cat. "What do we wager?"

"Most people don't wager anything, it's a fun way to pass the time. Sometimes people really like bragging rights."

The Cat nodded, as if he understood that part at least. Maybe I'd get him to play a round with Indigo and me after her lessons.

"Let me read those instructions again." He stared at

the page of instructions. They were super simple. You rolled the dice and moved your meeple that many spaces. Whatever was on the space, you did. If it had a ladder, you climbed it. If it had a snake, you slid down it. The first person to one hundred won.

"This is all about rolling a die," he muttered. "If you are good at rolling a die, this game is simple."

"I mean, you can't get good at rolling a die; it's based on luck," I added, shaking my head..

The Cat smiled at me. No idea how he did it, but he smiled. It reminded me of a shark.

"We should play the game; I bet it will even be fun."

Yep, the Cat knew something I didn't, and now I wasn't sure introducing him to things from my world was the right idea. Maybe something like a roleplaying game would be better.

THE DRAGON NOTICED the bracelet and said nothing. I wanted to speak with her about it, but there wasn't a chance. For someone like the dragon, the magic would be easier to trace.

Sable mentioning it came from her family would interest the dragon, since they hadn't dug into her background at all as far as I knew. The non-magical, after all, should be left alone.

By that one little gift, it was clear her sibling knew about magic. He'd gotten her a protective bracelet, after all.

I found the color of the gems to be interesting. Green,

purple, and black were three colors that represented many things, but at the moment tied most closely to Sable, Indigo, and I. Yet, the brother didn't know of Indigo or me. That meant whomever he'd gotten it from had known much more about her than should be possible.

The shop blocked most magic, though the dragon had broken it by finding it when it didn't want to be found. Lady Twilight's connection to Indigo was stronger than most, and hopefully that was how she'd found the location.

Otherwise... I couldn't let my thoughts go in that direction. It led to hope, and hope was dangerous.

Sable didn't seem to understand how magic could be used to direct dice, and it was time she learned a few things about using magic. She had a growing spark of it, after all. Probably enough that she was uncommonly good at games that depended on such things as chance.

After all, when you were magically inclined and untrained, objects tended to do what you wanted more often than not. Maybe I could teach her a few things. They would keep her safer, once the contract was up.

CHAPTER

THIRTEEN

I didn't know where I kept going wrong. Usually, I ruled at board games with my family. I'd always been decent at games, even when they were mostly luck. Heck, the dice games that were all luck were the best, usually. Still, today I couldn't seem to catch a break.

I sighed as Indigo joined us after her lesson with Lady Twilight.

My die landed on a five, usually a great number, except five spaces ahead was a snake, and I slid down from sixty-four to sixty.

Indigo chirped like it was the most hilarious thing and flew to pick up the die, then she dropped it. It crashed into the board, showing a three, and she landed on spot fifty-one, which included a ladder, which she then climbed up to sixty-seven.

The happy dance she did in the air made me smile. Though, I swore each time the die got back to me they were just a little smaller, like Indigo had practiced her shrinking magic on it.

The Cat batted the die with his paw and it rolled across the board, somehow missing the meeples. A two glared up at me, and my eyes narrowed. His piece moved from sixty-nine to seventy-one, then climbed to ninety-one.

I wondered if this was how my brothers felt playing board games with me at home. This time I hoped I'd get a six. I needed to regain some ground on the board. To my surprise, I rolled a six and moved to sixty-six.

Progress was progress.

Indigo rolled low, and then it was the Cat's turn. If he rolled a two, four, or a six he'd be sent down a snake and give Indigo or me a chance to catch up. That's all that I needed to happen.

He batted the die across the board and a six popped up. He made a sound almost like a growl, but cut it off. Down his black meeple went, from ninety-eight to seventy-eight. Though, if he rolled a two on his next turn, he'd win.

My eyes narrowed at the potential play, but it was my turn. This time the die was definitely smaller in my hands.

"Indigo, are you making the die smaller?" I asked lightly.

She wouldn't meet my eyes and flew up farther in the sky.

"You know that doesn't help you roll the numbers that you need."

The Cat chuckled. "It might."

My head snapped in his direction. "How's that possible?"

"If she is infusing it with her magic and will, anything could be possible. Those with magic can do such things. You just have to want it more than anyone else who is trying to infuse the object with their will."

"So, by making it smaller, it's more attuned to her?" I asked, trying to connect the dots.

The Cat didn't reply, but his tail flickered in the air.

"Indigo, you must return the die to its correct size." I used my stern voice, and she flew down and landed on the island.

She poked at the die in my hands and I felt a tingle where my fingers touched the die. Then, suddenly, it was the normal size again.

"Thank you," I said, giving her a scratch under her chin. That seemed to be the permission she needed to crawl up my shoulder and take a seat. I chuckled as I rolled the die.

A five brought me to a ladder and up to ninety-one, right where the Cat had been one turn earlier. Indigo went next, pushing the die off my hand instead of climbing off my shoulder. Her energy level decreased from undoing her magic, which was interesting.

Again, Indigo rolled low but didn't really seem to care, as she snuggled under my hair.

Then the Cat rolled the die. It landed on a freaking two, and up he went to one-hundred, winning the game.

The Cat chuckled as he sat down on the island and looked at me. "That was fun, next time you should invite the dragons. I bet all sorts of magic would take place."

My lips parted, then closed again before I grabbed the meeples and folded up the board game. Next time, it'd need to be a different game, something not based on luck as much.

Indigo snorted at the Cats' comment, but said nothing. Her eyes kept fluttering.

"How about I tuck you in for a nap?" I asked.

I left the game where it was in the kitchen, then headed up to my room and tucked her into the heated blanket inside her cat tree. It took only seconds before she was out like a light. Then I marched back to the kitchen.

The Cat waited next to the board game, which was now unfolded again.

"Alright, how did you do it?" I asked.

"I told you, intention and will."

"You mean, when you rolled the die, you..." I picked up the die and thought about all the times I'd used magic in the shop. Most of the time it wasn't my magic, it was the shop's magic. I held onto the plastic cube with one hand, staring at it with a frown.

Intention and will. It shouldn't be hard.

I tossed it across the board. It bounced once, then landed on a three. That wasn't my goal.

"Actual intention and will," growled the Cat, glaring at me. "This should be easy for you."

After picking it back up I let it roll again, this time focusing on the number five. The die moved across the board and landed on the number four.

"Well, I must be doing something wrong," I muttered.

"You might need to practice more," said the Cat. Though this time he sounded confused, and given his comment, that made sense. He believed this should be easy for me, and it wasn't.

I spent the next ten minutes rolling the die and trying to get it to land on the number I wanted.

Nothing.

Not once did it land on the number that I had been focused on.

"I'm gonna call it." I started packing the board game up.

The Cat kept staring at the box before he shook his head. "Next time we can invite the dragons. They will keep you on your toes."

I giggled, thinking of Lord Bennit or Lady Borsal playing Snakes and Ladders. "If I'm inviting the dragons, I'll pick someone that isn't as much about luck. Something like Catan."

Though as soon as I said it, I paused.

Playing board games with dragons might not be the best thing. They were probably competitive. Not to mention, a game like that might be above what Indigo could do.

"I wonder what age Indigo would be at if she was human...?" I asked.

The Cat's tail flickered. "Older than you would think. Though, I'm not sure how fast you humans develop. I bet she's smarter than that little girl that loves the dinosaur books."

"You mean Molly," I added. Molly was in school already. I bet Indigo would love to go to a human school. She'd eat up all of that knowledge. An idea sparked, and I dashed upstairs, a smile on my face.

It shouldn't have been hard for Sable to make the die land on what she wanted. The magic sat there inside her, but she couldn't pull on it easily. Something stood in her way.

I didn't understand what it was, but I would find out. Sable needed to be able to protect herself. With all these dragons around, it was more important than ever.

CHAPTER
FOURTEEN

The laptop sat on the counter as I moved between tabs. The idea had struck yesterday, and I finally had some good choices after doing way too much research. Now, I needed to chat with the dragons and see if it was a good idea after all. Indigo would have another lesson here pretty soon, and I'd talk to them about it then.

The first roadblock would be to see if Indigo could learn to use a computer or not. It might not make sense to her. Yet, if she could, then this idea might work. While the dragons wanted to teach her all about being a dragon and magic, learning about humans and how we worked would be good as well.

That led me to online homeschooling. At least on my planet, it was an option for kindergarten through twelfth grade. While things like Earth history wouldn't be super exciting, math and science were always excellent subjects to learn.

"Are you signing Indigo up for more learning?" The Cat's voice next to me made me jump. At some point, he'd leaped up on the counter, and I hadn't noticed.

"I was thinking about it." I clicked on a link. "There are a few placement tests she can take, and I can see where her current reading levels and such are at." I turned to look at the Cat. "Unless you think it's a bad idea…"

He chuckled. "It's a great way to show up the dragons."

I paused. "Maybe it's not a great idea then…"

"It's a perfect idea." The Cat chuckled as his tail switched back and forth. Even his whiskers vibrated with excitement. "You must do it."

"As long as I can figure this out…" Yet the Cat wasn't even listening.

"I bet she will love extra lessons. Book Dragons want to know everything. They see themselves as the masters of knowledge. I know of a story about one who just concentrated on learning about flowers. Every type of flower across several worlds. They are the leading flower expert in this part of the tree. They trade for rare seeds and cuttings like its pure gold."

"So, signing Indigo up for an online Earth school wouldn't be weird? She really likes the stories I tell her, and she gets through the stories the dragons send her very quickly." I ran my fingers through my hair. "It doesn't help that time passes weirdly here."

"If Indigo lived with her dragon family, she'd be learning all the time. Either with other dragons her age, or by following family members around."

The Cat's words reassured me and I pulled the placement tests up again. This online school was text based, so students didn't need to get on video. There were video lessons, along with digital textbooks and printable worksheets, but it all seemed straightforward.

"Once she's up from this next growth spurt, I'll see what she thinks." I scratched the Cat's ears, as he moved closer. "I bet she's going to be super excited."

My mind raced at the thoughts of what she'd need for school.

I should see if I could get her a laptop, so she wasn't using mine. Though, she'd need to learn how to use a mouse, since the trackpad would be hard for her claws. Or, maybe her claws would be too hard on the trackpad. Either way, a mouse seemed like a better choice.

"Does that mean you are done working on your laptop, and I can now watch more of my show?" asked the Cat.

I started laughing as I pulled up the show about Elves, Rings, and the fight of good versus evil.

"You can totally watch the show. I think I'm going to go read a book in the hot tub on the deck. The sun is shining."

The Cat nodded.

There were only a few more episodes left of the show that the Cat hadn't watched, and I'd need to find something to suggest once he was done, but for now it was time for me to relax.

There was nothing like a hot tub to take away my worries.

Sable headed upstairs while I clicked on the link. It took me longer than I'd like to figure out how to start the next episode, but I could do it all on my own. Introducing book dragons to the magic of Earth would change things, and cause some chaos. It excited me.

Annoying dragons was so much fun.

The show had just started when something drew my attention to the front door. We weren't expecting any visitors today, but something white slid underneath it. I paused the magical show and jumped off the counter to give it a good sniff.

I paused as the scent reached me.

Home.

In an instant I yanked the letter out from under the edge of the door and struggled to open it. Despite the difficulty, I didn't dare call for Sable. While her hands would make this easier, it had my name on the outside. My true name.

Only a few beings knew it, which meant it was from the others. One of the Fey Lords.

Felimid,

I hope this letter finds you well.

While I have written to you before, I never know what might reach you in your banishment. Time has marched forward, yet it has retreated, as well.

The dragons have returned to the Fey Wilds, the demons are gone, and the others wake for the first time in centuries.

These pesky dragons are young and brash. Who knows what they are up to in your lands? We cannot tell, for they are not our lands.

May the Towering Forest wait for you.
Nymeria

My claws dug into the wood floor, and I trembled. My lands were gone, and I didn't need any dragons sniffing around the edges of what was left. They were the only ones who could potentially poach my home from me with me not there.

Fire burned through me, and my claws slashed out, tearing into the parchment paper. It only took seconds before all that remained were shreds of white flakes. Still, I trembled.

How dare someone try to take my home? My people? This couldn't stand.

Yet the heat trickled away as I slumped to the floor. What could I do from here? I couldn't leave this building, let alone chase off a dragon. My banishment weighed on me. Was there anything I could do?

FIFTEEN

Indigo woke me up way before the sun was up, as she crawled under the covers and took over a portion of my pillow. She nudged me as she curled up in a ball, then went back to sleep.

Still, it left a smile on my face as I dozed off again, back to dreamland.

Next time I awoke, the sun just peeked in through the skylights, and little snores indicated that Indigo slept still. I carefully got out of bed and got ready for the day. Before I headed out the door, I moved closer to the front of the bed where she slept.

"Hey Indigo, I'm going to go make breakfast..." I whispered lightly.

Her green eyes snapped open, and she was suddenly airborne, heading straight for my shoulder. She chirped twice as she landed. *"Breakfast!"*

The weight on my shoulder had increased, but she still looked the same size as before. The growth spurt must have been magical or mental. Though, it all felt a little fuzzy to me. She ate normal foods and also consumed knowledge to grow up.

Brighter light than normal streamed into the shop as I headed toward the stairs, not paying too much attention to the main area. Work could come second; both Indigo and I were hungry.

My stomach growled as I entered the kitchen and decided to make pancakes. They were from a mix, so super easy, and I could make as many of them as I wanted.

"Let's do pancakes this morning," I said in a bright and cheery voice. It didn't take long to grab the mix out and have the pan heating on the stove.

Indigo flew the maple syrup out to the island, along with forks and knives. It took a few trips, but I could feel how proud she was to help out. I gave her a thumbs up as I added the plates for the three of us, plus a serving plate. I didn't see the Cat anywhere, and my eyes narrowed.

"Cat, the first pancakes are almost done..." I called out down the hallway.

Indigo added a chirp as well, but nothing came in response.

Hopefully, he was just running slow this morning.

The first pancake went to Indigo, and I cut it for her into bite-size pieces. She carefully added plenty of syrup to her plate, but didn't let it overflow. The next one went to my plate, and I munched on it as I quickly made a stack of pancakes in the center of the island.

Then they were all cooked, but still no Cat.

I ate another pancake as Indigo flew one from the center stack to her plate. I almost offered to grab it for her, but the look of determination on her face stopped me. It was just too precious.

It landed on the plate and didn't splatter syrup all over, and I gave her a nod.

"Cut it up?" she asked.

"Of course," I said, quickly cutting the pancake into pieces she could grab with her claws.

The Cat jumped onto the counter as I finished. He gave me a nod, but I could tell something was up. His eyes landed on Indigo and then flashed back to me.

"Can I have a pancake?" he asked.

I nodded and added one to his plate before adding butter and just a little syrup. Just how he liked them.

"Thank you," he mumbled, not meeting my eyes.

Indigo chomped down on her breakfast, being super careful to not get sticky syrup everywhere.

I gave the Cat a look and mouthed my words, asking if he was okay.

He nodded, but his eyes went to Indigo again. "We have a customer this morning. It should be a pretty normal morning."

I ate my pancake, wondering what the afternoon held if that was all he wanted to say out loud. Something was coming for my little dragon, and it wasn't going to be good.

"More pancake?"

Somehow Indigo had fished her second pancake without my noticing. I added another to her plate and cut it up before she flew it over.

She chirped happily.

The Cat flinched.

Yep, something this afternoon would rock her world.

Breakfast went quickly after that, and I found myself at the counter with the Cat, making lattes for both of us.

Indigo flew around the room in giant circles stretching her wings. She'd gotten faster and flew much more smoothly through the air.

The Cat padded closer to me and waited for me to top his teacup with the espresso. "This afternoon will be rough," he mumbled so low I almost didn't hear it.

I nodded. "We'll get through it. That's what families do."

The Cat stared at me for a few seconds, his bright green eyes studying me before he nodded.

He dove right into his teacup as I finished making my coffee.

I sat on my stool sipping my latte, watching Indigo fly with such joy. There was only one thing that'd interrupt this, and I didn't want to even think about it.

The Cat nudged me after a few moments, and I realized I'd been staring. His teacup sat empty. "You ready?"

"Yes, let's have a good morning."

He nodded solemnly as the door unlocked.

It only took seconds for the bell to jingle, and Indigo quickly dove toward us and the counter. She landed as the door opened and in flew a small flying creature.

It had small wings like a butterfly, and sharp pointed ears, but other than that looked like a tiny human. She flew to the counter, a soft humming noise coming from her wings.

Her eyes grew wide as she saw Indigo, but she landed with a smile.

Indigo stepped away from the creature to give her space.

"Welcome to the shop, how can I help you?" I asked in a soft voice.

A small squeak came from the woman, who smiled brightly. "I'd like to buy some ground coffee. The big bag," she added after a moment.

I nodded and glanced at the Cat, noticing the full bags behind the counter that hadn't been there before. I set it down next to the tiny fairy person and moved to the register.

The fairy pulled a bag off her shoulder and dumped out a pile of red and white mushrooms.

Indigo moved forward to sniff them, but the Cat growled.

Indigo froze, along with the fairy.

"They are toxic, Sable will handle them. Humans can touch them," he explained.

"Don't worry, he just didn't want the little one to get sick," I explained to the fairy.

She nodded and reached for the coffee. Somehow it shrunk down and vanished inside her shoulder bag. She gave me a nod and headed to the door before I could do anything at the register.

Indigo stayed far away from the mushrooms.

"Should I grab gloves, or just wash my hands?" I asked.

"Just wash your hands, they're completely non-toxic to humans."

I headed into the storage room and there was a canister on the shelf with a picture of the mushrooms on it. I picked them up and tossed them inside the empty container, before I washed my hands and sprayed down the counter.

The Cat moved closer to sniff before nodding his head. "All cleaned up."

"What are these, anyway?" I asked holding up the canister.

"Toads love to eat them."

CHAPTER

SIXTEEN

"So, the fairy loves coffee, and toads eat mushrooms?" I asked, just to confirm.

The Cat nodded. "My guess is that a toad will be by sometime soon to purchase the mushrooms."

"Why don't the toads get them directly from the fairies?" I set the canister on the shelf behind the counter attached to the wall. It was cute, though I wondered how big the toads were.

"That's the problem, they'll also eat the fairies. So, they don't go near one another."

My mouth opened, and then I closed it. I did not need to learn about the toad versus fairy fights that must be happening. Yet, why were the fairies willing to trade for them, then?

I shook my head and shrugged. "Alright, that was a quick morning. Unless you meant the toad will be by…"

The Cat turned to look at me as the bells on the door jingled again. This time his head snapped around, and his tail froze in the air.

Lord Bennit entered the store, and it reminded me of the first time I'd seen him. He'd aged, and his eyes didn't sparkle as much as they had the last time I'd seen him. Instead, he walked slowly as he entered, followed by Lady Twilight.

Indigo jumped off the counter and flew to meet them before I could say anything.

"They're early," said the Cat softly. He stepped closer to me, just enough so the edges of his fur tickled my hand.

"Welcome, Lord Bennit, Lady Twilight," I said with a smile, though I knew this wasn't going to be a happy meeting.

Indigo didn't pick up on the emotion. Instead, she flew around like she was hyped up on sugar and seeing her best friend.

Lady Twilight gave her a soft smile.

"Betty, can we get a seating area?" I asked under my breath.

I wanted somewhere comfortable for all of us to sit down. The area to the right of the register shifted, the case sitting near the wall sank into the floor while a loveseat and two chairs appeared. A fireplace popped up, with a soft red glow, though it wasn't fire in the center. The shop hated actual flames.

"Thank you, dear," said Lord Bennit. He motioned over to the loveseat and sat down with Lady Twilight.

I slowly moved out from behind the counter and sat in one of the chairs. Tension hung in the air, and I resisted saying anything.

The Cat followed and jumped up on the armrest, sticking close to me.

Indigo slowed down her mad sprint and landed on the coffee table, chirping once what sounded like a question.

Lord Bennit let out a sigh, and she leaped over to land on his knee, her head tilted to one side. "I have some bad news, little one."

She crawled closer to his hand, not saying a word.

"Your mother has rejoined the leylines and the great tree." Lord Bennit's eyes glistened, but no tears fell.

A heartbreaking sound came from the small dragon, and her scales shivered in the light.

"Mother?" she chirped.

"The one who bore your egg, my daughter." His voice broke on the last word, and I couldn't help myself. I leaned forward and set a hand on his knee.

Indigo crept closer and nudged his hand, though she turned to look at me.

At that moment, I wondered if Indigo remembered her mother at all, but I didn't dare voice that to the grieving dragon on the couch.

Lady Twilight set a hand on his back.

"Joined the great tree?" asked Indigo.

Lady Twilight smiled softly. "Remember the story about the great tree that all the leylines connect to? How it twists and turns through all the worlds, like mighty rivers and streams that connect all of us? Dragons join with the leylines and travel back to the tree when it is time."

Indigo nodded slowly. *"To help the tree we go."*

"Exactly, little one. Your mother has made her journey, which means we won't get to see her again."

Indigo stared at Lord Bennit, who slowly regained control over himself. He didn't shed a tear, but I wouldn't blame him if he did. Suddenly, Indigo launched herself upward and slammed into his chest. Caught off guard his arms slowly wrapped around her.

"We still here."

"We are, little one, we are." His hands held onto her softly as she sat there on his chest, just lying there.

I sat back in my chair, still wanting to give him a hug, even if I knew he was an ancient, powerful dragon. I couldn't imagine the pain that he felt, losing a child.

All of us sat in silence for a few moments before Indigo pulled away. Her head snapped toward me, her eyes growing big.

"Sable won't leave, right?" Her claws dug into Lord Bennit's robe as she flung herself my way.

"I'm not going anywhere anytime soon," I whispered as she landed in my arms.

Indigo's scales shivered again. *"Not dragon, no tree for you."*

I chuckled, trying to lighten the mood. "I have a long time until I need to think about that, Indigo. Until then, I will be here for you. I promise."

The Cat took a strangled breath at my words, as did the dragons.

There were two things I'd learned about the magical world: first, don't name things unless you mean it, and second, the same went for promises.

While it might mean distance from my family, someday they would understand.

Indigo needed me right now. In the future she might not, but until then I'd be here for her. Whether it was at the shop, or somewhere else, I'd find a way. After all, the dragons called me kin. That meant family, and I held on to my family.

"Sable..." started Lord Bennit. Yet his voice cut off as Lady Twilight set a hand on his arm.

"As Sable said, Indigo. You don't need to worry about her leaving." The dragon's voice came out like a grandma's, that tone you didn't dare contradict.

Indigo settled in my arms with a nod, then looked at Lord Bennit. *"Will you be okay?"*

A small smile came over his face. "She was not the first of my children to leave, little one. Dragons live a long time, but I have lived longer than most. I will be okay in time."

He must have seen so much pain, so much loss, in his countless years, and now here was more, yet he continued, helping where he could. At that moment, my heart broke even more for him, and I understood the anxiety the Cat had shown earlier. Still, we were family, too, and we were here to share the grief with him. It had to be enough.

CHAPTER

SEVENTEEN

"Lord Felix, can the shop access the leylines directly?" asked Lord Bennit. "We hoped to give a song with Indigo, to the great tree."

The Cat slowly nodded and glanced at me before looking away.

"Only if they agree."

I wasn't exactly sure who they were, but I could guess.

He jumped to the floor from the armrest, and padded toward the fire.

As far as I knew, now, the Cat didn't do much active magic. Sometimes he did magic over artifacts, when he created something, but around the shop in general, he rarely used magic.

Now, the fireplace twisted and the smell of leaves filled the air. It opened up, and the dragons on the couch stood.

I followed suit, clutching Indigo to my chest as an archway appeared.

Bright white light filled the space, like a river trickling over rocks through the archway. It vanished into the floor two feet in front of the archway.

Indigo gasped.

I blinked several times before I could really see the flow of light.

"Indigo, will you join us?" asked Lady Twilight as she held out her arms.

Indigo nudged me and then jumped to the elder dragon. Then they stepped forward, while everything in me warned me to stay back.

The Cat stood suddenly by my feet, though I didn't know how he had moved without me seeing him. His paw rested on my foot, almost like a warning.

The two dragons twisted as they stepped forward, as space itself distorted. Instead of two humans with magic around them, they were dragons in full glory.

One was bright blue, the other was a midnight purple. Indigo sat on Lady Twilight's nose, like she belonged there.

They moved with such grace as they touched the leyline.

Music rose into the air like a physical force as it danced along my arms. My hair floated upward as it continued. Warmth, love, and hope dug into me, like I was sinking into the hot tub on the roof.

Time no longer had meaning, running forever and also not moving at all, until the music ended.

Within seconds of the last note fading, the dragons were gone, along with the archway.

Lord Bennit and Lady Twilight stood there with

Indigo in their arms. The fireplace with the warm glow was back in place, and my mouth felt dry.

"It is done," said Lord Bennit. "We sang her goodbye, until we meet again within the great tree."

Indigo stayed quiet, looking thoughtful.

"We should get going," added Lady Twilight. "That was powerful magic for one so young."

Indigo chirped and jumped out of the elder's arms, heading for me again, though this time she landed on my shoulder like a bird perch.

It took longer for my mind to work again than I could have hoped, but eventually I got the words out.

"When will you be back for lessons?" I asked. I knew Indigo had hoped to have one today, once the Cat mentioned the dragons were coming, but whatever that had been was different.

Lady Twilight glanced at Lord Bennit before answering. "Soon. I will be back soon."

He smiled at me, though it didn't touch his eyes. "Thank you for standing witness."

I couldn't stop myself, and I hurried closer to give him a quick hug.

To my surprise, he wrapped his arms around me and held me tight, reminding me of my father.

Indigo chirped near my ear, and I'm pretty sure she nudged him.

I pulled away after a few moments, to see a surprised look on Lady Twilight's face that quickly vanished. "You are welcome to visit anytime. Well, anytime that we aren't working."

"I appreciate the invitation. I know you do important

work here." He nodded at me and then at the Cat, before heading toward the door.

Lady Twilight quickly followed. "I'll see you soon, Indigo. Remember to keep up on your stories."

"Of course."

Then they were gone, leaving the three of us in the shop alone.

"He's going to come around even more now," mumbled the Cat.

I shrugged, not caring. "We work most of the time, and he is family."

Not that the job was time-consuming. Usually, it was half days, sometimes longer if I wanted to get more done. Today, I wouldn't suggest we see what was next on the to-do list.

"How about we do something fun, like watch a movie?" I asked, testing the waters. "Something heart-warming. I can make popcorn."

"Popcorn is amazing!" Then the little dragon took off from my shoulder toward the kitchen. *"I make popcorn!"*

As she flew down the hall, I glanced at the Cat. "Do you think she remembers her mom?"

"I don't know. Dragons are resilient creatures."

I let out a sigh.

"She will be fine, Sable."

"I know. She has us after all, but still I worry about her. Maybe I'll start that school program sooner rather than later. It will distract her either way."

"Do what you think is best." The Cat jumped up onto the counter, heading toward the kitchen. "Are movies more of the magic from your world?"

"They are like TV shows, but longer and usually self-contained with one story line, though sometimes you get a series like with the shows." My mind raced at what would be a good choice to watch with Indigo. I kept going to a happy dragon cartoon series with dragon riders and one of the best black dragons ever, but I wasn't sure.

I found myself glancing back at the fireplace. That warm feeling from seeing the light and hearing the song rested inside me. I felt strange, almost unanchored to the ground beneath me.

"Sable, you coming?" asked the Cat. He stared at me from the other side of the counter.

"Yeah...that light was strange," I mumbled.

"You saw light?" he asked, waiting for me to catch up.

"A stream of light, almost like it trickled over rocks before vanishing into the floor."

The Cat huffed.

The smell of something burning caused me to dash forward into the kitchen, leaving the Cat behind.

My PAW HOVERED in the air as my thoughts fought to catch up.

Sable saw the leylines, like one of the dragons or fey. My assumption was she'd see a doorway, or maybe the image of a tree. Usually that was what people saw, if they caught a glimpse between the worlds.

That, or utter darkness that shook their souls.

I knew she wouldn't be one of those. But to actually see the ley lines... most Travelers didn't even have that ability anymore.

It was another part of the mystery of her, and I had to get to solving that, or I wouldn't be able to protect her. And I had to protect her.

CHAPTER
EIGHTEEN

The first sip of warm coffee sent a thrill through me.

I'd slept well, but somehow still felt tired. Whispers of the dragons' singing echoed through my dreams, along with flowing rivers of light. The intensity lingered and it made getting great sleep hard.

Indigo nuzzled my chin.

I needed to be careful to not knock her over. While I'd listened to her snores early this morning, now all she wanted was to be attached to me.

"So, what is today going to be?" I asked as the Cat jumped up on the counter.

"The same thing as normal," grumbled the Cat as his black tail flickered through the air.

I paused before opening my mouth.

It felt like he wasn't in a good mood, and I didn't want to poke any more than I needed to. Hopefully, he meant it was something easy.

96

At least it wasn't a coffee shop day, since the shop looked normal.

The normal rows of bookshelves along the back wall were there, along with a few additional ones. Lots of bookshelves, actually, even the main table that sat in the middle of the room in front of the counter was loaded up with bookshelves.

The setup reminded me of something, but I couldn't put my finger on it. It didn't take long for the bells on the front door to ring, and a man covered in a flowing robe of dark green entered.

He looked familiar.

Everything clicked in the time it took him to get to the register with his basket.

"You!" I knew exactly what'd happened last time.

"Me?" he asked with a sharp grin. His large brown eyes somehow still looked sad, even as the rest of him screamed trouble.

"You're the Bookseller."

Laughter rushed out of him so fast, that he almost bent over. His multiple earrings sparkled in the sunlight from the skylight, highlighting his elven ears.

"I see, you remember me."

"You're kinda hard to forget." Not to mention he was the one who gave us the cold book that'd caused all sorts of trouble. Then again, Indigo wouldn't be here if that hadn't happened.

"And you are the Shopkeeper..." His voice trailed off as he said it, and his eyes narrowed.

Indigo peeked out from behind my dark hair, which was down for the day.

"Hello..." she squeaked.

"Oh my, now, that is a book dragon..." He took the remaining two steps forward and set his basket on the counter. "Maybe you are why I am here today."

The Cat padded closer, sniffing the basket. Indigo released her hold on me and scrambled off my shoulder with haste to sniff it as well.

He shook his head at her but she ignored him.

"Tell him to get to it," grumbled the Cat as he moved back from the basket, nudging Indigo away as well.

Indigo retreated, keeping close to the Cat.

The Bookseller's eyes glowed.

"Well now, I have a whole stack of rare books," he said as he opened the basket and pulled out a whole stack. Six thick books he set on the counter before pulling out another four. "Most of them are from your wanted list."

"Wanted list?" I asked.

The Cat nodded his head. "I sent him a list of books I'm looking for. Ones to remove from circulation, or ones that others want but can't find."

Indigo darted forward, but before she could move a step she froze.

"Can you grab her?" asked the Cat. "She shouldn't touch some of these."

I quickly picked the little dragon up, and she unfroze as soon as her feet left the counter. "Once he is gone we can look at the books," I told her.

The little dragon huffed at me but didn't resist. Instead, she glared at the Cat.

The Bookseller chuckled again, and he pulled out a

few more books. These books were smaller, with strange symbols on the front. One had a golden dragon embossed on the cover.

"I assume you have what I'm looking for this time…?" The brown eyes stayed on the Cat, who nodded.

"Sable, go get the blue box from the storage room," ordered the Cat.

I set Indigo back on my shoulder and quickly headed to the door in the hallway. Inside the room was only a small blue box covered in a thick cloth. It was heavier than it looked, and I carefully brought it out and added it to the counter.

His eyes stayed stuck to it as soon as it came into view.

"It seems you're being rather generous with me." His fingers reached toward the box, shifting into talons as they approached.

A growl came from my shoulder and he paused, then blinked. The talons retreated rapidly, becoming normal fingers.

"It's for all of the books on the counter," added the Cat. I quickly repeated the terms.

The Bookseller nodded frantically. "The bargain is struck."

Then the box was gone and the basket back in his arms as he retreated to the door.

Somehow he had moved without moving.

"Great doing business with you, Shopkeeper." The image of the Bookkeeper flickered, showing the tall, shirtless creature with deep, dark skin and puffy pants. "Good luck with your lands… Toodles!"

The door slammed shut behind him, the bells silent.

The Cat let out an angry growl, which then turned into a sigh.

"Your lands?" I asked after a moment. I knew that the Cat was a lord, but I hadn't really thought about where he'd come from.

Indigo practically vibrated in my arms staring at the books on the counter.

The Cat padded closer and touched half of them with a paw. "Put these in the storage room, then she can look at the rest of them."

My eyes narrowed as he ignored my question, but I quickly did as he asked.

As soon as the storage room door closed, Indigo nudged the book with the dragon on the cover open.

"Anything I should be worried about?" I asked, just to confirm.

"The book's about the various types of dragons. It was written by a book dragon long ago. The Clan of Knowledge is looking for a copy." His voice sounded bored, and his whiskers twitched.

"I meant about his comment..."

The Cat turned away, but paused before reaching the edge of the counter. "Nothing for you to worry about."

Then he jumped down, vanishing from sight.

I rolled my eyes and let out a sigh. If he didn't want to talk about it, I couldn't make him. That much I'd learned over the months spent in the shop.

"*Pretty...*" squeaked Indigo.

I turned to look at the book she'd opened.

Inside, a brightly colored dragon flew across the

page. Then as she tapped it, it flew off the page and in a circle in the air. The brightly colored scales shifted in the light as it flew.

My jaw dropped as I leaned closer. It only lasted two minutes, but I couldn't look away from the small flying creature.

"Looks like you found a magical book about dragons," I said, wishing I could read it for a while. "Though, I bet you already know what it's going to say."

"Only learned about the best dragons, not these…"

Now that sounded a little elitist, but I kept my mouth shut. All the fairy tales said dragons were proud creatures, and I wasn't going to get into a discussion with Indigo about how all dragons were awesome, versus only some.

Indigo breathed out her nose and the page turned on its own to a different picture of a dragon.

That was new. Indigo could turn pages with magic. I wondered what else Lady Twilight was teaching her.

As soon as I saw the Bookseller on the schedule for today I knew he'd rattle me. It didn't matter that he had books we needed to remove from the various worlds. As soon as we relieved him of his burden, guarding that cursed book, he went back to his old ways.

Such a shame.

All of Nymeria's children were like that, playing at being Fey Lords, which they could never be.

Sable's concern had caused me to hesitate, but there was much I couldn't explain.

All I could think about was my people, and what was happening in the Fey Wilds.

I padded my way up the stairs to look at the only connection I had. The oak tree stood in its container, the same as it was yesterday. The last time a leaf had been lost, it'd sent me into a spiral, and the lack of any change right now steadied me.

At least Indigo and Sable would enjoy the dragon book. Now I had something to hold over the dragons, leverage to discover if they truly were messing with what was left of my lands.

Yet, that single red leaf still grew from the tree. If the dragons were my enemies, why was Liluth still alive?

CHAPTER

NINETEEN

A shiver went down my spine just thinking of the Bookseller. Yet, he was gone.

On the one hand, I was thankful that Indigo ended up in my life, but on the other, that evil book had almost killed me.

Not really, but it felt like it.

Or at least like something inside me had almost withered away.

I sipped what was left of my coffee and closed my eyes to enjoy it.

Indigo flipped through the dragon book for the fifth time. While the magical floating images kept distracting me, I needed more caffeine, and maybe some hot tub time.

The Cat had vanished somewhere to do whatever he did, which was the go-ahead that my duties were done for the day.

I loved my life.

My job was awesome, and some days were long, but most times, it was pretty simple. Do whatever the task for the day was, then spend time with Indigo.

"Sable…" The Cat's voice echoed from the balcony above, and for once he sounded concerned.

"Yes, Cat?" I replied. I knew his name, but it felt weird to think it, let alone say it. Plus, it didn't linger. I couldn't remember it without focusing on it for several moments.

"Did you invite anyone over?"

My coffee cup paused on the way to my lips, and my lips parted. "What? I don't invite people over…"

I finished my cup and turned toward Betty, needing more caffeine to deal with whatever the Cat was concerned about.

"Well, that's not what the book says…" He jumped onto the counter with force and almost flew off the far side. His loss of control caused me to take this a little more seriously.

"So? My brothers stopped by without a problem." I ground the espresso beans. "What's the problem this time?"

The bells on the door rang, and the Cat jumped back on the counter, knocking into Indigo. She chirped as she went tumbling off the back near my feet. Her chirp cut off as I turned to the door.

"Welcome to the sho…" My voice trailed off as I turned to look at who'd entered.

"Sable - surprise!" Standing in a red puffy jacket and bright green earmuffs was Jackie. She was one of my oldest childhood friends from back home.

"Whoa, Jackie..." I blinked twice, then quickly glanced at my feet to see the Cat, sitting right next to Indigo, who stared up at me with wide eyes.

"What are you doing here?" I moved the last stack of three books closer to the register and leaned to the counter. I quickly stacked the dragon book on top.

Jackie chuckled in that bright voice I remembered from joking around at school.

"Your mom mentioned you were working in the area. She gave me the address of the shop." Her eyes traveled around the space.

"Talk about a bookstore..." She turned slowly in a circle.

Taking a few seconds to steady my racing thoughts, I continued to make my shots of espresso.

"Uh, let me grab you some coffee and we can chat..." Out of the corner of my eye, I checked her out. Her auburn hair and green eyes were the same as I remembered. Not to mention the freckles, though she'd grown into them and they complemented her fair skin quite nicely.

Seeing the Cat's tail puffed as he tried to sneak Indigo down the hallway, I assumed Jackie shouldn't be here.

"I can't believe my mom's sending my friends to come and check on me."

"I'm only visiting the city for a couple of hours," she replied, looking at the stacks of books on the center table. She chuckled slightly. "Unfortunately, I'm moving back home."

I set my coffee cup on the counter, now filled with an Americano, as I quickly made another.

"Wait—didn't you swear to leave and never come back?" I flashed her a grin, but she didn't return it.

Instead, she chuckled softly, almost sadly.

"That was the plan, but finding a job has been rough." She shrugged, moving back in front of the counter. "My parents invited me to come back home and stay in the apartment over the barn."

"And that led to chatting with my mom?"

"Oh, no, that was about the job with your brother, Umber. He's looking for help on the farm; she's the one trying to fill the spot."

"Let me finish the coffee and we can go back to the kitchen." I filled a bright green mug with hot water and topped it off with the espresso.

"Can I get some cream and sugar in that?" she asked, watching me.

I nodded with a smile before fixing her drink. Then I grabbed both cups.

"Come on back," I said, holding out the coffee. The Cat and Indigo were nowhere to be seen in the hallway, which was important. As I passed the stairs, I saw paws and a set of talons on the very top step.

"This looks like a nice gig. How did you find it?" she asked as we entered the kitchen.

"Job board. I lucked out, though my family wouldn't think so," I mumbled as I sat down at the island. I set her coffee cup in front of one of the other stools.

Jackie took a seat and grabbed the coffee, unzipping her jacket. "Well, your family has always been close, and

I think your mother wanted you to come home and take over the clinic."

This time I snorted. "There wasn't a chance I was going to continue to study medicine."

My mother ran the clinic in town. She was the closest thing to a town doctor we had, and she was the school nurse as well.

"Plus, she'd do anything for me to return home."

"Don't knock her. Without this job with Umber, I'm not sure what I'd do." Jackie took a sip of her drink. "This is good."

"Yeah, we only use the best beans..." Then again, I wasn't sure what world we even got our coffee beans from. They just kind of showed up. It occurred to me that I wasn't even sure it was, technically, coffee, but it smelled like it, tasted amazing, and I decided to just let that particular mystery go.

"So, how long are you in town?"

"Only the day, I just wanted to stop by and see you. My car's parked out front, full of my stuff. Whatever didn't fit got sold or donated."

"Well, you can let my mother know I'm doing fine. I love my job, and I'll be here until my contract is up. I can't give up the room and board, plus the other benefits." A dark shape padded down the hallway, but before I panicked, I realized it was the Cat. Jackie turned to look and saw him.

"Oh my, look at that handsome fellow." She glanced back at me. "You always wanted a cat or two."

My laughter spilled out as the Cat jumped onto the island. If only she knew.

The Cat glared at me as she reached out to pet him. Him purring took over from my laughter.

I smiled, and then noticed a purple shadow dart toward the front of the shop.

As long as Indigo stayed out of the kitchen, this would all work out.

TWENTY

"So, you basically run the bookstore?" asked Jackie, breaking my train of thought.

"Yeah, pretty much. I keep up on inventory, and sometimes we have events." I motioned toward the front of the shop. "Right now I'm working on an inventory project and getting a new load of books put away from a large estate sale."

She chuckled. "This must be a dream come true for you. I know you loved the coffee shop job you had, but you've wanted a bookstore since we were kids."

All I could think about was Indigo and whatever she was doing out front. I hoped she was heading to her hideaway to listen to a book.

The Cat didn't even glance toward the front. Instead, he lay down in front of Jackie, who kept petting him.

"I mean, it's a pretty perfect job for me." I leaned across the table, trying to come up with something that was safe to talk about. "Plus, there is a hot tub on the roof deck. Like, you can't beat that."

"Okay, I'm jealous. You get all of this, and I get to dig in the dirt with your brother."

Dots connected in my mind. "Wait, didn't you have a crush on him when we were teenagers?"

Her cheeks blazed a bright red, and I grinned. "Oh, the crush is still there..."

"I bet he's involved with someone..." She downed a good amount of coffee, wrapping both her hands around her mug.

The Cat tilted his head in my direction as he spoke, "Are you just going to gossip with her? Get her to leave..."

I couldn't respond and ignored him for the moment. "He recently ended a long relationship, and as far as I know he is available."

"What about you? Any crushes I should know about?" The Cat pawed at the air and Jackie patted his belly.

I finished my coffee before replying. "Nothing like that for me. Not right now, anyway. I have too much on my plate, with managing the shop."

I hadn't even thought about looking to date some-one, given that I couldn't leave the shop. The only people who regularly came in were the delivery guy, and then Molly's dad, neither of which I wanted to get involved with. Well, there were the dragons as well, but that'd be slightly weird.

"I can be a crazy young cat person, for now at least."

This time the Cat glared at me while talking, "Cat person? You aren't a cat person."

Normally having conversations where people couldn't hear him wasn't bad, but this time his running commentary was a bit too much. My mind went to the massive painting in my room of him from the cat person. I might just be a crazy cat lady after all.

Jackie shook her head with a small smile.

"We have to keep in better touch. I can fill you in on all the small-town drama." She rolled her eyes. "Not that anything happens at home."

"Isn't that why we both left?" I asked. "Nothing kept us interested in staying."

Both of our families were upset that we'd left, but that hadn't stopped us. We wanted to see the bigger world. I knew I'd seen a much bigger world since taking this job.

"That's what we said," added Jackie with a soft smile. "Growing up changes things, that's for sure."

"I might go back after my contract is up, but who knows? Maybe the next time I'll be home is your wedding..."

Jackie laughed, this time rolling her eyes. "Talk about jumping the gun."

A loud bang like a book falling to the floor came from the front of the shop, drawing all three of our attention.

The Cat jumped to his feet. "I told her to stay upstairs."

"Gotta love falling books," I mumbled quickly.

"Well, I just wanted to stop in and see how you were doing. I gotta get back on the road. As is, it's gonna take a few days to get home. I somehow keep adding stops."

"I wonder why," I said, getting to my feet as she did as well.

The Cat jumped from the island and headed to the front of the shop faster than we did.

"How many folks are you going to visit with?" I asked, trying to slow her down.

"A few from school, no one else from back home." She walked over to the sink and placed her cup inside. "It's strange, almost everyone else returned, or didn't leave."

"Really?" I wasn't sure what she was talking about, and tilted my head in her direction.

Jackie turned to face me, zipping her coat up. "We're the only ones who are still living away."

I took the lead, slowly walking down the hallway to the front, delaying as much as possible.

The dragon book no longer sat on the top of the stack on the counter.

I swallowed as I slowly walked around the counter, but it wasn't on the floor either. Indigo and the Cat were nowhere nearby as we headed to the door.

"That's weird, but not unexpected, really. If you love the small-town feel, we have it." My mind raced, trying to come up with an example. "I mean, the adults have gatherings every holiday to celebrate, drink, and be merry."

"There was nothing exciting for us as kids, but maybe it will be different now." Her eyes lingered on the bookshelves on the far wall.

The winter holidays were next. "Remember, the Solstice holiday is next. You'll get to see what the big fuss was always about."

Jackie's face brightened as she zipped up her fluffy

jacket. "That's right, I'm old enough to join in this year." She chuckled slightly. "I can tell you all about the ball, or whatever it is. Not to mention, I'll keep you in the loop with how your family is doing. I know they aren't fans of technology."

"Tell me about it, our text thread gathers dust every so often." We both paused by the door, and I opened my arms for a hug. By the time she pulled away, I felt like I'd pulled it off, albeit with a little help from the Cat.

Normal bookstore, check!

She opened the door and then did a double take. "Oh, no! I think you might have a rat problem."

I twisted about, seeing a shadow near the far bookshelf. My eyes grew wide at the flash of purple. "Oh, the Cat can deal with that, I'm sure..."

A loud squeak came from that area. *"I am not a rat!"*

The patter of claws on the floor caused me to inhale deeply.

Don't you dare, Indigo!

TWENTY-ONE

"It was great seeing you, but I need to get back to work on inventory." I grabbed the edge of the door and opened it wider, mentally urging her to leave already.

Her car was stuffed to the brim right outside the front of the shop.

"I'll keep in touch!"

"Same!" I said with a fake grin, before closing the door and locking it.

That was too close.

I let out a sigh before turning to Indigo, who was dragging the dragon book across the floor.

"You couldn't wait until she was gone?" I asked, taking a step forward.

"My book! Wanted it now!"

"We can't let normal people see you," I said with a frown, picking the book up and setting it near the door to her hideaway. The small door wouldn't fit the book, but magic might take care of it.

She huffed.

"Indigo," I whispered lightly as she flew from the floor up to the opening to her space. "I just worry."

At the tone of my voice, her head hung a little low, and she peeked down from the top of the bookcase.

"Sorry, no worries," she replied, her tail dragging behind her. *"I forgot to use my shadow magic."*

"It's okay, you're still little, and she didn't see you, this time. In the future, be more careful." I patted her on the top of the head.

Indigo nodded, then her head vanished from sight.

When the delivery guys were here, she remembered, but not when a random friend from home showed up. Then again, that book was pretty amazing, with the magical drawings.

Her hideaway was a private space, but I couldn't help but wonder about all she had inside there. My assumption was books and a place to rest, but I didn't know. It wasn't like I could visit.

"Cat, I thought you raced out here to hide her?" I asked, searching for him.

"That isn't my problem," he said. His voice came down from above and still sounded concerned.

I shook my head, walking back to the counter and picking up the rest of the books before popping them into the storage room. By the time I made it to the top of the steps, the dragon book and Indigo were gone.

Somehow the book had made it inside her little space.

The Cat sat near the small oak tree, staring up at it. It hadn't changed as far as I could tell. That one bright red leaf, with the rest green, stood out and it made me pause.

I didn't want to intrude on his space, but I did want to know.

"So, yeah. I didn't invite Jackie for a visit," I started.

"That much was clear." He turned to face me, his green eyes glowing. "Though, I'm not sure that was who the book warned me about."

He padded to me and rubbed against my ankle.

I bent down and picked him up. "Not my fault, I swear. My family can be a little crazy."

Pulling him close, I cuddled him toward my chest.

He purred in response.

"Is Indigo being a little angsty today? It's like she's hit her teenage phase..." While the dragon had apologized, the outburst was still out of character.

"What is a teenager?" asked the Cat.

"The worst time in a human's life," I explained, while sitting in the chair next to the tree. "Everything sucks and you're stuck in that weird place between being a kid and an adult. Not to mention acne."

"Indigo is too young to be in the adolescent phase yet." He stood up and circled twice before sitting down on my lap. "More likely, she wants the book for her hoard. She's young to create one, though I wondered if hers was going to be those books she listens to."

"I mean, it's a pretty awesome book. I'd want it for my hoard, if I had one." I wasn't a big collector of things in general, but that was a nice book.

The Cat chuckled lightly. "That book belongs to the shop, not to her. It might be why she's grumpy. She knows it doesn't belong to her, and she can't do anything about it."

"Can't I just give it to her?" I asked, a little confused.

"No, it will remain in the shop for the time being. She can read it, but she doesn't own it."

A long list of questions ran through my head, starting with 'What difference does it make who owns it' and ending with 'Why do you care,' but I resisted asking.

The Cat broke the small silent pause as my brain raced. "I'm wondering who the next visitor is going to be."

"I mean, we can order Chinese food. The delivery driver knows our location pretty well." I didn't look down at the Cat, but I knew he glared at me.

"That isn't how the book works. Usually, I have more information."

"Is it broken?"

Again more glaring from the Cat. "You can't break a book from the Fates."

"This would be easier if I could read the book," I added lightly.

He looked away and purred. "Chinese food for lunch would be tasty, though, if you wanted to order some."

I chuckled at the change of topic. "Of course. I'll get our regular order."

I swore the shop knew what we got by heart, since I rarely deviated from it and we got Chinese at least once a week. Plus, it was so easy just to hit the reorder button in the app.

"Chinese?" squeaked a voice from below, and I couldn't help but laugh.

"Yes, I will get your soup dumplings that you love," I called out. "Though we have some time before lunch."

I CALMED down in Sable's lap as she scratched behind one of my ears. Whatever was coming hadn't happened yet, but the item on the task list in the book made little sense. I thought it had to do with the unexpected guest that had just left, but Sable's friend hadn't crossed the item off. The only hint I had was 'Unexpected visitor'.

The Fates must be playing a cruel game on me right now, since the book was being so vague. Between worrying about that and what was going on with my lands, I didn't know what to do with myself. Both items were things outside of my control, and even with all my centuries of practice, out of control was not a place any Fey Lord liked to be.

Plus, I now had another item on my list to figure out. What was a crazy cat lady, and why did Jackie think Sable was one of them?

Maybe I should get rid of that picture of me she'd hung up in her room. Having it hung up did make her rather strange.

TWENTY-TWO

I lost myself in my thoughts as I petted the Cat. Jackie heading home was almost unbelievable, yet she'd stopped by and we'd spoken about it.

If my life hadn't become so magical, I wouldn't believe it.

Now, who knew?

Yet, her comment lingered about everyone either not leaving or eventually returning. After all, my mother swore I'd be back, yet here I sat.

I didn't know how long I sat there with the Cat, but eventually he jumped over to his cat house, and I made my way downstairs to order the food.

Not to mention, make a cup of tea. Tea sounded good, and would be a pleasant change from all the coffee I'd been drinking. By the time I made it down to the front counter, the shop had changed to the default layout.

The tall bookshelves in the back were like always, not overflowing, and the large table in the middle had a tasteful arrangement of books instead of disorganized piles. Everything was nice and neat. Two fluffy chairs sat near the right wall, instead of the children's area. The fireplace from before stood on the wall with crystals glowing inside.

"I love a good fireplace..." I muttered as I heated the water before pouring it into the mug. The metal tea ball floated to the surface until I poked it down.

Quietly, I walked over and sat down in a chair, staring at the fake fire. The crystal still sent warmth into the room, and it made the entire space feel cozy.

"Betty, you are fantastic at making this place feel like a home, even though it's a shop."

A blast of warmth flooded out from the fireplace, and I giggled.

A squeak announced Indigo right before she landed on the armrest.

"Feels inviting."

"It really does..." I said with a smile.

Indigo slowly climbed onto my shoulder, careful to not jostle my mug. It was clear she still felt bad about earlier.

"Soon the winter Solstice will be here," I said. Jackie's visit had reminded me that my family, well, my mother, expected me to be home for the holiday and the family dinner.

That couldn't happen, and somehow I needed to explain it to her. I let my mind brainstorm as I sipped on the rich tea. It was a minty blend that didn't get bitter from steeping too long.

"Party, like your birthday?" asked the dragon.

"It's a gathering, but not focused on one person. It's more about the food and company. There are songs people sing, and special cookies that only come out that one time of year." I sipped on my tea. "You would enjoy it."

"We can go!" Indigo leaped off my shoulder and flew around the room in a large circle before landing on the armrest again.

"Not this year, but maybe next year. We can decorate the enormous tree and you can see all the pretty lights in town." Decorating for the holidays could be fun.

The doorknob rattled, cutting off my rambling. I set my mug down before frantically jolting toward the door.

"Coming!"

The Chinese delivery guy was unusually quick. The door unlocked as I approached, and I swung it open to get the plastic bag.

"You were..." my words stopped as I blinked at the person on the other side. It wasn't the delivery guy. All I saw was a mouth filled with sharp teeth and an outstretched hand with pointed talons.

Panic rushed through me, and I wished them away.

Bright light pulsed out in a wave from the bracelet on my wrist. The golden light slammed into the creature and shoved it back across the snow.

I slammed the door shut and locked it as my heart pounded in my chest.

Stumbling backward, I didn't even hear Indigo until she flew right in my face. I landed in a chair that hadn't been there before as the Cat appeared near my feet.

"Sable!" Bright green eyes stared at me before he

raced to the door, peering out the window. "What happened?"

Squeaks came from Indigo, too fast for me to follow. Then a shimmering image appeared floating in the air in front of the Cat. It showed me opening the door, and then paused as I stared at the creature.

Now that it wasn't in my face, I noticed more detail. The creature stood taller than me, with armor and a sword strapped to its back. Deep black scales covered it under the armor, and it didn't wear shoes. Both fingers and toes were sharp talons.

"What was it?" I asked, clutching my bracelet to my chest.

"A dragonling..." muttered the Cat. "I've never met one before."

His head tilted sideways as the image moved. It showed the golden wave of light flash out of my bracelet and hit the dragonling.

"You did magic..." This time his eyes went to me.

The bracelet glowed, and I didn't know what to say.

"Dragonling?! Are they okay?" Indigo's comment cut the silence in half as I jumped to my feet.

"Oh, no..."

"They are probably the unexpected visitor," said the Cat. "All I know is that they are normally warriors, on the more orderly side of things. They usually work with the Fates, whether or not they know it..."

I quickly reached out to the door to yank it open, but it remained locked.

"Betty, I might have overreacted and we need to make sure they're okay."

The door remained locked, but an impression that felt like the shop was asking if I was sure hit me.

"I'm sure. Plus, I can blast him again and you can eat him if necessary."

A second later the door unlocked, and I yanked it open.

The dragonling stood a few feet away from the opening.

"Are you okay?" I asked. "You surprised me is all..."

He scratched the back of his head, staring at the door.

"A fine blast of magic, that. I didn't mean to surprise you." He shrugged, letting his hand fall. "I heard this place might have the knowledge I'm looking for, if I may enter?"

That's when I realized I still stood in the doorway.

"Come on in," I said, turning toward the counter. I took one step forward and suddenly found myself stepping behind the register.

Yet, the Dragonling hadn't entered the shop.

The Cat also stood near the base of the counter, and Indigo rested on top.

"It's all good, Betty..." I whispered reassuringly, while patting the wooden countertop.

The dragonling entered the shop, glancing around with wide eyes. "So many books..."

"So, what are you looking for?"

The dragonling took a moment to answer, turning around in a circle to see the whole shop. "Maps...I'm looking for a hidden place."

"Well, you're already in some luck, since this shop is hard to find," I replied with a grin.

The Cat, sitting next me, went still, then his tail flickered through the air. "There are a few maps rolled up in the corner near the window."

I pointed toward the rolls of paper. "There are some maps over there."

I tried to take a step in that direction away from the counter, but my feet didn't move. It felt like the floorboards were stuck to my shoes.

"Betty…"

"Maps? That would be helpful." One moment he was in the middle of the room, the next he was pulling the tubes of paper out, then he was in front of the counter setting them down.

Indigo jerked backward, drawing the dragonling's attention.

"Oh, hello little one." He bobbed his head at her before setting a map on the counter and unrolling it. "Oh, wow…"

The map showed some world I didn't know.

"This is wondrous." A claw pointed at a location with a weird tree holding a book. "That's where we are right now."

Indigo leaned as far as her neck would let her, staring at the map.

He traced along the edge of a mountain range toward a circle of stones. "Yes - this is what I need to finish my quest."

Quest - he was on an actual quest.

His golden eyes rose to study me. "What will this cost me?"

"Knowledge!" Indigo commented before the Cat or I could say anything. Both of us turned to glance at her. *"Knowledge of what you find!"*

TWENTY-THREE

"Indigo..."

The Cat grumbled near my hand. "That's a good price."

My head swiveled to look at him, before turning back to the dragonling. "What she said. Knowledge of what you find, and what you are seeking."

"The little one is wise." The dragonling bowed his head. "I will return when I finish my quest."

With that, the door jingled as he vanished from sight.

"Okay, so what just happened?" I asked before turning toward the Cat. "And how didn't you know that he was going to show up?"

"Sometimes the book doesn't give details." The Cat's tail flickered in the air a few times. "Usually, it's more useful than it was today, but dragonlings are strange creatures, an offshoot of dragons. From what I know, they're hard to track when they are on a quest. They might have magic that prevents it."

"Even from the Fates?"

The Cat didn't respond. Instead, he sat down on the counter.

I held up the bracelet, which wasn't glowing anymore. "How did I do that?"

"*Magic!*"

I chuckled at Indigo's bright response, trying to settle the panic in me. The bookstore had magic that I used, but it wasn't mine; I didn't have magic.

"I'm not magical, Indigo…"

"That wave pushing him back would indicate otherwise," interrupted the Cat. His green eyes flickered toward me, and then Indigo. "The dragon stone wouldn't have worked if you didn't have some sort of magic. The same went for seeing the job application, though both only need the tiniest seed."

I sat on the stool trying to get my brain to work. "So, you're saying you knew I had magic this whole time?"

"Everyone usually has some sort of magic; just ask Indigo."

"*Lady Twilight said so.*" Indigo scrambled next to my hands, which rested on the counter.

I didn't dare contradict her statement about Lady Twilight, but magic didn't exist on my world.

"Every living thing has some magic from the tree. We all come from there." Her purple scales glittered in the sunlight coming from above. "Not all can use it, and most are not very strong, but all have it."

Maybe there was just a little magic inside me.

She danced a little. "*But you can use it! Which means you can freely visit the clan lands someday!*"

I reached up and rubbed my forehead. More questions were racing through my head as Indigo danced around the counter, before her excitement was too much and she took off into the air.

"I knew you were magic! You smell like a dragon. Baby dragon, smaller than me, but a dragon!"

"She doesn't smell like a dragon," said the Cat.

"Does too!"

The Cat only glared at her in response before turning to me. "Maybe dragons do become like teenagers from your world."

His tail jerked to one side before he turned away from the little dragon.

"Teenagers?"

"Back to my magic. I have magic and can use it to blast people?" I held up the bracelet. "This let me use it?"

"Just like the leaf and feather on your necklace let you call for the dragons, or use the magic of the archangel, items can unlock certain abilities," explained the Cat.

Indigo flew circles around the Cat, but he completely ignored her. Total teenager behavior.

Shaking my head, I tried to wrap my mind around all of this and explain what was going on inside my head.

"Those are powerful magical items, from very magical people. This came from my brother... He's the least magical person there is." While Cerulean worked one of the most adventurous jobs I knew, that didn't mean he was magic.

The bracelet probably came from some artist he found in a small village. The more I thought about it, the more it made sense. He bought it and thought it would make a good gift for me.

"Indigo how about fewer circles? You might make yourself dizzy," I said.

"What is dizzy?"

I closed my eyes for a second before opening them, trying to figure out how to explain it to the dragon.

The Cat's head snapped toward the door. "That will be food."

Two seconds later, someone knocked on the wooden frame. This time when I stepped in that direction I was free to move. It didn't take long to get to the door and open it. The delivery guy stood on the other side of the door with our food. The smell of the Chinese food filled the shop as I headed to the kitchen.

"Food, and then we can continue this conversation, because I need carbs."

Thankfully, Indigo took off flying toward the kitchen.

The Cat remained on the counter watching me. "How long do the teenage years last for humans?"

I chuckled, carrying the bags of food.

"According to my mother, until we're thirty, but realistically only about ten years. Some get over it sooner than others..." My voice trailed off as I thought about the other time humans threw tantrums. "Toddlers are a lot like teenagers, though, and that's only a few years."

The Cat jumped off the counter and walked beside me down the hall. He hopped up on the island as we approached.

The big bowl I used for Indigo's dumpling soup,

along with the normal plates for the Cat and I, were already sitting in the center.

Indigo waited, shifting from side to side next to her bowl.

I unpacked the food and poured her soup into the bowl.

Surprisingly, she didn't try to swim it in. Instead, she dunked her head in it and drank some broth.

"Don't want to swim in your food?" I asked with a small smile.

"Lady Twilight said it isn't proper..."

"Well, we do have the hot tub on the roof when we want to relax in some hot water." That sounded like the perfect afternoon. I plated up the spicy chicken for the Cat and some noodles for me.

Indigo chirped positively.

"Alright," I said, setting the plate in front of the Cat. "How do I learn to use this magic that I have?"

The Cat blinked before taking a bite of the food.

I dug into my noodles, hoping this wasn't going to devolve into a staring match.

"Practice, just like anything else." He said after a few moments of eating.

"Lady Twilight says magic is easy," chirped Indigo, with a bite of dumpling in her mouth. Pieces tumbled back out into her soup. *"You need to picture it to make it happen."*

"You need to finish swallowing your food before you speak," I added, looking away from the mess she'd made on the counter.

"She isn't wrong," said the Cat. "Magic is all about

intention. Earlier, how did you feel when you used the bracelet?"

I paused with my fork in the air, noodles dangling from the end, then set it back down on my plate. "Panicked. All I saw for a second was that demon. I just wanted him away."

"So, he was pushed away," explained the Cat. He went back to his food as I thought about it some more.

I chewed on my noodles, trying to wrap my head around it.

It seemed too easy. Just think about what I want, and it happens?

Inside the shop, Betty responded to my thoughts and requests. Usually before I could voice them, but that was because the shop knew my preferences, like the plates and bowls we always used for Chinese being on the table.

"Tell her about energy..." squeaked Indigo.

I blinked at the little dragon as she moved away from her bowl. Somehow in the little time that had passed, she had finished the entire bowl and cleaned up the mess she'd made.

The dragon walked over to the bag of egg rolls, and using one claw, she carefully opened the top before pulling one out with her mouth.

The Cat let out a sigh before pulling away from his chicken. "Magic costs energy. That gold wave you saw was that energy. Indigo has shadow magic, like Lady Twilight. For you, it's gold. You only contain so much of it, and when you do magic, you use it."

"Mana, you're talking about mana..." I'd played

enough video games to know the general idea of what the Cat was trying to explain.

"See, she knows," he added, speaking to Indigo, then went back to his food.

I didn't know any specifics. Those were games, and this was real life. My life wasn't a video game, and I didn't have a way to track how much mana I had or used at once.

"What else can I do with my magic?" I asked, grabbing an egg roll for myself, and still not entirely sure I wanted to know the answer.

Every time I asked a question, it led to more I didn't understand. I already had to contend with the fact that I had magic, and something was up with my brother.

Wasn't that enough for a single day?

CHAPTER
TWENTY-FOUR

The Cat turned and stared at me before responding. I wasn't sure if it was a dumb question, or if he was looking at my soul—either could fit the situation.

"It depends on your Mana capacity, and the strength of your magic." He longingly looked at his chicken before continuing. "The more complex the action you are trying to accomplish, the more strength and Mana you need."

"It's why dragons are the best," interrupted Indigo. The egg roll she'd dragged away was nowhere to be seen. *"We have lots of both."*

"Dragons are not the only creatures strong with magic," growled the Cat. He shook his head after a moment and focused back on his chicken. "Dragons always think they are on top of the list. A full archangel, as only one example, would outclass many dragons."

It felt like he had plenty more he wanted to say to the young dragon, but was resisting.

I wolfed down a bunch of my noodles. "So, Indigo... What can you do with your shadow magic?"

The little book dragon's eyes opened wide.

"Watch this!" She launched herself into the air and then she faded, but only partially, leaving a faint outline of her flying around the room.

I leaned toward the Cat. "Should we be able to see her still?"

"Most wouldn't be able to." His tail flickered in the air before he finished his plate. "Can I have some noodles?"

I nodded and poured a pile on his plate.

"Did you see me?" She flapped her wings faster as she flew around. *"I vanished!"*

"Yep, you vanished! I know you are good at disappearing into shadows." I pointed toward my necklace. "Plus, you helped Lady Twilight shrink the feather."

Indigo shook her head as she landed. *"I watched, but I can only shrink non-magical things for now."*

That reminded me of the dice slowly getting smaller as we played the board game. "I guess you'll be able to teach me how to use magic," I said jokingly to Indigo.

"Absolutely not," growled the Cat. His voice hung in the air. "I know someone who can help you, though."

Indigo went from smiley to crestfallen, and the Cat stuttered. "It's...because Sable can't learn dragon magic. She needs someone who can teach her type of magic."

"Lady Twilight can help," stated Indigo.

"The Lady Dragon can teach you magic, little one. Sable needs her own teacher." The Cat quickly turned toward the noodles I'd given him. Each time he took a bite of food, it vanished from the plate.

For a second I saw an outline of what I swore were

much bigger teeth. I hadn't seen that before, and it was almost like the outline of Indigo I'd still been able to see when she'd vanished while flying.

I reached out to Indigo and scratched under her chin, which perked her up. "Plus, Lady Twilight needs to focus on you. We can't be taking up all of her time, she is an important dragon."

The top of the island rippled, and my phone rose next to my hand. I blinked, and then it vibrated as a message appeared.

"Thanks, Betty…" I whispered.

The Cat watched as I snagged it to see the messages. It also distracted Indigo from talking about how awesome dragons were.

I had four, no, five missed messages from Cerulean asking how I was doing, and what I was up to. It was a private thread without anyone else. As I read through them, another one came in with just a question mark.

I shook my head in confusion. Cerulean never texted me. Heck, him even showing up with the gift for me was out of the ordinary.

Before I could respond, the phone started buzzing again. This time, his name flashed across the screen with him calling. I narrowed my eyes as I answered the phone.

"Hello…" I said hesitantly, wondering if one of my other brothers had borrowed his phone.

"Hey Sable, how are things going?" asked Cerulean, sounding a little too cheerful. "I realized we haven't chatted since my visit."

I paused for a second, my head tilting to one side.

It drew Indigo's attention, along with the Cat's.

"I'm fine, just eating some Chinese food for lunch, then I need to keep working on inventory. It's been a boring week."

"Oh, nothing out of the ordinary?" In the phone call's background, the whistle of wind echoed loudly for a moment.

"No... Just a normal day. Where are you?" I wanted to ask more about his location, and the noise in the background. This whole thing was just too weird.

"Working, but I had a quick break, so I wanted to call, especially since you didn't respond to the texts."

I leaned back on the stool, careful to not fall. "I keep my phone in my room while working, I only caught your call since I started my lunch break."

"Well, if everything is okay, I gotta get back to work." Someone yelled in the distance, and Cerulean responded, saying something about the storm coming in. "Talk to you later."

My phone beeped, and he ended the call before I said goodbye.

"Who was that?" asked Indigo while creeping closer.

"My brother." I quickly opened the text messages back up and sent along a reply.

Sable: I hope your day goes well! Don't die!

Cerulean: Of course I won't.

"He's being very weird." The edge of the bracelet he had gotten me poked out from under my sleeve. "Cat, is it possible that my brother knew something happened with the bracelet?"

"Anything is possible. The question you wanted to ask is whether it's probable." The Cat licked his empty plate. "Only you can answer that."

"You should try some more magic. Make me fly backward," squeaked Indigo. Her voice cut across my thoughts as she giggled. *"Make wind."*

"Maybe up on the roof, once I crawl into the hot tub. I don't want to make a mess of the shop. I might miss and hit a bookshelf." Though I bet Betty would straighten anything up that got out of order, I didn't want to create more work for the shop. "Let me first make a drink to bring up."

Indigo quickly launched herself toward the door, singing about warm waves and strong winds.

I shook my head as I packed up the leftovers.

The Cat remained on the island.

"Are you going to join us on the roof?"

"No, thank you. You can deal with the teenager." He jumped off the counter and padded out of the kitchen before vanishing.

Still, the text message thread with my brother made me wonder. Was it possible he knew about magic? Somehow, I needed to find a way to ask.

ALL I COULD COME up with was that she didn't want to know the truth.

Mortals sometimes didn't. Otherwise, there were too

many shady moments surrounding her brother to not connect some dots.

Eventually, she'd ask me outright, and I didn't know what to say.

Neither Lady Twilight, nor Lord Bennit, had commented on her family, even after dangling morsels of potential family power with the bracelet.

I stepped into my study, before leaping onto the table. The constant hum from the golden book agitated me, but I ignored it like always.

Sable needed to be my focus right now.

The magic she used appeared gold.

Something about that tickled in the back of my mind, something important. Shaking my head, a tome flew off the shelves and landed in front of me.

Time to discover what.

CHAPTER

TWENTY-FIVE

"*Waffles...*" whispered a quiet voice next to my ear.

Laughter, a group of women singing, and golden light everywhere. Whispers of voices I almost recognized and very familiar people. Dark shapes of people near a fire talking, and something about stones.

"*Waffles,*" came again.

I blinked in my dark room, yawning. The dream fled. The thick blankets covered me, just leaving my foot and my head uncovered.

"*Can we have waffles for breakfast?*" A warm snout pressed right next to my ear, almost tickling me.

Thankfully, I recognized Indigo. Groaning, I wrapped my arm around her, causing her to chuckle, before I dragged her under the covers.

"Waffles in the morning," I mumbled. "Sleep right now." After I closed my eyes, I felt her snuggles under my chin, her scales feeling softer than they should.

Something nudged me again, interrupting the dream that involved elves, magic, and little pink flowers.

"You said waffles!"

This time when I opened my eyes, the bright sunlight streaming in from above kept them open. "I'm moving, I'm moving."

Indigo pounced across my bed and then jumped high in the air before soaring out my open door. Chirping echoed from the shop as she flew around the open space.

It didn't take long for me to get up, dressed, and ready for work. Before Indigo could bug me again, I was staring into the oven, watching the waffles like a hawk.

Indigo kept flying around the room, trying to draw my attention, but I resisted. I didn't want the waffles to burn. They were just a little too big for the toaster—the waffles, not Indigo. Though, she wouldn't fit in the toaster either.

I rubbed my eyes, trying to wake up. Indigo and I had spent too long in the hot tub trying to get my magic to work again. All it left me with was a headache, and weird dreams once I finally fell asleep.

My bright blue mug with stars already sat empty, and I needed to make another.

First, the waffles, or I might have a very upset dragon on my hands. It didn't matter that she was the size of a cat. I didn't want to see what she could do with those claws.

I yanked the oven open and pulled out the large waffle using the tips of my fingers, which burned slightly in the process. Then I did it again for the second and third one, stacking them on a plate.

"Tongs exist for a reason," said the Cat, jumping onto the island.

"Yeah, yeah... I'm a little tired today," I mumbled, setting the plate on the island.

The Cat stared at me, then the waffles.

"Weird dreams, and Indigo really wanted waffles." I yanked the waffles out of the way as she crash landed on the island. "Woah, woah, woah, Indigo...!"

"Sorry..."

"Do you want butter and syrup?" I tossed a waffle on my plate, and another on the Cat's.

"Yes, please." The Cat nudged Indigo toward her normal sitting area.

I fixed mine and the Cat's waffles, cutting them up and adding lots of butter and syrup, before setting the Cat's plate in front of him.

Then I stared at Indigo for a moment. "How do you want your waffle?"

"I make!"

I opened my mouth and then closed it before setting the whole waffle on her plate and grabbing my fork.

Both the Cat and I watched Indigo as we dug into our food. She carefully used her front claws to 'cut' up her waffle. By cut up, I mean rip into uneven pieces. Some were as big as her head, others much smaller. Then the syrup bottle wobbled in the air all by itself.

I resisted helping and instead took a few bites of my waffle. Inside my head, I shouted words of encouragement as Indigo concentrated on using her magic.

Buttery, maple goodness exploded in my mouth and

it helped wake me up even more. "Waffles were a good idea, thank you Indigo."

The syrup bottle wobbled back to the countertop after dumping some on her plate.

Indigo smiled in glee and did a small happy dance.

"Waffles are the best." Indigo stuck her head in the pile of shredded waffle bits to grab a piece. Then, she dipped it into syrup before swallowing it whole.

"Bacon is the best," said the Cat.

"Ooooo... bacon."

"Bacon is totally the best," I agreed. "But I don't have any precooked bacon in the freezer. Meanwhile, I have an entire stack of these waffles that just need to be baked in the oven quickly." I usually needed to unthaw them first, but magically they had already been unthawed and waiting on the counter for me to pop in the oven this morning.

"So, are you ready for today?" I asked the Cat.

The coffee shop layout had greeted me this morning as I made myself an Americano. Usually, that put the Cat into a grumpy mood.

The Cat's tail twitched in the air a few times before he responded. "Today will be interesting. I'm curious to see who shows up. All the book said was 'A pleasant moment can change everything.'"

"That sounds like a fortune cookie." My fork hovered in midair. "A particularly unhelpful fortune cookie, at that."

I finished my waffle quickly, wanting more caffeine rather than a slow breakfast. Both the Cat's and Indigo's plates were still full of waffles.

"I'm going to go make a mocha. Do you want one?"

"Yes, please."

"Hot chocolate?" asked Indigo, her snout dripping in syrup.

"Of course, just make sure you wash your face off before you go flying around."

The little dragon nodded, and a drip of syrup went flying.

I walked to the front of the shop where the lovely espresso machine sat.

"Betty, thank you for cleaning up all the syrup." I patted the machine, even though it didn't really make sense. Still, for me the machine represented the shop.

From there, I quickly ground up some beans and pulled out a teacup for the Cat. It was the one with the soft pink roses along the edge. I admired it for a second, then got to work to make us all something warm, yummy, and most importantly, caffeinated.

Hopefully, the cryptic book was hinting at a pleasant, easy day.

I could use it.

CHAPTER

TWENTY-SIX

The scent of chocolate and coffee hit a spot inside me I couldn't explain. Even a regular hot chocolate had much of the same feeling, but with the coffee and the promise of extra caffeine, the experience was sublime. It had something to do with the warm milk... and probably the whipped cream on top as well.

Indigo licked at the whipped cream on the top of her hot chocolate, having learned that she only got one serving of the treat on any given day. Slowly, she licked her snout off before running her nose through the top again.

The Cat also drank his mocha, but much faster than Indigo and I. His small cup made it a little easier.

My giant mug was about the size of his head, after all.

Small changes around the room drew my attention to the coffee shop version of the shop, which I'd found when I'd woken this morning.

A few extra plants hung from the window, and the

144

artwork on the walls was different. This time it was all small prints, twelve by twelve inches hung like a checkerboard on the righthand wall.

The bells rang as the door swung open revealing the troll, who always seemed to be my first customer. He chatted with someone over his shoulder as he entered, making me smile. It was Samantha. Young love for the win!

"Good morning, welcome to Meow," I said as I started on his Americano and her vanilla latte.

He flashed me a smile as they placed their books on the long table before approaching the register.

I set both drinks on the counter in mugs. His was a dark green, while hers was a soft blue.

"Morning y'all, I hope you like the drinks," I said, taking his card to check them out.

"You are amazing," said Samantha, her voice soft. Her eyes sparkled as she picked up her drink. "Every time I come here, it's like coming to a friend's house that you don't want to leave."

"Thank you, it means alot." I blushed as I tapped the card before handing it back to him. I added a rewards card with two punches on it.

Indigo chirped twice in agreement, making the two trolls laugh before they headed to their books.

I sipped my mocha, checking the two out from the corner of my eye. No gold outline this week. So, they weren't the moment we were aiming for, though they were a pleasant moment.

The next time the bell rang, it indicated the morning

rush, with a consistent flow of people in all shapes and sizes, not to mention colors.

Indigo hung around after her hot chocolate ran out, and the Elven girls admired her as they bought coffee and tea. She posed for them multiple times, and when they asked if they could pet her, she'd enthusiastically nodded her head. At the moment, she napped on their table as they worked on their economics project.

The Cat vanished after the trolls left the counter, but I spotted him on the balcony watching everything from above. His green eyes flickered around the space from where he lay.

Overall, it really was just a relaxing morning.

I ran out of chocolate chip cookies within two hours of opening, and the peanut butter went soon after.

To my surprise, the next person through the door was the baker, Sandra.

She carried two totes in her arms, and I rushed around the counter to help hold the door. A younger woman followed her, carrying two as well.

"Sandra, I wasn't expecting you this morning... I must have forgotten about an order..." I glanced up at the balcony, but the Cat had vanished. I found him on the counter next to the register, his eyes on the totes.

"Nonsense, I have the order form in my pocket." She set the totes on the counter and the other two followed. Sandra held it out to me. "I just need the totes from the last order, and we can get out of your hair."

I rushed behind the counter to find them already stacked on the floor. Snatching them up, I passed them over. A quick glance inside the totes showed that half the batch of cookies was baked, while the rest were dough balls.

"Thank you again," I said with a smile.

"Thank you!" Sandra chuckled. "You helped my shop when I needed it most."

She smiled and motioned for the young girl to head out.

"I thought it was a bookstore," the younger woman whispered as she took the lead out of the shop.

"Meow is a special place," Sandra responded before the door shut behind her.

I stared at the totes with my mouth open, my mind catching up to the fact we weren't on earth, yet Sandra had been here.

"Are you going to put some of those out?" asked the Cat. "Don't the ones still shaped like balls go in the freezer?"

His voice snapped me out of my stupor and I picked up the uncooked dough balls to bring to the kitchen. "Yeah, I'm moving."

In the kitchen I set them on the island and they sank down, vanishing from sight, as I rushed back out front.

A pair of tongs sat behind the counter, and I used them to put out the fresh cookies. There were a dozen chocolate chip, more peanut butter, and ones that had drizzles of icing and smelled like cinnamon.

The totes contained more than fit in the stands on the counter, and I set the containers on the floor out of sight. They were gone before I could think about it.

Fresh cookies brought plenty of attention from everyone in the shop. The trolls got refills on their drinks, plus cookies, while the elves all switched to tea and tried the new one. A large group of magical humans gathered at the far end of the long table the trolls sat at. They all bought cookies as well.

Once things settled down, I nudged the Cat.

"Cat, I thought Sandra was from Earth?" I whispered, wondering how we were in two places at once.

"That doesn't mean she doesn't know about magic."

"Still, she didn't freak out at all." I tried to keep my voice low. The Cat said non-magical people couldn't be shown magic without consequences. Yet, there were trolls in the shop.

"One thing I've learned is that people will keep your secrets, especially when they consider you an important part of their story. Your reviews saved Sandra's shop. How was that not magical?"

I let the Cat's words sit in my mind as a woman and a little girl entered the coffee shop. The little girl dragged her mother inside by the hand. The group of humans glanced their way, smiling. One waved at the little girl, who waved back in excitement.

"You're the witch from Halloween!" The little girl's voice carried through the shop, but most didn't even turn to look.

The humans at the end of the table snapped to attention though, staring at the little girl, then at me.

CHAPTER

TWENTY-SEVEN

"I remember you," I said with a soft smile, thinking of her empty bucket. "Are you here for another cookie?"

"I've been dreaming of magic, and I knew we had to go searching for it today," said Angela.

"We mean no harm." Her mother glanced uneasily at the Cat, and her hand tightened around the little girl's. "Angela, what cookie do you want?"

The girl spun around, letting go of her mother, and stared at the stands on the counter, barely able to see the edges.

My thoughts raced, and a short stool rose from the floor next to the end of the counter.

"We have chocolate chip, peanut butter, and a cinnamon cookie of some kind," I said as I motioned near the end of the counter. "There should be a little stool you can stand on at the end."

Angela's head vanished, then appeared taller at the edge of the counter. "Oh, they all look so good. Mommy, can I have two? A chocolate chip and cinnamonmon one?"

The girl mispronounced cinnamon in the most adorable way, adding too many 'mon's to the end of the word.

Her mother let out a sigh, then nodded. "It's cinnamon, can you try again?"

"That's what I said." Angela didn't repeat the word.

"For here or to go?" I asked, interrupting the exchange.

The girl flashed me a grin.

"Here's fine. Can you steam a milk for her? And I'll take a large coffee, to go."

The Cat ignored the mother's pointed looks. His gaze turned to watch the trolls still studying on the long table next to the windows.

Warm sunlight poured in the windows, making the green of the plates almost glow.

I plated the cookies and set them near the edge of the counter. The steamed milk went into a to-go cup with a lid, the same for the large coffee.

"Is that a dragon?" Angela's voice came out in awe. "It's purple!"

Indigo landed on the counter, blinking at the little girl.

The little book dragon took a step to her, chirping and holding her head up.

The elves had gotten up and headed out the door without me realizing it.

"That's Indigo. She's a special dragon," I said with a smile as Indigo jumped into the air and circled the little girl's head. I leaned down closer to the little girl. "She's a book dragon. They love knowledge."

Angela's mouth dropped open and her eyes widened like saucers. "I love books, too! We can be best friends!"

I chuckled at the scene.

The mother picked up the drinks. "Angela, grab your cookies. We need to make sure we stay on time for your appointment."

"I'm moving." She grabbed the plate of cookies and stepped off the stool, her head vanishing from view until she stepped far enough away from the counter.

Indigo kept flying overhead as her mother led the way to a small table near the bookshelves.

The little girl barely watched where she headed, instead keeping her eyes on the small dragon.

For a split second, a golden outline surrounded the little girl.

"Well, that's one thing off my list," I mumbled.

"Hmmm," purred the Cat.

"They are the thing for today, you know." I sipped my drink, savoring the moment and wondering what needed to happen with the little girl.

Indigo flew over to the bookshelves and pulled out one of her favorite books, one that involved dragons. It wasn't the special book, but a normal one from my world about dragons and spicy salsa. Given how smart Indigo was, it was under their reading level, but they still loved it.

Angela's eyes lit up and she broke a piece of her cookie off for Indigo. Then she started reading the book to the dragon.

Her mother blinked with wide eyes and sipped her coffee in disbelief.

The Cat padded closer and rubbed his head against my arms where they were resting on the counter.

I scratched behind his ears, making him purr in contentment.

"The pleasant moment," I said, motioning with my mug at the scene in front of us. "You can't tell me that isn't cute. Two kids of very different species trying to talk about the books they love."

He turned to watch the scene, saying nothing.

For a moment, I thought he wasn't paying attention, then I realized he stared at the scene like he didn't understand it at all.

I patted his head.

"It could be a human thing, finding something like that cute and special." My last sip emptied my mug. "Do you want another coffee?"

His tail flickered in the air before turning my way. "No, thank you."

He then turned and jumped off the counter and headed down the hallway. It didn't take long before he appeared back on the balcony overlooking the shop.

I grinned to myself as I started on my own refill.

Cute.

What did cute even mean?

I didn't understand what Sable implied about the two children interacting. That happened all the time at different points across the many worlds. Why was this instance cute?

It made little sense, and Sable had picked up on my confusion.

Heading back up the stairs to watch things from above was the easier choice, rather than asking the questions inside my head. Pleasant, yes. Right now the shop felt pleasant. The various patrons all chattered softly and focused on their own lives, not to mention drinking Sable's fantastic beverages.

The cookies added sweetly to that. I'd placed the order when I realized the freezer didn't have a back stock of Sable's favorite cookies. Given how she put up with me, she deserved a treat as well.

Unknown to her, time ticked by. Her contract had passed the halfway point, with all the jumping around various worlds and time spent working. While it had only recently hit the winter holidays on her world, the timekeeping abilities of the shop said it was otherwise.

I loved snow, but hated winter, and rarely let the season appear in my lands. Sometimes, if one of my children asked for it during the season, I'd let the soft fluffy flakes fall for a night. It always snowed for the Solstice, that was the one time the snow brought happiness and joy to all my children.

Bitter cold and ice were a different story. I preferred the soft sunlight of late spring, and the warm breeze smelling of new life. The heat of summer always hung heavy in the air, so spring it was for my home. If I could only have the light snow of a late spring snow storm, that'd be different.

The floorboards beneath me creaked, and I realized the path my thoughts had taken. Shaking my head, I padded away from watching the coffee shop down the hallway to my room.

The warm fire awaited me.

Sable could handle the rest of the day. I didn't want to think about how lonely the shop would feel without her.

CHAPTER

TWENTY-EIGHT

Snow settled on the roof of the skylight and I snuggled deeper into the covers. My flannel pajamas were fuzzy, and the blanket added a nice extra layer. Today had been a perfect day in the coffee shop.

A soft chirp came from near my head, and I turned to look at Indigo.

"It's called snow," I explained. "It's like rain, but cold, and melts when it touches warm things."

"*Pretty...*" she chirped softly.

Light barely crept into the room from above, but what did come in made the snow seem even more magical. Yet, the flakes slowly piled up on the window, making it hard to see.

"Let's go watch it on the roof," I whispered as I sat up in bed.

Indigo jumped into the air, flying to the door as I hurried to catch up.

I opened it just in time as she headed into the hallway. Out in the shop, more snow piled up on the skylights in the main area, and across the way I could see it on the rooftop deck.

Indigo flew across the open space while I crept along the walkway. I didn't know if the Cat was awake, but if not, I hoped we wouldn't wake him. It could be midnight or close to dawn, and I didn't have a clue.

The comfortable chair next to the plants faced the wall of windows that observed the roof. I sat in the chair, pulling my feet up and tucking them under me before Indigo landed in my lap.

The snow gathered on top of the wooden hot tub cover and the deck chairs placed around the roof. The wall surrounding the rooftop deck provided a dark background to see each bright white flake as it fell. Moonlight streamed down from above, making the snow magically glow.

"Maybe later today you can go play out in the snow," I said. "Though, you need to remember it will be cold."

Indigo shivered. *"Maybe play in hot tub."*

I chuckled. "Sitting in the hot tub as it snows could be fun as well, though we'll want to be careful about getting in and out. To make sure we don't get too cold."

The wind picked up, and snowflakes blew across the area.

I hummed in pleasure, almost wishing I had some hot chocolate to sip on, but I didn't want to get up from the chair.

"The winter season is here," whispered the Cat, as he slowly padded into view near the edge of the window. He stared out at the snow, before turning toward us in the chair and pouncing onto the armrest.

"The Solstice snow was different, almost pleasant."

"Do you celebrate any winter holidays?" I asked.

"My people celebrate the Solstice with food and songs." He let his voice trail off and I didn't push for more information.

Indigo nudged me.

"My family also celebrates the Solstice with lots of food. We also burn a huge fire, and hang stockings up for small gifts from Saint Nick."

"Saint Nick?" asked Indigo. *"Who's he?"*

Even the Cat stared at me in the darkness, green eyes floating in darkness, waiting for an answer.

"As my father would say, Saint Nicholas is an old god that rewards those who keep the old traditions alive. He visits all the houses on the night of the Solstice, and places gifts in the stockings of children. The adults sneak small gifts into each other's stockings, to show love and friendship.

"My mother makes sure we burn a yule log each year and read of the battle of the Oak King and the Holly King."

"Oak King?" asked the Cat.

"Yes, the Oak King rules over the spring and summer, while the Holly King rules over the fall and winter. They fight every year at the equinox times, and each then rests while the other rules. The secret is that one cannot exist without the other, creating a balance through the seasons."

"Have you seen one of these Kings?" asked Indigo, her eyes wide.

I shook my head lightly. "No, I haven't seen the

Kings, but they are out there somewhere, in the circle of birth, life, and death."

"Can we have stockings?"

"Of course we can have stockings to celebrate the Solstice. Maybe I can even see if I can get the recipe for the cookies my brother makes each year. They are like a snickerdoodle, but better. Do the Clan of Knowledge have winter traditions?"

Indigo shook her head with a sad chirp. *"Dragon celebrations are about learning and growing."* She snuggled closer to me. *"Not like cake and presents."*

It took me a moment to remember my birthday. The date that Indigo showed up was listed on my calendar, maybe I'd throw her a cute little dragon party for it. However, for now I needed to figure out what to do about the Solstice. "What about you, Cat? Anything to add?"

The Cat's tail flickered in the air. "Nothing for me."

I snorted.

That's what he thought. If we were doing stockings, he was getting a stocking. Maybe even one with paw prints on it and an oak leaf. I'd need to see what I could find online, or maybe order from that lady that knitted things.

The snow continued to fall as my thoughts wandered about what to get for the Cat and for Indigo. They already had cat trees. Plus, whatever it was I got needed to fit in the stockings, that was part of the challenge. You had to follow the rules with whatever you chose to give.

Either way, this was going to be fun. We had plenty of time until the Solstice for me to figure this out.

A soft snore came from my chest and I realized Indigo had drifted off to sleep.

The Cat moved from a sitting position to lying down next to me on the chair. His head rested on his paws, as he continued to watch the snowfall.

The moonlight drifted over everything, and I let my head rest on the other side of the chair. While this wasn't as comfortable as my bed, the magical night with my chosen family was worth it.

TWENTY-NINE

Snow continued to fall as I stood guard. Sable joined Indigo in falling back to sleep. The two of them were lost in hopefully sweet dreams.

I didn't know of this Saint Nicholas.

Though I'd heard stories of the Oak King and the Holly King, they were of the fey variety from a far off world. Then again, stories twisted between the worlds, with similar tales even in the farthest lands.

Magic gathered in the shop, and I didn't poke at it. Sometimes the shop did things I couldn't understand, and this had happened more often with Sable than any other shopkeeper before.

Hopefully, it would bring her joy.

I wanted her to be happy.

Daylight crept in through the windows, reflecting off the

160

snow on the roof and filling the space with bright light. Chirping came from somewhere behind me.

"Magic happened!" Indigo's voice echoed from the hallway behind me and I forced myself to stretch before climbing to my feet. The chair hadn't been the best place to sleep, but I wouldn't give up the moment last night for a few aches.

I climbed to my feet and headed toward the noise, knowing that soon I could drink a warm coffee.

Yet, I paused as light streamed in from a new location.

The hallway, which normally only sometimes had an arched door that led to what I suspected was the Cat's private area, had another door. This one didn't have an archway, and instead had thick wooden beams framing it out.

I stepped inside in surprise.

Tall bookcases covered the wall on the right, the same golden wood from downstairs. A large stone fireplace took up the wall to the left, with a giant fluffy couch shaped in an L in front of it. A dark green rug covered the floor, with wooden floorboards peeking out from the edges.

Yet, to the back was a wall of solid windows.

Giant, tall dark evergreen trees dotted a landscape covered in snow. Mountains rose in the distance, along with grey clouds that didn't block out the sun.

The entire room felt cozy and warm.

Indigo flew around the room, only pausing to stare at each new thing before moving on.

"This is a new space," added the Cat, who jumped up on the big couch.

I nodded, but said nothing. This room was literally a dream come true.

"This should be impossible," I whispered.

The Cat snorted. "Magic is real."

"Still..." I slowly walked inside and around the couch to take a seat in front of the fireplace. "I dreamed of a room like this being in my grownup house when I was young."

My gaze darted every which way as I sank into the fluffy couch.

Now this I could sleep on.

"We can hang stockings here!" Indigo said as she landed on the mantle.

I giggled. "That mantle has plenty of room for stockings."

It was giant and could fit enough stockings for my entire family. The fireplace was massive, though a fire didn't burn in the center. Instead, it was full of crystals that glowed that same red color as flame, and warmth drifted out of the opening just like an actual fire.

The same went for the lanterns hanging from the ceiling. No open flames in any of them. Instead, each had one of those crystals sitting in the center.

I didn't know what to do as I sat on the couch. It felt like this couldn't be real, yet it was as real as the shop.

"This is amazing," I whispered as I sat there.

The Cat moved closer, carefully moving along the back of the couch. "The shop appreciates you."

Warmth blasted from the fireplace directly at the Cat, who dodged backward.

I couldn't help the giggles that came out.

"I might have understated that," mumbled the Cat as he moved back into the spot he'd been in.

"This is going to be an amazing room for the Solstice. I can see it now, with stockings and decorations." I wished my family could see this space, but that wasn't possible. I knew they were preparing for the holiday season, and I still hadn't told them I wasn't going to make it.

Missing my birthday had been one thing, but missing the Solstice was completely different.

Still, looking between the Cat and Indigo I knew it'd be a delightful holiday. The first one for the little dragon, and she deserved for it to be something special. I thought of her stocking again, and all the little things I needed to do to make it extra special. The Cat, too!

Somehow, he had something to do with this. Otherwise, how would a room I'd dreamed about for years appear in the shop?

Something had changed with him over the last several weeks. He'd acted sweeter around me.

I snuggled deeper into the couch, and the Cat jumped down from the back to near me before crawling into my lap.

He purred loudly as I petted his back.

"Watching the snow from here will be more comfortable," he said.

"That's true," I replied, glancing over at the wall of windows.

The dark forest reminded me of ancient stories about magical castles and libraries. Then again, this was a magical shop that appeared all over, with real magic.

I held up my hand, admiring the bracelet. Heck, I could even do real magic.

Indigo eventually landed on the couch and yanked on a blanket that rested on the back. She yanked it down with her mouth and over to where I sat with the Cat. *"We rest here."*

I chuckled. "Indigo, it's the morning. We need to eat breakfast and then open the shop." Yet, I pulled the blanket closer and tucked it around her. "You can nap here, though. I'll make breakfast for you that you can eat whenever."

"Best magic," she chirped.

"Yes, it is," I whispered. This room was perfect, almost too perfect. The various rooms the shop created were all put to shame with this one. It matched me so well. I wanted it. And not just for now. Forever.

I let out a small sigh, but snapped it off as Indigo snored. She'd fallen asleep so quickly, and I didn't want to wake her. Maybe another growth spurt was on the way.

"You ready for breakfast?" I asked the Cat.

He stared up at me from my lap. "Food is tasty."

I lifted him up into my arms, pulling him close before standing. Slowly, I walked around the edge of the couch and to the door. I paused in the doorway, glancing over the room again, to make sure it hadn't changed.

Stockings would look perfect on the mantle. I needed

to buy them as soon as possible. It was less than two weeks until the Solstice.

THIRTY

Excitement and energy filled me as I exited the new room.

My thoughts revolved around holiday shopping, and everyone I had to get a gift for on my list.

That all skidded to a halt as I walked out to the balcony.

I must have made a sound, because Indigo slowly flew out of the living room, though I'd left her napping soundly on the couch.

The shop didn't quite look, well, normal. In fact, it didn't look like any of the several normals I'd become used to.

While the bookshelves against the back were filled with colorful spines, the large center table had an assortment of things like art supplies, craft kits, and handmade merchandise. It reminded me of when those forest folks were looking for mating gifts, except everything was in English.

Plants covered the giant window facing the front of the store, along with candles. Chocolates in pretty boxes, along with an assortment of other candies, were in a glass case near the register. Seeds and gardening supplies, like a bright blue watering can, sat near the right wall.

It took seconds for me to bypass the counter and start wandering the shop. So many goodies were out on display, and I did have that list to get through.

"Breakfast?" asked Indigo after a few moments of flying around overhead.

"Sure, but I'm going to need to do some shopping later, after we're done for the day. This will make my Solstice shopping much easier."

Before I headed to the kitchen, I made myself a hot peppermint mocha. I patted Betty on the top, smiling. "Today's going to be a good day, I can feel it."

Into the kitchen I went, to scramble some eggs and make bacon.

"You're in a happy mood," said the Cat as he jumped up onto the island.

"You have good timing, and yeah, I am," I replied as I set down the tall plate of bacon.

From the new living room to the shop of my dreams, it felt like today was perfect.

Indigo landed near her plate of scrambled eggs, which I'd already dished up. She daintily tried to eat them, each bite super small instead of her normal habit of putting her head all the way into her food.

I stacked two slices of bacon on the edge of her plate before I plated up the remaining scrambled eggs for the

Cat. I paused, studying the plate of bacon, before grabbing three slices of my own.

By the time I set the plate in front of him, he'd already eaten half of his first slice of bacon.

I added another couple of pieces to his plate.

"The store looks different, and I can't wait to see what it brings. Or, rather, who," I said, as I added another couple of pieces to his plate. "I just have a great feeling about today."

The rest of breakfast was quiet except for the crunch of bacon. As always, all of the bacon somehow vanished by the time we were done. That seemed to be a thing, no matter how much I made. It was delicious, though, so I couldn't really fault anyone.

The Cat led the way out to the front counter, his tail flickering around in agitation.

"Can I get a coffee, please?" he asked.

I pulled out his teacup as Indigo happily chirped about an audiobook she was listening to. It involved something about manners and fancy dresses. It made her newfound eating habit make a little more sense, though I didn't point out that manners for a human might be somewhat different from manners for a dragon.

For the Cat, I made a basic vanilla latte with extra foam on top and set it carefully down in front of him.

He glanced up at me, his green eyes looking pleased before he started lapping it up.

"Hot chocolate?" I asked Indigo as she continued to fly around, a little slower now.

She gave a negative chirp before looking longingly at her hideaway.

"Feel free to listen to your book," I added with a chuckle, wiping down the counter. "I think we can manage today without you."

Indigo happily flew circles overhead before darting over to her hideaway, vanishing from sight.

"That's for the best," said the Cat, padding over to my elbow before sitting next to me. "It wasn't clear if this was a magical day or not."

"Huh."

I glanced around the store, trying to figure out if anything on display had magic. Nothing looked magical at first glance, but then again some things had hidden secrets. The gems in my bracelets sparkled to make the point.

"That's not good, that you don't know." My mood dampened, thinking about how the Cat seemed to have less and less information about our days lately. "Well, Indigo will have a fun day no matter what."

I pushed my concern for the Cat aside as I sipped my peppermint mocha.

Anticipation ran through me as I sat on my stool, imagining the post-day browse through the goodies the shop had on display. I couldn't wait to go shopping after work, though the things I wanted to get for the Cat and Indigo weren't going to be found here. But, for my parents and friends for sure I'd find something.

"Are you ready?" asked the Cat, snapping me out of my daydreams.

"Yes, let's do this."

As we waited, the bright morning sunlight streamed in the front windows and skylights. The Cat snoozed on the counter after I finished my drink, curled up in a cute little ball of fur. I wouldn't ever tell him I found him cute, of course, but he was.

Immediately, I made another peppermint mocha for myself, this time adding some whipped cream and sprinkles to the top. I caught a flash of green from the Cat, so I put some on a spoon and casually set it next to him.

The spoon was licked clean the next time I glanced at it.

Finally, the bells hanging from the front door rang.

In walked a young woman, about my age, wrapped in a black wool coat. Snow dusted her shoulders, and her nose appeared to be a little red from the cold. She wore a green knitted hat that made her eyes pop.

"Welcome to Meow," I said with a smile.

"This is such a cute shop!" she gushed, her head trying to turn in every direction at once. "I'll totally find something for Mom here."

As she stepped in, I noticed the rolling suitcase she dragged behind her and the backpack over one shoulder.

"You can leave that by the door if you'd like," I added.

She nodded and set it off to one side before checking her phone.

My eyes widened, and I casually went to check mine to see if I had service, but I'd forgotten it upstairs since it usually didn't work.

"Did you want a coffee by any chance?" I mentally kicked myself for leaving my phone upstairs. "I can get one started."

"Oh, yes please, can I get a peppermint mocha?" she

asked as she glanced around the shop. "I can smell yours from here."

"Of course." I got to work, keeping track of her out of the corner of my eye.

She strolled through the bookshelves, reading over each of the titles and pausing in the section with the farm and garden tag.

I made a note to check that section out later, for my brother and his new assistant.

After I added whipped cream and chocolate shavings to the top, I placed the to-go cup on the counter, not wanting to rush her.

Eventually, she wandered over to the main table with two books in her arms. She smiled, looking over the items before making her way to the counter.

"I think just these two books." She seemed uncertain as she set the books down.

"You mentioned you're shopping for your Mom, right?" I asked, looking over the books, one of which was a farming memoir. One I'd read, actually, and thought was pretty good.

"Her birthday is coming up, and I'm suddenly free to head home for it." She didn't sound happy about it, but tried to smile a little.

"Is everything okay?" I asked as I moved the to-go cup closer to the two books and set a lid beside it.

"I wish." She snorted. "I quit my job yesterday, because my long-term ex-boyfriend got the promotion I'd been working for. So, it's been a week."

That was an understatement.

"That's pretty rough," I said, wanting to give her a hug. "Maybe this is a chance for a new start?"

"To be honest, I wasn't happy at the job anyway." She leaned against the counter. "It felt soul-sucking."

"I've totally been there. You never know what can be waiting right around the corner, though." I smirked, thinking of this place. "Believe me, sometimes the perfect position just falls in your lap like magic."

Not that I was speaking from experience or anything.

CHAPTER

THIRTY-ONE

"I gotta trust in the universe, I guess." She tapped the farming book. "Thankfully, I have enough savings that I can take a break and relax till summer. Hell, even my roommate was glad to see me go, since she wanted to move her boyfriend—well, fiancé, now—in."

"That's a pretty direct kick in the pants from the universe," I said, eyes wide. Like, that many things all at once? Totally had to be magic of some sort. Or Fate.

Maybe.

"Hmmm," she said, staring at the book under her fingertips. "Maybe I'll help my Mom with her giant garden this spring. Spend some more time with my family, and see if anyone has any job recommendations. Something different."

"Spend as much time as you can with your family. You never know if an amazing position will open up and you'll need to move far away." I swallowed lightly after I spoke, feeling like I'd put a little too much emotion into that statement.

The Cat suddenly rubbed against my elbow, purring loudly.

"Oh, hey, big man. Aren't you a gorgeous cat," she said, petting him on his head.

I chuckled at the scene.

Then I froze, staring at her hands. A slight golden sheen covered the very tips of each finger. There was something here, something important I needed to do, but I didn't know what.

"Do you like gardening?" I asked, trying to figure out why the golden outline had started forming.

"I'm not sure. I've always helped my mom. Though," she leaned forward against the counter with a very bright smile. "There is nothing like a homegrown tomato."

"Yeah?" I asked, thinking of the garden boxes on the roof. Maybe I could grow a real tomato for Indigo to try.

"Pure magic." She did the whole chef's kiss thing with her golden fingers. "I swear."

Suddenly, something glittered out of the corner of my eye near the gardening supplies.

"You know, we have some seeds and gardening stuff on sale over on the wall," I said pointing. "It's the wrong season for it, but you might find a few treats for yourself, or another gift for your mom."

She jerked up and turned to face the wall. Her whole hands practically glowed as she headed in that direction.

I wished I could follow, but instead I petted the Cat, who stared at me rather strangely.

He purred under my fingertips, though, so I let it go until later.

Slowly, the young woman poked through the various supplies we had, then started going through a giant box that had seeds written on the side of it.

"Oh, this would be perfect!" she said, pulling out an envelope. Then another.

It took a few more minutes before she came back to the counter. She added six seed packets on top of the books, all marked down to 50 cents each. One of them glowed golden.

I picked them up along with the books, moving them closer to the register. I scanned in the barcodes on the seeds, pausing briefly on the golden packet.

"Magical Sunflower Seeds, huh?" I asked, flipping the packet over as my fingers buzzed at the touch. It appeared to be the same as any old seed packet, but it glowed in my vision, and the name literally said magical.

The front included a picture of bright yellow flowers with purple streaks starting from the ends of the petals, reaching toward the center.

"I haven't seen anything like them." She slid her backpack off her shoulder and pulled out her wallet.

"Do you want a bag?" I asked as I finished ringing up the merchandise and adding the coffee to the order.

"No, thank you. I'll put it all in here."

I tapped her credit card and it was approved.

She put everything away in her backpack.

As soon as she zipped it closed, the golden glow on her hands vanished like it'd never been there.

"Oh, my coffee," she said, glancing at her watch. "I better hurry or I'm going to miss the bus. Thanks again!"

"Of course," I said with a smile. "I hope you find what you're looking for, and good luck!"

She took a sip of the mocha as she was rushing out the door, barely pausing to grab her suitcase on the way out.

The bells jingled as the door closed behind her.

I almost leaped over the counter as I rushed to the seed box. Those seeds reminded me of the ones I'd sent to my brother. My family had asked for more, and maybe we had some.

I rifled through the box, looking at the various flowers and vegetables that we had, pulling a tomato packet to set it aside. This spring I'd definitely grow them so Indigo could taste test them.

Nope. The box didn't have any more of those seeds, which was a bummer. Still, at least I'd figured out what needed to happen today.

"Hey Cat, was that the only person on our list today?"

He didn't answer and I turned to look at the counter. The lock turned on the door and I shrugged my shoulders. That was enough of a response for me.

Time to shop.

MAGIC HAD GATHERED around Sable as soon as the girl had started petting me. It tasted strange, and appeared as a golden metallic color.

A color I hated.

They had something to do with this, and it made my slightly pleasant mood at seeing Sable so happy go away.

I padded up the stairs, only pausing to make sure the door locked at her question. As far as the book was concerned, that was the only customer today. However, given how it gave me less and less information every day, I didn't really know.

It worried me.

The lack of direction and that golden color surrounding Sable made me nervous, and it was time to do something about it.

I resisted the urge to check on my tree, and the leaves still holding on to dear life. I hoped my children would prosper, but right now I couldn't help them. I could help Sable keep clear of a disaster waiting to happen, though.

The archway appeared on the wall just beyond the new room that made Sable so excited. Her hopes and dreams for the space made the shop happy. Happier than it'd been in a long time.

I worried about the shop, and what would happen when Sable's contract was up. Betty, as Sable called it, tuned in to Sable more than it had any other Shopkeeper before. Disconnecting that might have some bad ramifi-cations.

I huffed. I'd figure out a way to keep the shop safe.

Not like my poor land.

I shook my head, clearing those dark thoughts as I entered my workshop. Leaping up on the counter took only seconds. The book lay open in the middle of it, golden light glimmering above it, coming from the pages themselves.

I'd had to move it here after Sable saw it on the counter so long ago. I couldn't risk her trying to read it.

"You listen to me. Stay away from her," I growled, my voice coming out more like my old self. "Once her contract is up, she will be free to go back home to her family and the people that care. You have no claim!"

The glimmering light above the book shifted and darkened, but it didn't respond.

Just like always.

THIRTY-TWO

I stared at the pile on the counter, smirking to myself.

So far, I'd only picked out things for Umber, since he was the easiest one to shop for. I'd found a cute cookbook based on a cute cozy farming video game, a packet of rare flower seeds from the box, and a bar of chocolate from the case. The seeds looked pretty hard to find, based on a quick internet search I did on my laptop, which also sat on the wooden counter.

Betty had grabbed it for me, which was sweet of the shop. I needed to figure out how to gift a shop something for the Solstice, one way or another.

I'd found a book about basic farming and how to grow things, which was perfect for Jackie, who now worked for Umber. Plus some chocolate.

Actually, a stack of chocolate bars sat on the counter, one for each of my brothers and parents, but that couldn't be the only thing I sent to people. On the center table, I found a pair of knitted purple fingerless gloves that I picked out for my mother. The clinic she worked at got cold some days.

For my father, I snagged a wood carving kit, since it was the type of thing he'd enjoy. He was always looking for the next hobby.

The art supplies, including some glittering paint, were for Cyan, along with a cool new fantasy book about dragons. The first three books in the series were out, but for now I'd send the first book, and the other two for his birthday, which was right after the new year.

That left Onyx and Cerulean.

They were the hardest people to shop for. Onyx, my oldest brother, appreciated food, or things homemade, neither being anything I'd had any talent in in the past. But this year, I could send him some cookies. It'd surprise him and prove to everyone that I really could bake something. I'd leave out the fact that the dough was frozen.

That left Cerulean.

He didn't like stuff, and he traveled all over the world for his job. But, he always gave the best gifts, picked out for each person.

I stared at the shelves, trying to come up with something for him. Something that'd really make him smile, and that he'd appreciate. Obviously, he wanted to connect more with me, given the text messages and recent phone call.

My fingers tapped on the closest shelf, but nothing came to mind.

Indigo popped her head out, chirping.

"Book is done," she said. *"Is there more?"*

I chuckled and headed to my laptop, pulling the stool closer.

She leaped into the air and landed next to the pile of stuff. Her eyes grew wide at the stack of chocolates.

"Those are not for you; they're for the rest of my family."

Indigo nodded solemnly before staring at my laptop screen.

I pulled up the audiobook account that I used, to see what she'd been listening to. Surprisingly, it was a young adult series about a finishing school of assassins, and there were only four books.

"There are three more books that you can listen to in that series."

"Yay! Can I get?" she asked in a very sweet tone.

"Of course." It took only a few clicks and the books were purchased. "Your music player should sync."

I wasn't sure how Lady Twilight did it, but whatever magic she placed in the MP3 player, it somehow suddenly just worked when I bought audiobooks for her. I didn't need to send them over. However, it made me wonder if all the audiobooks I bought would head her way. I wasn't an audio listener, but some of my ebooks were a little spicy for the tiny dragon.

"Thank you!" Indigo flew off without a backward glance.

She definitely lived up to the bookdragon name, though I wasn't sure if fantasy books were the type of knowledge Lady Twilight and Lord Bennit wanted her to learn.

"I know what to get her..." Two clicks later, and Indigo's present was in my shopping cart. She'd turned out to be surprisingly easy to shop for.

Though, I tossed a few cute-to-me things in my cart as well. A handmade seller had tiny scarfs for cats on her crafts page, and I bought two immediately. One was a bright green, to match the Cat's eyes, and the other gold for Indigo. Not that they'd ever wear them, but still I couldn't resist.

That still left Cerulean, and the Cat. Oh, plus Betty as well.

"Three's not bad," I muttered to myself. My fingers tapped on the counter a bit more before I added some additional catnip to my cart. It still wasn't enough.

I snagged my cell phone and hit Cyan's name. Thankfully, he picked up.

"Wow, you're calling me? Are you okay?" He joked.

"Ha, ha, very funny," I replied, though he wasn't wrong. I never called him. "I'm trying to figure something out for Cerulean for the Solstice."

He snorted.

I could practically see his smile in my head.

"What will ya give me for the info?"

"Oh, come on." I pouted even though he couldn't see it. "You aren't gonna help me out?"

"Bribes work best, you know."

"Fine, I'll send you some extra goodies." I eyed the two other books in the series that I'd marked for his birthday. They could go early. "Promise it's worth it."

"Concert tickets to the Blazing Cactus. I'll go halfsies with you, two hundred and fifty dollars for each of us. They were a little pricey for my blood on my own."

I glared at the phone before responding. "Fine, I'll send you some cash."

"Perfect! Now that's taken care of!"

"Love you." I'd bet he'd already asked a few of the others to go in on it, but everyone had turned him down. Lucky jerk.

"Same, sis." Then he hung up.

I shook my head as I mentally crossed that off my list. Those would be a little steep for my usual budget, but given how much money I'd stocked away working here, I could afford it. For once, I could afford to be someone who gave the best presents. I loved that feeling.

I sent the money over via a cash app, with a smile. My bank account had the most money it'd ever had.

It felt really good.

Scooting around the counter, I started scanning each item at the register. The total didn't even make me whine. I paid with my credit card, still smiling.

All I had left was the Cat, and the more I thought about it, the more I had the perfect idea for him. It involved the new room, and a projector.

I snagged one of the woven baskets by the door and piled all of the gifts inside to bring them up to my room. My online cart needed to be finalized, but I still had to add things like wrapping paper and bows. All of the fun stuff to make the presents look pretty. Not to mention some cards.

I made a mental note to bake cookies soon, and I'd need to send everything out, probably the same day. My next day off was close enough that I'd do that then.

As I set the basket on the floor a weird feeling crept

up my spine, like someone was staring at me or talking behind my back. I turned to peek at the door.

"Cat?"

There wasn't a reply, but the feeling went away.

I needed to have a chat with him about just vanishing on me and using his words more often, but first I opened my laptop to get his Solstice gifts.

"Hey, Betty, I have an idea of something you can add to that really cool room you built for me..."

THIRTY-THREE

"It's time, Indigo," I said, as I picked up the dishes and set them in the sink. This morning I'd kept breakfast simple. I'd just microwaved frozen pancakes that I had made a few weeks ago. I added our great maple syrup and some sliced bananas to spruce them up.

"It's time to decorate the living room, and the tree!"

I didn't know where Betty had gotten the tree.

The small blue spruce magically grew from the floorboards and filled the living room with that strong evergreen scent. The fireplace provided a pleasant warmth, even without the flames and smoke.

The boxes had arrived late yesterday from the online shopping store that everyone used. They'd had everything I wanted, and of course it was all delivered, which made my life easier.

I climbed the stairs with Indigo going on ahead. I carefully carried my mug and the Cat's teacup. Once upstairs in the living room, I set both on the coffee table in front of the couch.

The beautiful tree stood in front of the windows, but first my focus was on my coffee. I needed more caffeine to do this without thinking too hard about my family.

"So, what are we doing today?" asked the Cat, following his teacup with his eyes.

"Decorating for the Solstice. We have the tree, then I need to wrap presents for my family and bake some cookies."

"And you need my help because..."

I glared at him. "It will be fun. All you need to do is drink your coffee with cream and sit on the couch."

The Cat glanced away from my look, moving closer to his coffee.

The first box I opened had all sorts of ornaments in it, but not the lights. Two boxes later, I found the lights, all the wrapping paper, and ribbons. The last two boxes held surprises for later.

I grabbed my phone and turned on some classical music. The sounds of a string quartet filled the space, and somehow it started snowing outside the windows.

"*Lights,*" chirped Indigo as she flew about, only getting slightly tangled in a string of them she latched onto in the box.

"If you fly the end up to the top, we can wrap them in the branches. They will look pretty once they're on."

It took a few tries, but Indigo figured out what I meant and dropped the correct socket near the tip of the tree while I held the rest of the cord of lights.

My eyes widened as the tree suddenly began to turn in place. It made putting the lights on as easy as could be. We just needed to slowly lower the mess of them to get an acceptable distance between each row.

"Next we have ornaments." I held up one of the glittering snowflakes in a bright white.

Indigo dived at my hand, grabbing the hook and flying high in the air. Glitter drifted through the room from the cheap ornament. These were harder for her to put on the branches, and she accidentally dropped one, but it didn't break. It only left a pile of the sparkles behind.

"Try again!" She flew down to the floor and scooped it back up her claws, covered in white glitter.

Glitter flew everywhere, but I didn't mind. Instead, I grabbed a few round balls in various colors. I used them to fill in gaps in the natural tree, focusing on places Indigo wasn't putting the snowflakes.

A box of golden oak leaves sat in the bottom and I pulled them out, setting the open container off to one side in view of the Cat perched on the back of the couch.

I didn't say anything, and instead went back to putting the metallic balls in various open spots on the tree.

Out of the corner of my eye, I spotted the Cat putting a golden oak leaf on a lower branch. Yet, when I casually glanced at the couch, he was back in his perch, just watching us.

I chuckled to myself, but didn't say anything.

Instead, I hummed with the music, just relaxing into the fun activity. Back home when we decorated the tree, things were different. Everyone got one section to decorate, and when we were done, it looked like stripes on the poor plant. You could always tell who did what section. This tree wasn't like that, and I reminded myself that was okay.

A few more oak leaves appeared on the tree in various places, following flashes of black fur.

Between the three of us, the tree slowly filled in with the silver snowflakes, plastic metallic balls, and the golden oak leaves. I needed to move a few things here or there, to balance them out, but it looked good.

"No more snow?" asked Indigo, perched near the box she had slowly emptied.

I pulled out one big golden star I'd kept off to one side.

"What about this?" I asked with a smile.

Indigo's eyes grew big looking at the star. It was half her size.

"Do you think you can place this up on the tiptop of the tree?"

"Yes!" She nodded her head and jumped up on my shoulder before launching herself in the air. She flew around the top of the tree, looking at where the star needed to go, before flying to the star in my outstretched hand.

Indigo hovered over the top with her wings beating carefully before settling it in place.

Seconds after she flew back toward me, I hit the floor button for the lights and they flickered on. Soft white lights made the colorful ornaments glow and the snowflakes sparkle.

"Ohhhh, it's so pretty," whispered Indigo as she settled

on my shoulder. She stared at the tree with her eyes wide. *"Magic tree."*

I nodded. "My world has some magic. You just need to know where to look."

I took a step back to grab my coffee, and she fluttered over to the back of the couch next to the Cat, not looking away from the tree.

The last of my warm latte tasted perfect as I watched the two of them.

The Cat's green eyes didn't leave the tree, either. Hopefully, he wasn't like a normal Cat who liked to climb trees and knock things off them.

I sent my intent to Betty and one of the boxes sank into the floor without either of them noticing.

"I'm going to get started on cookies. I'll be back soon."

Still, the two of them watched the tree in awe.

"Betty, you are fantastic at creating magical moments," I whispered as I left the room and headed down the balcony.

A warmth rushed through the floorboards and up my socks.

It made me smile, as I focused on only thinking about the good today, and not the fact that we had less than a week and a half 'til the Solstice and I still hadn't spoken to my mother.

THIRTY-FOUR

By the time I walked into the kitchen, the cookie dough was sitting on the counter along with cookie sheets, and the oven was preheated.

"You are amazing..." I chuckled and patted the counter. With the tree decorated upstairs, all that was left was cookies, wrapping presents, and decorating the living room. Actually, that was a lot more to get done, though I had plenty of time today to do it.

I scooped cookie dough onto trays. It wasn't complicated. Balls of cookie dough were placed three inches apart and then baked in the oven for the required time.

In no time at all I had chocolate chip cookies, plus peanut butter. I added two dozen of the cinnamon from the oven onto the island.

I'd forgotten to make another cup of coffee when I'd come down, so I took a moment to scoot to the front of the shop.

I went for a mocha with a little peppermint, and

some whipped cream on top. Picking up my mug, I headed back into the kitchen to box the cookies up in the seasonal tins I'd gotten.

Giant snowflakes covered one of the larger tins, and that was the one going to Onyx. I packed some of each of the cookies into that one tin and wrapped a ribbon around the top, keeping it in place with a small piece of tape. The name was easy enough.

The rest of the cookies I put on a large platter that I'd take upstairs once I was ready. The soft music still played in the living room, and I could barely hear it if I strained.

"This will be okay," I whispered to myself.

Another rush of warmth rose from the floorboards.

"I'm okay, Betty…" I let out a sigh. "Once I wrap and pack up all the presents, I'll need to call my mom and let her know I'm not coming home for the holiday. And that is okay. I've come to terms with it. It's just that the conversation is going to suck, you know?"

I wasn't sure if the shop understood, but I appreciated the warmth soaking in my toes.

"I appreciate your help today with the tree and making cookies. You make this place feel like home."

I still had plenty of time before I needed to make the call. Instead, I picked up the tin and my coffee mug and headed for the stairs.

With Betty's help, none of this had taken long. It wasn't even lunchtime yet. Back upstairs, I found the Cat napping next to Indigo, who clutched a golden oak leaf in her claws. She lay next to him with her eyes closed, snoring ever so lightly.

I didn't wake them as I set the tin down and pulled out the wrapping paper. The coffee table was the best place to get all the gifts for my family wrapped. The basket of things I'd gotten earlier in the week rose from the floor next to me.

Then I very slowly got to work cutting wrapping paper. Some people could wrap gifts and make them look amazing. I could do okay, but I needed to be very intentional about it and take my time. Otherwise, it looked like a two-year-old did it.

I started with the easy one, the books. I'd slowly move onto harder items after that.

Indigo stopped snoring at one point and watched what I was doing.

I placed a small square of wrapping paper in front of her and she tried to fold it with her claws. It didn't go so well, but she kept at it.

Eventually, my pile of presents sat in the center of the coffee table, wrapped with name tags and even ribbons with bows. I might have gone a little overboard, but it provided me more time to put off the phone call.

"Are you mailing those today?" asked the Cat, snapping me out of my thoughts.

"I am," I said with a frown, glancing at the time. "I scheduled a pickup with the delivery guy. I still need to get them into a box and labeled for delivery to mom's."

It was a good reminder that I couldn't just zone out right now. Especially not if I wanted the package to get to my family on time, and not have it cost hundreds of dollars to ship, though for once I could afford it.

I grabbed the cardboard box and carefully stacked

the wrapped presents inside, using tissue paper to fill in any gaps and protect the bows.

"Me too!" Indigo held up a roughly star-shaped object she'd made out of the wrapping paper.

"That's pretty," I said, taking it from her claws. "I can add it to the box, or hang it in your room, which do you prefer?"

Indigo's eyes grew wide as she looked between the cardboard box and me.

"I can make you a paper star for your room if you want..."

"Give to family, my present." Indigo nodded her head at her statement and I added it to the box.

I set it on top, though it'd probably get moved around during shipping. Who knew what my family would make of it, but it didn't matter.

"They'll love it," I told the little dragon. I'd need to weigh the package and get it taped up, but I still had a few hours until the pickup time.

"I'll make you a star," I said, pulling a piece of white paper with snowflakes on it closer. I cut it into a square and then slowly folded an origami star. It was one of the few things I could fold like that.

"Ohhhh... can has more?" she asked, claws outstretched for the one I'd made.

I chuckled as I cut out several more squares and got to work folding them.

Indigo watched like I was a superhero as I made each star for her cat tower. The pile slowly grew bigger, and she flew around the room holding one in her claws.

Eventually, the alarm on my phone went off, and I paused the folding.

"Time to get the box mailed," I muttered to myself. I taped the box up and carried it downstairs, careful not to trip.

A scale sat on the counter by the time I got there, and I weighed it before printing the label with the label maker that happened to be next to the scale.

I slapped the sticker on the box and headed to the front door to unlock it. I'd just turned back to the counter when someone knocked on the door.

Quickly turning, I caught sight of the delivery guy on the other side. I waved quickly at Adam and pulled it open.

"You have perfect timing; let me grab the box."

"I can get it," he said with a smile. He followed behind me, which made me nervous, but I caught sight of the Cat watching from the balcony.

Adam grabbed the box after scanning the barcode on the box. "This looks good, have a nice one today!"

"You too," I followed him out this time and locked the door behind him.

Indigo chirped from upstairs. *"Stars, more stars..."*

I chuckled and headed in that direction.

Sable did her best to hide her emotions today with a bright facade, but the shop could feel it, and so could I. Packing the box up and getting it out the door brought her down a little more, but Indigo didn't even notice.

Maybe there was something I could do to make this better. Just a little.

I'd need to be sneaky, even for a Fey Lord. But I was sure I could do it.

THIRTY-FIVE

Indigo slept calmly in her cat tree, which now had paper stars hanging from the upper portions with fishing line. They twirled whenever she flew back, making the glitter sparkle in the light.

I snuck out of the room quietly to not wake her and closed the door, but didn't latch it so she could get out when she wanted. Slowly, I made my way back to the living room, keeping an eye out for the Cat. He wasn't on the balcony or in the room when I entered.

"Hey, Betty, can you warn me if the Cat comes in?" I asked, quietly.

A burst of warmth under my feet made me smile as I opened one of the other boxes from earlier. Inside sat a bunch of hand-knitted stockings I'd ordered from online. I pulled the first out, which was a bright white with red writing.

'Indigo', in a pretty slanted writing, blazed across the front. It had small purple dragons flying along the cuff. I hung it from the hook attached to the mantle, smiling.

The next one was for the Cat. The body was dark green with white writing. One side had 'Cat' on it, while the other said 'Felix'. The white trim had a black cat decorating it. I hung it up next to Indigo's, with the Cat side facing out.

The second to last stocking had my name on it. It was blue with white writing on it. My name practically glowed on the front, and golden stars decorated the white cuff. I paused, staring at it, before pulling out the order slip.

"That's strange..." I whispered. I hadn't ordered the cuff decoration on mine. Maybe the knitter wanted something there. I hung it up next to the Cat's stocking.

The last one was a bright red with green writing. 'Betty' stretched across the front, and coffee cups decorated the cuff. It was exactly as I'd imagined. I hung it up next to the other three, smiling.

The blast of warmth that came out of the fireplace almost knocked me over as I giggled.

"I'm glad you like it, Betty..."

I added some dark green garland to the mantle with a strand of red beads wrapped around it, to give it a little more presence. Standing back, I declared the fireplace to be done.

"So, did you get the secret project up?" I whispered into the room.

A controller appeared on the coffee table with all the required buttons. I did a little happy dance, knowing that my gift for the Cat was complete, along with the one for Indigo.

I hoped both would enjoy their presents, even if they weren't wrapped under the tree.

Still, I needed to get some things to fill their stockings with. Small things that'd be cute or useful.

Then I had nothing else to distract me from making the phone call I'd been dreading. I really didn't want to do this. I tossed myself back on the fluffy couch and pulled my phone out of my pocket.

To my surprise, I had a text from Cyan asking to call him. I dialed his number.

"Hey, I just got your message," I said, staring at the fireplace.

"Glad I caught you... Are you coming home for the holiday?"

I hadn't expected him to be so blunt.

"No, I can't get the time off that week..."

"Ugh, that's not great..." said Cyan. He sounded conflicted and slightly worried.

I sat up.

"Okay, what's going on?"

"You should call and talk to Dad. It really isn't my place to discuss it, but maybe, just like, call him right now? He...one sec..." His voice cut off, and I heard him walking somewhere.

"Yeah, he's in his study, alone. Now's your best shot."

"Okay. I'll call him."

Cyan hung up the phone, and I quickly hit my dad in my contacts list. It rang a few times before he picked it up.

"Hey Dad, how are you doing?" I asked on high alert.

"Wow, calling your old man, I feel special." He chuckled. "I'm...not doing okay."

My hands shook, and I switched the call to speaker phone.

"You gotta give me more than that."

"I'm having a few health problems. Nothing serious that your mother can't handle, but I'm spending more time resting than I'd like."

I'd always pictured my father as a healthy man. He practically hadn't aged—no white hair, no slowdown. Nothing like that. So this threw me.

"Are you going to be okay?" I asked, tucking my feet underneath me and pulling a throw blanket into my lap for something to hold onto.

"Yeah, it's just going to take some time to recover. Just a few weeks and I'll be back on my feet."

My eyes narrowed. "Are you downplaying this, right now?"

He didn't answer immediately. Then he sighed. "A little, but I expect you're not going to be home for the Solstice, and I didn't want you to worry."

"I'm not. I wish I could, but I can't get the time off that week." I leaned back, staring at the ceiling. "Of course I'm going to worry. I love you. What's wrong? For real, I mean?"

"It's a small lump that is going to be removed."

Everything inside me froze.

"Cancer. That's what you're not saying."

"We don't know yet, and your mother doesn't think so. I trust her more than anyone."

"Maybe you should see a more modern doctor than

mom…" I added softly. My mother was a fantastic nurse, with several credentials, but she also practiced some very far out there new-age type things.

"I'm going to pretend you didn't say that and get upset," he said sternly. "You mean well, and I know that, but don't you dare put down your mother's skills. I'm not worried about this, just feeling down."

"I might be able to figure out…"

"No, do not put your job at risk over this. While I want to see you, and so does your mother, this isn't big enough to risk your job." His voice came out very matter-a-fact. "To prove it, I'll even be the one to discuss you not coming home with your mother."

"Dad…you don't need to do that." This totally felt like something I should discuss with the Cat and see if I could go home for a night.

"I know, but I love you and want you to not worry…" His voice trailed off, and then he continued with a brighter tone. "Have you started writing in your journal yet?"

"Not yet, but I'll make sure to soon." I'd forgotten about the gift for my birthday.

"You better." He chuckled. "I saw that and had to get it for you. I know it's not my normal type of birthday gift."

"It's perfect," I said thinking of everything happening in my life. I had plenty to write.

"Well, I need to go talk to your mother. I hope you have a fantastic Solstice."

"You too. I love you."

"Love you!"

I hung up the phone, unsure of what to do. While Dad talking to Mom was such a relief, this health thing of his worried me. Even if he didn't want me to worry.

"Everything will be alright," I whispered to myself.

I HATED TECHNOLOGY. Maybe it'd be more pleasant if I had thumbs, or hands, again. The tablet in front of me made me want to yell, but I couldn't do that without Sable finding out what I was up to. The email thing frustrated me, too, but the shop helped me as best it could.

Words flowed across the screen, as best as I could get them to.

The email address the shop pulled from Sable's computer. I didn't know, or care, how that worked. Only that the shop could do it.

Hopefully this would help, ramifications be damned.

THIRTY-SIX

First coffee, then breakfast.

The warm scent of coffee filled the air as I ground the beans to make the espresso. A nice, normal day sounded great at the moment. Everyone else still slept, as far as I could tell.

Indigo snored from her cat tree as I got up and got ready for the day, and I didn't see anything of the Cat.

The shop felt quiet.

Sunlight barely peeked in from the skylights, and the sound of the grinder felt muffled. It was like Betty agreed with me on how things felt.

I knew it was early. Yet, I felt great, and I'd climbed out of bed before my normal time. For once I started with an Americano, then at the last minute I added a splash of cream before I left the counter.

Warmth from my mug felt great as I padded my way into the kitchen to decide on something for breakfast. We had plenty of eggs and frozen waffles, but I wanted something else. Something better.

Then it hit me. Eggs Benedict.

There wasn't a chance I could make it. Though it sounded so perfect, I knew it was beyond me. I'd never gotten a hollandaise to come out right, and poaching eggs was not a skill I'd mastered. Somehow, I always overcooked them, no matter the method I tried.

My stomach growled while thinking about it, and I headed back out front to see what places I could order breakfast from. Within two clicks on the tablet, I had options. Five minutes later, and I'd placed a rather large breakfast order for the three of us.

The one thing I counted on was Betty keeping everything nice and warm while the others slept.

I sat at the counter, staring over the shop as I sipped my coffee. Bits of sunlight filled the area in a golden light. That light made everything feel like magic. Like everything would be alright with my dad.

"I am so lucky…"

The floorboards under my feet warmed up at my statement, and a shadow by the door caused me to jump up. I raced to meet the delivery person before they could knock.

The six foot tall blue person handed me the bag without blinking, then went on his way. The shops lining the street had signs in various languages I didn't recognize, and soft music came from somewhere.

With a sigh, I closed the door, wondering what world I'd just ordered breakfast from.

Maybe someday I could explore other worlds and see what else was out there. I carried the giant plastic bag to the kitchen and pulled out various cardboard containers.

Though, they didn't feel like cardboard, really, and the plastic bag felt strange as well.

The bag dissolved into nothingness after I removed all the containers. The cardboard felt more like wood. Inside, each container was filled to the brim.

One had crispy, hot diced potatoes with onions, another had poached eggs, slightly too big to be from the chickens I knew. A third was filled with sliced bread of some kind, and not the English muffins I was used to. The last though, was a pale golden color. I touched it with my finger and tasted the sauce.

Pure goodness rippled through me, and I resisted eating right then. Instead, I let Betty put everything in storage so it would stay the perfect temperature until everyone woke up to share this bounty together.

That sauce, though.

Whatever world this was, I needed to somehow make my way back to it. I quickly rushed back to the front counter and favorited the restaurant. We definitely needed to eat from here again, and I hadn't even tasted everything.

Breakfast was gonna be good.

I silently made my way to the rooftop deck to watch the sunrise, even with the walls. Yet, as I stepped out they faded away, and more of the town I'd glimpsed from the delivery came into view. The bright yellow light peeked over the horizon, and I sat down to enjoy my coffee along with the slow awakening of the foreign place.

That music came from the same direction as the sun. It was soft, almost like someone singing quietly. Yet, I couldn't make out any of the words. It softened even more as the sun crested the horizon.

There wasn't anyone in the streets, and I really could only see the tops of some shops, but in the distance a pyramid stretched upward in a soft green color. The golden light hit different areas, and black designs formed on the surface.

After the sun rose high enough that pure heat hit me, I finally got up and headed inside. The walls shimmered back into view and a rush of cool air met me. Which was good, since I didn't want to be sweating all day.

Indigo chirped from downstairs, and I quickly made my way to the kitchen. Both the Cat and Indigo sat on the island, talking to one another. They glanced in my direction as I entered.

"Found you!" Indigo's wings fluttered.

"I watched the sunrise on the deck."

"What about breakfast?" asked the Cat, sniffing the air.

"I ordered food from a local place," I said, pulling open the fridge. Plates rose on the island, already made up.

Piles of roasted crispy potatoes next to toasted bread, with poached eggs on top and that amazing sauce over everything.

I drooled and snagged my stool before digging in, getting a forkful of the sauce, egg and the crispy bread all together.

The first bite melted in my mouth as the tangy cream sauce took over. Then the yolk pushed that aside as I chewed, followed by a nutty flavor from the bread.

Energy rushed through me as I swallowed. I had to pause, eyes wide at the sensation.

"What was that?" I asked.

"It has magical effects." The Cat glanced up at me with sauce and egg yolk on his face. "Where did you order this from?"

"No clue. It was listed on the register, and highly rated." I carefully grabbed a piece of potato and dabbed it in the sauce. Spice took over from the potato, but it didn't linger.

Indigo chirped twice, her front two paws almost in the center of the plate as she ate, way too fast.

I did the opposite and slowly lingered over every bite, enjoying the flavors and the rush of energy that made my fingers tingle.

Both the Cat and Indigo finished before I did, and the Cat jumped off the island and vanished to the front of the shop. It took several minutes for him to come back. By that time, I'd cleaned my plate with the last bite.

My lonely Americano sat next to my plate, and I picked it up to take a sip.

"That was an expensive meal," added the Cat, as he landed back on the island. "From a world I've never heard of."

"How much?" I asked, trying to picture the prices the register had shown, but unable to remember clearly.

"More than your salary for the day."

THIRTY-SEVEN

I spit out my coffee for the first time in my life, my inside full of panic. "That cost more than my salary?! It was three eggs, potatoes, and toast!"

"Yes, almost double." The Cat studied me with his bright green eyes. "I'm still uncertain what world we are currently on, but the currency conversion is terrible. At least we aren't doing business here today."

What the heck?

Indigo chirped twice, asking about the area.

"All I know is they have a green pyramid that has dark writing that appears when the sun hits it." My brain couldn't move past the fact that breakfast had cost more than I got paid in a day. "Why does everything cost so much?"

My fingers tapped on the island faster than ever before.

"Sable, calm down," growled the Cat. "That was magical food. It might have con..."

Indigo launched herself off her plate, and it shattered into a multitude of pieces. Her wings flapped in panic as she flew higher and slammed into the ceiling.

I dove and caught her, but accidentally stumbled on the stool, sending it flying into the glass door of the oven, which rippled like water.

Indigo landed in my arms, twitching. Electricity sparkled along her scales, sending shocks into my skin.

"CAT!"

"She's fine, just a little overloaded." His voice came out as calm as ever, yet Indigo had shattered a plate and Betty had stopped me from breaking the oven.

What the heck had that food done?

Again, a rush of energy went down my arms and I resisted curling them around Indigo.

She cracked open an eyelid and then rapidly blinked. *"Sparkles!"*

Bright light flickered above me like fireflies, and I felt myself leaning closer to them.

The shocks from Indigo stopped as she let out a massive burp.

"Are you okay?" All I needed was to have damaged her from food, and then have the clans come after me.

"Tasty food, want more!"

"Nope, nope, nope. We are not eating there again." I climbed to my feet, keeping Indigo close. "Betty, can we leave this place now?"

The warmth from the floorboards wasn't reassuring.

The Cat jumped from the island, his eyes wide, then he scrambled across the floor to the front of the shop.

"Not possible," he grumbled, as his paws ran above the floor.

I turned to follow, but he literally ran through the wall and vanished.

"Betty?"

Again a rush of warmth, but not a confirmation, more a feeling that she couldn't leave this place yet.

"You've got to be kidding me."

For the first time, I paused and stared up at the balcony overhead. The Cat's voice had come from the direction of his hidden room. He never raised his voice like that.

Something had gone wrong.

"Sable..." This time the Cat's voice came a little softer, but his green eyes flickered from between two pieces of a railing. "What did you do? Our customer for today... changed."

"Changed? Is that even possible...?" I set Indigo on the counter with a frown, yet she jumped up as soon as I let her go.

This time she didn't hit the ceiling because of the added height in this room. Then she zoomed toward her hideaway, a gust of air blowing in her wake.

The book didn't change, did it?

I tapped on the counter and my coffee mug rose from the wood, still nice and warm but with barely anything left.

"Thank you, Betty."

"Stop thanking things," grumbled the Cat as he appeared in the doorway, before leaping to the counter.

He missed.

Somehow, the Cat missed the counter.

He landed on his paws on the other side, just barely missing the table in the center of the room. He blinked in shock at the display.

"What was in that food?" I asked.

"What did the order say?" he replied, his paws touching the ground like bits might be lava.

I hurried to the register and quickly flicked through the apps to the one I'd used.

"Eggs Benedict for the Adventuring Party... Hearty enough to satisfy any appetite, except perhaps a dragon. This magical meal enhances your basic stats, with a tilt toward Strength."

"That is a strange description..." The Cat landed on the counter this time, and carefully joined me at the register to peer at the tablet. "What kind of world are we even on?"

"I don't know, you're the expert here."

This time, his tail flickered in the air, back and forth. Then he tapped his paws on the counter like he was making muffins.

"Cat, are you okay?" I reached out to touch him and he nuzzled my hand.

"I feel weird." He twitched a few times as he resisted moving closer to my hand. Finally he laid down. "I'm not moving until this wears off."

"What about the customer on this planet?"

"I don't need to move." The Cat glared at me, but then glanced away.

"Okay, so what did the book say?" I finished my mug of coffee carefully, to make sure I didn't break it. If the food increased my strength, based on the description of the meal, then I needed to be very careful.

I gazed longingly at the espresso machine, but I didn't dare use it. If it broke, I'd cry.

"They are just buying something we have in stock. It isn't a big deal. Somehow it's more important than what we had scheduled."

That sounded like a pretty simple day, something we could quickly get done then maybe even get back on track by doing the task that was meant for today in the afternoon. Given how early it was, there shouldn't be a rush yet.

"Then, what's the rush? We can wait until the food-stuff wears off, and then deal with the customer." It felt like a suitable compromise, though I really wanted a better coffee. An Americano was tasty, but a latte always won out in my book.

Maybe I'd carefully use the coffee machine.

I brushed the button to grind the beans, and with barely a touch it got to work. So far, so good. Next was to steam the milk.

"It might not work that way," grumbled the Cat.

He twisted about and I couldn't help but watch. His goal of not moving had shattered pretty quickly. Still, I tried not to judge as he stared at the people walking down the street on the other side of the window.

Wait, people were walking down the street, and we could see them?

"That's not normal..."

I twisted about to look, completely forgetting the steaming wand and metal pitcher in my hands.

Steam shot out everywhere as the wand on Betty bent, and the metal pitcher dented inward at the pressure of my fingers.

CHAPTER

THIRTY-EIGHT

The steamer quickly shut off, and thankfully it didn't get anywhere close to my skin. I'd burned myself in the past with the steamer wand, and this was a lucky break.

"Thanks, Betty," I mumbled under my breath as I set the metal pitcher on the counter.

Hot milk dribbled down the sides of the metal container and I cringed.

It sank down, vanishing from sight, and I forced myself to turn to look at Betty. The damage wasn't bad-bad, just kinda bad. The steamer wand was bent in the wrong direction, and the tip was flatted where I'd pinched it.

It hurt just looking at it.

My fingers tingled, and I felt slightly sick to my stomach. The lovely breakfast now felt like a brick in my stomach.

"Sable, are you ready?" asked the Cat.

"What?" I glanced over at him to find him staring at

the front door and the shadow within the doorframe. "Shoot!"

The door swung open as they raised their hand toward the doorknob. In walked a tall woman with an undercut on her chin length hair. Her skin flickered. One moment it appeared like normal, brownish skin, but then it sparked and became a deep blue with bright white cracks trailing down it.

She paused and glanced down at herself, and the flickering. "Ah, guess a magical shop wouldn't like glamours."

"They tend not to work in here," I confirmed, even though I knew that wasn't always true. I resisted looking at the espresso machine. "Welcome to the shop. How can I help you?"

My eyes stayed focused on her as she headed for the front counter. Yet, she paused almost mid-step as Indigo leaped into the air. Her bright blue eyes landed on the little dragon and she watched her circle overhead.

"Hey, little one, I bet you can smell my magic..."

Indigo chirped twice and added more. *She smells like power and storms!*

"Is she friendly?" asked the woman.

"Yes, generally, but she has a mind of her own."

"Most dragons do..." The woman held up a hand to Indigo. "I'm Kyra, little one. I mean no harm."

I snuck a glance at the espresso maker and found it gone. Completely gone from the counter. I resisted asking the Cat about it, and instead focused on Kyra.

"So, what brings you in?"

"I need to feed my sword," replied Kyra.

Indigo swooped down and landed on her shoulder.

The cracks in Kyra's skin glowed for a moment near where Indigo landed.

"*Her magic tickles, like the sky,*" added Indigo.

Kyra didn't respond to the dragon. "You are so pretty, little one. I bet you love to soar with the dust devils in the canyons."

"What does your sword eat?" I asked, interrupting the moment. I found myself slightly jealous, and tried to ignore it. This was only momentary, it wasn't like Indigo would be going anywhere.

"Probably metal of some kind, along with gems," said the Cat, his eyes narrowed at Kyra. "What is so important about her?"

"I need silver shavings and amethyst dust, along with lightning glass." She stepped closer to the counter, though her eyes remained on the dragon, who kept sniffing her. "Do you want to see my sword?"

Before anyone could respond, she pulled the sword off her back. I hadn't even noticed it, or the leather armor that covered her like a crop top. The glowing skin had distracted me, plus how she acted with Indigo.

She laid the sword on the counter.

"Dragons also like it."

Indigo climbed down her arm and sniffed at the sword as she made her way to the counter.

"*Old magic,*" whispered Indigo in the softest voice I'd ever heard from her.

I blinked twice as golden light formed, then crept along the edges. It then stretched from the sword to Kyra herself.

"Ancient magic," added the Cat, snapping me out of the zone.

The golden light vanished.

The sword and Kyra herself were important, especially if the amount of golden light increased with a higher need.

"We should have all of that in the storeroom," said the Cat as he nudged me with his nose.

"Let me go get some." I spun and quickly headed to the door that led to the storeroom.

Inside, the massive shelves and bins were full. Yet, in the center of the room a wooden table held a box that already appeared open. Four bags of various colors sat next to it.

I picked one up to see the tag.

"Silver shavings...amethyst dust, and lightning glass. Plus, crystallized Zephyr's breath..." That bag was the lightest, and I felt the pulse of magic inside. It overshadowed the hum from the amethyst bag.

I slowly brought all four out to the front of the shop.

"I found something else that you might want as well."

"Put that back in the storage room," growled the Cat, as I placed the bags on the counter. "That is dangerous material."

Yet, the sword started glowing a bright purple color as soon as the bags hit the counter.

"That's new," whispered Kyra as she leaned forward. She lightly touched the blade of the sword. "You doing okay?"

It took a moment before I realized she had asked the sword, and not me.

Indigo moved closer to the blade, her snout almost touching it.

"You should have put that away," whispered the Cat.

I ignored him. Everything else felt like it had been the correct thing to do. Even Betty thought so, since she'd pulled it out of storage all ready to go.

"Okay, I want whatever is in that fourth bag. He said he needs it to not fade." Kyra glanced up at me. "What does it cost?"

"Not sure, give me a moment..."

The Cat wouldn't look at me and focused on the bag instead.

I stepped over to the register, and my mouth dropped. "Uh... Cat?"

He glanced up at me and away.

"Can you please check what this is asking for?" This time I let the concern fill my voice.

The Cat padded in my direction and he put his paws on the edge of the register peering at the screen.

"I told you it was dangerous. That price tag is what I expected."

"That's just strange," I whispered quietly, rubbing my fingers together.

"I mean, a plant gave you its heart in a pot, and you didn't seem to care."

My mouth opened then closed before I just went for it.

"I need some of your hair..."

THIRTY-NINE

I felt awkward asking for hair.

"How much?" asked Kyra without missing a beat. "I unfortunately cut it recently, but I can totally pay that as long as I have enough."

"It says several strands," I read off the register.

"Not an issue." Within seconds, Kyra separated out the longest strands she had left and braided them, before using her knife to cut the bunch near her scalp.

I didn't know what to say as I took the bundle. Her hair tingled in my hands, like I'd touched a battery to my tongue.

"Do you have a tub I can use?" she asked, picking up the bag.

"Sure, I bet I have one..." I reached under the counter, unsure of where to place the hair. I set it off to one side and, behold, there was a tub long enough for her sword to fit inside under the counter. I pulled the plastic container out, careful to not squeeze the edges too hard.

"That will work." Kyra picked up the sword and

placed it inside, followed by opening all four bags and dumping them into the container. The silver shavings, amethyst dust, and lightning glass all made sense. Though, the lightning glass looked like pebbles with sharp edges, and I wasn't sure what it really was.

The crystalized Zephyr's breath made absolutely no sense. A bubble floated out of the bag and shattered into what looked like little bits of glass when it hit the sword.

Kyra then used the same knife to cut the edge of her arm and drip some blue blood inside.

I couldn't look away as she pulled a water bag out of nowhere and poured water into the mixture.

"Hopefully it works," she muttered, focusing on the sword.

"You don't know if it'll work?" I asked, grabbing Indigo away from the tub as she tried to stick her head inside.

The dragon glared at me.

"It's not like it comes with much instruction. It only told me it needed to be fed, and then it wanted that when you brought it out."

"So you talk to your sword?" I couldn't help but ask her about it.

"You talk to your cat?" Kyra shrugged, her eyes still on the container. "It's a weird world we live in."

Indigo chirped. "*And dragons.*"

"You are right..." I shouldn't find it weird that she didn't know how to do magic. I was still learning, and felt like I'd be learning more all the time. "It is a weird world...speaking of. Why does the pyramid look different in the sun?"

Kyra's eyes flickered to me in confusion. "What do you mean? Sunlight doesn't change..."

The sword started glowing again, this time a bright white, almost silver, as the liquid lowered in the tub.

Magic tingled in the air, and I stepped back, pulling Indigo off the counter.

The Cat jumped to the floor.

Kyra leaned in closer, and the light almost danced along her skin. The crackles glowed even brighter on her body, and she smiled. Tears gathered at the corners of her eyes as the light danced. Whispers tickled at the edge of what I could hear.

"Daughter, keep...the path...truth."

What I made out felt broken, but it wasn't for me. It was for her.

I blinked as the golden shimmer of magic returned, connecting the sword and the strange woman. A feeling of rightness echoed through the room as all the things blinked out, including the golden shimmer.

Kyra wiped the tears away and swallowed hard before picking up the sword. She slung it into a hidden sheath on her bag and it vanished from sight. Her eyes met mine.

"I owe you way more than hair. If you need me, I will come. Just sing my name." The next words she spoke felt more like lyrics dancing on the wind.

Images flashed in my mind of a flower petal made of lightning dancing alone in a breeze. Then it stopped, and we were back in the shop. Yet, it felt like her name flickered in the back of my mind. I knew I could sing that if I needed to, even though generally I wasn't a very good singer.

"Stay safe, both of you."

Kyra nodded at Indigo in my arms, then turned and headed out of the shop. The door shut quietly behind her, and it felt like all the energy left the room.

"What was that?" I sank down to the stool and set Indigo back on the counter.

"The last storm elemental, by my guess," said the Cat as he leaped up on the counter. "I believe the souls of her ancestors are in that blade."

"What did we do?" Her name danced in the back of my mind before quieting. Yet, I knew I'd be able to recall it without a problem if the need arose.

"Not a clue, but it must have been important." The Cat shivered just once, as green light flowed over his fur.

Indigo glanced between the two of us, like we were dumb. "*Family matters.*"

"Yeah, her family is in the blade." I couldn't imagine carrying my family around with me like that.

"*Magic added to bond.*" Indigo frantically shook her head no. "*She spoke to her mother.*"

I swallowed hard at that, as understanding rippled through me. "Oh..."

Indigo crept closer to me, and I patted her head lightly.

"*Someday, I speak to mother.*" Indigo said with full confidence. "*When bigger.*"

"I hope you get the chance," I whispered.

"*I will, Grandpa said so.*"

This time I nodded. It must be a dragon thing, or a magic thing I didn't know about.

Especially since dragons returned to the tree when they passed away. I still didn't really understand what the tree was, besides that the leylines led there and the leylines connected the worlds. Or at least, that's what the books said.

The whole thing felt so strange. Then again, magic existed, so what did I know? It felt like I couldn't learn it all, and so I just went with the flow. My basic needs were met, and my life was so amazing. I could handle not understanding things most of the time. Other things, I wanted to know about badly.

My eyes flickered to the Cat, and back to the door.

"So, what's next on the docket?" I asked, thinking of the day we were originally supposed to have.

"I think we should call it a day," grumbled the Cat.

"It's still early!" Then I remembered what was missing, and twisted back to the espresso machine. "Cat, where is Betty?"

"Probably getting fixed. Did the steam go everywhere?"

"Yes, but that was only the steaming wand. It should..."

The counter rippled upward and the beautiful espresso machine slowly rose from the wooden counter back to where it was before.

"Okay, that's better..." I mumbled before taking a deep breath. My shoulders felt like they were up to my ears. "Maybe you're right, and we should take the rest of the day off."

"I am always right. The sign says so."

By the time I glanced over, the Cat had vanished, and Indigo was flying toward her hideaway. I guessed some relaxing time was needed after that event.

Between the name floating around in my mind and how tasty breakfast had been, I didn't really know what to do with myself.

Though, I really wanted to order more of that food from the breakfast place, now that the immediate effects had lessened somewhat. Maybe something that I didn't need to learn how to use to avoid breaking the shop.

Still, I needed to figure out my magic, and soon. Not to mention what the heck was going on with my brother.

I pulled back my sleeve and stared at the bracelet around my wrist. The stones glimmered, especially the green one, which wasn't normal.

Why would we need to be on this world, and what did we need her hair for? The bigger question that I couldn't ask was, why did I need her name?

CHAPTER
FORTY

"You will meet your magic teacher today," said the Cat, as he jumped onto the island.

I almost flung scrambled eggs everywhere as I spun to look at him.

Indigo chirped in a panic, since she stood beside the stove, watching the cooking process from the counter. She'd asked nicely if she could learn to make breakfast, so we were starting with the basics.

"What do you mean?" I asked, turning back to stir the still wet eggs. The heat was low, so as not to cook the eggs too fast.

Indigo mimicked the same stirring motion I made with the smallest kid-sized spatula I could find online. If I'd known she'd get into cooking, her Solstice gifts would have been different.

"Someone answered the call to teach you about magic," said the Cat in a slow, are-you-dumb kind of voice. "I told you I'd find someone, since the dragons aren't the best way for you to learn."

"*Lady Twilight?*" asked Indigo.

"I don't know when the dragon will be back for classes, though it has been a while," I said with a frown. Usually, they seemed to show up every couple of weeks, but the last visit about Indigo's mom had been intense. "Maybe she'll come this week to show you some new things."

"*She gave me more audiobooks,*" said Indigo, shaking her head. "*But I want to see her.*"

I nodded as I turned the stove off and showed her how the eggs were cooked all the way through.

"Tomorrow, you can try to make a scrambled egg while I help."

That caused Indigo to launch herself from the counter, leaping over to the island chirping as loud as she could.

The Cat glared at her, his green eyes burning at the sound.

Indigo didn't care.

I set out plates and then piled two of them high with eggs, while the third got a slightly smaller pile. The toaster popped up the six pieces of toast, and I quickly slathered them with butter plus cinnamon and sugar before cutting them into triangles. One piece got cut into mini triangles as well. Those were for Indigo.

I dug into my food, waiting for the Cat to say anything else about this magic teacher. Instead, he slowly consumed his food. I stared, but he ignored me.

"Anything I should know about this teacher?"

The Cat's eyes landed on Indigo, then shifted back to

me. Whatever he had to say, he didn't want to say in front of the dragon.

"So, Indigo, are you going to listen to your new stories?"

"*Yes! After breakfast, I want to finish, so visit.*" She carefully picked up a tiny triangle of toast and took a large bit of it. Her wings fluttered behind her.

"That's true," I said between bites. "Once you have done all the homework, Lady Twilight might visit to check up on how you are doing."

Breakfast was quick, though I saved a piece of toast to carry out to the counter to have with another cup of coffee. I'd slept great, but felt like I'd need the caffeine to help perk myself up. I quickly steamed the milk, making lattes for both the Cat and myself.

Indigo flew directly to her hideaway, not even asking for a hot chocolate.

"Well, that's one dedicated learner," I muttered. While I loved learning, it wasn't like that. Then again, dragon stories had to be much more exciting, compared to what I'd learned in school. That reminded me of the online elementary and middle school classes I'd found for Indigo. I made a mental note to ask Lady Twilight about them, since I hadn't registered her yet.

The shop had the small seating area off to the right, while the rest of it was still packed with bookshelves. The large center table was missing, and a bright green rug lay on the floor, stretching to the fake fireplace to the right.

I sat on my stool and faced the Cat as he lapped up his teacup of caffeine goodness.

"So, about this teacher…"

The Cat sighed and pulled away from the now empty cup.

"They were a friend, once…" he hesitated, whiskers twitching. "They won't be able to recognize me, and I'd appreciate it if you try not to speak about me… but… if you could ask about my lands, I'd appreciate it."

The Cat paused, like he was waiting for someone to do something to him. His whole body went rigid, and then relaxed, licking a paw nonchalantly.

I nodded, but didn't comment, not wanting to trigger any ramifications to the Cat. The rest of my toast lasted only a few seconds before it was gone. Crumbs remained on the counter, which I went to sweep up, but they vanished.

"Thanks, Betty."

The door jingled, and I smiled, ready for this adventure.

In walked a slender humanoid in robes of deep green. The embroidered constellations moved all over it in an entrancing pattern. Yet, the most distracting thing was the ears. A pair of extraordinarily long, velvety rabbit's ears twitched and swiveled independently on either side of the being's head.

I couldn't look away.

The ears twisted in my direction.

"Is this the place?" she asked.

"Welcome to Meow, the Magical Emporium of Wares…" I said, trying to get my bearings.

Her face was humanoid, and kind brown eyes stared at me.

"I feel like that's a clue to this strange mystery I find myself in." She sniffed, her small upturned nose twitching. "So much magic in this place. Magic I recognize hints of."

"I'm Sable, the Shopkeeper."

"Ah, then this is the place," she muttered stepping forward. Her eyes landed on the Cat and moved on without even pausing. "I received a message from an old friend directing me here. It claimed that I'd find an interesting student, who needed to be taught."

"I was told a teacher would appear today, if that helps." I didn't know what else to say, and more importantly, what not to.

"My name is Professor Eira, and I would like to know how you know the Fey Lord." She lifted an oak leaf out of her pocket and set it on the table. Instead of hands, she had soft-furred paws with dexterous claws. "My old friend vanished under unfortunate circumstances, and I search for him still."

The Cat froze behind me, and I wanted to scream that he was right there, but I resisted.

"I wish I could help, but..." I didn't know what to do, and the Cat only stared at the lady in front of me. My eyes landed on the oak leaf.

Her ears twitched as her brown eyes stared into my soul.

"You speak the truth, so I am here to teach you about magic. What do you know?"

CHAPTER

FORTY-ONE

I went to speak, but she held up a paw, interrupting me.

"Let me guess," she said quietly. Her dark eyes studying my face. "You are new to magic, yet work in a very magical shop."

She leaned forward, reaching out with a paw. "Can you touch my paw?"

I glanced at the Cat out of the corner of my eye, and he nodded slightly. So, I reached out. Warmth blazed from the woman and rushed up my fingertips.

Then she suddenly jerked back, taking a step away.

"Dragons, Fates, Angels and Stones!"

"*I'm a dragon,*" chirped Indigo, as she stuck her head out of her hideaway. "*Teacher!*"

The bookdragon launched herself to Professor Eira, then at the last minute twisted in mid-air to land on the counter.

"*You have a teacher, strange magic!*" Indigo stared up at the Professor, whose eyes went wide.

229

"That's a baby dragon," she whispered, taking a step back.

"*Bookdragon!*"

"What type of dragon is she? You can't just kidnap dragons, you know," she said leaning closer before shaking her head, like she couldn't help herself. "The magic makes more sense now."

"I didn't kidnap Indigo. I am her aunt, and the Clan of Lore has blessed the arrangement." I picked Indigo up, pulling her close.

"She can't understand dragon, so she doesn't know what you're saying," I said to the little dragon.

"*Not fun,*" chirped Indigo, wiggling in my arms. "*Stories better.*"

"Yes, go get your homework done before your teacher shows up," I said, redirecting Indigo back to her hideaway.

She jumped and took off flying back the way she'd come.

The Professor watched her go. "So, that's where the dragon protection comes into play, and why you have dragon magic all over you."

The Cat hadn't warned me to keep anything secret but him.

"They taught me their language with magic, and I have a few magical artifacts from various people. The dragons, and a feather from an archangel."

The professor blinked a few times and motioned to the chairs by the fireplace. "How about we sit and chat?"

"Would you like some coffee?" I asked.

"No, thank you. I find caffeine can play with the flow

of my magic too much." She turned and glided over to a chair.

I quickly followed, bringing my latte with me.

The Cat crept along by my feet and jumped up to sit on the armrest of my chair.

"So, how have you used magic so far?" she asked, clenching her paws together.

"Accidentally," I said, lifting the bracelet. "I sent a customer flying out the door by accident. I felt terrible."

"That's it?" Her head tilted to one side.

"Well, I've used it a little while experimenting with Indigo. My current instruction, just a few words, really, said magic is all about intention. I need to really want something, and then make it happen." I leaned back in the chair and tried to relax, even though talking about all of this still didn't feel real.

The Professor's ears twitched again, and she nodded. "Those are some early signs of what happens before a child's magic finds its place. Yet, you are old for that to be happening."

"Its place?" I asked, taking a sip of my coffee.

"All magic comes from the leylines. I assume you know what those are?"

I nodded quickly.

"Well, from there different beings use magic differently. Dragons use leyline magic, just like Fey Lords. Usually, one species on each planet can use raw magic. From there, other species become more specialized. An example are healers, who can use healing magic to restore injuries, or Wind Walkers who can travel by air."

"Is that why Dragons and Fey Lords don't get along? They both use the same type of magic?"

The Cat's tail brushed the back of my arm.

"Fey Lords are complex individuals, and also places at the same time. They connect with their homes more than any other being. Almost all Fey Lords create other beings, companions that they think of as their children. My friend created elves to live in his towering forest. They... become protective of their people." She paused and shook her head. "It can be their downfall.

"Angels are similar," she continued. "They belong to different hosts, and each have abilities based on the host they come from. They draw power directly from the leylines, too."

She motioned to me with a paw. "You have energy around you of many of the species that draw directly from the leylines, and your magic hasn't focused in one area, maybe because of that."

"What does that make me?"

"A mystery, and one I'm excited to solve." She clapped her paws together. "I've decided I will teach you how to use raw magic, the same magic that gathers around you."

I finished my coffee cup and set it on the coffee table. "That sounds amazing."

"You might not think that once we have finished your lesson for today," she said with a smile. "First, you need to learn how to reach the magic inside of you, without feeling."

What? I didn't say it aloud, but a sneaking suspicion came to mind.

"You need to learn to breathe and meditate."

Bingo. There it was.

"Close your eyes and focus on your breathing. Eventually, you will find your sixth sense, your magical sense."

I closed my eyes and tried to focus on my breathing. Instead, every little thing distracted me. The smell of espresso in the air, the faint breathing from the Cat, warmth from the fake fireplace. My fingers rested on the velvet of the armchair, which suddenly felt itchy.

"Ignore all the little sensations and look inward to that feeling of warmth from your chest." Her voice swept through my mind like a cool breeze, pushing back everything that I felt.

An image of the gold outlines I'd started noticing on people came to mind, and my brain focused on that. The bright shimmery color and a feeling of warmth pulsed from under my collarbones, and then it was all I felt.

I suddenly snapped away from it, blinking.

"What was that?" I asked, my voice coming out brittle.

Professor Eira smiled at me, her eyes holding curiosity. "What was what? Did you touch it?"

"I did, but then lost it," I mumbled, trying to think about what had broken my concentration.

"That is superb for a first try," she said with a bright smile, her ears twitching. "You'll need to keep working on it and practice each day. Your goal is to touch the magic, not to do anything with it. Just to touch it."

The Cat stared at her, then his gaze flickered back to me. His eyes begged me to not forget.

"You mentioned you came because a friend asked you to. Do you know what happened to his lands?" My question hung in the air.

She blinked twice, and both ears turned toward me, then her eyes narrowed before they suddenly grew wide.

FORTY-TWO

"I feel like I should answer you, but a part of me wants to resist," she said, before shaking her head. "One of the Lord's Children has gone missing, the eldest, and it is expected she has rejoined the tree. Though some whisper of dark deeds, of the dragons stealing her away."

I nodded, though I knew Liluth was with Lady Twilight's clan, hidden with magic on her protected lands.

"His former domain is still a twisted land that none may enter. All who do end up right where they started. Demons invaded the Fey Wilds some months ago, but were pushed back before the King was defeated." She leaned back in her chair with a frown. "War is on the horizon between the Queens. They don't appreciate that the dragons have returned from self exile, and that they visit with friends within the Fey Wilds. Other Fey Lords have close ties with them, but the far Queens don't agree with that."

The Cat's tail twitched, twice. Hopefully, he'd gotten what he wanted. Now it was time for me to learn more.

"What do you know about how the Lord was banished?" I asked softly. This could be my chance to figure out how to free the Cat.

"It was my fault." Professor Eira wrapped her paws around her midsection, not looking at me.

The Cat froze.

"I should have stopped him. My oldest friend. I warned him, but he didn't listen. I should have made him listen."

"Listen to what…"

"*That* magic, the magic he wanted to use, wasn't for him. The raw, most potent magic of the leylines themselves is for those Fate Bound: the Travelers, the Wanderers, the Seers, and the like." Tears gathered at the corners of her eyes. "He protected me and offered me sanctuary from those who hunted my kind, and I failed him."

She sniffed a few times, and all I wanted to do was offer her a hug, but I didn't know her.

Warmth blazed from the fireplace, like a sudden gust of wind.

"Betty doesn't want you to be sad," I said, motioning to the shop.

She wiped her eyes and sat up a little straighter. "I apologize for my outburst, I'm not sure where it came from."

I reached out with a hand and set it on the armrest next to her. "You miss your friend. But you shouldn't blame yourself; he made his own decisions."

"But he wouldn't even have thought of it if I hadn't

mentioned it." She swallowed hard, wiping her eyes some more.

"He made his own choices, and I doubt he'd want a friend to be weighed down by his decisions." I kept my voice firm, hoping it was the correct thing to say.

The Cat hadn't moved, almost like he couldn't. His tail hung limply down the side of the armrest. His eyes didn't move from the Professor, curled in on herself.

The bells on the door rang as it opened.

My head snapped in that direction to find Lady Twilight entering. Her purple eyes glowed brightly, though her smile fell as she took in the fact that someone else was in the shop with me.

"Oh, I hope I'm not interrupting," she said, stopping once the door closed.

Indigo suddenly appeared, flying out of her hideaway and speaking so fast I couldn't follow the conversation.

Lady Twilight laughed, sending a feeling of warmth through the room. "Ah, to be that young again, and have such a thirst for knowledge!"

She turned to face me again, this time her eyes landing on Professor Eira. "My apologies for interrupting your meeting. Usually this sort of thing doesn't happen here."

"I'd think not," said the Cat, drawing the attention of the dragon.

Professor Eira didn't notice at all.

"Hey, Indigo, how about you show Lady Twilight the Solstice tree?" I asked, motioning upstairs.

Indigo's eyes grew wide, and she dashed through the air to the stairs, directing Lady Twilight to follow.

Her head tilted toward me. "Are you sure?"

"Of course, you're family. You should see the room, it's pretty amazing."

Lady Twilight followed Indigo, stepping around the counter gingerly, almost like she was waiting for something to happen.

The Cat grumbled under his breath, but he appeared more lively than he had for the last little bit, and that mattered.

Then the Elder Dragon vanished into the hallway and up the stairs.

Professor Eira blinked multiple times, her ears twitching back and forth. Her voice came out, barely above a whisper. "That was a dragon..."

"Yes, Indigo's grandmother, kind of. You know what? Close enough. Her grandmother."

Her mouth opened, then shut, and her eyes darted all over the place before settling on me again. "You will make a good student."

"I'll try my best."

"Keep up the practice with the meditation, and I'll come by in a week or so. By then, you should be able to find your source with ease. If not, we'll need to come at this from a different direction." She nodded a few times, like she was thinking about something important. "I'm going to leave you to your guest."

"Well, she's teaching Indigo dragon magic, so she's not really my guest. I didn't think you'd run into her, though." I didn't want the lesson to end already, plus I finally was learning more about the Cat as a Fey Lord.

She stood up, her ears twitching again. "That's okay. You have much to learn, but practice is the first big step."

"Should I do anything with my magic when I can sense it?" I lifted the bracelet up. "I've funneled it through this before."

"You can if you wish, though I'd prefer if you didn't teach yourself any bad habits. Instead, take notes and write down the moments your magic comes to the surface naturally." She gave me a pointed stare. "Every time it appears, write it down. It will help us figure out what direction your magic is inclined to prefer."

"I have a journal I can use." My mind went to the journal my father had gotten me for my birthday, that I hadn't started to use. "I can make a list of all the times I remember, too."

"All the times?" asked the Cat.

I ignored him. "Thanks for coming in."

"Of course," she said, bowing in my direction. "I'd hoped to hear more about my friend, but now's not the time."

She got up and hurried to the door, leaving without looking back.

"What other times?" asked the Cat again.

"I told you about them," I muttered, turning to the counter and heading to join Indigo and Lady Twilight upstairs.

I found the dragon staring out the large windows, with the snow still coming down outside.

"Ah, sorry about that, I didn't realize the shop would let others come in while I was with someone," I said.

Indigo perched on Lady Twilight's shoulder. The two

created a striking image against the falling snow. Lone guardians protecting the forest.

"Indigo, can you show me your practice with shadows?" asked Lady Twilight.

Indigo nodded and then dove into Lady Twilight's shadow, vanishing from sight.

"What the…" I mumbled.

"That will only distract her for so long," whispered Lady Twilight, though her lips didn't move at all. "I have a favor to ask."

The Cat rubbed up against my ankle, and I glanced down at him before looking back at the dragon.

"What type of favor?" More importantly, why did Lady Twilight need a favor from me? I didn't have anything she couldn't get on her own.

"Lord Bennit is struggling with the loss of his daughter, Indigo's mother." She let out a sigh. "All of his descendants are meeting to try to snap him out of the state he's in."

"And you want Indigo to go…" Oh. That made sense. She nodded.

"Will she come back?" I asked, ignoring the sharp pain inside me.

"We won't stop her. I'll make sure of it, even if Lord Bennit doesn't come back to us." Her voice remained soft and her lips didn't move.

My eyes opened wide. "It's that bad?"

"Dragons can fade from grief and rejoin the tree, especially when they are, shall we say, advancing in years…" she explained softly.

Indigo couldn't lose her grandfather as well. I couldn't let that happen.

FORTY-THREE

Indigo popped out of the Cats shadow, and he batted her with his paw. She turned around and chased after his tail as it flickered.

"If she wants to join you, then she can go." I nodded, swallowing the lump.

This was too important to prevent, not that I really could have stopped the Elder Dragon from doing what she wanted. Lord Bennit was important. I didn't want Indigo to lose her grandfather; she was too young for such a thing, given that they were dragons.

"Go where?" asked Indigo.

"To see your grandfather," I whispered, trying to smile.

"But, what about the Solstice?" asked Indigo with alarm, as her eyes grew wide. She jumped up, flying to my shoulder. *"We celebrate together. Tree and socks!"*

The stockings were hanging from the mantle, but I hadn't filled them yet. I still needed to get a few more things for each of them.

"Maybe you can get him to come for our small gathering," I said with a smile, patting her side as she landed. "I can get him a stocking."

She rubbed her head against my neck like the Cat did sometimes. *"Maybe... Invite him. Not leave."*

"Hey, it's okay if you leave," I said, running my hand down her spine.

"But, you not come?"

"Not right now." I let out a sigh. "Someday, you'll show me the dragon lands, but you need to go there first."

I lifted her off my shoulder and held her in my arms. I glanced at Lady Twilight, needing her to hop in if she really wanted Indigo to go with her. Light from the tree made Indigo's scales almost glow.

"Indigo, asking your grandfather to come to the celebration you are having will do good." She reached out for the little dragon. "I promise I'll bring you back in time for your celebration. You don't need to find your way on your own."

"But safe here, with Sable and Cat!"

My lips parted, but I didn't have anything to add. My heart broke in two. Even with how important Lord Bennit was, I wasn't going to make her go.

"You will be safe with Lady Twilight," said the Cat. "Your great-grandmother will always protect you, just like me."

"Promise?" she asked in a trembling voice.

"I promise," said Lady Twilight.

I hadn't realized that Indigo wanted to stay here

because she felt safe and protected. Now, I wish I hadn't said she could go.

Indigo flew out of my hands to Lady Twilight. *"Short visit."*

"Of course," said Lady Twilight. "You need to be back in time for the holiday."

Indigo grumbled under her breath, sounding like the Cat.

I almost chuckled.

"I'll show you both out," said the Cat.

Lady Twilight's purple eyes stared at me, and she nodded. "We won't be gone long, to us, but I know things are different with the shop."

"We'll be fine. I'll be waiting."

I couldn't watch as she left the room. Instead, I stared at the snow falling. The woods looked the same as always. Dark pine trees were covered in bright snow. A brush of warmth came from the floor, almost like a question.

"It's okay, Betty," I said. "I know she'll be back. You're not getting rid of us that easily."

I wrapped my arms around myself, smiling at the soft glow of the tree to my right. I turned and headed to the couch, and the fireplace.

"She'll be back before I know it," I whispered to myself.

"She will," said the Cat, as he leaped onto the back of the couch near my head. He stepped down onto my shoulder, then into my lap. "You should take this time to do all the non-kid-friendly things."

"I don't think we have anything like that." Nothing came to mind.

"What about horror movies?" asked the Cat.

I shivered. "I'm not a fan, but I can set some up for you."

He turned around in a circle before lying down in my lap. I couldn't help but pet him as he began to purr.

My mug, filled with hot chocolate, appeared on the coffee table and I chuckled.

"Thank you, Betty, you are amazing." I picked the mug up and took a sip.

The Cat nudged my hand, and I patted him lightly with my free hand.

"So, Professor Eira...you protected her?" I said, adding a questioning tilt to the end.

"Yes. Her kind was hunted down so others could absorb their magic," said the Cat. "Her kind can see all the various types of magic a person has. Those were some very dark days. She might even be the last of her kind."

"So you hid her." This was the Cat that I wanted to save. One who treasured those he cared about.

"My children loved her. Liluth, in particular; they were friends."

"And she thinks Liluth's dead." That wouldn't do. "Maybe I can tell her that isn't the case? Somehow let it slip that the dragons might know something about her location?"

The Cat didn't answer as I stared into the glowing red crystals.

My empty journal appeared on the coffee table next, along with my favorite pen.

"Betty, I'll be okay, though reminding me about my homework is good. I'll need to keep in mind that I have to meditate every evening."

"Morning, too," said the Cat.

"The Professor didn't say that..." I grumbled.

Hopefully, meditation became easier, and whatever had snapped me out of it the first time didn't happen again. I pulled the journal over to the couch along with my pen, but instead of writing in it I sipped on the hot chocolate and petted the Cat.

"When do you think the Professor will be back? Oh, wait, probably a week." She'd mentioned me needing a week to practice. The Solstice was only just over a week away. That was a week of time on my planet, per my phone, which didn't always update depending on the day.

"I hope she comes back," The words slipped out.

"Indigo isn't going to leave you for long. She loves you." The Cat circled in my lap, then started making muffins on my leg before he settled down.

"You too," I whispered, hoping he was right. Otherwise, this was going to be a horrible Solstice.

FORTY-FOUR

Five Days.

Was it sad that the first thing I thought about was that we only had five days until the Solstice, and Indigo wasn't back yet? Not to mention, the professor hadn't been back yet.

At least I had the distraction of writing in my journal about my magic, and forcing myself to practice meditating each morning and evening.

I sat on the fluffy couch facing the snowy windows in the living room. A warm mug of coffee waited for me on the coffee table. Hints of it floated through the air, tempting me.

Unfortunately, I'd discovered the Professor was correct. Meditation went so much smoother if I hadn't had a cup yet.

So it was my treat. My precious treat, waiting for me to reach a good point with focusing on my magic.

It sat in the middle of my chest, a warm pulsing light. Golden, with spots of white. Touching it felt like warm rays of sunshine after several days of rain. Happiness and joy filled me during the moments I sat trying to touch it.

As I withdrew, my mood dropped.

The little bookdragon would hate having to do meditation, but she'd love snuggling with me on the couch.

I pulled my treat closer to me, cupping both my hands around the dark blue mug with stars. Warmth flowed from the mug to my hands, and I sipped on the warm latte. Cinnamon burst in my mouth, along with some sweet maple.

Absolutely perfect.

The snow drifted slowly to the ground outside, still covering the massive dark green trees in the distance. The Solstice tree sparkled with the lights.

I let out a sigh, then took a deep breath.

I trusted Lady Twilight. Indigo would be back.

Slowly, I climbed to my feet and headed to the kitchen to make breakfast.

Betty pre-heated the oven to the correct temperature, and the bacon was ready to be tossed inside. I got that started, then pulled out the eggs to make a quick scramble.

"How is your magic training coming?" asked the Cat.

I glanced over my shoulder and found him staring at me from the island.

"I think I have the meditation practice down."

"You think, or you know?" he asked in a strange tone.

"I have the meditation practice down," I said more confidently.

The Cat nodded, and his tail flicked back and forth in the air behind him.

After cracking several eggs into the pan, I stirred it, making sure to keep them light and fluffy. I tried not to think about how Indigo had been learning how to make scrambled eggs. I had to remind myself she still would learn how to make scrambled eggs, as soon as she was back.

"Are you ready for the Lord and Lady to attend the party?"

The Cat's question hung in the air, and it took way too long to sink in.

"You're that certain she will be back on time?" I asked softly.

"Of course. You had better be prepared for the dragons..." He said the word dragons with a hint of distaste.

I smiled to myself and nodded, making a list of things I needed to do if we really were going to have guests for the gathering in five days. That brought a rather important question to the front of my mind.

"What the heck do I get the dragons?" I glanced at the Cat, but he wasn't paying attention to me anymore. Instead, his gaze was fixed on the oven.

The timer went off, and I quickly pulled the pan out of the oven, before going back to the eggs. By the time I piled the food up, I realized I'd made way too much. It was just that sort of day.

"I hope you want lots of bacon," I mumbled.

"I am never going to say no to bacon." He immediately started crunching down on it.

After breakfast, I made a second mug of the cinnamon maple latte along with a small one for the

Cat's teacup. He sneezed, then quickly finished the rest of it.

"Thank you for the coffee," he said, padding closer to my elbow as it rested on the counter. "It was tasty."

"Of course," I said, and patted him on the head, looking over the bookshelves that filled the store. "What's today look like?"

"Easy day..."

The shop's layout was the normal bookstore one, though the tomes on the shelves felt different. Energy rose in several places, some areas more than others. The sunlight coming in from above felt different as well, like the color was off slightly.

"Woah," I whispered at the purple sky above the skylights. "That's new."

"Hmmm?" asked the Cat, glancing up.

"The sky's different..."

"What do you see?" demanded the Cat. His body radiated power, and warmth, almost making me feel like he was a flame.

"A purple sky..." I scratched under his chin. "It's nothing to worry about."

His eyes focused on the skylights, but he said nothing else. The power coming off him reduced until I couldn't feel it.

"You ready?" I asked him.

"Of course," he said, taking a step back.

The door unlocked, and I sipped at my coffee, letting the maple flavor wash over me.

Green.

The smell of a forest and wild flowers filled the shop

as the tiny lady stepped inside. The bells softly jingled behind her, slightly muted. Her emerald eyes were ovals as she glanced around the shop.

"Oh my," she whispered. "Look at these books!"

She was shorter than me, and a cascade of vibrant green leaves and moss took the place of her hair. Two bright pink flowers seemed to be near where I expected ears to be.

"Welcome to the shop. How can I help you?"

Her eyes landed on me, and suddenly she almost appeared even smaller as she took a step back. Scared.

CHAPTER
FORTY-FIVE

"You can completely ignore me," I said, trying to save the small green woman's mood. "I'm just here if you want to buy anything."

She blinked twice, then nodded. "Okay. I've just never seen anyone like you before."

"Same, actually, but if you like books, this is the place."

A wave of happiness came over her face again, and she stood back up, staring at the shelves. She took a few steps to the closest shelf and ran a finger down the spine of the cloth binding.

Light green mist rose from the back of the book, but she didn't seem to notice as she stepped to the right, still tracing titles with her finger.

I did my best to not stare at her as I sipped my coffee.

Bark covered her arms, and flowing moss made up the bulk of her clothing.

The Cat rubbed himself along my arm, and I set my coffee mug down to pet him.

From each of the books she touched, a magical haze rose. Then she turned to the genre shelves. The first one read 'Stories,' then I swore I saw an Urban Fantasy section and titles I totally recognized.

She squealed and started creating a small stack of books in her arms. Her stack reached five books, and she turned toward the counter, rushing over.

"I'm taking these," she set them down, then bounced back to the shelves. This time she reluctantly pulled herself away from the Urban Fantasy section. The next books she looked through were again cloth bound. After a couple of minutes, she headed back to the first book-shelf and grabbed two large tomes.

One caught my eye on the third bookshelf, with a faint golden outline. Yet, she headed back my way without stopping there. She set the two she'd selected on the counter.

"I think that's it," she peeked at me, then glanced at the Urban Fantasy books. "Are humans really like that outside of the stories?"

"What do you mean?" I asked, trying to figure out the question based on the books she had.

"Warriors and mages, ready to save the world!" Her voice rang through the shop, all excited.

I chuckled. "Some are, others like me are Shop-keepers in magical bookshops."

"I've read so many human stories, whenever I can get my hands on the books that is..." She nodded slowly. "I bet you read about other people as well."

"I do. I read all sorts of stories about dragons and Fey." I tapped the cover of the book. "There's nothing wrong with reading these books, though. All knowledge, all stories, are worthwhile."

"I know," she mumbled, glancing down at her hands. "But I feel like I need to keep broadening my horizons."

Bingo.

"You know, there's a book over there that is calling out to you, but you didn't pick it up…"

"Really?" She glanced up, her eyes glowing.

"Third bookshelf."

She raced in that direction, going directly to the book that glowed. "I'm not sure I have enough to pay for all of them. That's why I left this one behind."

"It's on the house…"

The Cat coughed beside me.

"Sometimes you just gotta get a book."

She pulled a bag out of nowhere, and set it next to the books.

I pulled the pile closer to the register and scanned the Urban Fantasy books, then the other cloth bound books popped up on their own. Though, the titles weren't listed.

"This says, five gold," I read off from the screen. I never knew how people were going to pay.

After placing five round golden tokens on the counter, I packed a bag with all of her purchases and held it out to her.

"Hopefully, I see you again," I said. Any book lover was welcome here, as long as they weren't looking for evil books.

"Me too!" she said with a smile. "The last bookshop I found after wandering out of my woods was too far off in a different world. They didn't have the Urban Fantasy books I wanted. Thankfully, you were at the perfect place."

"We're pretty good at that." I chuckled, thinking about how we moved about.

She turned, then hesitated. "My name is Whisperleaf..."

"It's nice to meet you. I'm Sable, the Shopkeeper."

Whisperleaf nodded and headed to the door, carrying her bag. She paused at the door, and turned to look at me. I felt like she used some sort of magic, but I didn't know what. Instead, she nodded again, and walked out.

"You shouldn't give your name out like that," mumbled the Cat, sniffing my mug.

"Did she mean any harm?" I asked, looking down at him before moving back to Betty and starting another round of drinks.

"Well, no, she can't harm any other. Her kind is bound to their forests, so she doesn't get to leave very often."

"Then what was the problem?"

"The problem is, you didn't know that," he said, padding closer. "Please be careful. Names have power."

I stared at the now closed door, trying to think how to describe what I'd felt.

"She didn't feel dangerous." I ground the beans before packing them, and pulling the espresso shots. I split them between the Cat's teacup and my empty mug, then grabbed the milk. "She felt lonely."

"Lonely?" asked the Cat.

"Yeah, lonely, and like books were her only friends." I needed to explain why I did what I did. Maybe it'd help him. "That's why I gave her my name."

The Cat didn't respond, just watched as I finished making the coffee for both of us.

My journal appeared on the counter, and the Cat studied me as I grabbed a pen to detail what had happened.

Because that was magic. I'd seen it, and my magic had told me she needed that book. That it was important. I quickly wrote it down, then snapped the journal shut.

"So, what else is on the schedule today?" I asked, ready for another distraction.

The teacup was empty, and the Cat was nowhere to be seen.

"Okay, that means shopping for gifts for the dragons."

The skylights still showed the purple flickering sky, but maybe that wasn't the world the Whisperleaf was from at all. Betty was like that sometimes.

My laptop appeared on the counter, and I pulled up the online shopping store everyone used back home. A quick glance at the skyline showed that the sky was blue again. Hopefully, I had enough time to order something and get it shipped.

Maybe something funny.

The perfect idea came to me for Lord Bennit, from Indigo. I'd need to show her before she 'gave' it to him, but she'd love it. A smile covered my face as I placed the order, along with rush shipping.

The Solstice would be fun.

FORTY-SIX

To my surprise, after lunch the bell on the front door rang as I searched for gifts for the dragons from me. Professor Eira crept in, her nose twitching as if she was searching for something.

"It's just us," I said with a smile. "Indigo is off on an adventure with Lady Twilight and Lord Bennit."

Her ears turned a few times before she confidently stepped inside.

"Good to know."

"Welcome to the shop. I didn't realize that you'd be here today. I thought I had another couple of days," I said while shutting my laptop, and stepped around the counter.

"For some reason, something told me to try to stop by today to see how you were doing with your practice."

The bookcases against the far wall shifted, vanishing from sight to be replaced with the fake fireplace, and the couch and arm chairs.

She stared at it while it happened, mumbling under her breath. "That's Fey magic."

"Betty does it," I explained as I walked over to the couch. The skylights had shifted back to the strange purple sky.

She quickly followed, noticing the boots I wore. "You also have magical boots."

"Working here has its perks." The boots were one of my prized possessions, which also included the necklace and bracelet. I didn't add that the perks included laundry, student loan repayment, and learning life-changing magic.

"I can feel the difference in your sensitivity," she said, as she sat across from me. "You've found the way to access your magic. Can you show me?"

I nodded, then closed my eyes. Within seconds, I reached the warm sun, sitting inside my chest.

"Good, good."

I opened my eyes, smiling.

"Can you do it without closing your eyes?" she asked with a half smile.

I opened my lips but snapped them shut to try it. It felt like starting at the beginning again. I fought against closing my eyes, and eventually touched the edges of my magic after several moments.

"I'll need to practice that..."

"That, along with pulling on your magic." She chuckled. Then she did something. A feeling of heat came from her center and bobbed around her ears.

"What was that?" I asked, staring at her ears.

The feeling went away immediately. "You felt that?"

"You mean the warm magic in your ears? Yeah…" I leaned forward, wondering what she had been doing.

The haze of magic around her at that moment had reminded me of Whisperleaf touching the books, but more concentrated. Like this was active, while that had been passive.

"I've kept track of the instances of magic in my life as well," I said, letting my earlier question drop when she didn't answer it. My journal appeared on the table next to the couch and I held it out to her. "I've detailed everything in here."

Her paws carefully took the journal with a bow. "I will keep this secret with my life."

Bright white warmth crossed the room, touching me, the journal, and the Professor. It took a second, if that, but it happened.

"What did you do?"

The Professor jerked. "You felt the oath?"

Her eyes glittered as she quickly flipped open the journal and started at the beginning. Pages turned faster than anything I'd seen before, and then she handed it back.

"Magical sensitivity has increased, along with moments of Fate sense." She caught my concern. "Those are moments that the Fates express."

"The Fates…" I whispered, thinking about the Cat.

"I don't see any more mentions of stone magic, though," she motioned to the bracelet.

"I've only been working on meditating." I wasn't sure what she meant by stone magic. "Can you explain stone magic a little bit more?"

"Of course. Like I explained last time, Dragons and Fey have their own magics, similar to the Fates. Stone magic is a way to funnel magic of any form, including the magic that is around all life. Different stones can cause different reactions. I will need to find some books on it to give to you..." Her voice faded as a pile of books rose from the table beside her.

She quickly sorted the stack. "This one for sure... This one is outdated... Not this one."

By the time she finished, four books stood in the yes pile, while the other ten or so were in the no pile.

"Your Betty is pretty amazing," she said carefully.

"She's not my Betty. Though, she's family, just like the Cat."

"Cat?" she asked, tilting her head to the side.

"Yeah, the black Cat from the counter the other day." I tried to figure out how to back peddle.

"I think I remember seeing a Cat..." A weird expression crossed over her face, and she blinked a few times. Her ears twitched, and magic gathered around them before vanishing. "What were we... Ah, yes, stone magic."

A hand went to the side of her head, and she rubbed the area under one ear.

"Are you okay?" I asked, wondering why talking about the Cat affected her so.

"I think I need to cut our lesson short." She stood up and pointed to the books. "Study the books on stone magic, and practice accessing your magic without meditating, but keep up your meditation, too."

"I will." I stood up and reached out to help steady her, but she jerked back.

"'Till next time," she said before rushing out the door.

"Well, I messed that up."

"Just a little," said the Cat, drawing my attention up. He stood on the balcony, watching from between the railing. "You can't talk about me with her. She got hit with memory magic."

"Will she be okay?" I'd screwed up for sure.

"Yes, just be careful in the future."

I nodded and grabbed my journal to document my lesson, and the use of magic. No point in stopping recording my observations. Hopefully, they'd help in the future.

"Maybe I'll make some cookies to take upstairs, to help me study."

A plate of peanut butter cookies appeared on the table, making me laugh.

"Thank you, Betty. You are so amazing!"

I wondered at the shop's most recent antics. It responded to Sable instantly, even things she thought about, or ways to make her life easier than ever before. However, I wondered how Professor Eira was so wrong about the Fate magic. She hadn't realized it came from the shop, not Sable.

It couldn't be coming from her. Sable wasn't a Fate Worker. I wouldn't allow it.

FORTY-SEVEN

Snores from the Cat woke me up at my normal time. He lay next to my pillow, a black blob highlighted by my bright white sheets in the morning light. The Cat normally didn't sleep in my room, but with Indigo gone, I appreciated it.

It made me smile as I stretched, careful not to wake him. I needed to shower, so I quietly slipped out from under my blanket and headed to my bathroom. By the time I'd used up an ungodly amount of hot water, the Cat was gone from my blankets.

Still, the picture of him sleeping there stayed in my mind as I got dressed, and then laced up the world's most comfortable boots.

Letting my thoughts drift, I sat on my bed and reached for the core of my magic. It took only seconds, so I let it go. Then I focused on my bracelet. Carefully, my attention went to the center stone, trying to pull from my core and make the stone glow. After a few moments, the stone brightened.

I let out a breath, and it went out.

"Okay, try again..."

I practiced for another ten minutes before the sunlight coming in from the skylight made it clear I needed to get moving.

On the balcony, I paused, studying the shop below. It reminded me of something, but I couldn't figure out what. The tall dark bookshelves still graced each of the walls, and books sat on the back wall, but the wall to the right had large glass jars on each shelf.

I hurried down the steps to get a better view. Betty still sat in her place, and I headed her way to make a coffee as I took in the view. Shelving on the wall behind the counter with the various teas was back, along with cookies on the counter under glass domes.

Actually, almost everything was under glass, which was very strange.

I kept that in the back of my mind as I decided to go with a classic mocha. Melting the chocolate took a moment, but the decadent smell hung in the air, reminding me of a candy shop.

"That's it!"

"What?" asked the Cat jumping on the counter.

"The shop reminds me of an old fashioned candy shop, but without candy..." Under the jars sat things like powers, herbs, and all sorts of potential ingredients. At least, I thought so.

"A candy shop?" The Cat glanced around the space, then back at me as his whiskers twitched.

"Haven't you ever been to a candy shop? With, like, chocolates, and hard candies, maybe some toffees?" I started rambling about candies, then paused when I noticed the Cat's head tilted.

"Let's just say old candy shops are amazing." I made a note to grab some old fashioned hard candies to add to his stocking. Maybe the dragon's stockings as well. They probably hadn't been to one either.

Maybe it was an Earth thing?

I finished melting the chocolate into the milk and pulled a shot of espresso.

"What are your thoughts on breakfast?" I asked the Cat.

"Bacon." Direct and to the point.

"We've been eating a lot of bacon," I muttered, but my stomach growled just thinking about it. Hopefully, we still had some in stock. I needed to do another grocery order soon, especially if we kept going through this much bacon.

Breakfast didn't take long with the help of Betty.

The amount of bacon we consumed couldn't be healthy. Tomorrow, I wouldn't make bacon. I repeated it inside my head multiple times to try to convince myself.

Taking a breath, I spoke out loud. "Hey Betty, how about tomorrow we do oatmeal with berries and honey instead of bacon?"

I felt the confirmation from the shop and the glare coming from the Cat.

His green eyes stared at me as I pulled his flowery teacup out and set it on the counter. I decided to make him a mocha with lots of whipped cream on top, since Indigo wasn't here. She couldn't get jealous.

"Watch, you'll make bacon tomorrow," grumbled the Cat, almost soft enough for me not to hear it.

I chuckled to myself as I added a bit more whipped cream to the top.

"So, what's on the agenda for today?" I asked as I stored the whipped cream back in the tiny fridge under the counter.

He glared at me yet again as he lapped at the cream.

This time, I lifted an eyebrow in response.

"You'll find out why everything is under glass."

Oh, snarky Cat.

Two could play this game. See if I made him any more coffee today.

I nodded and sat on the stool, sipping my own mug, which might have been topped with more whipped cream than it should have been, given the bacon. Indigo needed to come back soon or all the calories would catch up to me.

"Well, I'm ready to open the shop," I said in a nice and confident voice.

The Cat wasn't done with his coffee, and his head jerked up. "Wait!"

The lock moved, but didn't unlock all the way.

"Imps, today is imps," muttered the Cat, before going back to this drink.

"What are imps?" I asked, thinking of what I knew from movies, though it could be wrong.

"Mischievous little buggers. I don't have a clue why they need to come here today. They've never needed the shop before."

That was the longest rant from the Cat I'd ever heard,

and to make it worse, he had some whipped cream on a whisker. It bobbed as his tail flickered.

It took everything in me to not giggle. I swallowed, getting control of myself before speaking.

"We can handle this." I was a professional after all. How bad could Imps be?

FORTY-EIGHT

"That's what you think," said the Cat, finishing his coffee. Then, in a softer voice, "Can you hide my teacup?"

"Of course," I placed it under the counter, but it suddenly sank into the wooden shelf. Safe and sound.

"So, about these imps... what should I be aware of?" I asked, trying to figure out a little more about these people.

The bells on the door jingled, but it didn't open. Or if it did, it was quick enough for me not to notice.

"Here we go," grumbled the Cat as his eyes darted around the room, landing on the jars on the righthand wall.

Something small glittered near the lid of a jar, about the size of my fist. Then it shot across the room to the bookshelf at the back. One book suddenly pulled free before falling to the floor.

I stood from my stool.

"Welcome to the shop, how can I help you?" I asked, taking a step to the end of the counter.

"Don't you dare move from behind the counter," growled the Cat. "They can be dangerous."

His words made me pause my movement as I studied the direction of the glittering light.

It darted to the counter and paused in front of the sign. The one I hadn't really thought about in a very long time. It read:

> Do not upset the Cat
> The Cat is always right
> Do not go behind the counter
> Do not upset the Cat

It didn't move from its position in the air. The glow surrounding it failed as it hovered there. Then, suddenly, it wasn't just the size of my fist.

A small horned humanoid creature stood there with small dragonish wings rising from its back, wearing a pair of jeans. It even had brown hair and eyes, though it now appeared to be the size of the Cat.

"I need some herbs..." drawled the imp. "Some moonflower and silverweed."

"I can help with that," I said with a smile.

"In the canisters behind you," whispered the Cat in my mind.

I turned and grabbed two of the small envelopes sitting on the shelf behind me. "How much do you need?"

"A scoop each."

That unit of measurement wasn't a great one, but I pulled each canister from the shelves and set them on the counter. Then I carefully opened the moonflower. Small round flower buds filled the glass container, though when I opened the lid, light pulsed out of the top.

I added one scoop to the envelope, then sealed it, before moving to the silverweed. This one reminded me of shavings from some metal, yet somehow it smelled like grass. Still, I did the same as the first.

After I placed the canister back on the shelf behind me, I glanced up to find the Cat gone. The imp remained where he was, watching each of my actions.

Under my eyelashes I spotted a dark shadow racing across the floor to the book that had been dropped earlier. The book shifted a few inches closer to the door.

I said nothing as I stepped closer to the register.

"Alright, just the two herbs?" I asked, glancing back at the imp, waiting to see what he would do.

"Yep."

The two items appeared on the screen of the register, along with an amount.

"Three gold bullion," I said out loud.

The imp nodded and tossed three bright gold coins to the counter. One rolled off the back edge of the counter.

I pressed my lips together as displeasure rippled through my body. I hated it when people tossed money down on the counter, not even bothering to count it. Or, god forbid, a stack of coins that was probably right, then took off with their coffee. Your drawer was always short, and you had to deal with your boss being mean.

"That was rude," I stated, unable to help myself. I held up the envelopes pitched between two fingers.

Why did these imps need to be here today? What needed to happen?

A whimper came from beyond what I could see, and the imp flinched. His eyes grew wide, but he didn't leave.

I tapped the counter, and the book sprang from the wood, appearing under my finger.

The Cat followed, leaping up, with something glittery dangling in his mouth.

"Ah, was this something you planned on getting?" I asked the imp pinched in the Cat's teeth.

Neither of them said anything.

"I guess we aren't doing business, are we?" I said as the missing golden bullion also appeared on the counter. "Take your coins and go..."

I nodded to the Cat, and he opened his mouth.

A smaller imp flew and hid behind the larger one, still in its small glittery form.

I grabbed the book and the envelopes, turning toward the hallway.

"Wait!"

I resisted smirking as I turned back.

Sweat dripped from his forehead. "I need the herbs and the book."

"Well, what do you have to pay..." There was something missing... That golden light hadn't appeared yet.

"I..." He emptied out his pockets, showing four gold bullion and a leaf, outlined in gold.

"This is all I have, I swear..." The light behind him bobbed in the air. "My brother, too..."

I approached the counter, and I set the envelopes on it, along with the book.

"Are you sure?" I kept my voice level and stared at him.

Two more leaves appeared next to the first. All three had the golden outline.

"That will do. You get the book and these two envelopes, we get the three bullion and the three leaves."

The imp frantically nodded.

I handed over the items, and he snatched them before darting to the door with the smaller light stuck on his shoulder.

The door snapped open and closed behind them.

The three leaves glowed on the counter.

FORTY-NINE

"What did the imps buy, anyway?" I asked while studying the leaves.

The bright green oak leaves glowed in magic, and not just the outline that normally let me know something needed to happen with them. The green color didn't match what I knew of oak trees. Even in the spring, when the leaves first burst forth, they weren't this bright, vibrant color. But who knew what type of a magical tree these could be from?

"Items needed for making a small magical explosion," said the Cat, nonchalantly.

"Really?" My head snapped in his direction with a frown.

"The book gave instructions for magical explosions, plus the moonflower and silverweed create bursts of color."

"You mean fireworks, they bought what is needed to make fireworks." That made sense for a trickster. I wasn't sure if I should have sold the items to the imp.

Yet, for some reason these leaves were important. I touched one with just the tip of my finger, and it buzzed.

"Cat, do you know anything about these?" I asked, poking the leaf. "They're magic, and make my fingers tingle."

It didn't feel bad, kind of like when you pressed a battery to your tongue. Or like a cool shiver up your spine on a hot day. I poked it again to make sure.

The Cat stared at the tip of my finger and padded closer to my hand. He sniffed the air as his tail flickered back and forth, again and again.

"What are they?" he asked quietly. "Describe them."

I paused, removing my fingers. "Three large oak leaves, each the size of my hand. What do you see?"

The Cat stepped closer, his paw almost touching one. He swatted at the air and his paw passed completely through the leaf without a sign.

"Nothing. I see and sense nothing..." said the Cat, curiously.

"You literally just touched it," I whispered.

He jerked his paw back, but the leaf hadn't moved at all.

I picked it up, still feeling the tingling where I touched it. I waved it in front of his face.

He leaned forward, but the leaf passed right through him, like an illusion.

"The imp must have played a trick on you," said the Cat, turning to look at the door. "They have magic and are strong with illusions. I warned you they are tricky buggers."

The Cat appeared not worried at all, but still I

collected the three leaves and placed them on top of Betty. They stood out against the bright red color. The golden glimmer remained.

I'd see what the Professor, or one of the dragons, thought the next time they came in.

"Well, at least we're done with them," I said with a smile. "Anything else on the to-do list for today?"

The Cat sighed and turned away from where I'd held up the leaf.

"Not that I know of, though that hasn't meant much lately," he grumbled, yet a feeling of sadness registered instead of annoyance.

I immediately scooped him into my arms and snuggled him. Maybe him sleeping next to my pillow had less to do with me, and more to do with him.

"Hey, you are an amazing, magical Cat who happens to be a stuck Fey Lord. But you have me, and maybe even bacon tomorrow morning..." Normally we ignored the whole he-was-a-fey-lord thing, but it felt important to say it.

The Cat jerked back, but let me give him head scratches.

"You're lucky you can cook and make coffee..." mumbled the Cat, and he turned to give me an easier reach to his right cheek.

"You mean, I have thumbs." I rolled my eyes and continued to give him scratches until he jumped down.

"You have the rest of the day free..."

"Sounds good," I said, while thinking about what candy to get for him and the dragons. Candy buttons for sure, along with bubble gum and a ring pop. Maybe even some black licorice, and some pixy stix, and definitely some old fashioned salt water taffy.

My fingers tapped on the counter next to my cup as a few different varieties came to mind. My laptop rose from the countertop, and I smiled.

"Thank you, Betty," I whispered as I quickly started a shopping cart with two-day shipping, so everything would show up on time for the Solstice.

Other ideas popped into my head of presents to get for the dragons. Indigo was coming home and going to bring her family. It had to happen, and I needed to be prepared.

No matter what.

It was hidden from me.

Hopefully, Sable hadn't caught my untruth, but I didn't know what else to tell her. Nothing in the store should be hidden. It shouldn't be possible, not with what the store was. Yet, Betty... I destroyed the thought from entering my head. I warned Sable time and time again to not name things.

Names gave power. Was this an effect?

It couldn't be. My reach couldn't be that far gone.

Could it?

Ice crept up my spine as I jumped up the stairs and made my way to the tree. Time slowed down, and I didn't dare look up until I stood in front of the pot. My tail twitched as I suddenly glanced up, almost holding my breath.

It stood there the same as yesterday.

The same leaves, same scent, and the same pot binding it in place.

Relief.

What was left of my people were still safe.

The cat tree stood next to the pot, towering high above it with the scent of that herb. It calmed me and helped me sleep. One such as I didn't sleep like a normal being. Yet, as time ticked by, more and more I caved to the little pleasures of being a cat.

How long until I...

Again I destroyed the thought before it could finish. Names and words were power. I dared not think it, or whisper it.

But if it wasn't the shop or my power, that only left *them*.

FIFTY

"So, what's on the schedule today?" I asked the Cat while sipping my mocha, which contained way too much chocolate.

The shop appeared in its coffeehouse form. The long wooden table rested near the window, and bookshelves lined the far wall. It was one of my favorite kinds of days.

Whipped cream towered on top of his teacup, and I didn't expect a response for several moments. Not that he usually had information about coffeeshop days. Normally, I just went with the flow, keeping an eye out for magic.

The Cat lapped at the whipped cream, seemingly in a cheerful mood, which honestly helped my own.

My brain froze seeing a stand with cinnamon rolls piled on it next to the register. It took two seconds to pull one onto a plate and take a giant bite. Cinnamon and cream cheese frosting burst in my mouth, making me want to groan.

By the time I finished it and licked my fingers, the Cat sat staring at me.

"What? It was amazing..."

The Cat shook his head and turned to the door, while I headed into the kitchen to clean my hands.

By the time I got back, he appeared to be napping.

"So, no input on today?" I asked.

He opened one eye at me. "You do better with these types of days than I do."

He wasn't wrong.

The door's lock snapped open, and I prepared myself to handle the morning rush. Yet, it didn't really come. The students who usually filled the space, just didn't.

A couple of people came in for coffee to go, but not any of the regulars.

Time ticked by slower than I'd have liked, and I wondered if we were even in the same place as normal. The truth was, I had no way of telling.

A loud group of shifters entered, their way-too-bright eyes giving them away.

"Can we lot get a whole round of coffees?" asked a younger guy at the head of the pack. "Seven, just black, to go. We don't want to miss our ride."

I quickly got to work on the Americanos, since I didn't do drip. "Oh, you guys going on a trip?"

"Just home to our pack for the holidays," muttered the guy, keeping an eye on the rest of them, who were talking way too quickly for me to follow.

"Oh, the semester must be out," I said, figuring out why we were so slow.

He gave me a strange look.

"I must have spaced about it. Caught up in my own plans, you know?"

"Yeah, the last day was yesterday." He nodded. "Guys, quiet down a little..."

The entire group of them quieted down and started grabbing coffees off the counter as I set them down. It didn't take long before he tapped his credit card, left me a tip, and they were on their way.

"Well, today's going to be boring," I mumbled to myself as the door jingled again.

This time a quiet Elven girl came in with a heavy coat and a backpack over one shoulder. Her ears pointed to the ceiling, and her eyes darted all over as she headed to the counter.

"Can I get something warm and sweet?" she asked.

"Sure. Do you want lots of caffeine, or something a little less caffeinated?" I asked, thinking of different things.

"Some coffee isn't bad..."

I quickly started on a mocha, but with only one shot. "I hope you like chocolate."

She nodded, and as she did her eyes landed on the Cat and she smiled.

"He's friendly, if you want to pet him," I said as I steamed the milk with chocolate.

She reached out and scratched under his chin. The Cat's tail twitched, and he began purring. She chuckled at his antics.

"Are you staying, or do you want it to go?" I asked, my fingers hovering over a thick mug.

"I'll hang out for a while, I have some time to kill."

I yanked out a dark green mug and tossed in the shot before I filled it with the steamed milk. "One nice mocha, just for you."

She smiled brilliantly at me and tapped her credit card to pay. Carefully, she picked up the mug and headed to the long table facing the window.

I tried my best to not stare at her as she situated herself. It didn't take long for her to grab a pad of paper out, along with some pencils. The art book sparkled a bit out of the corner of my eye, but I didn't ask about it, not yet.

The Cat stared at her, not even being subtle about it.

I sipped on my mug and grabbed my book out from beneath the counter. It was pulp fantasy, but both distracting and something I could put down if something came up.

"She's sick," said the Cat, almost like he spoke to himself in disbelief. "When she petted me, I knew..."

There really wasn't a way to respond, since no one else was in the shop.

He turned to look at me, and meowed.

The woman stopped her drawing and glanced up as I reached out to the Cat.

"Hey kitty, you doing okay?" I asked him.

He meowed again, before turning back to the table the woman sat at and jumping off the counter. It didn't take long for him to leap onto her table and lay down next to her mug.

"Watch out, he might steal some of your drink," I called out.

"No worries, he's adorable." She leaned closer to the Cat. "Aren't you..."

Now the Cat left me in a horrible situation. Did she know she was sick? Was that why she was here? Yet, it was her art book that glittered a bit.

My thoughts were interrupted as the door opened and a familiar troll strolled inside.

I smiled as he approached the counter, already working on the Americano.

"Are you staying today, or getting coffee to go?" I asked.

"Staying, I'm not leaving for the holidays. Not worth it to go home for me."

I nodded. "So, what's your name? I figure I should get you a custom mug at this point."

"My name's Fred." He chuckled and smiled. "Well, this place is my favorite place to get coffee and study."

I wasn't sure he looked like a Fred, but I went with it. "How's Samantha doing?"

"Good, really good." His eyes brightened. "I'm going to meet her parents after the holidays."

"Woah, big step there."

"Like my mom says, when you know, you just know."

"Well, enjoy." I finished making his Americano and handed over the forest green mug.

He turned around and headed to the table, then he paused, blinking, at seeing someone already at the long table.

"Allisa! I thought you were taking the semester off?"

FIFTY-ONE

llisa rolled her eyes. "My parents want me to, but I don't really care."

Fred sat down near her, but not in her space. He pulled out a textbook, but kept glancing in her direction. "I mean, have the healers figured out what's wrong?"

"No..." She shook her head. "My grandmother wants me to visit the edges of the old forest, and speak with some elders. She remembers something similar happening to others, but it was before her time."

"I'm sorry," he said with a soft smile. "But you're strong and you'll beat this, whatever it is."

She shrugged her shoulders and held out the drawing. "What do you think?"

That's when I spotted the Cat. His nose reached out and he touched her mug. Magic tingled and the mug suddenly lit up, yet neither the troll nor the elf noticed. The Cat slumped back on the table like he'd suddenly lost all of his bones.

The two kept chatting about classes, oblivious to what had just happened.

Then Fred went back to his textbook and notes, while Allisa flipped to a new page and started a new sketch.

Whatever the Cat did, it didn't change the fact that the sketchbook still sparkled.

"Did you sip my drink, little man?" Allisa asked the Cat. She petted him for several moments as I tried to focus on my book and figure out how to ask about her sketchbook.

Yet, she suddenly grabbed a pencil and started on a new page.

The story couldn't hold my attention, and now I worried about the Cat as he just lay there, though he was still breathing.

The door jingled, and a crowd of others took my attention off the situation. All were humans getting drinks to go and nothing special. The mid-morning rush definitely took off.

The Cat almost spooked me into dropping a drink when he leaped up onto the counter near the register and went to sleep.

The cinnamon rolls sold quickly until a single one waited, all by itself, mocking me whenever I spotted it. I did not need another sweet treat, especially after the last few days without Indigo. The number of treats I'd allowed myself exceeded my limits.

Finally, the rush slowed down, and I started thinking about lunch. I knew for dinner I wanted to order Chinese, so ordering food for lunch was a no go. No one needed anything, and I darted into the back to make a sandwich, which didn't take long. I left one on the counter for the Cat.

By the time I got back out front, another troll had entered the shop. This one I didn't recognize at all. They waved at Fred, and approached the counter with a smile.

"Welcome, what can I get started for you?" I asked.

"Can I get a vanilla latte and that last cinnamon roll?"

"Of course, coming right up." I quickly got to work grabbing a mug and steaming the milk. "How's your day going?"

"Awesome, I aced my last final and now I get to relax until classes are back in session." He smiled brightly, and his horns gleamed.

I nodded as I set his drink on the counter and grabbed a plate for the treat. Thankfully, I had tongs to use and handed the gooey deliciousness over once he tapped his credit card.

"Yo, Allisa, I thought you were headed home," he said, turning and catching sight of the woman. He sat down right next to her as she rolled her eyes at him. "Woah, that's an exceptional sketch."

That golden outline shimmered again, then went out as the two of them began talking.

"Okay," I muttered under my breath and then checked on the Cat.

He still slept, and I gave his head a pat. He lifted it and cracked open an eye before closing it again.

Something felt wrong with the Cat, but I didn't know

what to do. If the coffee shop wasn't open, I'd take him upstairs and cuddle with him on the couch. Maybe get him some food. But with the shop open, all I could do was sit here and wait...

"Can I get a tea?" asked Allisa, her sketchbook under her arm. Her voice knocked me out of my panicky mood.

"Of course, let me grab you a new mug..."

"Actually, can I get it to go?" She smiled and set her nice ceramic mug on the counter. "I can't spend all day sketching, after all."

"What'd you sketch?" I asked as I grabbed a to-go cup. I motioned to the various tea canisters on the back wall.

She pulled the sketchbook out and flipped open to a page covered with pencil marks.

Gold flashed along the edges as she flipped it around to show me.

She'd sketched the face of a man. He had sharp pointed ears, and eyes that stared into my soul. Something about him felt familiar.

"Who is he?" I asked. "You're really talented."

"No clue, his face flashed in my mind while working today." She paused, glancing at the canisters. "Can I get the spiced apple?"

"Of course." I pulled it down and used tongs to grab a tea bag from inside before putting it into the cup. I poured hot water over it, but not boiling water since I didn't want to burn the tea. Then I set a timer for 4 minutes.

"It will be done in a jiffy... If you want something

sweet, I can toss a little maple syrup into it. It goes with the apple perfectly."

She leaned forward with a smile. "Yes, please."

I added a jiggle of syrup and stirred it slowly with a spoon as I waited for the timer to go off. When it did, I removed the tea bag and added the lid. When I turned back, I found the Cat eyeing the sketchbook.

"Here you go," I set the drink on the counter and rang it up.

Allisa tapped her card and gave the Cat one last pat before she put the sketchbook in her bag and grabbed her cup.

"Thank you!"

"Have a good day!"

The Cat didn't move, just staring at her as she left the shop.

It shouldn't have been possible.

But I did it anyway.

As soon as she touched my fur, I knew what was wrong. The healers wouldn't be able to fix it. The magic that connected her to her people, and eventually to me, had frayed. Her connection to the ley lines had frayed. Without that, as a person of a magical race she would slowly fade, then die.

I couldn't let that happen.

So I fixed it.

My bones felt on fire as I shoved past the limits

placed on me. Everything inside me turned to nothing as I waited for my punishment.

Yet, it didn't come.

They didn't come.

And then...

I stared as she left the shop, that sketch still with her. That beautiful, lost, ancient image of what I used to be.

Impossible.

FIFTY-TWO

Fred and the other troll left after another hour, and other foot traffic in the shop died down. Not much later, the shop was empty, and I took my chance.

"Hey Betty, can you lock the door?"

The click removed the stress from my shoulders, and I turned to the Cat, who hadn't really moved all day. His sandwich from lunch still sat on the counter in the kitchen, and I left it there after picking him up.

"How does Chinese sound for dinner?" I said, and I held him close.

"Tasty..." He didn't fight me at all. "I'll be okay; I'm just tired."

He closed his green eyes and rested in my arms.

I took the moment to place the repeat order and scratch behind his ear. Once the order was confirmed, I headed up the steps to the living room before placing him on the couch with a blanket tucked under him. Warmth from the stones in the fireplace gave the place a pleasant mood as I hurried back downstairs.

A loud knock had me switching from heading to the kitchen and to the front door instead. The familiar delivery guy stood outside, and I rushed to unlock it to take the bags of food. He gave me a nod before hurrying on his way.

"Betty, however you do that, it's amazing," I whispered as I pivoted back to the kitchen. The heavy bag reminded me we'd have way too much food, since Indigo wasn't here.

I snagged the sandwich I'd left on the counter and tossed it in the fridge. The bags on the counter were gone when I turned around. A rush of warmth came from the floor, along with the impression to breathe.

I paused, taking a deep breath.

"Thanks, Betty... I just get worried about him, especially when I don't know how to help." My focus switched to trying to let my brain relax and not rush through things. That Cat said he was just tired. Yet, he'd done something to that elf who was sick.

This time I moved slower and with a purpose as I headed back upstairs to the living room.

The Cat remained in his spot on the couch, with the soft blanket tucked around his curled up form.

Various plates of Chinese sat on the coffee table, distributed based on what we normally ate. Indigo's soup wasn't present, but two plates both containing the spicy chicken, noodles, and egg rolls looked delightful.

I smiled and grabbed my plate, suddenly staring.

Snow still fell beyond the glass in the windows, and the lights on the tree sparkled softly. My hidden surprise for Indigo called for me to use it, but I ignored it, wanting to not use it until I could give her the present.

The same went for the Cat's present, but again, I'd wait until the Solstice. Hopefully, both of them would enjoy their gifts.

Using chopsticks, I slowly ate the chicken and the noodles until the Cat stirred.

His eyes opened, and he gazed at the warm plate of Chinese on the coffee table.

"Oh, food..."

"Yep, you'll need to eat up, it's the spicy chicken you love," I said after swallowing a bite. The restaurant had really outdone themselves with our order today. Everything was perfect.

He lifted himself up slowly and leaped over to the coffee table with ease, but then he lowered himself next to his plate. Normally, he stood while eating.

Yet, it didn't take long for food to vanish off his plate.

At that I relaxed even further. He was eating, awake, and doing as well as I could hope. That had to mean something.

"You're staring..." grumbled the Cat in between bites.

My chopsticks paused halfway to my mouth with a piece of chicken in them. I lowered them back to my bowl. "I worry about you..."

"I am fine, and the food is good." The Cat continued chowing down on the massive plate.

"Good... Do you want to talk about today?" I ate a couple of bites.

The Cat didn't respond for several moments.

"There is nothing to talk about."

"Okay. Well, Allisa was pretty nice, and whatever you did, helped... I guess?"

The Cat paused, then nodded. "She will be fine now."

The silence stretched out, and I finished my plate before setting it on the coffee table. I left my egg roll for last, crunching down on it, careful to not get crumbs everywhere.

"That sketch was fantastic. I wonder who it was? He had tall ears like the dragons, and kind of like Liluth."

"The ears were not like the dragons; the dragons copied..." His voice trailed off, and he stared at his plate for a moment without continuing. "The Fey Lords."

I leaned back on the couch, watching the Cat, who suddenly seemed quiet.

"Well, isn't that a chicken and the egg problem... The dragons would say the Fey Lords copied them, while the Fey Lords would say the dragons copied them."

"That isn't the dragon's natural form, it's one they decide to shift into. The Fey Lords' natural forms normally included the ears. They were created with them." The Cat paused like he couldn't believe the words had come out of his mouth.

"You okay?" I asked, finishing up my egg roll.

He nodded slowly, looking thoughtful.

"I'll ask one of the dragons when they return Indigo about the ears, and see what they say..." At least I'd distracted him with the conversation about the sketch. I wanted to ask more about it, but the Cat still seemed to be in a weird space.

"You could believe me, you know. I am an expert on

this topic, after all." The Cat said as he glared at me before chomping down on the rest of his chicken.

"I mean, your ears are a little pointed, though kind of fuzzy compared to the drawing."

The Cat's tail twitched erratically, as he coughed like he'd swallowed the bite wrong before crouching down like he was going to launch himself at me.

"I surrender," I said, grabbing a pillow and holding it out in front of me. I peeked above it and found him back on the couch, his plate completely cleared.

"Not funny..." he grumbled.

"No, hilarious."

The Cat rolled his eyes at me as I chuckled some more. At least he appeared more normal now.

However, I couldn't help but wonder what Fey Lord it was that Allisa had sketched. And if it could possibly be who I thought it was.

FIFTY-THREE

I didn't want to get up. Only a couple more days until, hopefully, we'd be closed for two days around the Solstice. More importantly, Indigo would be back.

But today, my comfortable bed kept me locked under my heavy blanket, even as the sun streamed in from above.

Something leaped onto the end of my comfortable hiding place near my feet and padded up next to my leg.

"We have the same number of tasks to get done, whether you get up now or later," said the Cat.

I couldn't see him, but I felt him move closer to my head.

"It doesn't matter to me how long it takes, but each one needs to be done before the holiday."

"Ugh," I grunted as he pulled down the top of my blanket and stared directly in my face. Cat breath washed over me.

"I'm getting up." I finally sat up and yawned while stretching upward.

It wasn't until I was in the hot, steamy shower that the Cat's words sank in. From there, I quickly finished washing my hair, getting clean, and then yanking on clothing.

"Cat…" He wasn't in my room anymore. Instead of rushing, I took my time lacing my boots up and brushing out my hair. It hung damply down around my shoulders.

I decided to do something about it and tried to focus on the energy inside my core. This time it only took a second to find the magical ball.

Now, directing some of it to my hair took a little longer. I imagined my hair perfectly dried with my wavy curls. Warmth washed over me as energy left my chest and faded.

"Sable?"

The Cat's voice caused me to open my eyes as I wobbled.

"What did you do?" he asked, staring up at me as I sat on the end of my bed. He leaped closer, staring at my head with his head tilted to one side. Totally cute, if I wasn't completely panicking that I'd fried my hair.

Yet, when I reached up, my fingertips touched soft curls.

My only mirror stood over the sink, and I headed that way.

"I decided to try something…" My voice trailed off as I stared as intently as the Cat had. My dark curls were there, nice and springy, with very little frizz. Yet, my hair had also turned a deep purple. Almost an amethyst color.

"You look like you did when you colored your hair," said the Cat, following me.

"I didn't mean to do that," I said, touching the ends of my hair. It still felt soft. "I'm not upset about it, but I didn't mean to…"

The Cat wound around my feet, and I bent down to pick him up.

"Let's do breakfast, and you can explain to me what you meant about the tasks-getting-done-no-matter-what comment."

The Cat sniffed at my hair, and I ignored it.

"You have realized that time passes differently in the shop, correct?" he asked right near my ear.

"Kind of."

"The task list takes the same amount of time to do, even if we rest in between."

"Where do we go for my days off?" I finally asked.

The Cat didn't answer as I climbed down the stairs and turned toward the kitchen. Needing my hands to make breakfast, I set him on the counter.

"We aren't exactly anywhere; we just are," he finally replied.

"So right now, we're just hanging out in space, outside of time?" I asked, trying to wrap my head around what he was saying.

The preheated oven beeped and a pan already sat on the counter right next to a package of bacon. I chuckled to myself as I laid it out on the pan before tossing the pan into the oven.

"Something like that."

After washing my hands, I pulled some frozen waffles out of the freezer, letting my mind come up with my question.

"What's around us?"

"The Leylines," said the Cat, without a care in the world.

This time I paused, thinking of everything I'd learned so far about them. No matter how I thought about it, it didn't make sense that we were just chilling inside them.

"We're surrounded by magic, is what you're saying?"

"Yes, and no." The Cat shook his head. "We aren't inside the leylines, just in a place most people can't access. Only Travelers can."

"And us."

The boots I wore were copies of a set made for a Traveler, if I remembered correctly.

The waffles I popped into the oven on the rack above the bacon. They'd taste faintly like the delicious smoked meat, but I didn't care. Bacon and maple syrup were a gift.

"Is that where Betty's magic comes from? The leylines around us, that we aren't inside of..."

"The magic of the shop comes from the artifacts we have stored, ones that are being destroyed for the greater good, and the ambient mana in the air here." The Cat stared at the oven as he spoke.

"So, while we rest here, time doesn't pass..." Sometimes it felt like time passed, and other times it didn't. More than once I'd gotten the day of the week wrong when we checked back in on my homeworld. Especially when I sent an email, I always had to triple-check the date.

"Mostly."

That wasn't helpful.

The oven timer went off, and I carefully grabbed the pan out with an oven mitt. The waffles needed another couple of minutes, so I laid the bacon out on paper towels to rest.

When I turned back to the island, the maple syrup and butter were already out, along with plates, and a fork with a knife for me.

"Thank you, Betty."

The Cat glared at me for a second, and I removed the waffles, setting one on his plate. They were giant, crispy on the outside and hopefully fluffy on the inside.

I buttered both waffles and cut them up into bite-sized pieces before I drizzled the surgery goodness over them. The bacon I left on its platter and just set between us.

"So, what task is waiting for us today?" I asked after taking a bite of crunchy bacon.

"Some writer is visiting."

I tried to remember what the shop had looked like as I came out of my room, but realized I hadn't glanced over the balcony.

"An event, or just a random person?"

The Cat's tail flickered in the air as he ate, not answering me.

I'd also forgotten to make myself some caffeine before breakfast, but surprisingly, I didn't have a caffeine headache. I resolved to fix the caffeine deficiency as soon as the food was properly devoured.

Bacon was halfway to my mouth when I realized I'd said we'd have oatmeal for breakfast today, not waffles and bacon.

The Cat won that round.

I'D SLIPPED UP and spoken about the magical nature of the shop, because nothing stopped me. It wasn't until she kept asking questions that I realized some of these weren't things she should know. No mortal should.

Then again, she'd used magic on herself for her hair, and it worked.

I'd felt the draw of mana, along with the intent. I hadn't expected it to work.

Now, though, her hair glimmered with mana. Though she didn't notice that part, only the color.

I wondered what the Professor would see when she glanced at Sable now. Hopefully, she'd get a chance before it wore off. Whatever was happening, I needed to understand it in order to protect her.

CHAPTER

FIFTY-FOUR

Caffeine called my name as I finished up breakfast and headed to the espresso machine to make something tasty. Maple lingered in the air, and I went with a maple latte, one for each of us, even though the Cat's fit in the teacup.

I sipped slowly on the hot beverage as I studied the setup of the shop. Lots of bookshelves, and books were stacked all over the place. This layout tied with the coffee shop layout as one of my favorites. If only the two would combine, I'd be in heaven.

It also answered my question on the type of day it'd be. Something with only one person, or maybe a couple, and not a large event filled with people. Not that I minded hosting larger events at the bookshop. That was how I'd found the cookie vendor, after all.

"Do you know anything about this writer?" I asked, hoping to discover more about how today should go.

The Cat lapped at his teacup, his tail flicking in response and giving me absolutely nothing.

300

Rolling my eyes, I took another sip of my warm beverage and I felt the store asking if it was time.

I smiled and nodded as the door unlocked. Part of me wondered if the shop popped into existence seconds before the person entering spotted the building, since it always felt like they showed up right after opening.

The bells hanging from the handle jingled, and I set my coffee cup down.

The embroidered floral pattern of the dress stuck out like a sore thumb, followed by the oversized glasses, but the extra large cardigan appeared comfortable as heck.

"Welcome to the shop! Let me know if I can help you!"

The woman's head snapped in my direction and a light green shade of eye peeked at me before darting around the shop and taking in every detail.

I tried not to stare at the canvas tote she carried, a dark blue over one shoulder. The brown messy bun with a pen through it reminded me of nights spent studying before exams to get my useless degree. Yet, she was older than a college student, though maybe not by much. The dress definitely gave off age more than her unlined face.

She waved at me as she headed directly to the first shelf.

I sipped my coffee, but kept watch out of the corner of my eye.

She slowly trailed her fingers along the spines of the books.

Eventually, I stopped paying too much attention as I sipped my coffee, since she was taking her time with each bookshelf, reading each of the titles before moving on.

The Cat lay down next to my arm, not even paying attention to the woman. Instead, he shut his eyes and slept.

The benefits of being a Cat, and not a shopkeeper.

Warmth from the sunlight streaming in from the skylights made it hard to keep my eyes open. To stay awake, I snagged out one of the books the Professor had given me to study. Time to learn more about stone magic.

The bracelet gleamed on my wrist and I wondered what type of stones they were. There was the black one, the green one, and a purple one. I only knew for certain that the purple was amethyst.

"Hey, Cat, what stones are in my bracelet?" I asked under my breath.

"Green aventurine, obsidian, and amethyst," he responded, without even opening his eyes. "Good to see you are studying."

Flipping the pages ahead, I paused on the obsidian page to read about the types of magic it could be used for.

Obsidian is born from the fiery heart of a world and is a protective stone. The dark glassy surface whispers about its abilities with protective barrier magic, grounding and absorbing negative energy, and reflection magic.

It is a powerful tool best used with respect and intention for protection and grounding.

That stone had shot out a powerful burst of energy, though it might have been a barrier that I'd pushed quickly at that poor customer. Even though it'd been gold in color, it'd come from that stone, I was fairly certain.

I couldn't help but flip to the others.

Amethyst, with its soothing violet hues, is a stone of mental and spiritual clarity. The crystal acts as a bridge between the conscious and subconscious, enhancing intuition, rational thought, and attacks against the mind.

It's best used for meditation practice and restful sleep.

The description made me pause. Had I seen the golden outline before I received the bracelet? I tried thinking back and pulled out my notebook from under the counter that listed the times I'd used or seen magic.

Tapping my fingers on the counter helped settle things as I processed that the amethyst might be helping me notice things.

The break from the book let me check on the writer, who'd made it to the second shelf of books, but still hadn't chosen anything. She didn't pay any attention to me, her focus fully on the titles she read, her lips forming each of the words before moving on to the next.

That left one more stone to read about.

Green aventurine shimmers with the essence of spring and vibrant magical vitality. It acts as a catalyst, nurturing both

*personal growth and magical abilities. It's a stone of opti-
mism, renewal, and the potential of life.*

*It is best used to strengthen the flow of magical energy within
the body, revitalizing and empowering the practitioner. Like
a nourishing spring rain, it fosters growth.*

I stared at the bracelet containing protective magic, mental clarity, and magical growth. When I'd received it, I'd thought the colors reflected my life, though my brother didn't know that. Now, I wondered at the abilities each of the stones would help me with. I'd already used the obsidian, but maybe the other two provided benefits as well.

The scrape of a book sliding off a shelf brought my attention back to my actual job, managing the shop.

The writer stood at the end of the second row of shelves, flipping through a bright yellow book with cream pages. Nothing stood out about it, and I frowned, thinking about why she might be in the shop in the first place.

Something needed to happen, surely, but what?

FIFTY-FIVE

Nothing in the shop leaped out at me, and the writer snapped the book closed sliding it back onto the shelf with a loud sigh.

"Is there anything you're looking for in particular?" I asked, closing my own book and notebook before sliding them under the counter. I didn't need questions about them.

The woman turned to glance at me with a frown. "I've lost my magic..."

I blinked and noticed the Cat stretch next to me.

"Your magic?"

"Yes," she said, taking several steps closer, her hand clutching her bag tightly. "I need to figure out a way to make my characters feel real again. For the magic in my stories to be almost touchable."

Relief rushed through me, and the Cat curled back up into a ball. Book magic, not magic magic.

"Do you believe in magic?" I asked, thinking quickly.

"I used to." She frowned, and her eyes drifted upward to the skylights. "I don't think I do anymore."

Taking a gamble, I turned to the espresso machine and started making a latte.

"Why don't you have a coffee and tell me about it?" Losing oneself was something I dealt with in school, especially since it felt like I'd only gone to escape my family. "Tell me why it feels like you lost your spark..."

Her face softened, and she approached the counter.

"I usually don't drink coffee, unless I'm writing," she whispered, like it was a secret.

"Then this can stay between you and me." I very quickly steamed the milk and poured it into a to-go cup. Something inside me said she wouldn't stay for too long after the conversation.

Once I added the espresso and a little sugar, I set it in front of her.

She leaned against the counter and took a sip. After a moment, she began.

"It's like I always felt like magic hid just around the corner. Like it was there, real, for me to touch, only just out of reach. And now...that's gone." She took another sip of coffee. "I miss that wonder."

"What if I told you this shop was magical, and you just didn't know it?"

"If only." She chuckled and smiled softly. "I have this feeling that I just need to find the right book, or story, to light my spark again."

"I can tell you a story," I whispered, leaning close. "It's about a magical bookstore and a tiny book dragon who lost her way. The tiny book dragon hid in the stacks, letting none see her but the shop's Cat and the Shopkeeper. Both kept the dragon's location secret, for fear that something bad would happen to the tiny dragon."

The lady chuckled and sipped on her coffee. She glanced around the shelves with a look.

I pointed to the tiny hole above the bookshelf, near the entrance. "That's her tiny hideaway."

The writer blinked a few times and then laughed out loud, yet something clicked into place.

"Oh, you got me there for a couple of minutes," she said, with a bright smile. "I'm going to keep looking through the shelves and find something interesting to read. Thank you for the coffee."

"Of course! It's our little secret." I leaned closer. "Just like the book dragon."

Again she paused, like she couldn't believe me, but something in her eyes felt different. A faint golden glow flickered inside before she turned away. She headed back to another shelf and moved a little quicker as she read the spines on each of the books.

The Cat rubbed up against my arm, and I scratched under his chin.

"You walk a fine line," he whispered.

I shrugged and didn't respond as I petted him. I sipped on the last of my latte, and wondered if I should have another.

More caffeine was always good, yet I remembered what the Professor said about it. That it interfered with magic. Given all the studying and practice I wanted to do, I should hold off.

The bells on the door jingled, and it snapped shut behind the woman, locking.

"I hope I helped her," I said under my breath. For the first time, someone didn't buy something from the shop. It felt weird, but if my little story about Indigo helped, then good.

"The book didn't say what she needed help with, only that she would show up," grumbled the Cat, rolling in a beam of sunlight. "At least she's gone now."

"Anything else today?" I asked, checking the time on my phone. It was early still, with plenty of time before lunch.

"Yes. Deliveries, and that tiny human."

"Molly?" I asked.

The little girl and her father hadn't been in for a long-time. As for deliveries, given the number of things I'd ordered over the last couple of days, my bank account was feeling it. Still, I couldn't help myself, not with gifts.

"If she's showing up, then the shop isn't..." My voice trailed off as some shelves sank into the wooden floor while others rose up, including the entire children's section, which hadn't been there before. The table floated up out of the wood until it stood just perfectly in place in the middle of the area.

While the shop changed in small ways sometimes, it usually didn't do a full reshuffle with me standing here.

The door unlocked right before a small form crashed into it, sending it flying open.

Molly dashed into the space with her pigtails flying as she raced directly to the children's section.

"Book day is the best day!" she chanted as she headed to the shelves.

A few minutes later her father came in the door, much less exuberantly. "Molly, what did I tell you about racing ahead?"

"But this is the bookstore! It's the safest place in the world..."

I chuckled as he waved at me before I pointed at the coffee machine. He nodded, looking tired.

I started an Americano for him and a small hot chocolate for Molly.

"You only get to pick out one book," he said, kneeling next to her.

"It's buy one, get one free," I called out as the Cat glared at me.

Her screech of joy made it totally worth it as she pulled several books off the shelves and started going through them one by one to figure out what she wanted to get.

"This one and that one."

"More dinosaurs?" he asked in a patient voice.

"Of course! Dinosaurs are amazing." She picked up the unchosen books, carefully putting them back into place. "They go roar! Just like dragons."

By the time they made it to the counter, both the coffee and the hot chocolate were ready to go. Molly's father placed the two books on top and I quickly rang them up. One of them came up free.

He handed over his card, but appeared exhausted.

"Are you doing okay?" I asked, trying not to stare at the dark circles.

"Long week of travel," he said with a frown. "But I'm home now."

"And he is going to read to me, and then I'm going to read to him," stated Molly, with all the certainty of her young age.

"That sounds like a delightful day..."

"After school and work, we will do that," he said with a chuckle. "School first."

"School is boring, unlike books," she said, carefully grabbing her drink.

Her father slid the books into a small backpack he was carrying. Given it was bright green with dinosaurs on it, I assumed it was hers.

"School should be just as fun as books, since you get to learn things," I added. It reminded me again of my ideas about schooling for Indigo.

Molly shrugged with an uncertain look. "Books are better."

"School is important," said her father. "Just like work."

"Books and reading time is more important." This time she glared at him.

He chuckled and nodded slowly. "You win."

My fingers tingled as I studied the two of them.

CHAPTER

FIFTY-SIX

Something about Molly's father drew my attention more than normal, especially with how tired he was. His answer about travel felt wrong, but I couldn't say why. It didn't take long before they both headed out.

Jingles from the bell on the door closing behind them made me smile. Molly had always been so happy about books and dinosaurs. Yet, as their presence left the store, I couldn't help but wonder.

"Cat, why are Molly and her Dad here so often?"

The Cat opened one eye and stared at me as his tail lazily traveled across the counter.

"No idea, but they don't hurt anyone."

I stared at the shut door, concerned.

Again, what the Cat said felt wrong, but there wasn't anything I could do about it. They were already gone this time, but the next time they were in I'd ask her father a few more questions. Maybe I could solve the mystery of why they needed a magical bookshop on the way to school some mornings.

I flipped open the book on rock magic and sighed before grabbing my mug. The maple was tasty, and I studied the stones in my bracelet.

Obsidian, amethyst, and green aventurine. Protective magic, intuition, and magical vitality. Me, Indigo, and the Cat. There were too many parallels between it and my life right now.

What had drawn my brother to pick this out for me?

I sipped on my drink, finishing it and moving to Betty. Taking my time, I made myself another coffee. We still had deliveries today before lunch. Then, I'd have time to practice actual magic.

By the time I finished prepping my drink, the door jingled open, and Adam rolled in with a cart filled with large boxes.

"Where would you like these, Sable?" He smiled as his bright blue eyes stared at me.

"The counter is fine," I replied with a grin, trying my best not to blush.

The Cat leaped off the counter and sat, staring at Adam as he got to work unloading the boxes from the cart.

However, as he piled the boxes higher and higher, I wondered about the packages. I hadn't ordered that much, and I had no idea what it could all be.

"This last one I'll leave on the floor," said Adam, nodding at the bookshelf. "It's heavy. Probably some new books."

"Yeah, this was unexpected," I mumbled, glancing in the direction that the Cat had gone. "I'll be doing inventory after this."

"Well, good luck." Adam turned and headed toward the door, pushing the trolley in front of him.

"Did you want a coffee?" I asked.

"Not today," he said with a wave. Then the door jangled shut behind him.

"This can't all be the candy," I whispered as I snagged a box cutter to open the packages. Doing a quick count, I came up with seven. I knew three of them were mine. The rest, I had no clue.

The first box was for me, and contained a few things I'd ordered to make the celebration even better. I quickly closed it so the Cat couldn't peek. The next two were for me as well, which was strange because I couldn't remember what I'd ordered.

My knife cut into the tape easily, exposing the packing paper that filled the inside. Slowly, I dug around, finding a strange, transparent yellow stone. I held it up to the sunlight, marveling at the color.

"That's citrine," said the Cat, unprompted. "A good choice for you."

The small stone would fit as a pendant, or on my necklace that contained my magical treasures.

"Did you order it?" I asked, searching the packing paper for a note, but I found nothing but a small velvet bag it must have slipped out of. Though, the box seemed unusually large for such a small object.

"I thought you did," he said.

"Nope. Must be a gift." I shook my head and set the box off to the side. The stone I placed on top of Betty in a small patch of sunlight, since the counter still had too many boxes on it.

"What's citrine good for?" I asked as I cut into the next box addressed to me. I immediately knew who this one was from. Several wrapped packages were inside.

"My dad sent a box for the Solstice…"

Besides the wrapped gifts, there were decorations, as well. Tall, bright white pillar candles, and a package of gold stars for a tree.

"Don't worry, Betty, we can put the candles out and just not light them…"

Warmth blazed up from the floorboards, and the candles sank into the small space on the counter as I set them down. I then added the box to the floor, and it followed.

"Can you put those up near the tree?" I asked the shop.

The Cat glared at me, but said nothing, his disapproval clear.

I'd deal with the rest of that box and the emotions that came with it after I finished going through the rest of the packages.

Four more.

The next box shimmered as I opened it, and the Cat suddenly pushed it closed with his nose, shoving the cardboard back into place.

"Let me deal with this one," he grumbled in a deep voice.

I stepped back at the tone.

The box lids opened as he batted at it.

For one second, all I saw was brown packing paper. A pulse of green flashed from across the room.

Everything in the shop stilled and became almost

transparent. Stars flicked around the room, then were gone and the shop appeared as it had. The brown packing paper shimmered, and earthenware jugs appeared, each sealed with various colors of wax.

"What was that?" I asked, my eyes flickering around the shop to the locations I swore had been stars a moment before. Nothing sparkled in that gold light I'd assumed was magic. Plus, that solid green wave of magic from the Cat, that was a first.

"It is safe now. That was a protective ward."

"What was it protecting?" I tried to spot the magic on the jugs, but nothing appeared.

CHAPTER

FIFTY-SEVEN

"The jars, from being spotted." The Cat's paws rested on the edge of the box as he studied each of the jars. "I've been searching for these for ages."

"They don't look that impressive to me," I said, as I reached toward the box to lift one out.

"Don't!"

I froze at his command, though it wasn't reinforced with magic like in the past.

"They're dangerous, and filled with the remains of destroyed worlds." His words hung in the air like a confession you couldn't put back in the box.

"There are ashes from dead worlds in those jugs?" I asked quietly, thinking of the urn we'd had for a little bit after my grandmother died. We had waited until spring to sprinkle her ashes over the fields. It was her last wish, to return to the land she loved.

"Not like that," he explained. "These are what's left after a place has been destroyed."

"Kinda sounds like that."

316

"These are remains of the magics lost." The Cat glanced at me, this time confused. "They can be used as a powerful magical ingredient."

"How were they harvested? And, what is actually in there?" Again, I pressed the issue. Something about the jugs felt wrong, and not just because they had forced the Cat to use magic.

The Cat paused and stared at them. I didn't interrupt.

I waited quietly, trying to figure out on my end what made my skin inch about them.

A hot itch, like a bug bite that you accidentally scratched and now you can't help but think about all the time. Nothing magical came up on my senses, but something bothered me.

"Why are you asking?" This time, the Cat's voice came out soft, almost like a whisper.

"They feel wrong, like my skin's itching." I paused, then it came to me. "They remind me of that book, the cold one. But these are too hot. Why were you searching for them?"

Again, the Cat went quiet, staring at the jars. It felt like he wasn't even in the room with me anymore.

Was Sable right? The jars were so close, and the magic inside called to me. I'd started my search long before my imprisonment. It had begun my study into ways to protect my people. Ways to gain more power, to stop demon-kind from hurting any more of my children.

Yet...

Wasn't that what destroyed them in the end? My lust for power. In the end, my people were dying, exiled, and scattered to other lands while I was bound to this shop, unable to help them at all.

The magic didn't feel like the book to me, but I couldn't even touch it in this form. It would have destroyed this shape.

These five jars made her feel the same way as the book had. Even now, the uncertainty and hesitation was clear in how she leaned away.

Her fingers rubbed together anxiously, and at the sight I wanted to headbutt her elbow. Sooth her nervous energy.

The shop responded, the darkest corners growing brighter.

Could I trust myself to make this choice?

With the power inside those jugs, I could heal my tree and help my people. I'd thought that the last time as well.

"I want to use them," I whispered, and the words hit her like a wave. Her face fell, and her lips tightened into a frown. "But I don't know if I trust myself. With these, I could do so much for my people. I need to help my children."

I let my paws fall from the box.

"We will find a different way," she said, as her hand wrapped around me, lifting me away from the box and the counter. She pulled me close and patted my head.

I couldn't look away from the containers, or respond to her.

"I think we need to return these to the source of magic," she said confidently.

"You mean the leylines themselves, the tree."

Warmth pulsed from the shop as the fireplace appeared and twisted without any input from me.

It lengthened, growing taller like an old mirror, exposing the gap between.

Sable stepped forward and folded the top of the cardboard, closing the box. With the jars out of sight, I felt better, more at ease.

I NEEDED to remove the magic jars from the shop as soon as possible. Each passing moment caused my skin to burn even more. As soon as the top closed, it lessened, and I set the Cat down on the counter. Yet, I kept him in sight as I hefted the box up. It felt lighter than it should.

Somehow, it didn't want to go closer to the fireplace. The box grew heavier with each step, and I gritted my teeth to keep moving.

I yanked on the magic inside me and it responded. Strength flowed from my core into my limbs, and a bright golden light flashed from the bracelet. It enclosed the box, suddenly making it lighter.

Then I tossed it into the opening over the river of bright silver and gold light.

The box disintegrated almost instantly, and the five jars floated for a moment in the air. Cracks formed in the clay, and bright light peeked between the edges. Silver and golden light rose to meet them as they crashed into the river below.

Then they were gone.

The fireplace shrunk down to its normal size before becoming a bookshelf.

Releasing a sigh, I turned back to the counter and the three remaining boxes. A flash of golden light shimmered on top of Betty, and one of the golden oak leaves vanished.

The Cat didn't even twitch.

I paused just for a second, then let it go. The Cat couldn't see the leaves anyway, and I didn't need to add anything else to complicate this day.

"We did good, Cat..."

He head-butted my hand as soon as I walked close enough, taking my spot behind the counter. I scratched his ears for a few moments before picking up the box cutter.

"Hopefully, the rest of this is pretty normal stuff." Yet, there was only one box on the counter left, and then the box on the floor that Adam had warned me was heavy. One of the boxes had gone missing.

FIFTY-EIGHT

A blast of warmth from the floor made me relax. Betty had moved that other box, so it must not contain anything to be too worried about. The next box was filled with bundles of dried herbs and flowers, each tied with twine and labeled with various properties.

"That's for restocking," said the Cat, sounding like his normal self. "It's cheaper from the supplier here. We'll be selling that later to a recurring customer."

He sniffed at the bundles, then sneezed.

"Don't sneeze on the merchandise," I said, closing the box and picking it up to take to the storeroom.

For once, the storeroom had other boxes sitting on the shelves, making me pause. Most of the boxes weren't cardboard and instead were some sort of clear plastic, letting me see inside. Tall wooden spears rested against the far wall, while another shelf held a bunch of velvet pouches. A third had a stack of wooden wands from a children's story.

I exited slowly, tilting my head to the side.

"Hey, Cat, the storage room had stuff in it."

The Cat blinked up at me from next to the last box, which now rested on the counter.

He lowered his head and spoke slowly, "The storage room has always had stuff in it. Merchandise, ingredients, that sort of thing."

I headed directly to the box and my box cutter.

"Not for me. I always put the stuff away on empty shelves, or things that we needed appeared when we needed them."

Again, the Cat glanced at me like I was weird.

"Never mind." This box was books, like Adam had said, but books I recognized. Various fantasy paperbacks, along with a few hardcovers. All stuff from my world that I read in my free time. "Is this merchandise, or for me?"

The Cat jumped up and landed on a book.

"Merchandise. Books like this sell well on other worlds, but we normally ship them out in large lots once or twice a year," said the Cat.

"Urban fantasy books?" I asked just to confirm.

"Yes. I don't get the appeal, but if the stories are like the show, they might be interesting."

It came to me that he was talking about the Elven show, with the rings. It was a good one, but I didn't know how much of it he had seen. Hopefully, that meant he would like his gift.

"So, this can go into the storeroom? Or should I put them on that one bookshelf?" There was one bookshelf that sometimes came out full of these.

That plant person had really enjoyed them. She'd

been nice, though I couldn't remember her name for some reason.

"The shop can take care of them," he said before nodding at me. "You need to practice your magic before the Professor comes back."

He stared pointedly at the citrine resting on top of Betty before jumping off the counter and heading for the kitchen.

My stomach grumbled, letting me know it had to be close to lunchtime.

"How about I make some grilled cheese sandwiches first, then I can practice and get back to studying?"

The Cat didn't say anything, just kept marching away from me with his tail in the air.

The box sank into the counter, and I patted Betty on the top. It gave me an excuse to really get a look at the rock, plus the two oak leaves that remained. I hadn't imagined one of them fading into gold sparks.

"What are you for?" I whispered to myself, poking one of them. Then I snagged the yellow crystal and stuck it in my pocket. Off to the kitchen I went to make some lunch.

I DIDN'T ESCAPE Sable until she rested on one of those ridiculously long chairs on the roof in the sun. She at least had her books on magic that the Professor had assigned, along with the stone that had appeared.

The grilled cheese sandwich was tasty, though it sat in my stomach like a rock. I stared out the window as she used golden energy shaped like shields to shove a small ball around that was floating on the surface of the water in the hot tub.

Even now, her progress amazed me. It'd taken me years to learn to use my innate abilities, yet she took to the stone magic with ease. Then again, she should have been able to use it since she was young, if it was innate.

I turned away from the smile on her face to peek at the tree.

It still sat there, one single yellow leaf with a few other green ones. It felt small and weak. Using the dust to fertilize it would have filled the tree with energy, maybe even enough to break free of its cage.

Yet, I'd let her destroy it.

Destroy lost magics and give them back to the source.

I didn't regret it, but I worried about my own decisions. I couldn't ask those who knew if I'd made the right call. That left Sable, and maybe I trusted her. She'd asked me to. But she didn't know what that meant. The ramifications of that.

Could I trust her to figure this out and free me?

I KNEW he stared at me through the glass, yet I didn't look in his direction. Hopefully, he'd figure out whatever was bothering him. Though, today had been a weird one, even on the scale of the shop. Those jars.

I shivered and missed bouncing the ball with the shield.

This couldn't be what the Cat had meant when he'd mentioned practicing magic, but it was fun. I wondered if I could play ping pong like this, and maybe beat my brothers for once. I was the worst player in our family.

The box of Solstice gifts sat in the living room. I'd noticed them as I walked by, but I hadn't stopped in yet to figure out how I wanted them to go under the tree.

I missed my family, but felt okay with staying here. Not that I really had a choice, besides breaking the contract, but I couldn't do that to the Cat or to Indigo. Both needed me.

That's really what it came down to.

I felt like I needed to be here. Like the shop was the place to be. Especially once Indigo came home, things would fall back into place. Plus, I'd get to hear all about the dragon lands and how cool they were.

I just needed her to come back. We had one more day. One more workday, then the Solstice would be here.

"She'll come back, right, Betty?" Warmth blazed from under me, making me chuckle. The citrine sparkled in the sunlight, and I pulled the book closer. "Let's see what I can do with you."

FIFTY-NINE

My coffee this morning was strong, but strange dreams had haunted me all night, and I needed it.

Weird flashes of people I knew, then sudden jumps to others.

Kind of like my mind was traveling along a web connecting people, but I didn't understand the connections. My old friend from college jumped to a sweet old lady crossing the street, then a cute little dog, followed by someone I recognized, but didn't know.

It didn't make sense.

The smooth coffee this morning helped ease how rough my mind felt. The looks from the Cat over the cereal bowl didn't help. I didn't have it in me to make a hot breakfast. Not even bacon, where Betty did most of the work. Instead, we both had a tasty cereal that reminded me of French toast and milk.

The Cat's bowl sat near mine, already licked clean.

He'd liked that I added a splash of cream into his. Mine, not so much.

I needed to finish eating breakfast, but my hand stayed wrapped around my coffee mug. The dark blue mug and bright gold stars brought me comfort. The warmth steadied me.

A headbutt brought me back to the present and away from the memories of my weird dreams.

"Are you okay?" asked the Cat, rubbing his head near my wrist.

I couldn't help but give his ear some scratches.

"I'm okay, I've just got strange dreams from last night on my mind." I set my coffee mug down and pulled my cereal bowl closer. "I feel like I slept. Like, I'm not tired...the dreams were just weird."

I grabbed my spoon and stirred my cereal around before taking a big bite. It was slightly soggy, but I didn't mind. Parts were still crunchy.

The Cat's green eyes stayed on me as he purred next to my coffee mug.

"What kind of dreams?" he asked insistently.

"Just people and connections." I twirled my spoon in the air. "Also, I couldn't get the citrine to do anything. It drank energy in, but there was no physical manifestation of magic."

"What were you trying to do?" he asked.

I paused and thought about it for a second, not having an answer. I'd pushed energy into the stone, which sucked it up, but then it didn't do anything.

"Well, I guess I charged it..." I hadn't given the energy any direction to go or do.

"Intentions matter."

The Cat's words rolled around inside my head as I finished up the cereal. It didn't take me long before I placed my bowl in the sink and snagged my coffee mug back. My coffee stayed warm no matter what, and I had to admit that was the pinnacle of magic sometimes.

What were my intentions for the citrine? I knew it brought light to places, and manifested power. It dispelled negative energy.

Now that it was charged, what would I do with it?

I had no clue, but it'd made a good talisman for the Solstice. For the next year, lots of powers manifesting and dispelling all negative energy felt like a great idea.

"What's today?" I asked, pushing thoughts of tomorrow away.

First things first, I needed to get through today and then finish wrapping gifts—and stuffing stockings. I couldn't bring myself to do it last night; instead, I'd focused on magic practice.

Now, I had to get that done tonight.

"Magic," answered the Cat, without looking at me. His head twisted toward the storage room. "Can you get the powdered amethyst and the box of herb bundles that came yesterday?"

For a split second I thought he was joking, and then he continued his request. With a shrug I headed into the storage room, still surprised by all of the stuff that fit inside the shelves. This time, I noticed a narrow archway that led to even more shelves, though I didn't head in that direction.

The herbs were right where I left them, though the

box wasn't cardboard anymore. Instead, it was made of some sort of clear substance which wasn't plastic, but wasn't glass either.

I snagged the box, along with a second one that hummed. The label read crystal powders, and everything inside hid within white tins.

Once back near the island I set things down.

The Cat nodded at the boxes.

"Now, I need a bowl."

"Does the type matter?" I asked, thinking of a metal mixing bowl from a cupboard.

"No."

The exact mixing bowl I thought of suddenly rose from the island next to the boxes. It nudged the Cat's tail, and he glared.

As soon as I opened the lid, the humming became louder. Small cursive letters decorated the tops of each lid with what type of stone it contained. I snagged the amethyst and quickly closed the box to reduce the noise.

"What herbs do we need?" I asked.

The clear box of bundled herbs made me hesitate. For some reason, when herbs were in nice labeled canisters, they didn't worry me, but these didn't have labels or anything.

"We need coarse salt, ground silver, and Beesmalt." The Cat pointed his nose back at the box of crystal powders. "The ground silver should also be in there."

I opened that one back up, ignoring the humming, and found the right container. By that point a bowl of coarse salt had appeared. That left the box of herbs.

"Which one is the Beesmalt?"

"Look for the bundle with black and yellow leaves, like a bee."

I glanced into the box without opening it and spotted it before going into the box. The clear sides were helpful in that regard.

Then, I lined everything up on the island. First the salt, then the stone, the silver, and lastly the herb.

The Cat stared at the order I'd put things in and nodded. "That's...correct...but only start with a sprinkle of the salt. I'll tell you when to stop."

I sprinkled salt in until he nodded, then I added the powdered silver. He didn't stop me and I dumped the entire container into the mixing bowl. That earned a nod as well.

"The stone you need to be careful with. Only add a touch."

I carefully opened the box, which hummed even louder, making my fingers tingle. I grabbed a pinch and added it to the bowl.

"Good. Now the entire herb bundle," he ordered.

"Done." This type of magic made me nervous, since I didn't understand it.

"Swish the bowl around so the herbs get coated..."

The herbs were in a tight bundle, with some sort of black thread keeping it together. Still, I swirled the bowl around, letting the ground amethyst, salt, and silver mingle with the bundle.

The Cat watched intently.

"Stop."

I froze, waiting to see what would happen.

CHAPTER

SIXTY

The Cat padded closer to the bowl, then stuck his nose in. It barely touched the herbs before everything glowed a bright white and the humming climbed higher.

I shook my head to try and clear the sound away.

Then it suddenly stopped.

The light vanished as well, leaving the bundle of herbs behind. Now, instead of just the black and yellow, the bundle had threads of purple and silver in it as well.

"Strange," whispered the Cat, sniffing the bundle. "It is done."

I picked up the box of tins and then went to grab the box of herbs.

"The herbs you can leave; we will be selling them today."

"Alright..."

It didn't take any time at all to clean up the counter, leaving the box of herbs and adding the now more colorful Beesmalt back to it.

"So, what'd we just do?" I asked, picking up my mug. "Also, do you want some coffee?"

"Coffee would be nice," said the Cat as he leaped off the island and headed to the front of the shop.

After grabbing the box of herbs, I followed, noticing he hadn't answered my first question, as usual.

The shop adjusted itself while we ate breakfast.

While bookshelves still wrapped around the room on each of the walls, the spaces between things had increased. The aisles were bigger, and the table normally in the center of the shop was gone.

While there wasn't a ceiling over the shop, since it opened to the second story, the doorway height increased.

"Are we expecting giants?" I asked in a slightly concerned manner.

"Not giants. Just a bigger-than-usual customer."

I said nothing as I placed the box of herbs back on the counter.

"You can lay those out, though I bet he buys them all," said the Cat as he padded closer to the espresso machine.

I nodded, but moved to make more caffeine first. My strong coffee had been a great way to wake up, and now I wanted something sweeter. The maple lattes had been perfect yesterday, so I went for the same today.

Once I filled his teacup, the Cat got to work lapping at the warm beverage.

I took a moment to lay the herbs out on the counter, keeping all of the bundles in a line. Then I hid the strange clear box behind the counter.

Finally, I sat on my stool and sipped my warm beverage. The latte had turned out pretty close to perfect. "Now, that's a tasty coffee…"

"It is…"

Now I stared at the Cat. He wasn't one to compliment things.

"Are you doing okay?" I asked, wondering about his mood.

"I'm fine. They will be here soon, if you are prepared…"

Now I needed to be prepared for this customer? Last time he'd acted this strangely it was the first time with the trolls, and I'd freaked out. It'd also been my first customer. I wasn't nearly as naive now.

I nodded, and the bells rang almost immediately as a tall figure stepped inside the shop. The clop of hooves echoed with each step.

A tall head swiveled around, followed by a very naked chest, and then a… horse.

A centaur. A literal, half-human-half-horse centaur.

Behind him a much smaller centaur followed, with his head barely up to the first customer's leg. Lastly, a small human boy the same size as the smaller centaur came in.

"Boys, be careful. This is a treat. You must respect this space and the things inside it." The deep voice brokered no compromise as both boys nodded.

"Welcome to the Shop, how can I help you?" I asked, trying to not let my surprise show.

His head snapped in my direction, and he smiled.

"Ah, the Shopkeeper has changed," he said before his eyes landed on the Cat. "But some things stay the same."

He stepped into the center of the shop with his tail flicking behind him, as the two boys headed to the bookshelves. The one with only two legs darted ahead of the other, more nimble in the tight space.

"I see that you already have the herbs ready... I hope that the boys can still wander?" he asked this time, his voice much lower.

"Of course. You can take your time..." Like I was going to stop two kids from exploring a magical shop.

His shoulders relaxed. "Good. They've been well-behaved all winter, and I promised they could come with me as a reward."

"Did you have a rough winter?" I asked, sipping my coffee.

"We had deep snow this year. The green of spring is welcome, and the herbs will help those who fell ill." He smiled as the boys wandered about.

I motioned to the coffee. "Would you like a cup of coffee?"

His head tilted to one side.

The Cat answered before he could. "That wouldn't be a good idea. No chocolate, either."

"Ah, nevermind. I didn't realize it wasn't a good idea for your people."

He nodded. "I haven't heard of it before, but I trust in the judgement of the Cat."

"You know the Cat?" I asked, surprised that he spoke about him.

The man chuckled. "The Cat has helped my people

for several years. The shop appeared one late winter, when mold destroyed the herbs we had in storage. It came again after a horrible flood, where we lost several people. This place has saved our clan multiple times, including our young ones."

"Father, can we get a book?"

We both turned to look as the young centaur held up a blue bound book.

"It's about how to grow things," he said with a hushed breath. "I think Mother would enjoy it."

The father shook his head no.

Yet, my eyes stayed on the book, the edges of which had a slight sheen to them. The more I stared, the more it came into view. A bright golden edge connected the book to both boys. The two legged one was hiding behind his brother, or half-brother, or whatever.

"We are here for herbs, that is what we can afford." He turned back and motioned to the counter. "We will take all of these. The Beesmalt feels extra charged."

"They may have the book, as well..." The words fell from my lips.

The Cat's head twisted to look at me. His green eyes glowed as his tail flickered behind him.

"We couldn't take it," answered the man, unsure of my offer.

"It is a gift for them." My head tilted toward the boys, both of whom heard me.

"Father, can we?" asked the centaur again.

"Please?" came a soft whisper from the other boy.

CHAPTER

SIXTY-ONE

"Sable," whispered the Cat as his claws dug into the counter. "You can't just do something like that."

I ignored him and nodded at the father.

"They are meant to have it," I said. This time, my voice came out stronger, making it clear I wasn't going to take no for an answer.

Both boys stared at me with deep green eyes I hadn't noticed before.

Finally, the father nodded.

"How much for the herbs?" he asked, hesitantly.

I walked over to the register, ignoring the Cat's eyes as they flicked between me and the boys, then the book on growing things.

"Five gems..." I read from what the screen said.

He placed five bright blue gems on the counter, and then scooped the bundle of herbs into a satchel I hadn't noticed on his back.

I picked the gems up and placed them into the drawer.

The human boy clutched the book to his chest as the father turned around carefully.

"Come boys, we must go..." He turned his head to me, and only me. "Thank you for the gift."

I nodded my head, and the boys waved before taking off out the door. The father quickly followed.

As soon as the door snapped shut, the Cat started talking.

"Sable, you can't just give knowledge to any child you meet. It can change things...in ways that we might not understand."

"The boys are meant to have that book." My voice came out firm.

"Sable, just because..."

"No." This time I stared at the Cat. "The boys came to the shop today to get that book. The father was just how it happened. I know he came for the herbs, but that wasn't the real reason for their visit."

His eyes stared at me, and his voice quietly whispered in my mind, "I don't understand."

"That golden light I sometimes see?" I'd written about it in my journal, and I knew he'd watched me take notes. "It connected them. That's how I knew."

The Cat's mouth snapped shut, and he glanced at the door before turning back to me.

I couldn't help but pick him up.

"I'll need to add it to my journal. It's like the other times it happened." I petted his head, and he began purring in my arms. "What else is on the schedule for today?"

"That's all for this morning..."

I nodded. "Good, I have a long to-do list to prepare for tomorrow. I can get started on that, then make lunch."

My mind had already jumped ahead to think about what we might eat, since the cereal wouldn't keep me full for long. Maybe I'd order some subs. My family usually had sandwiches the day before the holiday, since we'd be running around getting things ready. While I could make an okay sandwich, a really good sub would hit the spot.

"After lunch we have another customer, but it shouldn't be long," added the Cat. "Hopefully."

"Perfect..." I set him down on the counter, still smelling faintly like herbs, and quickly placed an order for subs for lunch. "I'm going to be busy in the living room, but it's a surprise, so don't peek."

The Cat blinked at me twice, then nodded.

Off I went up the stairs, hoping I had enough time to get a good amount of prep work done. Not to mention sorting through gifts I'd gotten, and trying to explain to Betty how to hang the gifts for the Cat, and for Indigo.

I knew there wasn't a chance the shop would under-stand modern technology. Though, maybe Betty would surprise me.

Fate magic.

I knew she had some small Fate magic, and she'd written about it in her journal, but this...this hard example I couldn't turn away from. The book had told me one thing about the centaurs, yet she had seen something else once they were in the shop.

That book might help the young ones learn to grow the herbs they needed, as the last clan member with that knowledge had died during the flood. They might not need the shop anymore after this.

All of those days in the golden book were potentially scratched out, and the tallies were checked off the massive list of things I needed to do to earn my freedom.

"Trust me," she'd said.

She'd asked me to trust her more than once. Though, that was hard when she spoke about freeing me without any clue of what it would entail.

Yet.

All those days the shop needed to sell herbs to them, done.

Maybe it was possible.

Maybe I could be free...

I shook my head and jumped off the counter. It wasn't any use to think of wishful things, since that wasn't how the Fates worked. They wanted me suffering, not hopeful.

At least Sable's mood had improved. Hopefully, lunch would be better than the sweet cereal thing we'd had for breakfast. I hadn't wanted to tell her how bad it was, for some reason.

I couldn't help myself as I jumped up the stairs and headed toward my workshop. The book lay there, waiting. I could flip through the pages and see what the future held, if it let me.

Sometimes, the book didn't care if I glanced ahead.

Especially in the early days, several shopkeepers ago. More recently, it gave me less and less information.

Since Sable.

Light rose from its pages as I entered the room, leaping onto the large table.

The golden pages shone with a bright white light as I padded closer. This morning's customer was checked off, and next to it rested a symbol I'd never seen before. A small knot.

"What?" I sniffed at the page as if it would reveal something, then I tried to flip forward. The page wouldn't turn. All that remained on this page was this afternoon's customer, which I'd seen this morning.

I sat down staring at the pages, wanting more information and trying to not let myself hope. Hope could be so cruel, especially as months turned into years, which turned into centuries. Hope was worse than the pain.

Wasn't it?

SIXTY-TWO

The knock on the door vibrated through the entire shop, though it took a second for me to realize what it was. Then, I took off across the living room and down the steps to reach the front door as quickly as possible.

I'd forgotten about the lunch delivery.

I skidded to a halt in front of the door as I recognized the person on the other side. It unlocked as I yanked it open, and Alas stood there. A paper bag rested in his arms, with the logo of the sub place on it.

"How did you get our lunch?" I asked, waving him inside.

His long, deep brown hair hung loose, though his pointed ears stuck out. There wasn't a chance the delivery guy hadn't noticed them. I mean, Alas was an elf, there wasn't any way around that.

"The guy dropped them off just as I arrived. I said I'd bring the package inside." His eyes darted around the shop, first to the chair in the window then the counter.

"Where is that old coot? We need to have a conversation."

"Cat! We have a guest!" Turning back to him, I grabbed the bag. "You can join us for lunch if you'd like, I ordered way too much food."

I headed to the kitchen to unwrap the subs and put out the plates.

Alas hesitated next to the counter. "Lass, I'm not sure I can come back there."

My eyes went to the sign I hadn't thought about in ages.

"If I invite you, and you promise me, the Cat, and Betty no harm, you're fine."

His eyes studied me for a moment, the deep brown flickering in color to a forest green.

"I agree." The sound rattled through the shop, and suddenly the Cat appeared at the top of the steps.

"What is going on?" he asked before spotting Alas. "What is he doing here?"

"No clue, but lunch is here." I headed into the kitchen and snagged out three plates before pulling the two giant subs out of the bags.

Lunch meat was stacked high on each foot long bread roll. One with roasted chicken, a little cheese, and veggies like tomatoes, lettuce, and peppers, plus a tasty sauce. The other had spicy salami, ham, and pepperoni with cheese, lettuce, tomato, and spicy peppers, plus oil and vinegar.

I grabbed a knife and cut each one into four pieces. At least this way, I wouldn't eat a whole sub by myself and feel too full afterward.

Alas crept inside the kitchen, with the Cat near his feet. He kept glancing up at Alas, then to me.

"What do you guys want? I have a full Italian sub, and then a roasted chicken." I glanced at them as they approached. Both seemed confused. "I'll give you one of each," I answered myself, looking at their faces.

I added a piece of each to their plates while I took two of the Italian. Then I sat on the stool, before jumping up and grabbing a pitcher of iced tea from the fridge.

Once I took out a cup for each of us, I sat down again.

Alas watched me curiously, as did the Cat. He glanced at the sandwich, and then back at the Cat, who didn't say anything.

"Alright, so what brings you in today?" I asked, before taking a bite of my sandwich.

Alas watched how I held the sandwich before carefully doing the same.

"I got the note. It was lost in my mail, but I found it."

"What note?" The Cat's head snapped in his direction. "I didn't send any notes..."

"He doesn't have a clue," I replied to Alas after chewing my bite. The sub hit the spot, and I sped up my next bite.

"Yeah, it wasn't from him, it was from Liluth. She told me not to worry about her, and that she was safe." He set the sandwich down. "I can't find her anywhere."

Now, that I hadn't seen coming, and I didn't know how to respond.

"Tell him she is safe," answered the Cat. "But he..."

"She's hanging out with the book dragons at the moment, until things change with..." A pressure hit my chest so fast I gasped. My lips wouldn't move, no matter what I did. Then it stopped.

I found the Cat next to my fingers, which had tried to dig into the island.

"He doesn't know who or what I am," whispered the Cat. "You can't tell him. They won't let you."

"You just got hit with a geas," said Alas as the Cat spoke, since he couldn't hear him. "Those are powerful, and dangerous."

"I'm okay," I whispered to both the Cat and Alas.

His fingers tapped on the island. "Why is Liluth with the book dragons?"

"She is with some family of mine." That I could say.

"You mean with the dragons from your birthday?" His eyes went wide, and he leaned back.

"Yes." I finished off the first half of the sub on my plate, doing my best to recover, though I noticed the Cat wasn't eating. "Are you not hungry? I thought you'd like the chicken?"

He took a bite, and his eyes widened before he took another.

"When will she be back?" Alas watched the interaction.

This time, I hesitated. "I don't know. I might be able to pass a message along the next time I see the dragons."

"She wouldn't just get up and leave like that," he mumbled. Then he paused, and his head tilted to one side before his eyes widened. Yet, he didn't speak. Instead, he took a big bite of the sandwich in front of him.

Maybe he'd connected the dots, but I didn't dare try

to say anything. I hated the feeling of being restricted, but knew that I couldn't fight whatever that had been.

"So, what's your interest in Liluth?" I asked. An idea came to me about why she'd send him a note and he'd rush over here looking for information. "Are you guys a thing?"

Silence hung over the island while a light red color crept up Alas's cheeks. I couldn't help but grin as I set my sandwich down.

The Cat finished off both pieces of his sandwich, and stared at the remaining portions in the center of the island.

"You don't need to tell me, I just wondered. I'll make sure to send that message as soon as I see the dragons tomorrow." I then turned to the Cat. "Or do you think they'll be here tonight?"

I wanted Indigo back, but tomorrow was the celebration, which I was still preparing for. I'd gotten lost in the time, and the box of candy sat open next to the fireplace in the living room. I needed to finish filling the stockings.

Plus, put the decor out that my family had sent, and their presents.

"I'd appreciate it if you send along the message that I'm worried about her," said Alas after several moments.

"You could do it yourself if you want. Tomorrow, I'm hosting a Solstice celebration. The dragons should be here for it."

It felt like the holiday would be a repeat of my birthday, but that was okay. It wasn't like there were a ton of people that I interacted with on a repeat basis that could go to something like this, with literal dragons there.

Maybe all Alas had done was make me some nice boots and come into the shop a couple of times, but he felt like a friend, and at least I knew he was allowed in that crowd. Plus, he was friends with the Cat.

"That would be welcome, thank you, Sable." He bowed his head in my direction and pushed his plate forward. "I need to get back to work if I am taking time off, however."

"I understand," I said, moving to take a stand, yet he quickly hurried out of the kitchen before I could follow him.

"He can see himself out," said the Cat. "You didn't need to invite him, you know."

"He is one of your friends; of course I invited him. I bet that's why he showed up today." I didn't know that for a fact, but it felt like it fit.

"He isn't our afternoon customer," added the Cat.

"Wait, what?"

SIXTY-THREE

"We have someone else coming in," answered the Cat, as he continued to stare at the last two sections of roasted chicken sub.

I picked them up and put them on his plate.

"Alright, I'll need to clean up from lunch and make myself a tea, but another customer should be good."

Either way, it'd be a good distraction from the fact that I now needed to find some extra stockings, to ensure that everyone attending had one.

It didn't take long for me to finish eating my sandwich and put the dishes in the sink. They didn't stay there long, as Betty put them into the dishwasher automatically. I knew I didn't even need to put them in the sink, but still, it felt like the polite thing to do.

Then once at the front counter, I snagged some fruity tea and brewed around four cups' worth before putting it in a teapot that matched the Cat's teacup. I hadn't seen it before, but it was too cute to not use.

The Cat joined me at the counter and he gave the teapot a strange look.

"The afternoon might be quick, but it might not," he said, distractedly.

"That's so very helpful..."

He glared at me.

"I'm just saying..." I paused then. "Is there anyone else I should invite to the holiday for you?"

It was only after I said it that I realized I shouldn't have asked the question. He didn't have anyone who knew who he really was. There wasn't anyone to ask to come.

He didn't say anything, just glanced at the door away from me.

"I'm sorry if that was insensitive. I only want the holiday to be good for you, as well." I felt bad about not thinking before I spoke.

The Cat nodded, which always felt strange, but didn't reply.

"I'm ready for whatever is next," I said, hoping to dissipate how awkward I felt.

The bells on the door jingled almost immediately, and I smiled. My face froze as a Cat-like being entered the shop, with the body of a lion and the face of a woman.

A Sphinx; it had to be a sphinx. As it turned, the wings became apparent, tucked tightly against its body. A fluffy fur covered its body, ending at the neck.

First a centaur, and now a sphinx.

"Welcome to the Shop, how can I help you?" I asked

in a cheerful voice. Though I hoped this wouldn't be all riddles and puns, I did my best to be prepared.

The space hadn't changed from earlier, which made sense given how massive the creature was. Only slightly bigger than the centaur from earlier, but still definitely bigger than our usual customers.

The sphinx turned and smiled at me, her teeth razor sharp, though her eyes drew me in. They were an almost impossibly bright blue, with a golden iris. So freaking pretty.

"I am looking for a few books, and a break from the challengers." Her voice came out in an almost singsong manner.

"Challengers?" I asked, trying to think what she meant.

"Ah, yes. Those who wish to reach the portal I protect." She turned to face the bookshelves, her eyes wide. "When all who come to see you only want one thing, life gets a little boring."

I nodded, understanding how that could feel. Though, with the number of beings who came in looking for a really good book, part of me felt like I should start up a book club. Each quarter I could send out a new and interesting book for those who didn't get out much.

"Do you get to take a break often?" I asked. I wanted to know more about this creature.

"Only when I have someone who can watch my spot." She chuckled before I could ask. "It's not often. Maybe every couple hundred years."

"That's horrible." I couldn't imagine being stuck in the same place for that long without anything to do. It reminded me of the Cat's punishment. "Well, if you want any suggestions or have any series that you've been reading, I can search for the next book for you."

She paused, and her head swiveled to watch me, like an owl. "You can do that?"

"I can try my best."

Next thing I knew, my pen flashed across my notepad of series names and various books she'd read.

It might've been easier for me to create a profile on one of the reading sites to find books for her, but while she read a ton, most of it was old, very old. Still, some trends popped out. Romance with some fantasy was big. Especially if the woman was strong, and the main character.

I made a list of recommendations, and I knew we had at least one series on the shelves.

"This shouldn't be hard," I said with a grin. "I have this one in stock, but I can get more for you as well."

"It might be a long time before I can pick them up," she said with a frown, her wings fluttering on her back.

"I might be able to solve that, but I need to ask a few people some things. Let me pull these off the shelves for now. Do you want a bag for them?"

"I have my own personal storage," she said carefully.

I nodded and hustled around the counter, along with the Sphinx, careful to stay away from her tail, which had a large stinger on it. I wasn't sure if that was normal, but it didn't matter. She wasn't trying to do me any harm.

My excitement grew when I found the complete series on the shelves of all five books and snagged them, along with a separate trilogy she might enjoy.

"So, I found that series, plus a trilogy that you might want as well." I set all eight books on the counter, then scooted back around. "Do you want me to grab more for you?"

"This should be good, I can't stay gone for too long." She smiled and purred. "Hopefully you find a way to get some more books to me."

I rang her up and the register said it cost a favor.

"It says it costs a favor," I said with a frown. Any time the payment wasn't something like a known currency, I wondered about the deal.

"That's about right," she nodded. "It's an easy price to pay, only a small one."

The books vanished off the counter and she slowly padded toward the door. "You have been helpful, Keeper."

Then she was gone, the bells jingling in her wake.

I realized the Cat hadn't said a word the entire time the Sphinx had shopped.

"Are you okay?" I asked, looking down at him by the register.

"Yes. Sphinx hate cats, as a rule." He shook his fur out almost like a dog. "It's better she didn't notice me. Last time, she talked for ages, and the Shopkeeper couldn't get what she wanted."

I sat on my stool and tapped my pen on the counter. The list of series in front of me was pretty long, but the idea of a book club stuck in my mind. So many of the different people who came in wanted books but couldn't come in often, and it felt like a shame.

"Cat, is there anyone that does deliveries across the various worlds of the Tree?" I asked.

He turned to look at me with a frown.

"You'd need to find a Wanderer, but they are even harder to find than Travelers…"

"A Wanderer…" I said slowly, thinking of what I'd read about them. "They can wander between worlds, and are protected by fate, right?"

"Something like that. Fate-touched, so people don't mess with them, though not truly protected. They are often formidable in their own right, though."

"Couldn't Betty's door just appear near the people who were members, and I hand the books out the door?"

The Cat blinked several times before answering. "The shop appears where it is needed. It's not controllable."

That was something to think about. I wasn't sure, but it felt like we had been conveniently available several times unrelated to the missions of the Fates. Like when Alas had come by earlier.

I mean, if I needed to deliver books, wouldn't that count?

"Was that all for today?" I asked, thinking of the stocking dilemma I had and putting the idea of a book club on the back burner.

SIXTY-FOUR

"That is all," said the Cat, stretching on the counter. "Like I said, last time she was here for hours searching for three books to buy."

"Guess I'm better at this job than the last guy." No wonder people were happy to see me behind the counter if he was that bad at the job.

"Understatement," muttered the Cat.

I turned to head to the stairs, but paused, thinking about her payment.

"What does a small favor from that particular Sphinx get the Shop?" I asked, trying to think about the payments that were tossed into the register.

"It depends on what the Shop needs. I know we've traded one before to someone who needed to enter the portal they guarded." The Cat didn't seem all that concerned. "The register charges what is fair for that being."

That only generated even more questions that I didn't dare get into right now.

Instead, I snagged the still-warm pot of tea and my mug before heading up the stairs. The soft warm light in the living room made me smile as I set my tea on the coffee table. The box of candy remained right where I'd left it.

Except now I needed an additional stocking, one for Alas.

I needed something for the Elven man, since I'd make stockings for Lady Twilight and Lord Bennit as well. Maybe just a regular red and white one would work.

"Betty, do you have any stockings hidden away somewhere?" I asked, hesitantly. I normally didn't ask for things outright, but I didn't have a clue what could be in storage.

The tabletop shuddered and a pair of stockings appeared, though they might actually just be giant socks of some kind. They appeared to be brand new, so I didn't think about it too hard.

They were a matching brown color, and didn't have the nice fuzzy section. Now I only needed to change the color, and maybe material.

Pulling out the citrine and taking a few breaths to steady myself, I decided to have intentions. Bright red stockings, with a white fuzzy band. I picked up the first in my hand, along with the stone, and closed my eyes, focusing on what I wanted.

"What are you trying to do?" asked the Cat, from right next to me.

My eyes snapped open to find him on the coffee table, staring at me and the sock clenched in my hands.

"I need it to be red and with a fuzzy band like the others," I said, motioning to the mantle.

The Cat's eyes darted in that direction, and he blinked like he hadn't noticed the decor. He let out a sigh, and stepped closer. "Stone magic isn't used for transformation in most cases. That's the hardest path for changing things."

He touched his nose to the stocking and it shimmered brightly with a green color. Once it faded, a deep green color replaced the brown. A thick band of a lighter green formed near the top.

That wasn't what I'd meant by red, but honestly it looked good.

"This is perfect. You are amazing..."

"Of course it is." His head snapped up, and he nodded, though he wobbled a little. "I think I will nap."

He curled up on the couch next to me, and within moments his breathing slowed.

With a shrug, I filled the stocking with some old fashioned candies from the box, along with a few modern treats like peanut-butter cups. I added it to the mantle, pleased that everyone would receive something for the holiday, even if it was only sweets.

I leaned back on the couch and pulled my mug close to sip on the fruity tea.

The warmth coming from the crystals in the fireplace felt like the real thing, casting a soft glow from that direction. This entire room felt homey. So much so that I just sat there for a while, relaxing, watching the light dance, and drinking my tea.

The Cat snored every now and then, but I didn't

wake him. Whatever magic he'd done had tuckered him out.

Yet, I still had one more box to deal with. The one from my family.

As soon as I finished the tea in my mug, I poured a second cup from the teapot, then moved toward the tree and the cardboard box.

I knelt on the floor and opened the lid, smiling at the colorful wrapping paper. Inside rested several gifts that I put under the tree, not looking to see who they were from. I'd do that tomorrow.

The pillar candles and ornaments I set off to one side, until all of the presents were under the tree. In the bottom of the box sat a tin much like the one I'd sent off to them, with cookies. This would be chocolates. Some caramel, some peppermint, and all super tasty from a local candy maker in our small town.

These I'd take back to the coffee table.

Next, I untied the twine that held the golden stars together. Seven golden stars came free, each with a name written in black. Tears crept toward the corners of my eyes as I read the names of each of my family members. This had to be from my mother.

Very carefully, I added each to my tree, including my own. I kept them close together near the top, thinking about how I'd need to get two more golden stars. One for Indigo, and one for the Cat.

Picking up the tin of chocolates and the pillar candles, I headed back to the couch, pausing next to the mantle. The three pillar candles I set on top, not lighting them, but the bright white wax added something to the room.

The chocolate tin went on the coffee table and I resisted opening it. If I opened it right now, I knew I'd eat most of the box. Like, I couldn't resist a box of chocolates like that. And they weren't for today, they were for tomorrow.

Instead, I stuck to my tea.

THE MUG DIDN'T SHATTER on the floor as it slipped from Sable's hand as she fell asleep. Instead, the wood reached up to catch it before it rose on the coffee table, like she'd placed it there.

Her emotions were all over the place this evening, and I worried.

Those dragons better bring Indigo back, or I'd find a way to war with them. It didn't matter what it took.

Still, I knew Sable wouldn't want that. She'd march into the dragon lands without a care in the world, and maybe even bring a gift. Just to find her ward.

At least I'd helped her with the stocking, though I didn't understand why it hung from the fireplace with things inside it... but it made her happy, and I could help.

My stomach grumbled, and I stretched before padding closer to Sable. We needed dinner.

SIXTY-FIVE

One second, I slept curled up in a ball, nice and cozy with a blanket wrapped around me. The next, something flung me into the air and I landed on my paws on the floor.

"It's morning!" Sable's voice cut through the strange dream, and I leaped back onto the end of her bed to find her smiling.

"Yes, that's clear." Stretching out felt good, as everything settled back into place. "Does that mean breakfast?"

"Of course," she said, blinking a few times. "I need to shower and such, but then breakfast. Probably bacon and maybe waffles..."

I didn't know how I'd lived without bacon before this, though waffles were only okay. I bet they'd be more interesting if I didn't get maple syrup on my whiskers. I padded out of her room and went to go check the book. It didn't matter what day it was, or that we were closed.

The day started with the book.

It rested in the same place as always on the table in the middle of my workshop. Yet, it sat closed.

No light, no fluttering of magic.

Nothing.

This hadn't happened before. I pawed at the book, trying to open it, but it didn't move. This wasn't good.

"You can't do this," I muttered. "Not today."

Then I smelled them.

"Enjoy the holiday..." The cold voice whispered around the room. Then it was gone.

I shivered, unable to help it, and darted out of my workshop and away from the cursed tomb.

They'd spoken to me. After all of these centuries of silence, they'd spoken to me.

I fled down the stairs just to get away, and almost crashed into the wall at the bottom as my foot slipped. The wall itself twisted to soften the impact, but still my heart pounded.

THE CAT MET me at the bottom of the stairs, which was unusual. He hit the wall, he'd been moving so fast, which had never happened before.

"Is everything okay?" I asked, leaning down to pick him up, since he seemed out of it.

"Fine..."

I petted him on the head and turned toward the counter. Some espresso felt like the correct thing to do. Though, part of me wondered what I'd mix in with it today.

Maple always went with waffles, and I was on a little bit of a maple latte kick, but today was special. Still, maple wasn't out of season during the Solstice, and I couldn't think of anything else I wanted more.

I set the Cat on the counter as I got to work whipping up the latte for me, and a small one for the Cat.

It didn't take long before I carried both our drinks into the kitchen. Yet, as soon as I set them down, someone pounded at the door to the shop. Out of the corner of my eye, I saw the Cat freeze, but I quickly headed to the front.

A familiar dragon Lord knocked on the door, which unlocked as soon as I recognized him. He opened the door before I got there.

Indigo burst into the room, flying directly toward me. She slammed into my chest, almost knocking me back as I wrapped my arms around her. Frantic chirping filled the air, along with a smattering of words, but I couldn't follow because of her excitement.

"I hope we aren't too early, but Indigo wanted breakfast," said Lord Bennit. The proud dragon appeared off. His white hair was scattered all over the place, but his blue eyes were clear. He carried his cane again in one hand, which I hadn't seen in a while. The weight of his presence flared around the room for a moment, but faded quickly.

"Of course, you are welcome," I said as the slightly larger little book dragon tried to curl up on my shoulder. "We are having bacon and waffles."

"*Bacon!*" Indigo's tiny voice made me smile, as relief that she'd come home flowed through me.

"Yep, lots of bacon." I prayed Betty had already preheated the oven, and that we had plenty to go around. "Is Lady Twilight joining us?"

"At a reasonable hour." Lord Bennit chuckled. "Indigo woke very early this morning to get here in time for food. She hasn't stopped talking about bacon."

Indigo launched herself off my shoulder toward the kitchen, and I trailed behind with Lord Bennit.

"How are you doing?" I asked quietly. The whole reason she'd gone was to help save him from despair.

"Better. Indigo reminds me of her mother so much." He paused and frowned. "She'd beat me over the head with a tree if she saw the state I was in, just like her mother."

"Good. I'd hate to lose a family member..."

He nodded and smiled. "Being around the young ones does help."

"Sable!" The Cat's voice echoed from the kitchen, and I picked up my speed.

I paused in the hallway before yanking out my phone and taking a picture. I couldn't help it.

Indigo had the Cat in a hug around his neck. He stared anywhere but at her as she hugged him. Now, that would need to go in my memory box somewhere.

The savory smell of bacon filled the room, and I noticed a pan of it already sat in the oven. The waffle maker rested on the counter with a bowl next to it.

"Grab a seat," I said to Lord Bennit. "Indigo, the Cat does need to breathe."

She let go, but then again I wasn't sure if what I'd

said was entirely true. Still, it wasn't like I could ask the Cat if breathing was optional.

"*I want lots of bacon!*" the little dragon piped.

"Of course, I'm making two pans, given that your grandfather is joining us."

"Don't feel like you need to go out of your way for me," added Lord Bennit.

I chuckled. "You'll understand once you try nice and crispy bacon."

Then I got to work making some waffles while glancing at Indigo, who couldn't help but keep flying around the kitchen. She paused as soon as the first waffle came off the iron and picked it up carefully in her claws, trying to bring it to Lord Bennit.

"Here, let me help," I said, grabbing a separate plate for him. The buzzer of the oven went off, and I pulled the first pan of bacon out to place on the counter. It needed to rest for a moment as the grease sputtered. Once it stopped, I placed each piece on a layer of paper towels.

The next two waffles were quicker, since the iron was nice and hot. These each came out perfectly golden brown. Then I carried the plates to the island.

I cut up the two waffles into quarters and placed two pieces on my plate, and one on Indigo's. The Cat got three.

Then I poured maple syrup on top of mine.

Indigo got a small side dish with the sticky golden substance.

Everyone stared at the stack of bacon as I placed it in the very center of the island. I snagged four pieces for me, and three for Indigo. She stared at mine, but didn't say anything.

"Eat your waffle first, then you can have more bacon."

The Cat also got four pieces, and I let Lord Bennit serve himself.

He watched me cut up my waffle as Indigo tore hers into small pieces, since the silverware was beyond her abilities with her claws. Each piece she dunked carefully in her little bowl of syrup, making sure each piece had the correct amount before she ate it.

I cared less about the correct ratios as I ate. Food helped distract me from the fact that I needed to entertain Lord Bennit until it was time for the celebration.

I tried not to watch as he tried bacon for the first time. Yet, he crunched into it with glee.

"Is it good?" I asked.

Indigo's head whipped around to also stare at him for the answer, like the world depended on his good opinion.

SIXTY-SIX

"This is good, it reminds me of when you roast an animal..." His voice trailed off as he realized he was about to say something probably impolite, and he changed his wording. "It's very good, and an easy preparation."

He added a few more pieces of bacon to his plate, and Indigo nodded.

I smirked to myself, glad that I'd found another to convert to loving breakfast foods. I cut into my waffle again and crunched down on a perfect bite, with both butter and syrup. My eyes drifted over to Indigo more than once, though it didn't look like anything had changed with her from her time away with the dragons.

Thankfully, she hadn't gotten any bigger. As it was, the big bowl for her dumpling soup could just barely hold her if she swam in tight circles.

It didn't take long for everyone to finish eating, though I noticed the Cat remained very quiet throughout the entire meal. He didn't even stare at Lord Bennit during that time.

"Can I get you some dragon tea?" I asked, as everyone finished up the last bites.

"That would be lovely," replied Lord Bennit with a smile.

The Cat blinked a few times in my direction, but again didn't comment.

I left everyone behind in the kitchen as I headed to the front of the shop. The tea canisters lined the wall behind the counter, and I pulled down the one with the dragon tag. Using the electric kettle, it didn't take long before it beeped at the correct temperature listed on the label.

Indigo flew through the air and landed on the wooden counter with several chirps of joy.

"I show grandpa my cave!" Then she launched herself into the air again, heading across the shop without a care.

Footsteps behind me alerted me to Lord Bennit coming to the front.

He chuckled at Indigo's flying speed.

"I'm not sure you can fit in her hideaway," I whispered, not wanting to burst Indigo's happiness bubble. "It's Indigo-sized."

"I can take care of that," he replied. Then I felt a blast of a cool wind and his form shimmered. One second, he looked like he always did with white hair and generally human features. Then, he became a dragon.

Yet, small.

Bigger than Indigo, and even the Cat, but not much

more than that. Bright blue shimmery scales covered him, and pure white eyes stared at me as he landed on the counter with a thud. His wings were tipped with silver ridges, and after only a moment he jumped into the air with another burst of a cool breeze, before racing after the young book dragon.

"Can all dragons become Indigo-sized?" I asked myself, as I filled the metal ball with tea.

"Dragons do what they want," said the Cat as he leaped on the counter. "It helps that he is a particularly powerful dragon."

I scratched the Cat's ears, and he sat down right next to me, rubbing his head on my arm.

"How are you doing this morning?"

He blinked, and his green eyes glowed brightly for a moment.

"I am unsettled." Each word came out slowly, like he didn't want to say them, but he made himself.

"Go on." I needed more than that to work with.

"They said to enjoy the holiday."

It took only a second for the words to sink in, and for me to understand what the Cat meant. Then I smiled brightly.

"That's amazing news! You can relax for today, and not worry about work at all." I picked him up and snuggled him close before putting him down.

"You just need to suffer the company of dragons," I joked.

He nodded slowly from where I put him down on the counter.

A timer went off for the tea, and mentally I thanked

Betty. I'd forgotten to set one for the dragon tea. I removed the metal ball and emptied out the tea before moving the mug to the center of the counter.

It'd stay warm, based on my prior experience.

Then I started making some more coffee for me and the Cat. A second round of loveliness sounded perfect. I pulled out his teacup with flowers on it and set it nearby, while I steamed the milk with a bit of heavy cream mixed in, sticking with the maple theme.

The Cat watched me make his latte, a little more relaxed than before.

"Why does it worry you that they told you to relax?" I finally asked, trying to understand his point of view a little better.

"They never speak. Never, in centuries. Only through the book do I receive instructions..."

"You mean, besides when they use power on you," I added, a little heat creeping into my voice.

"Don't tempt them," whispered the Cat in a choked voice, his tail flicking behind him.

"Enjoy this, and try to relax." I finished up the lattes and pointed at his. My mug sat nice and warm within my hands. The first sip warmed all of me, and I couldn't help but smile.

A smaller part of me wondered about the Fates, and the Cat's fear of them.

All I knew was that they existed, and dragons ignored them. Fey Lords as well, though they could get punished by them. I guessed dragons probably could, too, though I hadn't heard about anything like that.

Others had spoken about them in a reverent tone,

almost like they were gods of some type. They were also the Cat's keepers, and the ones that needed to agree to give him his freedom. That meant they were entities that could be interacted with, more like the ancient gods and goddesses from Greece or Rome on my world.

"You are very relaxed for needing to entertain the dragon until the Elder joins us."

The Cat's words caused me to chuckle with how formal he was being. He was completely right, I did need to keep Indigo's grandpa entertained.

"I don't have a clue. Usually, we all lounge around on the Solstice after breakfast, then snack on cookies and hot chocolate until we decide to do presents. Dinner was normally right in the middle of the afternoon, then relaxing until the town's celebration started as the sun went down."

I moved back to Betty and steamed some additional milk for a hot chocolate for Indigo, only enough to fill a teacup. I knew what I'd put in her stocking, and didn't want her to overload on too much sugar.

"What's for dinner?" asked the Cat, after lapping at his drink.

I paused with my lips parted before I snapped them shut. I'd thought about the stockings, presents, and the tree, along with decorating the living room upstairs, but not dinner. It had never been a thing I'd ever had to think about, and now I realized I'd forgotten.

"Well..."

SIXTY-SEVEN

I needed to think fast about food. The cookie situation was covered. I had enough frozen cookie dough to not have a problem for three Solstice celebrations.

While I could order Chinese take-out, we'd eaten so much of that recently I felt I needed to come up with something else.

I slipped off the stool and headed to the register before tapping away on the screen. It didn't take long for an option to come up that sounded tasty, and would be a new experience for us.

I picked several large items that were served family style, along with a few side dishes. Plus bread. Excitement gathered in me as I finished the order.

"Dinner is taken care of," I announced. Thankfully, the Cat had said something, otherwise I would have needed to find out quickly what Betty had in the store rooms.

"What are we having?" asked the Cat, creeping closer to me.

"It's a surprise." Thankfully, whatever world I ordered from it wasn't a holiday.

"I don't like surprises," grumbled the Cat.

"Well, then today might not be your day. Several surprises are in store, especially up in the living room." I couldn't help but think of his gift that Betty had helped me with, and Indigo's. Hopefully, they both liked their gifts. My bank account hadn't been thrilled, but they were worth it.

"When are you going to open the gifts from your family?" he asked.

Man, the Cat was asking the hard questions this morning.

"After everyone has left, but before bed. I'll then send a few messages over to them to see if people are around for a call." I didn't want to open those gifts in front of our guests.

I hadn't gotten everyone big gifts, only the Cat and Indigo, but at least everyone had a stocking. Though, I wondered when Alas would arrive. I hadn't given him a time to show up, I'd just invited him.

Chirping from the other side of the shop caught my attention as Indigo zoomed into view.

She sped up as she spotted the cups on the counter.

Right behind her flew the blue dragon, though the small form felt weird. I kept reminding myself not to cuddle the little blue dragon. Somehow, cuddling Lord Bennit like I cuddled Indigo felt wildly inappropriate, though he was cute in his small form.

Indigo landed, and behind her Lord Bennit shifted back to his humanoid form with the sharp pointed ears.

"You have a fantastic space, little one," said Lord Bennit, with a proud look. "Your collection of books has grown."

"*I have the best collection.*"

"Collection of books?" I asked.

Yet, before she replied, she stuck her snout into the hot chocolate in the teacup.

Lord Bennit grabbed the mug of tea I had made for him and responded for Indigo. "She's been collecting audiobooks, along with some physical books as well."

I'd been letting her get audiobooks on my account, and hadn't really thought about how many credits she used. She never went over my plan, but I made sure to have one of the larger ones. Plus, the dragons sent her books as well.

"I mean, that makes sense given she's part of your clan, right? You guys hoard knowledge..." After I said it, I realized I probably should have asked how all of that worked before making any assumptions.

Lord Bennit's chuckle made his mug shake in his hand, and he had to put it down.

Even Indigo stared at him, with hot chocolate dripping off her snout.

"We collect knowledge, and it makes us grow stronger..." He chuckled again a few more times. "But we don't hoard it. Well, most of my close clan doesn't."

"*The librarian!*" Indigo's chirp made me turn toward her. "*The librarian dragon! Tell story!*"

"I will," said Lord Bennit. "Several clans' members have created libraries on various worlds, where they gather rare books and make sure history isn't lost to time, or revised out of truth."

All I could picture were massive libraries with giant dragons in them, making sure no one forgot to return a book.

"Revised?" I asked.

"People love to change history," answered the Cat, before Lord Bennit could. "Especially those who gain control. They tend to want history to reinforce their own narrow view."

"And your clan helps resist that?"

"It depends on the world," added Lord Bennit. "When a dragon settles somewhere, you can expect a certain level of magic on that world. Our clan doesn't get involved in the small struggles of the short-lived on those worlds. Instead, we record, document, and provide access to the knowledge and lore we collect. Sometimes, peoples on those worlds fall into centuries where there is no one interested in truth, but sooner or later someone always comes to find out what really went before."

"But other clans do get involved?" I asked.

Lord Bennit looked hesitant for a moment.

"Yes, some dragon clans rule worlds as kings." The Cat's answer hung in the air.

I nodded. "That makes sense, that not all dragons are the same. The same goes for humans, and Fey Lords."

Something said at the conclave came to mind.

"Who are the clan's enemies?" I asked, remembering the parts of the clan that were in hiding. Hopefully, he didn't feel like I was asking too many questions.

Lord Bennit let out a sigh and sipped his tea. "I don't

understand how any of the long-lived could take this view, but there are those who don't like knowledge getting passed around. Or even preserved, sometimes."

"*Book burners!*" Indigo's addition almost caused me to jump.

"*You can't burn audio books,*" she said as she launched herself at me. "*Bad people burn books! Or scrolls, if they have scrolls.*"

She landed on my shoulder, feeling heavier than before as she carefully moved closer to my neck. "*Very bad people.*"

"Don't worry, no one will burn books in the shop," I added, to reassure her. Yet, I was thankful that was her definition of a bad person. It meant she really didn't think about the demons.

"There are some dragon clans that we don't get along with, but nothing to be concerned with. Dragons intermingle between clans, as dragonets on occasion are born to different clans, and need to leave their nests young."

"Wait, you mean dragons who grow from knowledge can be born outside the clan?" This hadn't been in any of the dragons books I'd read.

SIXTY-EIGHT

"Yes, that's how Lady Twilight joined the clan and started our line."

The door rattled as someone knocked on it. Lord Bennit twisted around to peer out, his shoulders relaxed.

"Who's that?" he asked.

I lurched around the counter toward the door and found a delivery guy on the other side. It wasn't our usual one, but he held up a cardboard box with lots of takeout containers inside.

"I have an order for Sable?" He asked after I opened the door, with a confused look on his face. He glanced at the front window, then back at me.

"That's me." I grabbed the cardboard box from his hands, but found Lord Bennit right behind me.

"Let me grab that," he said, taking it from me as the guy held out a phone for me to sign to confirm delivery.

I signed and added a tip before he hurried away. Once I closed the door, I turned to the front room to find the cardboard box already on the counter.

Both the Cat and Indigo sniffed at it.

"That's not Chinese," said the Cat in an accusatory voice.

"Nope, I went with something new, but tasty…" A knock behind me caused me to jump. Another one, already?

Alas stood on the other side of the door, wearing a grin and holding a bag over one shoulder, along with a basket in his other hand.

I opened the door to let him in, wondering about the bags.

"Happy Solstice!" he said in a cheerful voice.

"Same to you, and welcome!"

"Where should I set my things down?" he asked, glancing around and carefully not looking at the dragon or the Cat.

"We're going to head upstairs, but we're waiting for another to join us…"

The cardboard box on the counter slowly sank down into the wood, vanishing from sight.

I hoped Betty could rustle up a dining room table upstairs in the only room I'd decorated. I hadn't thought of that before now, but I knew she had one from my birthday celebration. I hoped she was taking care of that for me.

There were so many tasks I hadn't thought about, since someone else in my family was usually responsible for taking care of them.

Another knock came at the door behind me, and yet again I twisted around to see who stood there. This time, I recognized Lady Twilight's form.

The door unlocked at my thought, and she opened it.

"I hope I'm not late," she said with a bright smile, seeing everyone in the room.

"*Grandma!*" Indigo's voice echoed through the pause in conversation.

Lady Twilight chuckled and stepped inside as the purple dragon streaked through the air to her.

"I hope you don't mind, I brought a guest."

Behind her, a cloaked figure let down her hood, her tall ears pointing to the ceiling. My eyes widened as Liluth stepped inside the warm shop.

The bag slipped from Alas' hand and landed on the floor with a thud before it vanished.

"Alas?" she asked in a soft voice.

Then he moved. One moment, he still stood behind me, and the next his arms were wrapped around her and his face was buried in her neck.

He spoke in a soft language that I barely understood, and I twisted away as quickly as I could.

The Cat sat on the counter, staring at the sight, his eyes wide before he glanced in a different direction.

"We can all head upstairs to the living room," I said, drawing attention away from the two by the door.

"*The tree!*" Indigo stopped her frantic circling around Lady Twilight and headed up to the second story. Yet, after she vanished through the archway to the living room, a second doorway appeared on the first floor. The bookshelves on the right most wall faded as the opening sprang up.

"Fewer stairs, for the win!" I added, and motioned in the new direction.

Lord Bennit took the lead and headed in after Indigo, then Lady Twilight entered.

I followed, noticing the Cat had jumped off the counter. I hoped he would join us, but I wasn't sure with Liluth's appearance.

Yet, as I entered, he sat on the back of the couch. His eyes met mine, and as usual I couldn't read him. I hoped he was okay.

The room had shifted at some point.

The giant windows overlooking the dark evergreen forest were to the right, but now the tree sat smack dab in the middle. Two large soft couches faced the tree, with an opening where the fireplace still stood to the left. Heat drifted from the golden opening from several large crystals resting within the stonework.

I resisted the urge to pause as I counted the stockings. Yesterday, I'd added one for Alas, but now there were two that looked the same. Somehow, we had enough for everyone to have a stocking, including Liluth.

Beyond the couches, a round dining room table stood near even more windows, with just enough chairs for everyone. Plus two spaces without chairs, one for the Cat and one for Indigo. Dishes were laid out at each place setting, and several empty enormous platters sat in the center.

I sent all the thanks and praise to Betty, mentally, at the sight of the room. Somehow, they had pulled it off without me even asking. They just did all of this; expanding the room, adding new windows, and then pulling out the table.

Plus the stocking.

I couldn't get over the stocking. It'd taken so much for me and the Cat to get it to work, and yet somehow a second one exactly like the first was hanging there, ready to go. Hopefully, the candy inside would be okay.

"This is an amazing room," said Lady Twilight, drawing my attention away from the fireplace. "It feels like you."

It took a moment for me to realize that she had spoken to me.

"Betty created it for me. I really wanted an actual living room. Somehow, they got it just perfect."

Lady Twilight glanced at the Cat, then back at me and around the room. For a split second, her eyes darkened with what felt like confusion, before they cleared.

"It's nice and cozy. All it needs are bookshelves lining the wall for a book dragon."

I chuckled at that. Normally, the opening to the living room stood on the second floor, and the balcony had bookshelves on it. Yet, I understood what she meant. Bookcases could line the fireplace, taking it up another level.

Indigo chirped several times. *"Just needs audiobooks."*

"You mean speakers," I replied, trying really hard to not think about her gift that hid under the tree.

"Cookies!" Indigo darted across the room and landed on the coffee table I'd missed. Several enormous platters of cookies, and one of brownies, covered it between the two couches.

My coffee mug sat near them, and I headed in that direction.

"So, what's next?" asked the Cat as I approached.

"Well, we can share cookies and settle in, then stockings, then dinner. Unless people are hungry."

Indigo picked up a cookie and started eating it rapidly, even though we'd recently eaten breakfast.

"What are stockings?" asked Lord Bennit, taking a seat close to Indigo and the fireplace.

I motioned toward the mantle. "Everyone has a stocking with some small gifts and treats inside."

"Where did my gifts go?" asked Alas, as he and Liluth walked in the room holding hands. "My bag vanished at some point."

CHAPTER
SIXTY-NINE

"Gifts?" I asked, as I sat on the same couch as Lord Bennit, but nearer the tree.

"Yes, for the Solstice exchange," added Alas, glancing around but keeping pace with Liluth as she walked into the room.

"Your bag looks to be under the tree," said Lady Twilight. "I should add my contributions as well."

She marched over to the tree, and a few small boxes appeared under it.

I only had stockings for folks and not any gifts, except for the Cat and Indigo. I pushed the panic away and decided to not worry. Even the Fates had told the Cat to enjoy the day.

"Oh, I didn't realize the shop had a Cat..." said Liluth.

I froze, as did the Cat.

Indigo looked confused and tried to say something, but nothing came out of her snout.

"Little one, sometimes we can't discuss things, even if we are dragons," whispered Lord Bennit.

Indigo glared at him, then turned toward me. "*Why can't talk about Cat?*"

"That's not my call. If it was, we would," I explained. Honesty was the best with the little dragon.

This time both dragons turned to look at me with wide eyed looks on their faces. Even Alas and Liluth seemed surprised.

"What?"

"You spoke in the dragon language," said the Cat, with something that almost looked like a smirk on his face. "Even with the dragon stone and the magic, it's a language that most cannot learn. Understand, yes, but speak like you just did?"

The Cat shook his head.

I had done nothing differently, I had just spoken like I normally did. Yet, apparently it came out in another language. That could happen?

Indigo left the coffee table and cookies to sit in my lap.

"*You spoke!*" She glanced at Lord Bennit, then back at me. "*Like us! How?*"

"Probably magic," I answered with a chuckle and a shrug. "Plus, today's the Solstice. It's a magical day!"

"*Magic day?*" asked the little dragon.

"Yes. Remember, the Solstice is when the Oak King starts his rule, and he slowly ushers in spring. The days start to get longer after tonight. At the shop, it's usually nice weather whenever we are on the roof, unless we want snow, but back on my home world, everything is covered in snow right now."

Indigo nodded slowly as I spoke, listening to each word.

"But, magic?"

"My father always said today was one of the most magical days, right up there with the Summer Solstice and All Hallows Eve." I didn't know if I was still speaking in the dragon language or my own, but either way I tried to remember exactly what my father said about this holiday. I kept coming up with nothing, just this feeling that it was a magical evening.

"I know this tale," said Alas as he sat across from us on the other couch. Liluth stuck near him with a bright smile on her face. Yet, she kept glancing at the Cat, who still sat on the back of the couch behind me.

Alas's voice took on a musical lilt as he spoke. His fingers twitched like he normally held an instrument.

"Long, long ago, even before the oldest trees were tiny saplings, there were two brothers: the Oak King and the Holly King. The Oak King was bright, like the warm summer sun. He wore a crown of oak leaves and acorns, and when he walked, the flowers bloomed, and the trees grew tall. He loved the long days and the busy buzz of life."

The feeling of the hot summer sun washed over me, followed by the scent of flowers and the buzz of bees. For a moment, I felt like I stood in the middle of a field during the summer months back home.

"The Holly King was quiet, like the deep winter night. He wore a crown of prickly holly leaves and bright red berries, and when he walked, the world grew hushed and peaceful, ready for rest. He loved the long nights and the quiet magic of slumber."

Then my moment in the field shifted, night taking over with a cool breeze and fireflies filling the air. The smell of fall leaves and crisp winter mornings washed over me.

"Every year, these two brothers would take turns caring for the world."

Images of my brothers flashed through my mind. Each of them was doing what they were best at. Cyan painting on a canvas, Cerulean hiking through the mountains, Umber growing crops in his field, and Onyx sitting next to a fire, quietly writing in his journal.

"At the longest day, the Summer Solstice, the Oak King was at his strongest. But then, the Holly King would gently remind him it was time for the world to rest. Slowly, the days would grow shorter, and the nights would grow longer, as the Holly King's magic filled the air."

Summer Solstice passed in my mind, with all of us wearing flower crowns, and the bonfires lit within the town square.

"Then, at the longest night, the Winter Solstice, the Holly King was at his strongest. But the Oak King was waiting, for even in the darkest night, the promise of light remained. Slowly, the days would grow longer, and the nights shorter, as the Oak King's magic stirred the world awake."

The snow falling outside the window drew my attention as it slowly covered more of the dark green trees.

"And so, the Oak King and the Holly King danced

their yearly dance, a dance of light and dark, of growth and rest. They taught the world that everything has its time, and that even in the deepest winter, the warmth of summer is waiting to return."

For a second, everyone stayed quiet as the strange magic drifted in the air from Alas' tale. Then, finally, it dissipated.

Indigo hummed in awe. *"So, your magic is stirring because of the Solstice?"*

SEVENTY

I paused, listening to Indigo's question, and realized she spoke better and in more complete sentences. The days away with the dragons had helped her language skills.

"Maybe..."

"Magic stirs magic," answered Lady Twilight, at the same time as my response.

I glanced at her, wondering what she knew that she wasn't telling. With a dragon, it could be quite a lot.

Instead of responding, she didn't meet my eyes. I didn't push the issue. One thing I had learned was that magic didn't always make sense, at least not in the rational way math did. It leaned more toward the arts.

"Indigo, do you want to give out the stockings? Or..." The words were barely out of my mouth when she leaped off my lap and into the air.

"*Stocking time!*" she chirped in a way-too-sharp voice. She reached the stocking with the blue dragon on it and carefully lifted it up in the air. For a second she wobbled, then suddenly stabilized as she flew it over to Lord Bennit.

"Thank you, little one."

She chirped in response and went to the one with the black cat on it. That one she flew to the Cat behind me. He purred in response, and off she went.

Quickly she gave out stockings to Alas and Liluth, then Lady Twilight, before me. Last, she took her own.

"Oh, what is this?" asked Lord Bennit, pulling out the button candy.

"I stuffed them with old-fashioned candy and party favors..." I answered sheepishly, as he pulled out a wooden toy with a cup and a ball on a string.

Alas chuckled along with the Cat, as everyone quickly started trying various candies and toys. The ball and cup toy fascinated the dragons, including Indigo whose mouth got stuck shut with taffy.

While I'd filled my stocking as well, a few additional surprises hid inside.

Someone had stashed a bag of premium coffee inside. The writing on the back wasn't in English, but I knew how it smelled. I wanted to make some right now, but I resisted as I set it carefully on the couch beside me.

Lord Bennit carefully glanced away with a soft smile as he tried to get the rubber ball in the cup.

Indigo darted in and grabbed it with her claws, which was not the game at all.

The second surprise in my stocking felt soft. I pulled it out and found a cute little sweater. It had bright green leaves on it and wouldn't fit me if I tried.

"Oh, that was for Indigo," said Liluth with a chuckle.

"Hey Indigo!"

She flew my way, and glanced at the sweater, I held up.

"You have a holiday sweater."

Her eyes grew wide, and she skidded to a stop on my knees.

I carefully pulled it over her head and slid her wings through the spaces on the back. My fingers tingled with magic.

"It's a safety charm," whispered the Cat. "So, it won't get caught on anything, or it will unravel before it hurts her."

I nodded at his answer.

Indigo twisted about, trying to get a better look at herself before I pulled out my phone and snapped a picture.

Her eyes grew even wider, then she took off to tackle Liluth.

I wasn't actually sure if it was the wrong stocking to put it in at all. I bet if Indigo had pulled it out, she wouldn't have known what to do with it. Or she'd have been distracted by the candy, which I limited in her case, but still.

A cold glass container came out next, filled with a thick bright blue liquid. A stopper kept it shut.

"It's bubbles for the warm spring that Indigo mentioned on the roof," explained Lady Twilight. "It helps with relaxation, and creates pretty sparkles."

"Thank you," I said with a smile. Normally, you didn't use bubbles in a hot tub, but given the magical nature of it I wasn't worried.

Lady Twilight popped a cute little party popper, sending confetti in the air that Indigo flew through. Lord Bennit used one as well, followed by everyone else quickly finding the ones in their stockings and filling the air with the small bits of paper.

The Cat purred behind me, almost right behind my head. His stocking already sat empty, and the toys I'd gotten him were somehow gone. Yet, he smelled faintly of sweet candy, which warmed my heart.

"Having fun?" I whispered.

"Surprisingly, yes."

I couldn't remove my smile if I'd tried.

"*Presents?*" asked Indigo, flying my way.

"Yes, I have things for everyone," said Alas, jumping to his feet. He approached the tree and picked up the woven bag before I could say anything. "Indigo, this is for you."

The dragon zoomed over and took a small object from his hands. She then flew in my direction and slowly unfolded the mystery item. At first, it was just a scrap of leather, but then each time she unfolded a section it grew bigger, until it became a small bag with a leather strap.

"*A bag...*" she said in a hushed whisper before sticking her claws inside, then her entire arm. It somehow vanished. "*All the room! My player can fit!*"

Then she vanished, a puff of air all that remained as a streak flew toward a small dark shadow on the mantle.

"Well, you made her day," I said with a chuckle. I stuck my finger into the bag she'd left behind. I couldn't feel a bottom, though there should have been one.

"Space magic is hard for the little ones to learn," explained Lady Twilight. "She'll love having it."

"This is for you," said Alas before he tossed something my way.

I caught it reflexively and unfolded it to find a belt. I held it up, slightly unsure. The quality was amazing.

"It has space magic built in as well. After those boots I made for that Traveler, I wanted to learn the magic to do it myself."

"He'd been saying for ages he'd learn, and now he finally has," interrupted Liluth. "It just took him a few hundred years to get around to it."

"Hey, I had to recover from being an adventurer." He ran his fingers through his hair.

She chuckled at him, and he smiled.

"This is for the old coot."

The next thing he tossed, I caught and held it up to the Cat, who laughed.

Actually laughed, out loud.

CHAPTER

SEVENTY-ONE

"What is it?" I asked.

"A teacup with a leather case," said Alas with a grin. "Pull it out for him."

I found a flap and pulled out a beautiful teacup with a chip on the rim.

It was made of white porcelain, with pitch black paw prints along with some vines twisted about the edges. It didn't have a saucer.

It was beautiful.

I twisted it in the light, and the black shimmered like a nebula.

"Where did you get this?" I asked in a hushed whisper.

"Just something I found," he said. "I try to get them as souvenirs from various places I've gone."

I couldn't imagine a place where he could get something so custom.

"It will fit in the collection," said the Cat.

This time I translated it to Alas, since he couldn't understand the Cat.

Liluth watched with slightly confused eyes, glancing between the Cat and Alas, like there was some sort of puzzle she couldn't quite understand.

Indigo came flying out of nowhere with her MP3 player and the beat-up headphones, yet she almost whimpered when she landed.

The wire holding the earbuds together had snapped.

"*It broke?*" She held it up carefully, and her eyes watered. "*I put it on, and snap.*"

Her head had gotten a little larger as she grew, and at some point, they wouldn't work anymore anyway.

I hadn't expected them to break so soon, but I knew it would be coming.

"How about you grab your present from under the tree?" I said quietly, motioning to the tree.

"*Present?*" she asked, as Alas picked something up from under the tree and held it up to her.

She zoomed over and snagged it in her claws. Wrapping paper went everywhere as she tore it off mid-flight, until she just clutched a small Bluetooth speaker.

"*What is it?*" she asked.

I took it from her and synced the MP3 player and the speaker. Then I hit the play button. An audiobook started playing out loud.

"*Books! Stories!*" She twisted in the air with it in her claws. "*Thank you! Best present!*"

Indigo brought it over to Lady Twilight to look at, while the Cat padded off to Lord Bennit and Alas.

That left Liluth to me. Yet again, I found her eyes watching the Cat.

"He speaks to you?" she asked softly.

"Yes, I can understand him. The dragons as well, but that's all." I wasn't sure how much I could say without getting into trouble, but so far so good.

"Strange. Though the dragons can ignore many of the rules of the Tree, just like the Fey Lords."

This time I stayed quiet on the subject and went in a different direction. "How is staying with Lady Twilight?"

"Good. I miss Alas, but it was worth it." A smile came across Liluth's face. "Plus, I have access to so much knowledge. Her library is expansive. I don't think I could finish exploring it within a century."

"I know how that feels," I said while thinking of the stacks hidden within the shop. I hadn't wandered them since discovering the Cat was cursed. Between practicing my magic and prepping gifts for this gathering, my time had been spent well. "The shop has its own library."

"This place is very magical, and it feels different from the last time I was here. Especially this room."

Lady Twilight's comment and strange looks came back to me.

"How so?" I asked, wondering if she could explain it better. "My magical knowledge is limited, though I have a teacher now."

Liluth pressed her lips together before answering. "It feels like you."

I let myself think on that before responding. This wasn't an area where I'd done a bunch of magic; that was mostly on the roof and by the counter. Or my room, but that was really my space. This space the shop had created for me, which I appreciated. Maybe Betty made it even more for me than I'd thought.

"Betty created this space for me, that might be it."

Liluth didn't look convinced. "Ask your teacher about it, and see what they say."

"I'll ask the Professor," I added without thinking.

Again Liluth paused, glancing at me and then the Cat who nodded at something Lord Bennit said. Her lips parted, but she stopped herself.

Lady Twilight stood up from where she'd sat and moved closer to both of us. Indigo followed. The bluetooth speaker was turned off.

I held up her bag, which she hadn't grabbed yet.

"*Everything fits inside it,*" she said with a smile as she shoved the speaker into it, along with the MP3 player and the broken headphones.

"It's a fantastic present," I added.

"*I got you present,*" she said, glancing at Lady Twilight, who pulled something out of nowhere. She held a deep blue cloth-covered book out to me.

I took it carefully, my fingertips tingling from the magic. The edges glowed with a golden light for a split second before it vanished. Flipping it open, it stopped on a table of contents. Various titles were listed: How Dragonlets Grow: a Guide for new Parents, Worlds to Visit and Places of Knowledge, The Best Places to Shop, and several more.

"Is that what I think it is?" asked Liluth, her eyes wide.

"Probably," said Lady Twilight with a smirk.

I glanced at them both.

"It has all the books, and you can add more!"

It sounded like an ebook reader, though I wasn't sure how a magical one would work. "Oh, that's fantastic! How do I add books?"

"You just place the book between the pages and it will become part of this one," explained Lady Twilight.

"It's a library in your pocket," said Liluth with her eyes wide. "Only you can use it, unlike carrying around individual books in a space magic bag. They are a specialty of the Clan of Knowledge."

"And as she is one of us, Indigo thought it'd be a wonderful holiday gift..." said Lady Twilight. "She spent ages in my library adding books. I made an addition or two."

"The best gift, right?" Indigo asked. *"Better than the drink?"*

CHAPTER
SEVENTY-TWO

"Of course, better than the coffee beans," I said as she snuggled close, still wearing the space bag and the soft sweater.

The gift felt huge. Books that came from Lady Twilight's library, more knowledge that wasn't restricted by the shop.

"*Good,*" she chirped softly. Her head snuggled close to my neck, and it felt like a heated blanket before she pulled away. "*Speaker awesome!*"

"I'm glad you like the present."

"I'll be placing an order for several of those as well," said Lady Twilight. "I'd like one for my library."

Liluth nodded. "I know the world that some Elves went to has technology, but I know little about it. I wish I'd learned more, now."

"Well, I know it wasn't to my world..." I said with a shrug, then thought of the Cat's gift and smiled. "But I can help you find things to solve certain problems."

"I know that look," whispered Lady Twilight.

"Hey Indigo, can you grab that small gold package and take it over to the Cat?"

Indigo frantically nodded before climbing down my shoulder and retrieving the package from under the tree. It wasn't very big or heavy, and she handled it easily.

She approached the Cat and the conversation that Lord Bennit, Alas, and he were having before dropping it in front of him.

The Cat paused, then glanced at me with his head tilted.

Indigo then helped him with the wrapping paper, revealing a small controller.

"What is this?" he asked as everyone went quiet.

"Hey Betty, can you do the secret thing?" I asked, drawing everyone's attention.

A white screen slowly unraveled from the ceiling in front of the fireplace.

"Hit the play button," I added.

The Cat pressed a button on the remote, and a movie started playing. It involved hobbits, a ranger, and a ring. Everyone went quiet, staring at the screen with their mouths open.

"What is this magic?" asked Liluth, her voice hushed in awe.

"It's a movie. A way to tell stories from my world. This is a favorite of mine."

The Cat's eyes glowed in the light as they stayed fixated on the screen.

I pulled some candy out of my stocking and got comfortable.

Indigo moved to Lord Bennit's lap, who sat closer to the screen.

The sound came from hidden speakers that Betty had put in various locations. The shop had done all of the heavy lifting.

I'd bought the screen projector and the speakers, and explained what needed to happen based on the instructions that came with them. Somehow they were attached in the right places, and it sounded and looked fantastic. I didn't look too closely to figure it out.

As a wizard appeared on screen, I chuckled to myself, thinking about how magic worked in the movies versus in the shop, or on other worlds.

Once the first movie finished, all everyone could talk about was the Elven city and how realistic it was.

"I bet Elves might be like that on other worlds," said Liluth as she sat down at the dining room table. "Strange that they are all good at archery."

"Yes, it's like saying all dragons breathe fire," replied Lord Bennit, chuckling in glee.

I snagged a lid off the first serving plate, wondering about that.

Underneath, a giant pan of lasagna smelled amazing. Steam drifted up, and the melted cheese on top appeared perfect. I quickly cut slices before adding one to my plate and adding a slice to the Cat's plate beside me.

Then I passed the serving tray to Lady Twilight, who added some to Indigo's plate.

Rolls were passed around, as well as salad, roasted veggies, and mini meatballs.

In my house, we roasted meats for this meal, but for

last-minute ordering this would do. Cookies were always the dessert, though everyone had made a dent in them on the coffee table before we'd opened our stockings.

I wasn't sure much remained besides crumbs. I knew I'd eaten two brownies without thinking about it. They were just so good.

Not to mention, I always snacked while watching a movie. I couldn't help it.

"*Do wizards act like that?*" asked Indigo.

"The only wizard I know acts like that," answered Lady Twilight. "He is very snobby. Not my favorite person at all."

"I can't believe they don't have a bard," added Alas, taking a sip of his drink. "Someone to sing stories, keep them on track and heal injuries. All adventuring parties need one."

"At least they have a ranger who knows the lands," said Lord Bennit, passing the serving plate on. "But the interpretation of dwarves is strange."

"What are actual dwarves like?" I asked, before I tasted the lasagna.

"Smart fighters who usually use some sort of earth magic, though not always," explained Lord Bennit. "Some can turn their skin to rock as a defensive measure. The ones I know the best are scholars looking to get access to our Clans' resources."

"They are always asking to visit my library," grumbled Lady Twilight, shaking her head and making Indigo giggle. "I had to ban several who wanted to borrow books."

"*I saw a dwarf in the library. They tried to show me*

magic." Indigo turned to look at me. "*Your magic is better.*"

"I've been practicing and trying new things with my magic." Not that too much worked yet, but still I practiced.

"*More flying games?*" she asked, while fluttering her wings.

I chuckled. "Not right now, we have yummy food to eat."

The salad had a dressing on it that had a little spice, and I ate several large bites trying to figure out the flavors.

"This food is tasty," said Lord Bennit. "What is the pasta called?"

"It's lasagna, made with a meat sauce, with only a little spice." For once I could explain things instead of asking the questions. "Some people make it much hotter, but I like that this one highlights the other ingredients."

He nodded several times and took a second serving. "I like it."

"*Grandpa cooks,*" said Indigo as she tasted the food on her plate. "*He made me food when I visited.*"

"You like cooking?" asked Alas. "I seem to burn everything."

"Somehow, even water, if I remember correctly," added Liluth.

"*Water burns?*" asked Indigo, stopping mid bite with sauce and cheese all over her snout. "*How?*"

"You need to get it hot enough to evaporate," explained Lady Twilight. "Like, if you leave the kettle on too long, you can burn the kettle."

"*Strange,*" mumbled the little dragon before going back to her plate.

The Cat's plate emptied first, but he didn't ask for more. He just sat, watching the conversations at the table.

"Are holidays like this at your home?" he asked quietly.

"More hectic, with so many people. This is nice and calm, relaxing almost." I wondered how everyone's holiday back home was going, but didn't look at my phone. Living in the now was too important. While this wasn't my birth family, this was my family too, and they deserved for me to be here with them.

SEVENTY-THREE

It didn't take long before everyone stuffed themselves full of food and candy from the stockings. It was in the post-meal lull that Lord Bennit pulled out the last surprise from his stocking.

At first, he stared at it as my eyes flickered over to Indigo. She flew quickly in his direction, chirping.

I hadn't had a chance to warn her what 'she' got him as a present. The bright purple shirt had seemed like a great idea at the time, but now I worried.

Indigo chirped again and landed on his shoulder before nuzzling him, saying something. Lord Bennit nodded and the shirt vanished. His eyes caught mine, with tears at the edges. He smiled brightly and scratched under her chin.

"What did you get him?" asked the Cat quietly.

"A shirt that says 'World's Best Grandpa'."

"Ah, that makes the comment about the universe make sense," he added.

"Universe?"

"Well, he is a dragon. He will not be satisfied with just being the best of any one world now, is he?" The Cat's words lingered in my mind, making me want to chuckle.

If Lord Bennit took it as a challenge, that was okay to me. Maybe it'd help him with his grief. He had so much to live for.

Lady Twilight stood first.

"We best be getting on our way," she said. Her face, normally full of laughter, seemed pale and strained.

Then I remembered her magic kept Liluth safe outside of her lands. While I didn't understand what was happening, this had to weigh on her.

I stood with a smile, pushing back my chair. "Thank you for coming..."

From there Alas also stood, and soon, the three of them were at the door. I hugged each tightly before they headed out.

That left Lord Bennit with the three of us.

He hung back until the others left.

Indigo perched on his shoulder and gave him a nuzzle before flying back to the living room.

"Thank you for coming," I said with a grin.

"Thank you for letting her visit." He couldn't meet my eyes for a moment. "I know it had to be hard. I needed that push to get off the ledge."

I stepped closer to him, placing a hand on his arm. "Are you doing better?"

"As good as I can be." This time he met my eyes. "I won't let her, or you, down."

"We will be fine."

"Thank you again for the invitation to your holiday." He bowed his head then headed out the door. It snapped shut and locked behind him.

Chirping came from the living room and I slowly made my way back to the doorway. Indigo and the Cat pushed buttons on the controller, looking at the various movies they might watch.

All that remained under the tree were presents from my family. While part of me wanted to ignore them for now, I headed in that direction and took a seat on the floor. I pulled the first over to me.

A movie began, then I felt someone staring at me. The Cat perched on the back of the couch looking down, his bright green eyes glowing.

"My gift will come soon, it's just delayed," he whispered.

I nodded with a smile. "No worries, I know delays happen."

The Cat paused, then slowly nodded his head. "Yes, a delay..."

"What movie are you watching?" I asked.

"Something about training dragons..." His tail flickered before he turned back in that direction and padded away.

While that might not be a great movie for Indigo, the movie itself was amazing. Hopefully, she wouldn't be upset when she realized that it wasn't about dragons learning about things and more about humans learning about dragons.

My attention went back to the tree when nothing came from the direction of Indigo and the Cat.

The first present was a tin covered in snowflakes, and I knew what it contained. I cracked it open with a pop and the smell of chocolate filled the air. The rocky road fudge made me drool, even though I wasn't hungry. I popped a small piece in my mouth, chewing on the marshmallow and nutty goodness.

Then I forced myself to set it aside; otherwise, I might eat the entire box without really enjoying it.

My mother knew my weak spots with sweets.

A few different books from my father and Umber were tucked inside a colorful box — one about how to cook, another about container gardening.

Cerulean must have said something about my sad rooftop deck. I just couldn't be bothered to try to grow any plants out there. There were plenty of plants inside, and they took care of themselves. I was lucky enough to keep the plant next to my bed alive, and that was only because Betty controlled the sunlight it received.

And it was magical.

Onyx's gift was a sweater. Soft and green, with golden colors woven throughout. It might even have been handmade, and I couldn't help but toss it over my shirt. It felt like a warm hug. Tears crept to my eyes, but I ignored them, even though it smelled like my family home. I took a moment to just relax with it on.

Warmth pulsed up from the floor, and I opened my eyes and patted the wooden boards.

"I'm okay, Betty, just thinking of the rest of my family."

A small golden box remained from Cerulean. It reminded me of a jewelry box, but I didn't know what it could be. Another bracelet wasn't practical, and honestly, I didn't know how much more I'd wear. Unless it was magical, then all bets were off.

I popped the top off, and it must have been spring-loaded. Golden dust burst out everywhere like glitter.

"Freaking brothers." Laughter broke out as it swirled in the air. This time the tears won as they slowly trailed down my face. He'd freaking glitter-bombed me. The golden dust landed on the sweater, almost making it sparkle. More laughter poured out of me.

A chirp came from the couch and I gained enough control over my laughter to see Indigo staring at me.

"*More gifts?*" she asked.

"From my family," I explained. "My dad and brothers got me some books, a sweater, and some fudge."

"*Sparkles...*"

"That's from my brother. It's called glitter. Try not to get it on you." I waved a hand in the air, though most of it was already gone. Betty must have been on top of the cleanup.

Indigo didn't look convinced at all, and kept away from the bits that remained in the air. She blew out a gust of wind, pushing what remained away from the couch.

It headed in my direction, and I started laughing again.

POWER FLOATED INTO THE AIR, and I raced to the back of the couch to find Sable giggling like a maniac. Bits of magic floated around the room, swirling back toward Sable. The sparkles landed on her skin, soaking in.

What magic was this?

The shop didn't mind, and hadn't been alarmed.

Yet, I couldn't get a good feel for where it had come from, or what it was trying to do. All I knew was it felt like Sable, and readily absorbed into her aura, making it glow even brighter.

It left questions floating through my mind.

Who was Sable's brother?

SEVENTY-FOUR

I'd slept great, and my blankets were nice and warm, making it hard to want to move. Soft snores came from Indigo, who slept next to my head on a pillow. The light from above made her purple scales sparkle.

I smiled so hard my face hurt at the sight of her being back. I'd missed her more than I could explain. The soft green sweater lay folded on my end table next to the magical plant. Both reminded me of all that I wanted to get done today.

That forced me to slowly pull myself out of bed and into the bathroom for a long hot shower.

Indigo still slept as I dressed and headed out to the balcony to start my day.

Today was another day off, per the Cat, and the shop remained in the same configuration as yesterday. Except for the doorway to the living room, which had moved back to the second floor.

None of that mattered.

Betty needed to be the first stop, with something

caffeinated, warm and tasty. Grinding coffee beans made the shop smell so freaking good, I started humming to myself in joy. A nice slow morning felt like the perfect capstone for the holiday. Normally, back home, everyone got up late, but then there was a family dinner again. It always felt like a bit much to me.

This was more my style.

I steamed the milk with some dark chocolate and added it to my mug. Then I pulled the espresso, but before I could add it to my mug, the Cat jumped up on the counter.

"Good Morning," I said with a smile, pulling his teacup out from under the counter. I added some of my chocolate milk to his teacup and then split the espresso between the both of them. "You have good timing."

"Are you feeling okay?" asked the Cat, staring at me intently.

"I'm good. Slept in, and now I'm gonna go make breakfast. I'm thinking breakfast burritos. I have some ground breakfast sausage from the last grocery order I can fry up."

He continued to stare.

"Okay, what's up?" The Cat seemed concerned. "You're worrying me..."

His bright green eyes didn't blink enough, and his focus on me felt like he was waiting for something bad to happen. Then he turned away.

"Just making sure that you're okay," he mumbled quietly, before padding closer to his teacup and sniffing at it.

I narrowed my eyes and resisted asking for more.

Instead, I took a sip of my rich mocha. The chocolate goodness hit the spot as I headed into the kitchen, leaving the Cat on the counter. If he wanted to join me, he could, and maybe explain his weird behavior. Since this was weird, even for him.

Once in the kitchen, I got to work pulling out the ground breakfast sausage into a pan to fry it up. We had tortillas, cheese, frozen hash browns, and eggs, as well. It wouldn't take too long to make an epic burrito. Or at least, I hoped it wouldn't.

The instructions I'd read online made it seem easy to do. I'd even decided to not multitask. Though, the hash browns went into the oven, which should also simplify things. The sausage didn't take long, and scrambling the eggs went quickly. By the time the hash browns were ready, everything was prepared to start going into the tortillas.

I felt eyes on the back of my head, and found the Cat had joined me in the kitchen.

"Are you going to actually explain your staring today?" I asked, dividing up the eggs.

"Will my breakfast depend on it?" He asked.

"Maybe..." Though honestly, it wouldn't. I couldn't eat in front of someone and not offer them food. It made me feel weird.

"Some of your gifts had magic in them yesterday, and I wanted to know how it affected you."

I paused with the spatula in mid air. "Magic?"

The coffee beans came to mind, from Lord Bennit.

"Oh, I'm feeling fine." I shrugged and went back to piling food in the middle of the tortilla.

"Are you sure?" he asked, padding closer to me. Sniffing. "You are practically glowing with it."

"Really?" I kept working on making my breakfast, thinking about how I hadn't practiced magic at all today. Normally I did it in the morning, but today I'd slept in.

The Cat nodded.

"After breakfast, I can work on my homework and see what happens." My stomach rumbled, and I quickly rolled my burrito up.

"Can I get mine in a bowl?" he asked.

"Of course. Both you and Indigo might find it easier."

On cue, a chirp came from the hallway, and I smirked. Two breakfast burritos in bowls, and one giant burrito for me.

Indigo landed on the table and stared at me before heading to her bowl.

The Cat caught my eye before chomping down on his food.

I quickly went to town on my own breakfast, eating it faster than usual.

"That was tasty," said the Cat.

"*Yes, spicy tasty!*" Indigo chirped before launching herself into the air. "*Hot tub?*"

Okay, Indigo totally knew how I loved spending my days off of work.

"I need to get some magic practice in, but I can do that in the hot tub."

"Sable, this is serious," said the Cat.

"I can move the shields and move the water about, along with meditating. I promise."

He sighed and then jumped off the counter.

"*Cat?*" asked Indigo.

"He's worried about my magic glowing," I said, wondering what glowing magic did.

"*You are shiny!*" she said with a nod, before launching into the air and heading down the hallway.

My concern stepped up a notch at Indigo's statement, and I decided to hold off on drinking anymore caffeine before I meditated and tried to figure out what had worried the Cat.

Betty cleaned up the kitchen before I even stood up, everything sinking into the counter but my coffee mug.

"Thanks, Betty." A tiny pulse of energy rippled through the floorboards at my statement, which wasn't normal. It made my fingertips tingle.

Once up on the rooftop deck, I sank into my favorite chair and set the rest of my mug off to one side. The snow had vanished, and the deck had gone back to a nice sunny warm place.

Indigo flew around the deck before diving into the water, then back out of it into the sky. She splashed again into the water then back into the sky without slowing down too much. She flew so much better than before she'd visited her clan.

Taking a deep breath, I closed my eyes to the sunlight and tried to sink inside myself to find my center.

Quicker than normal I found a golden orb shining brightly in the usual place. It felt like a big, bright star radiating heat. While the star itself was bigger and brighter, the magic felt the same. Thankfully, that hadn't changed. Yet, I didn't understand how my magic had grown so much in such a short amount of time.

My eyes snapped open as something moved near me.

The Cat stared up at me from the end of the lounge chair.

"Yep, I'm practically glowing, which isn't normal," I said.

"Told you so." Yet, he didn't look pleased.

SABLE DIDN'T REALIZE JUST how strange such a jump in magical ability truly was. Yet, here she stood, suddenly more powerful than she'd been before she'd opened the gift from her brother. The golden sparks of magic had gone straight for her, and only her. A few had tried to get closer to Indigo, probably because parts of her felt like Sable, since they were so close to one another. And Sable had named the dragon, when she shouldn't have.

The bond between the two of them shouldn't be possible.

It was another one of those strange things about Sable. Like how her magic grew in capacity from something I still knew nothing about. Last night, I'd scoured my bookshelves for any mention of the possibility of what I'd seen. I couldn't find anything.

I didn't know, and that bothered me.

Still, I had time to get my questions answered. I just needed a way to talk to that brother of hers, without Sable as the intermediary.

I could be patient.

SEVENTY-FIVE

"*Magic!*" Indigo circled back in my direction, which I knew even though I couldn't see her. Somehow, I could feel it.

"Yep, this is weird." Feeling where people were was just crazy.

Indigo shimmered into view as she landed on the lounger next to the Cat. Now both stared at me.

"You guys aren't helping..."

"What feels different?" asked the Cat, his whiskers vibrating.

"I know where you guys are, even with my eyes closed." Even with my eyes open, I could somehow sense them. Like I had another way to feel things. It felt like a light pressure inside my head, almost like a homing beacon or something.

"Your sensitivity to magic has increased." The Cat stood up and padded closer, sniffing. "That's a good thing, it's a step forward in your journey."

I focused on the bracelet and the stones within

before sending a shield of golden magic into the air. It took nothing but the thought to send the small blast upward. It sparkled in the light before fading, but it sent a push of air out and my hair fluttered.

My eyes widened.

While I'd gotten good at that, I hadn't been that good.

"I need to write this down..."

My journal appeared near the Cat, and I quickly picked it up and started writing inside it. I needed to get my thoughts down and get this documented as soon as possible. I wanted to remember what I felt, to ask the Professor about it, and if they knew what was going on with me.

"What gifts had magic in them?" I asked, looking at the Cat. "I want to make a note..."

The Cat visibly hesitated and glanced away, staring across the rooftop deck.

I waited patiently.

Indigo chirped once.

The Cat sighed. "The dust from your brother, Cerulean."

My heart pounded in my chest as my world froze. That glitter bomb, I remembered it clearly. Golden sparkles floating in the light, making me giggle like crazy.

That was magic?

That was magic.

Cerulean knew about magic.

The bracelet weighed down my wrist, reminding me he'd gotten it for me as a gift. He'd been to the shop and stared at the Cat too long. His strange trips away from home as a mountain guide.

He actually knew. He had to.

Before I even connected the dots, my phone appeared in my hand and I hit his name. It rang, then I got his voicemail.

"I am out on a tour until after the New Year. Please leave a message and I will get back to you once I'm able."

I hung up.

"Sable..." The Cat nudged my knee, eyes wide. "Are you okay?"

Automatically, I picked him up and cuddled him in my arms.

"My brother knows about magic, and he got me magical gifts..."

Indigo chirped. *"Does this mean I can meet him?"*

Her question sidetracked me for a moment, but the Cat answered before I could.

"Sable needs a moment," he said to Indigo.

Indigo's eyes grew wide, and she raced to my side, climbing next to the Cat in my lap.

"Why didn't he say anything when he visited the shop?" I asked.

"Sable, you're smarter than this." He batted at my knee with a paw. "He needed to be sure. You remember that girl whose grandmother passed away?"

I nodded. Those who didn't know about magic were kept in the dark. I just didn't really think about how someone would find others who also knew about magic. Cerulean had to make sure I already knew about magic before discussing it with me.

I let out a sigh and Indigo snuggled closer.

"Okay, once he's back from his work trip, whatever it really is, I'll ask him about magic..."

The Cat nodded, pressing his lips together.

"*And I can meet him?*" asked Indigo, her wings fluttering.

"I mean, if he knows magic is real, it shouldn't be a problem, right?" This time I glanced at the Cat.

"As long as he knows, things will be fine."

"And if he doesn't?" I asked, as my fingers dug into my legs.

Indigo whimpered.

"He knows." The Cat's words landed like a brick in a pond.

My whole body froze again, before I relaxed.

Secrets. My brother was keeping secrets from me, yet he'd left hints for me to find and see if something came from them. First the bracelet. Then that call to make sure I was okay after I used it for the first time. His voice filled with concern, yet still not asking outright.

"What happens if you show magic to someone not magical?" This time I asked directly. There had to be a reason he'd acted so carefully.

Indigo beat the Cat to the punch. Her voice came out quietly. "*They forget. Sometimes they forget you.*"

"What?"

"Magic protects itself," explained the Cat. "It isn't exact, so sometimes they forget other things as well. So you need to be careful. Very careful."

"How do people usually go about these things,

then?" I couldn't imagine someone forgetting I existed. "In families like that girl's?"

"Families with magical knowledge do testing, usually when kids are very young, to see if they have potential. Magical races don't need to worry about that, of course, because awareness of magic is in their nature. Or, if non-magical people live on a magical world, where it is the norm, there aren't issues. It's only on worlds where magic isn't a known thing that you need to worry."

"He didn't want me to forget our family... Oh heck, I could have forgotten him if he screwed up." I swallowed hard.

Silence reigned on the rooftop for a moment before Indigo climbed off my lap and launched into the air, then back into the tub.

"So, what now?" I asked. Quietly, my stomach fluttered in turmoil at the delay in getting a hold of Cerulean. It would be a few weeks before he'd be back in service.

"Practice your magic, and run the shop." The Cat's tail flickered in the air as he slowly crawled out of my lap. "You are the Shopkeeper."

The Cat's words settled my anxiety. What did this really change? I was already learning about my magic, and I had a job to do.

An important job.

I needed to run the shop and take care of Indigo, along with the Cat. Not that he'd be pleased with those thoughts. The fact that he was stuck here in this bookshop away from his lands and people still weighed on me. Yet, I didn't know how to break whatever curse the fates had stuck him with.

He needed to make amends.

The only record I had about what that really meant was the book, and the Cat didn't want me to touch it.

I leaned back in the lounge chair and tapped my fingers on the journal with my notes about my magic.

"What are you thinking?" asked the Cat.

I didn't answer immediately, not wanting to worry him. "About magic, but it is my day off. I'll meditate, but then I want to rest for a bit in the hot tub. I still gotta call the rest of my family and thank them for the gifts."

The Cat nodded his head before standing. "I'm going to get some rest. Remember to practice."

"I'll meditate and practice."

"*Me too*," added Indigo. "*Dragon magic!*"

SEVENTY-SIX

Thinking of my family reminded me of the fudge I had stashed away. It'd go great with my mocha.

I closed my eyes and let my hands rest in my lap. Again I reached for the tiny star inside my chest and just let my thoughts rest on it, getting used to the new feel.

Minutes passed that way, and at some point the Cat wandered off. Indigo floated in the hot tub, or at least it felt like that.

When everything felt solid, I opened my eyes and took a deep breath.

Time for the hot tub, and some fudge. I probably should drink some water as well, to make sure I hydrated correctly.

Indigo snoozed while in the tub, floating with her wings out on either side of her. Her stomach faced up. Soft snores drifted into the air.

That was so meditation and dragon magic practice. Hopefully, she was safe sleeping in the tub. Though, with how her wings were spread out I wasn't sure she could flip over without waking.

I quietly headed inside to change, grab drinks and grab some snacks.

The doorway that led to the Cat's area wasn't in the place it sometimes showed up, and I frowned. He probably rested inside, which meant getting to the book wouldn't be possible.

Instead, I headed to the kitchen, snagging my phone out as I walked to give my folks a call.

My mom picked up rather quickly.

"Happy Solstice!" Her voice came out happier than I thought it would.

"Same to you! How did the family gathering go?"

"Amazing, just amazing. I wish you could have been here, but your job is your job..."

I stared at the phone, frozen, my hand outstretched to grab the box of cheese crackers.

"You sound very cheery, today..." I quickly added, trying to figure out why my mom was in such a good mood. This wasn't how I expected this conversation to go.

"Of course! The holidays always put me in a good mood. Though, Cerulean headed out early this morning, not even sticking around for breakfast."

"Do you know when he'll be back?" I asked, thinking of his voicemail.

"He didn't leave a note." I could practically feel my mother rolling her eyes. "But hopefully in time..."

"In time for what?"

"Hmmm?" mumbled my mother, as someone said something on the other end I couldn't make out. "Oh, nothing, we're talking of doing a family dinner next month."

My heart clenched at the thought of missing yet another thing. Yet, her good mood made me feel better.

"Oh, that sounds like fun. How's Dad's health stuff going?"

"He'll be fine," she answered immediately, the singsong quality vanishing from her tone. "I expect everything to be cleared up in no time."

Again, someone said something in the distance.

"Is everyone there?" I asked. "Does everyone want to chat?"

"I'm out right now, but I didn't want to miss your call. I should get back to it. I love you!"

Then she hung up.

"What was that?" I asked the empty room, before grabbing down the cheesy crackers and filling a bowl. "I didn't even get to thank her for the fudge."

I slipped my phone back into my pocket, wondering what the heck was going on back home. I didn't really have too many people I could call to see. Though, I could text Jackie. Snagging my phone, I did just that.

I sent her a quick message.

Hey Jackie, how are things at home? Is the new job with Umber working out?

I waited several seconds and didn't get a response.

"Strange. Maybe she's busy with her family."

Shaking my head, I put my phone on vibrate and grabbed the crackers, along with a glass of water. The fudge tin I added to my haul after I changed into my bathing suit.

Indigo woke up when I returned and slid into the water. Her eyes widened at the bowl of orange crackers I munched on, along with the fudge tin set off to one side.

"Cracker?"

I held one out to her, and she swam closer to take it in her mouth without getting it wet.

As she crunched down, crumbs fell into the water, but I ignored them. Somehow, they magically left the hot tub, but I didn't know how. Even when I focused on a crumb it literally vanished without a trace of magic.

Maybe the water itself was magic, and it wasn't Betty.

My phone vibrated on the table near the tub. I quickly picked it up.

Jackie: Things are good. Busy right now with learning the ropes and planning for the farm in the spring. So much to learn. Umber is a taskmaster.

Me: I'm glad the job's going well! Is everything okay with my fam? Weird convo with my mom.

Jackie: As far as I know! You really should come visit. I can't wait to hang out with you.

Me: I will in a few months. Work's busy.

I dodged the invite about going home and set the phone back on the table before grabbing a piece of fudge. Everyone really wanted me to head home for a visit.

Indigo crept closer to the bowl and dragged herself out of the tub to grab some more crackers. A few moments later, the bowl tipped to one side spilling crackers all over the table. She sheepishly glanced at me.

"I brought them for you," I added.

"*Really?*" she chirped.

"They are one of your favorite snacks."

At that, Indigo perked up and began to eat the crackers off the table without a care. Several of the orange things stuck to her wet scales. The sound of her crunching on them made me smile.

I ate two more pieces of fudge before leaning back and just letting my mind wander. A loud crash shot me upright, and I found Indigo hovering in the air with the bowl gone.

"*Sorry...*"

"It's all good." I relaxed back into my spot but felt Indigo head in my direction.

"*Can we practice magic now?*"

I knew what she wanted, and it wasn't long before I sent shields at her that sent her flying high above the tub before she shot back down like a bullet. Then her wings would catch another gust of wind from my shields.

The Cat crept to the open doorway, but he said nothing. I only knew he was there because of my new sensitivity. Hopefully, this counted as practicing my magic. Dinner needed to be early tonight, as my stomach growled, and I smiled.

Practice or not, this was fun.

SEVENTY-SEVEN

I flipped the pancake with my spatula and it landed perfectly in the pan.

"*Ten points,*" said Indigo, with a chirp from her position on the counter on the other side of the stove. She tried again to stir the scrambled eggs, but her claws made it hard to hold onto the spatula. "*Cooking hard.*"

"It'll be easier if I can find something for you to hold a little better," I said with a smile. "You can totally make eggs by yourself once we find the correct utensil."

Indigo nodded her head solemnly as she tightened her wings around her body.

I made a mental note to ask Lady Twilight about it when she came by next for dragon lessons. I kept forgetting the online schooling as well, though with the holidays it didn't make sense to start just yet.

My mental to-do list already felt heavy with all of the questions I needed to ask the Professor, and with trying to figure out what was going on with Cerulean.

"I don't think you will find something she can hold

any easier," added the Cat from the island. He watched our antics with a bored expression.

"I won't know unless I ask."

I flipped the pancake onto the stack piling up on the plate on the counter. While I'd already made ten, I planned on freezing some of these. That way I could heat them up quickly for breakfast on days that were more rushed. The frozen waffles had run out, and I didn't feel like trying again making another batch.

I ladled another scoop of pancake mix into the pan and scattered a bunch of fresh blueberries on top.

"*Can I have extra blueberries?*" asked Indigo.

"Of course," I replied. I added a second handful, along with some pecans. "We all could use some extra sweetness."

I'd gotten to bed late the night before, and then my dreams had been filled with golden light, along with trees. It hadn't made sense, and I felt like I hadn't slept enough.

The Cat perked up as I flipped the blueberry-laden pancake to cook the other side.

The last couple of pancakes were for us to eat this morning.

Indigo's version of scrambled eggs hadn't turned out too bad, and I turned off the stove before giving them one more good stir. They were warm enough, and cooked mostly through. As they sat on the hot pan, it'd finish cooking them.

Indigo leaped over to the island.

I added her pancake to her plate in front of her. Then

I added one more pancake to the pan, and again added extra blueberries and pecans.

This one was for the Cat.

I snagged a pancake off the stack and tossed it on my plate. The pan of eggs went to the center of the table, and I quickly flipped the Cat's pancakes before serving the eggs to everyone's plates.

The butter and maple syrup appeared on the island as well.

Indigo cut her pancake up with her claws with ease. The pieces were all the same size.

I added a pool of syrup to one side of my plate before covering my own still uncut pancake.

The Cat's pancake was done, so I added it to his plate. Then I cut it up into slightly larger pieces before adding syrup.

He nodded at me in thanks.

Then it was time to eat.

"How late were you up?" asked the Cat.

Indigo chirped twice before answering. "*I went to bed at bedtime.*"

She had gone to bed before me. I'd stayed up way too late in the living room, watching the snowfall and practicing my magic.

"I got some sleep, though I'm tired today."

The Cat huffed. "I hope you're not too tired. We have a customer this morning, and then deliveries this afternoon."

I took a big bite of my pancake while eyeing Indigo, picking each small piece up individually and dipping it to get the perfect amount of maple before eating it.

The Cat's food had vanished. He sat contently behind his plate.

"Do you want another?"

He shook his head no. "Coffee will be tasty, though."

"Once breakfast is done." Yet, I didn't rush eating. I didn't want Indigo to feel like she had to hurry up and eat. "Do you know when the Professor will be back?"

"I expect them in a few days." He eyed me. "You might want to make sure you get a good night's rest before then."

I shrugged. "I didn't stay up too late, I just had weird dreams."

The Cat's eyes stared at me, but when I stared back he glanced away. "Still?"

I rolled my eyes and finished off my plate before sipping my coffee.

The Cat hadn't been around when I'd made my first cup.

Once Indigo finished her plate, we all headed to the front of the shop. Indigo stopped at the counter and then leaped down to her dog bed on the floor before curling up without a peep.

"You okay?" I asked, given how early she went to bed. *"Tired."*

I glanced at the Cat, but he didn't seem worried as she quickly fell asleep, even as I ground some coffee beans for espresso.

The Cat sat down on the counter, glancing across the shop before tilting his head to one side.

"Wait, I thought today we were selling..." His words cut off as the shop changed.

The normal bookshop layout rippled, with the large table in the center sinking down before raising back up covered with plants. Books on the far wall all changed, taking on the earthy tones of green and brown spines.

Hanging plants drifted down through the ceiling, while the carpet on the floor under the big table disappeared.

I poured the milk, and while I glanced away just for a moment, the tone of the shop finished changing. It'd been a bookshop, but now it was more of a plant shop. Yet, it didn't have gardening supplies or tools, just plants, and books about plants and growing things.

Then I spotted the stack of clippers with plastic bags next to them.

"Cat, what exactly are we selling today?" I asked, trying to make sense of why my eyes kept being drawn to the clippers.

"Just a couple of plant clippings," said the Cat with a nod.

"People buy plant clippings?"

He didn't respond, just stared at Betty as I placed a teacup in front of him with a basic latte. The same thing I'd refilled my mug with.

Concern rippled through the shop and I turned toward the espresso machine. For a second, I swore I heard a voice.

"The coffee machine needs to be gone for this one," said the Cat, still staring at it. This time his eyes narrowed.

A questioning feeling flowed up from my fingers where they wrapped around my coffee mug.

"It's okay Betty, you'll be back after this customer." I patted the top of the machine. As I pulled my hand away, it sank down into the counter.

A spiky plant took its place, with a beautiful blue flower with seven petals, enclosed in a red metallic pot.

I chuckled at the sight.

"You ready?" asked the Cat, suddenly right next to my elbow.

"Sure?"

SEVENTY-EIGHT

The doorbell rang as the door flung open and several beings entered the shop. Each stood taller than me by at least a foot and had several arms. They walked on four arms, or, rather, legs, but they appeared just like the arms. Each was a deep blue color with suction cups covering them. Dark eyes glowed on either side of their heads.

I didn't dare speak as I processed the sight of the octopus-like creatures walking around the shop. Finally, I just pretended this happened every day.

"Welcome to the shop," I said in a cheery voice.

A tentacle waved in my direction. One spotted the clippers on the center table and darted in that direction. Within seconds, they got to work, taking cuttings of a few different plants and placing them in the plastic bags.

Bubbles erupted from one of the creatures hovering over a plant that I would have sworn was a cactus. The customer quickly snagged a bag and placed several clippings into it.

I couldn't keep up with watching all of them, and before long one headed in my direction with a few bags.

Ice crept up my spine as the creature towered over me, but I didn't let the smile fall or the fear show. They set the bags on the counter.

"Will this be all?" I asked.

More bubbles erupted, but somehow I knew it meant yes.

I rang up the cuttings with the pictures that appeared on the screen.

"Five stars," I read off from the register.

Five starfish, still slightly damp, appeared on the counter.

I didn't want to touch them. Not at all.

I nodded my head to the creature, who scooped the bags up and headed out of the shop. From there, the rest of them hurried to bring the bags to the counter. Each paid in live starfish.

The last one left, leaving me with a giant pile of bright purple starfish on the counter, water pooling beneath them.

"What was that?" I asked, trying to reconcile what had just happened.

The starfish sank into the wood on the counter, along with the water.

Finally, the Cat spoke. "That wasn't what the book said..."

He glanced at me, then around like he couldn't believe what just happened. "There was only supposed to be one."

"I mean, it was a quick stop..." It hadn't taken any

time for them to figure out what they wanted and get to work. "Why did they want the plants, anyway?"

"They are treats for the young ones..." He shook his head, opened his mouth then closed it. "They are a very rare species. I've never even heard of more than one appearing anywhere."

"Where do they live?" I wanted to know a little more about them.

"On the ocean planets. Worlds completely covered in water. Plants are a rarity, mostly floating around the world's oceans like large living rafts, but they discovered how to use the portals early on."

The Cat stared at the door, then back at Betty as it rose up from the counter. "I need to research this... This isn't right."

He jumped off the counter and then headed up the steps, completely ignoring me as he grumbled.

"Well, Betty, do you think we can move up those deliveries? Maybe wrap today up this morning?" The positive affirmation made me smile as the shop shifted yet again. This time it returned to the familiar sight of the bookshop I loved.

This time, I sipped on my coffee as the door swung open by itself. Instead of the new delivery guy, a rounded square on wheels rolled into the shop with giant googly eyes on it. It carefully navigated around the table in the center, then started beeping as flaps rose from the top.

"Please remove your package from the compartment."

I blinked at the sight, and the plastic square repeated

itself. Hurrying around the counter, I saw a small box inside the compartment. I quickly lifted it out, trying to figure out what the robot was.

"What are you?"

"I am Meep, a delivery robot. Thank you for accepting your package."

A chirp came from Indigo, who must have awoken at the sound. She dive-bombed the robot, landing on one of the flaps.

"*What is this?*" she asked, clutching a metal flap in her claws.

The robot beeped again, almost rocking a little. "Please step back so I can finish my route."

It beeped again, a little louder.

Indigo didn't move, but stuck her head inside the compartment.

"Indigo, you should leave it be. It has a job to do." I didn't understand where the robot came from, but it delivered things.

She huffed but flapped her wings and flew into the air.

The robot closed its flaps, but then Indigo landed back on top.

"Please remove the item from my top," said the robot in the same cool voice.

"What is that?" came from the Cat, who leaped up on the counter. He stared at the robot.

"I think it's a delivery robot." I still had the package in my hands. "Indigo, let it leave."

The Cat leaped to the top of it, joining Indigo.

The robot freaked out, spinning in a frantic circle.

"Cat hat! Cat hat!" The cool voice was replaced by a high-pitched yelling.

Both the Cat and Indigo slid off the top as the robot spun. Indigo took to the air, while the Cat landed on his paws. The robot frantically rolled across the floor to the door, which opened at its approach.

"Rude," said Indigo as it left the shop. She flew toward her hideaway, unfazed by the experience.

The Cat leaped up on the counter, his eyes on the package. "What's that?"

"Isn't this the delivery?" I asked, setting it down on the counter before reading the label. "Wait, this is supposed to go to an art gallery...called Flora's Gallery."

"What is going on today?" the Cat grumbled, sniffing the package.

"That poor robot," I said, moving closer to the windows, trying to see outside and failing. "Betty, can we return it?"

"I don't even know where we were," added the Cat. "It really didn't like cats."

"I mean, you don't even like cats," I mumbled, before changing the topic. "Doesn't Betty know where we are?"

A strange feeling came from the floor. It took a moment to figure it out. Uncertainty.

"Don't worry, Betty, we'll figure it out eventually." I gave the counter a quick pat.

"I think we should call it a day," said the Cat, his tail twitching in the air. "We can do the deliveries..."

The door opened before the Cat could finish his statement, and a familiar delivery guy entered.

"Hey Adam," I said with a grin, as he wheeled in a cart of boxes.

"Hey Sable, where can I stack these?" He asked. He smiled brightly, glancing around the shop before his eyes landed on the Cat. "Oh you have a shop Cat, that's amazing!"

"Oh, just by the door is good. I'm going to be having an early lunch."

"Less work for me," he said as he set them down on the floor and backed the dolly up. "Have a good one today!"

The door closed this time with a rattle.

The Cat glared at me.

"What?"

"I told you not to name things."

"It's too late for that," I mumbled, as the boxes lowered into the floor. "Wait, don't we need to unpack those?"

"It's all books," said the Cat. "The ones you ordered."

"You mean for my book club?" I asked, with a grin. Step one complete.

"Wait, book club?" The Cat let out a sigh. "I told you that you needed a Wanderer to be able to do that."

"I'm working on it with Betty. We'll figure it out," I said with a grin, still picturing me leaving boxes of books on the stoop and then pushing them out with the handle of a broom. I needed to work on a list to get people signed up for it.

The Sphinx for sure, plus I needed to go through other customers on the tablet to see if anyone else would fit. Like the plant lady.

I headed to the register to get started on compiling the potential customers that might be interested. Either way, the books would get put to use. All of them were from series that would bring joy to anyone who wanted books from Earth that involved magic, humans, and found family. Plus a few romantic moments.

CHAPTER

SEVENTY-NINE

I tapped my pen on the pad of paper. So far, I had listed the Sphinx, the Nymph, and some of the book dragons as possible customers for my book club. Though, the more I studied the list, the worse I felt. I didn't even have names for most of the people who came into the shop. Instead, I made guesses based on what they appeared to be, or asked the Cat.

Taking out a clean sheet of paper and pulling up a clipboard that appeared just as I thought about it, I created a sign-up list that I put near the register. The top only said the words 'Book Club'.

Hopefully, it'd remind me to say something to any of the fantastical creatures that came in who purchased books. Or maybe they'd see it and want to join. Before I put too much effort in, I'd want to get at least five beings interested. Next time the dragons stopped by, I'd ask them, and the same went for Professor Eira.

Just as I was thinking of the Professor, the door

rattled and then it popped open, letting the small rabbit-like woman inside.

"Oh, hello," she said with a confused look. "This wasn't where I had planned on going…"

I paused, my pen in the air ready to tap on the notepad again. The Cat hadn't mentioned her showing up today. The rest of today was supposed to be off. We'd done our 'errands', or tasks, whatever the Cat called the work we had to do for the fates.

Her eyes trailed around the shop before landing on me. "Well, hello Sable. I guess this has something to do with you."

She stepped in, letting the door close behind her as she shook her head for a moment. Her tall ears twitched, but then she smiled.

"Well, how has your homework been going?" she finally asked.

"I've been practicing," I said, as I snagged my journal from where it rested under the counter. "I've had a few strange occurrences with magical things that I'd love some insight on."

She nodded and motioned to where there was normally a seating area.

"How about we talk about them, and then I can see how your progress is going?" she asked, through her eyes kept flitting back to me. Her ears twitched a few more times before turning toward the right-hand wall.

I opened my lips to ask Betty about the chairs when the archway for the living room appeared without any input from me.

Out walked the Cat, who stared up at the Professor,

then turned to glance at me. "I meant to warn you that somehow things changed... again."

"And now I have a lesson?" I asked, quietly.

"Make sure you ask about the sparkles." He turned around and headed back into the archway. The doorway didn't vanish behind him.

I came out from around the counter and motioned to the room. "We can sit in the living room and work on the magic stuff."

I made sure to take my journal with me.

The Professor couldn't stop looking at the doorway itself, or the glass window and the forest beyond. She headed directly to the windows, bypassing the couch. She tapped the glass with a clawed paw, and it rippled, sending a shiver up my spine.

"Fascinating! This section of the building is actually on a different world. Somehow, it's stretched over completely different universes without an issue." She glanced over at me as I sat down on the couch. "And it's completely tied to you."

"Lady Twilight said something like that."

The Professor's eyes went wide, and she flinched.

"She's really nice for a dragon. Maybe you two could become pen pals," I suggested.

"Dragon magic tends to ignore most of the rules, just like Fey Lord magic, and the fates." She paused. "Well, they all follow the same set of rules, I guess, but the rules sometimes shift in ways that don't make sense to me, but must make sense to those with those types of magic. There must be rules, but those three types of beings, at least, seem to be able to...stretch them?"

The Cat's head popped up from the end of the couch. "Do you mind if I watch a show, or should I go somewhere else?"

I glared at him, and he jumped onto the couch, padding closer to my leg.

"Tell her about the present."

I resisted rolling my eyes and waited for her to join us in the seating area.

The Professor glanced back out the windows and then joined us. She sat across from me and clenched her hands together. "Your magic has grown, more quickly than it should have."

I let out a sigh, glanced at the Cat, then held out my journal.

"I wrote about it here. I received a present filled with what I thought was glitter. Instead, the Cat and Indigo said it was magic." I tapped my chest. "It changed my magical center."

She took the journal from me and carefully flipped through the pages, pausing here and there to read over sections.

"Is the increase across the board, or only to your stone magic?" she finally asked.

I paused, trying to figure out what she meant. "I mean, I only use my stone magic."

"What about your Fate magic?" she asked softly.

I shook my head, thinking of the golden light that covered some folks.

"Any other strange occurrences?" she asked in a probing manner.

Things had gone how things usually went, ignoring

the robot from this morning. That couldn't have been caused by random magic of mine.

"Not really, though it's hard to decide what is because of me, versus what normally happens in the shop. I haven't been here long enough to really know what's normal..." I glanced at the Cat for backup with this question. He'd know better than me if something strange happened.

"Today's been a strange day."

"We had a run in with a ton of squid-like creatures, when we thought it was only going to be one. They paid in a boatload of purple starfish."

"The Naserath?!" The words burst from the Professor.

The Cat nodded, causing the Professor's brown eyes to go wide as she leaned back on her couch.

"Is that the squid people, or the starfish?" I asked, trying to follow what was going on.

"The people," she said in a hushed voice. "They can travel between worlds. Usually they don't take a physical form. In the history books, it is spoken that they might have been the first Travelers, or the first form the Travelers took."

"So, why'd they all pay in purple starfish, then?"

"No clue." She shook her head. "That's a strange occurrence, definitely. Though, what it has to do with you I can't possibly guess. You've been practicing your meditation, that much is clear."

"Yes, I have...though the boost in power is an added bonus." I demonstrated with the golden shield. It appeared around me, casting a slight tint of golden light to the room. Then I caused it to vanish.

"That's substantial progress. Are you using any other stones, or sticking with the obsidian for the most part?" She glanced at my bracelet.

"I've been practicing with it the most." I scratched the back of my head. "I tried to use citrine to transform something, but that didn't work."

"I'd think not." She laughed. "Citrine is used for creating light, and finding one's way. You could make a lantern with it. Or use it to reinforce your shields. While the obsidian is good for physical shields, the citrine could help you create a magical shield."

"I hope I won't need help with a magical shield."

"You won't," grumbled the Cat. "You are protected in the shop."

This time he stared at the Professor, who wouldn't look at him. Her eyes darted away as one of her ears twitched. Instead, her head cocked to one side before she turned to look at me.

"The dragon magic is because of your charge, and the angelic is from the artifact. That leaves the Fate magic."

Every time she mentioned Fate magic, I was reminded of the golden outlines and glows that sometimes appeared when customers came into the shop. Like what happened with the centaurs, even though the Cat didn't agree with me giving the book to the kids. I'd known it was the right thing to do.

"What about strange dreams?" asked Eira, her paws twisting in her lap. "Fate magic sometimes manifests as strange dreams, or visions."

EIGHTY

I stared at her, with nothing to say for a moment.

"I'll take that as a yes," said Eira, her big brown eyes staring at me while her ears twitched. "Fate magic can take the shape of dreams you cannot control. Some see what's happening in other places, or what needs to happen. Others may see what has already happened, though they were not present."

"It's not like that." I shook my head, sending my hair all over.

The Cat's attention focused on me.

I sighed, and tried to think about how to explain what my dreams were like.

"It's more impressions, and feelings, with lots of golden light. Sometimes, everything feels like a tangled mess that needs to be cleaned up." I paused, trying to find the right words to describe my experience. "I don't see things, only feel them. And it's not only in dreams."

I motioned to the Cat. "I felt I needed to give that

book to the kids. It was meant to go with them, and if I didn't the tangle would have gotten worse, not better."

Again, I paused and stared at the forest outside the windows, and the snow that still fell.

"Like, the tangle feels better now. Less frustrating, and more smooth. Closer to how it should be."

"So, your Fate magic manifests as strings," said Eira. "When I say that, what emotion does it invoke?"

"Better than what you said about dreams." My fingers tapped on my knee and I tried to understand why speaking of this made me feel anxious.

That bubble of anxiety rested in my chest, and I tried poking it to figure it out.

Realization dawned on me. I knew why. I wanted to free the Cat, but truly didn't know if I'd be able to. I didn't understand if this power would stop me. The thought of letting him down made me anxious.

I let out my breath and nodded.

"I'm hesitant to talk about my Fate magic, since I don't understand it. Hunches come and go, along with golden light that hints at things that need to be adjusted. Yet, there aren't any guides for it. I don't know what it can and can't do, or when I might be punished for using it wrong."

"That's completely understandable. It's not like you're a Seer, with an established ability. You are definitely something else."

The one Seer who had come into the shop had left behind a crystal ball. It'd reacted to me, but the Cat was certain it needed to be stolen by two sisters. Even thinking about that frustrated me.

How could the Cat just trust the Fates like that? Especially after they'd trapped him in the shop? Yet, wasn't that what I'd asked of him when I gave that book away?

The magical book that told the Cat what to do was from the Fates. Was my golden magic the same thing?

I frowned and itched the back of my elbow. I wasn't really a fan of the Fates. I didn't approve of what they'd done to the Cat, or at least, that they'd kept him entrapped for so long.

"Don't look like that," said Eira.

"What?"

"You have the look of someone who is starting to dislike their magic. It's a look, and a feeling, I know well."

"But isn't this ability just doing the work of the Fates? Making me their slave, just as much as..."

"Not like that!" Eira frantically shook her head. "The Fates care about keeping the balance of the universe, by keeping the tree alive and strong. The oldest of stories say that the Fates are just individuals with strong fate magic. They grew into their station."

"So, the Fates aren't some gods or something? They were, or are, actual people?"

The Cat's head twisted to glare at the Professor, but she ignored him.

"That's what the oldest texts say, that they gained enough power that the tree itself asked for their help, and now they are the Fates." Professor Eira bowed her head for a moment before continuing. "They work for the tree directly, and so they have great power. It's easier for most beings to think of them as gods, and in the context of most religious beliefs, they are as powerful as gods, but they were once mortal."

"So, the Tree, which all the leylines run to, and the dragons return to when they die, made the Fates out of mortals?" It felt unbelievable to me, but at the same time, it felt right somehow.

"The Tree made everything. It creates new worlds as branches grow." Professor Eira smiled. "Advanced civilizations all know this."

"How do Travelers and Wanderers fit into this?" I asked, thinking of the other beings I knew about.

"Travelers can travel between the worlds along the branches of the Tree itself. They help maintain the lines between worlds. Wanderers...are different. Not much is known about them." She hesitated, and scratched one of her long ears.

"Wanderers feel the need to wander to new worlds, and have the ability, like Travelers, to do so. Yet, after they visit a place, even though they don't seem to do anything, the connection to the leylines is strengthened. Some help others as they see fit; others are solitary. They are either very rare, or very rarely come into contact with the peoples of the worlds. Either way, little is actually known about them."

Professor Eira's eye darted all over the room before returning back to me. "The Fates are just people tasked with keeping the roots of the Tree growing. When something goes out of balance, they nudge the correct individuals to take care of it. They only step in when necessary."

"Yet they..." My voice cut off, like someone put me on mute.

The Cat's claws dug into my thigh, but I barely felt it as I stopped trying to talk.

I took a deep breath before opening my mouth again. "Alright, I think I understand Fate magic. It doesn't do anything."

"Sable..." whispered the Cat. "Don't just cross it out of your mind because of me."

"Don't say that!" Again, Professor Eira's eyes darted all around the room. "I wouldn't have found you if the Fates hadn't nudged me in this direction. I almost ignored the letter I received, since it wasn't possible my friend had sent it."

"But you showed up..."

"Only because I was nudged." Her ears violently twitched. "Those types of nudges came from the Fates."

"Can we just move on?" I asked, this time looking directly at her.

She slowly nodded her head. "As long as you promise to not ignore your magic."

"I promise."

The Cat relaxed next to my leg, and set his head on my thigh, almost like a dog.

"So, what magic of mine increased from the gift?"

"Your Fate magic."

I closed my eyes and let my head fall back against the couch. More Fate magic felt like the worst thing that could happen. Then, my head snapped back.

"But my stone magic is easier to use, and it is stronger."

She scooted forward, and reached toward my hands with her furry paws. "Take my paws."

I did as she asked, surprised at how soft they were. My fingers warmed up where we touched, and I felt something like a question. And something inside me responded.

The Professor closed her eyes, and again I felt the same sensation.

This time I tried to figure out what she was trying to do.

Inside my chest, the glowing ball of magic separated from being a single star, dividing into more than one ball, then pulled back into that glowing force. As she asked the question a third time, the star rippled like a pool of water, and colors flashed by like an oil slick or a rainbow.

Yet, the bright golden glow mingled with each color, permeating everything.

EIGHTY-ONE

Professor Eira jerked back, yanking her paws from my hands, trembling. Her ears frantically twitched back and forth. The trembling didn't go away as her eyes widened, showing the whites.

"Are you okay?" I asked her.

I reached out to her, but she leaned away from me.

The Cat jumped over to her couch and started purring. At the same time, warmth pulsed up from the floor and into the couches.

Slowly, the trembling stopped, and she started to pet the Cat. Eventually, she glanced at me.

"Your Fate magic is interwoven with your stone magic. The dragon and angelic magic are separate, since they aren't naturally yours. They're from bonds you've formed, or steps you've undertaken to connect with those powers." She frowned. "Whatever that gift was, it reacted to your natural magic like it was always a part of you. Like a missing puzzle piece."

"So, my brother gave me a puzzle piece that someone

took from me when I was younger?" I tried to under-stand what she'd said, but it just didn't make sense. Even if my brother knew magic, how would he know about my own magic, unless it was something he'd messed with in the past?

"You were born on a world where magic wasn't common, wasn't known, correct?"

I nodded and waited for her to continue.

"More than likely, what happened is that your magic hid because of the lack of magic around you. Children aren't the best at keeping secrets. Magic can protect itself. That glitter might be from your world, something that let your magic know it's safe to come out."

She nodded twice, as though she was agreeing with her own statement.

"That makes the most sense," she concluded.

"But, I've used magic and been around it in the shop. Not to mention the dragon's gift." The amount of magic I'd interacted with since starting this job felt enormous. I slept next to a very magical plant, for goodness' sake, and helped take care of a book dragon.

"Your magic hid really deeply within your soul... I couldn't even sense the vastness when I checked before, and I am one of the best magical teachers across several worlds." Her cheeks turned a little pink as she spoke. "I don't like to brag, but it's true."

It fit, but that didn't mean I liked what it meant. My brother did know I had magic, and had done something to convince my magic that it was safe to come out of hiding.

A thought came to mind, one I didn't dare speak

aloud. I couldn't. It hurt too much. Yet, my brain wouldn't let it go. Did others in my family know about magic?

"You might be able to learn to direct your Fate magic. You can write down questions before you go to bed, or when you meditate. Basically, ask it to respond. Right now, you only use it when it appears, but that doesn't mean it isn't active all the time."

I didn't want to try to use it, but I would. I had to understand.

"I'll try," I promised.

"The goal is to figure out your trigger, to get it to work when you want it. To see if you are in a situation where something needs a nudge, even when it isn't so strong as to jump out at you, like it does now."

"A nudge to help the tree." It sounded ridiculous.

"A nudge to make the entire universe a better place."

I thought about the golden glow I'd seen between various people on coffee-shop days. I'd thought it was only a relationship that needed to form. Did it mean something else? Could I learn how to understand what that glow wanted?

"But, what can fall under that? What kinds of nudges does the Tree need?"

Professor Eira smiled, and she practically vibrated with happiness at the question. "So many things! It can be as simple as creating a bright spot in someone's day. Maybe you start a nudge that causes someone to fall in love, or learn a new fact that creates ripples. It might be small in the grand scheme of things, but that doesn't mean it doesn't make life better for that person. Or it might seem small now, and become huge in generations, even centuries, in ways you cannot predict, but the Tree expects."

She leaned closer to me. "I've read stories of those Fate touched who changed everything. They stopped wars, helped discover new branches of magic, and healed people. Fate never touched them directly, but through little nudges, to drive their natural tendencies into the right track."

That sounded like a ton of responsibility. A weight settled on my shoulders that I didn't like.

"I like my life how it is..." Working in the shop, trying to learn how to cook, and discovering new things I could do with my magic. Simple, not responsible for the whole universe of everything.

"That's what I'm saying, dear. If you learn how to activate your magic, you wouldn't need to do more than you are. Think about it. You nudge someone in the shop, who then goes on to great things."

"I'd never know."

"Doesn't that make it even better?" she asked.

She wasn't wrong. I enjoyed making everyone's day a little brighter. That was why the coffee shop days made me so happy. Who didn't enjoy a good cup of coffee? Who knew what they'd go on to do for the rest of their day?

A warmth spread throughout me, and that weight lessened. Just because I learned to use it, didn't mean I had to help everyone. But those who came into the shop, those I could help.

Especially if it helped free the Cat.

"You aren't required to solve the universe's problems," said the Cat, from where he rested near the Professor.

"I'll bring some stories about those that Fate has touched next time I come by, though I hadn't meant to come by this time..." She suddenly jumped up. "I have an appointment that I shouldn't miss."

I stood up, shaking my head at the turn today had taken. I snagged my journal off the table from where she had set it.

"I'll try to figure it out a little more actively before you come back."

She nodded, but clearly was distracted as I escorted her back to the front of the shop.

This time, when the door closed, I locked it behind her.

I turned to find the Cat staring at me from the archway to the living room.

"She is wrong; you don't need to practice it if you don't want to. We can figure out your brother's gift in a different way."

ALL OF THIS conversation about the Fates made my hackles raise. Sable didn't deserve to be responsible for their jobs. Eira's theory about the Fates getting raised to that position also didn't match what I knew about them. They didn't feel like others; not Fey Lords, Dragons or any of the most powerful beings created when new worlds formed.

The bonds that kept me here were beyond that. Beyond the ability of even the strongest, and I had been one of the strongest.

"I like the idea of helping those who come into the shop," answered Sable. Her eyebrows drew together, and she didn't sound completely certain. "That feeling of that book going to those boys, it felt right. I liked that feeling."

I couldn't disagree with that. All of those lines gone from the book, all of those days spent helping that tribe gone from my never ending list. Yet... Yet, Sable was more important than that.

"You shouldn't feel like you must do that, though. It isn't your responsibility." The words fell from my lips. More truthful than I wanted to be, but there they were. "Your contract is only for a year, then you will have other things to do."

She nodded slowly before she smiled at me. "That doesn't mean I can't focus on figuring it out for the rest of my contract. Plus, who says I won't visit my family and then sign up again?"

This time, she chuckled as she headed past me into the living room.

Inside, my soul felt frozen. Sable couldn't be allowed to sign another contract. She deserved to be free of this place. I found myself unable to move as the archway closed behind me, leaving me in the front of the shop.

It shouldn't be possible, but it was clear the shop didn't agree with me.

CHAPTER

EIGHTY-TWO

I held the pen above the paper in my journal, trying to figure out how to direct my dreams for the night. Professor Eira said it could work, and this felt like the easier way to start using my Fate abilities in a more active manner, versus just letting them flicker into existence.

Indigo chirped from her cat tree under the heated blanket I'd already turned on.

"Dream of food!"

I chuckled. "I'm thinking of something a little more important than food."

There were two majorly important things weighing on me at the moment, and one I wasn't ready to touch.

My pen flowed across the page, and I quickly scribbled down my thoughts.

How do I free the Cat from his bound existence to Betty?

I snapped the book closed before I could second guess myself, and set the journal on my bedside table. A bright pink bud on the magical cutting potted there caught my attention.

"Oh, you're finally blooming," I whispered as I lightly touched a petal. It vibrated as my skin made contact. "You are so pretty."

"*Flower soon?*" asked Indigo.

"I think so. At least, I assume it will, because of the bud." I knew I hadn't been watering it, and I hoped Betty took care of it like the other plants on the other side of the balcony.

"Hey, Betty, do you water the plants?" I asked softly.

A feeling of warmth and affirmation came from the floorboards.

"Good to know, and thank you. I'm terrible at keeping plants alive."

"*But good with dragons,*" said Indigo, before she laid her head on the opening and closed her eyes.

This time I kept my thoughts to myself. I could only hope I was doing all right with keeping her alive and teaching her.

I snuggled into my fuzzy blankets and stared up through the skylights. The lights dimmed automatically.

"Good night, Betty," I whispered into the silent room.

It didn't take long for the soft snores from Indigo to fill the room. I smiled and rolled over before falling asleep myself.

Next thing I knew, sunlight streamed down from above. I stretched, only slightly confused as the experiment didn't feel like a success. I couldn't remember anything from my dreams at all.

Indigo continued snoring as I dressed and headed out to the balcony, leaving the door barely cracked.

Golden sunlight filled the space, and I smiled at the coffee shop layout down below. Days like this weren't the Cat's favorite, but I loved them. All it needed was an archway and a bookshop off to one side. That'd be the perfect situation.

It took a moment to make it to Betty and start grinding some beans. I hummed to myself as I drizzled maple syrup into the milk before I steamed it. My mug waited for me on the counter, and I quickly pulled the drink together, making a flower design with the steamed milk.

The humming continued as I entered the kitchen, fully prepared to make some oatmeal and toss some berries on top. Something warm and comforting.

The Cat leaped up to the counter and sat in his normal spot as I dished the berries out, along with a little heavy cream. He got a bit more of the cream than the rest of us, but he was a cat, after all. I stirred his up and set it down in front of him.

"Thank you." His head tilted to one side. "You're in a good mood."

"I am. I slept great. Indigo is still out." I sat and took a spoonful of my oatmeal. Somehow, it tasted better than normal. "The dream thing didn't work, though."

The Cat didn't respond, but continued eating his breakfast. Yet, his tail shot up at my comment.

"Yeah, I tried writing a suggestion to direct my dreams, but nothing happened. At least I slept well."

The Cat paused his breakfast and glanced at me. Bits of oatmeal stuck to his chin. "What did you ask?"

For once, I laid it all out. "I wanted to know more about how to free you."

The Cat blinked twice. "You shouldn't be digging into that. I cannot be freed."

I rolled my eyes at the comment, stirring my oatmeal together. "I don't believe that."

We both went back to our food without speaking. Indigo's bowl sat on the island untouched, but it stayed warm.

"Do you want any coffee?" I asked, as I got up and headed to the front.

Yet, he didn't respond as the bells on the front door jingled.

In walked a college student with bright purple hair. It stuck up in a spiky do, drawing my attention away from the fact that we weren't open yet.

"I love your hair!"

"Thanks," she said, glancing around the coffee shop. "I haven't seen this place before, but I'd love to get some caffeine."

"You found the perfect place. For here, or to go?" I asked as I started grinding some beans.

"To go, I only have a quick break before more work." She approached the counter with a soft grin. "I'd like a latte, if you could. Do you have any maple?"

"Of course! One maple latte, coming up." I quickly got to work pulling out a to-go cup with a new design on it. Oak leaves dotted one side, while a paw print was on the other. "So, what do you do for work?"

"I work for a museum. I collect all sorts of things. Right now, I'm hunting for a couple of old books about curses and redemption."

"Please, tell me the curses get broken in the end?" I asked with a smile as I steamed the milk.

"I think it depends on the curse, and if the cursed being deserves redemption," her voice came out all soft.

"I mean, everyone deserves redemption." I couldn't help but think of the Cat. "Especially when they've been trying so hard, and making better choices. It doesn't wash away the pain they've caused, but if they have become a better person, for sure."

The shot finished, and I drizzled it into the to-go cup, trying to keep my hand steady. I'd already made one flower today, I wanted to make another.

"What would you do to help free the Cat?"

I didn't even pause at the absurdity of the question. "Whatever I could, he is family."

"Even fix what he broke?"

"Of course!"

Then it dawned on me what I'd just said.

I snapped my head around to look at the college student, but she was gone. Then I realized that the floor felt strange, and everything around me wobbled.

I gasped, sitting up in bed, sweat dripping down my back. Starlight made the room glow, and Indigo's snores came from her cat tree.

"What the heck was that?" I said to the room.

Yet, I knew. I'd asked for it, after all. That was the answer to my question about how to free the Cat.

CHAPTER
EIGHTY-THREE

It took longer than I'd have liked to fall back to sleep after the dream. This time, chirping woke me up as Indigo flew about the room.

"The flower! The flower!"

Next to my bed, the bud had opened during the night. Bright pink and coral petals surrounded a vibrant purple center, which glowed.

"That's gorgeous," I said, gazing at it.

A second bud had formed, along with another stem with leaves.

As beautiful as it was, it wasn't enough to distract me from my shower. Yet, as I let the hot water crash down, all that I could think about was the dream that had felt so real, but wasn't.

I didn't like it.

Not at all.

The questions the person had asked rattled around in my head. What lengths would I go to free the Cat, and would I fix what he broke?

It left one more question that I couldn't answer, and the only one who could, probably wouldn't.

What had the Cat, or, rather, the Fey Lord the Cat had once been, actually broken?

The tasks he had to do were one thing, yet something inside me said it was more than that. Something else had happened with whatever the Cat had tried to do to gain power, and it broke something big. That something needed to be fixed.

Now, I just needed to figure out what that something was.

By the time I'd washed my hair and pulled it back into a ponytail, I wasn't any closer to an answer, but I felt ready to go for the day.

Indigo beat me out the door, and as I came to the balcony, the sight of the coffee shop layout caused me to pause. My mug rested on the counter, waiting for me to make my coffee. And, yes, a maple latte sounded good.

The flower design in my cup turned out perfectly, just like I'd dreamed.

Still, everything wasn't the same. The Cat and Indigo chatted happily on the island when I entered the kitchen. Both went quiet at my approach, giving me the feeling they'd been talking about me.

"Morning guys," I said, as I pulled out a defrosted package of bacon. The oven and pan were ready to go when I turned to the counter. "What's the plan for today?"

"You saw the layout," grumbled the Cat. "One of those days that make little sense."

"Did the book give any instructions?" This time I turned to look at him as I slid the pan into the oven. "Any hints?"

The Cat jerked backward at my gaze.

"No." His eyes narrowed, and he stepped closer to me. "What happened?"

Indigo jerked back at his sudden movement, before taking to the air.

I tried to gather my thoughts as she landed on the counter next to the stove.

"*I make eggs!*"

"Sounds good, Indigo," I replied absently. Eggs and bacon would make a tasty breakfast, plus a relatively easy one, and, most importantly, not oatmeal.

"Don't ignore me." The Cat appeared on the other side of the stove. "What happened?"

"I had a strange dream that asked me questions. It isn't anything to worry about, but it proves the Professor's point. I can control my Fate magic."

His gaze focused on the side of my head, but I ignored it as I helped Indigo pull a pan out, along with the rest of the things needed for scrambled eggs.

Then the sensation vanished.

I peeked over and he wasn't on the counter anymore.

Indigo cracked the eggs in the pan, creating a mess, but it didn't take too long to remove all of the broken shells. Then she carefully used the spatula with her claws.

"*I need hands,*" she mumbled.

"You are perfect the way you are," I replied. I couldn't

imagine Indigo with hands, or in a human form. The other dragons had one, but she didn't. She wasn't old enough. "You are a growing book dragon, finding your way wonderfully."

"*I am perfect!*" Indigo nodded as she stirred the eggs, only splashing a little out of the pan.

The mess vanished as quickly as it was made. Betty was on top of things this morning.

Indigo's tail slid back and forth across the counter behind her, but she remained in place, stirring the eggs until they were done. Then she handed the spatula over and launched herself into the air.

I gave the eggs one final stir before plating them up, along with the bacon that came out of the oven at the perfect time.

Indigo dug into her plate as soon as I set it in front of her. She took small bites, keeping clean as she ate.

The Cat hadn't come back, and I grew slightly worried.

"Cat, the bacon is done!"

"I'm here..." He leaped up on the island, taking his normal place, yet he wouldn't meet my eyes. "The bacon smells good."

I studied him for a moment, but then started eating my breakfast. The bacon had come out perfectly crispy and melted in my mouth.

The Cat finished his food first, but waited for the both of us.

Indigo took off after using the sink to clean her face. She air dried on her way to the front. At least the drops of water were cleaned up immediately.

"You know, I worry she takes Betty for granted," I mumbled.

Warmth from the floor brushed that feeling away.

"Did the book give us anything else about today?" I asked.

The Cat met my eyes this time.

"No, just to open the coffee shop." He hesitated. "What happened in your dream?"

"Someone showed up and asked some questions about you, and if you deserved to be freed."

The Cat's tail flickered behind him until he leaped off the counter, saying nothing.

"I said you deserved to be freed." I quickly followed him, snagging my coffee mug. "And that I'd help you."

"You already help me by being the Shopkeeper." That Cat rested on the counter by the time I arrived out front. "Can I have a coffee?"

"Of course."

Indigo flew around the room in wide circles before doing barrel rolls. She was fully dry by this point, and just playing until we opened the shop.

I sipped my coffee before pulling his tea cup out from under the counter. It was the new one, with oak leaves and paw prints on it from the holiday. I paused and glanced at the top of Betty.

A single golden leaf rested on the top.

There had been three. Then two, I knew there had been two. Somehow, it was down to one.

SABLE MOVED to make my coffee, and I sniffed the air. Something felt different. Lighter, though I couldn't pinpoint what. Her magic felt the same, so it wasn't that. The dream had triggered no intense feelings, since the shop hadn't woken me up.

It was something else.

A difference in the shop I couldn't trace. Yet, it didn't feel bad. Instead, it felt right, like we'd just crossed a hard task off in the book. The book keeping track only mentioned today was a coffee-shop day. One of those days I hated, uncertain with what it'd bring and if we'd accomplish anything with it.

Yet, this time it wasn't the same.

Sable had fixed that.

On days like this, she figured out what needed doing and did it, all without me.

"Here you go," said Sable as she placed the teacup right in front of me.

Sweet maple wafted upward from the small vessel, and I grinned at the tiny flower she'd created on top. While I wished she could always be by my side as the Shopkeeper, I also knew that less than half a year remained on her contract. And she missed her family.

Her voice saying she'd visit them and then renew the contract came back to me. That must not happen. She needed to go free and figure out her magic, finding her own path.

The dragons would be happy for her to join them. As much as I disliked them, they believed her to be clan, just like she was family... I stopped that train of thought.

It wasn't useful.

At least it wouldn't be long now until my gift arrived. Hopefully, she enjoyed it.

"Are you just going to stare at your coffee?" asked Sable.

"You do a good job," I said, before I tasted the latte.

"Of course I do. I'm the Shopkeeper."

TONI'S NOTES

Thank you for reading the second book in the Meow Series.

I started writing this story several years ago as my personal escape - a quiet corner of the world where I could find a warm hug on the page. The story has flowed for weeks now, only a little at a time, but consistently, and as one story followed another, at some point it became the right time to bind them into volumes. Sharing this next volume in Sable's story is an absolute delight, and I hope you find yourself both comforted, and excited to learn more. It's your kind encouragement and comments, as always, that has kept me writing.

Our little book dragon, Indigo, holds a very special place in my heart. If you'd like a sweet, secret peek into her very first moments arriving at the shop, I invite you to join my newsletter! It's a simple, cozy way to stay in the loop with what I'm currently creating and all the on-going adventures in the garden. Check out bookhip.com/MMHZKBC to get the story!

For those who want to join me even earlier on the writing path, you can find me on Patreon or Ream. It's there that I share chapters of my new books as they come to life, including an upcoming series about a very special customer from Meow whose life is forever changed by their visit.

May your days be filled with warm tea and even warmer stories.

Cozy wishes, Toni

MORE BOOKS BY TONI BINNS

<u>Nexus Universe - Traveler Series</u>

If you enjoy Urban Fantasy with found family, slow burn romance, and unknown magic, check out the complete story!

- Traveler Forgotten (*Short Story*) - Available at tonibinns.com
- Choice of the Traveler
- Call of the Traveler
- Courage of the Traveler